FALCON'S CALL

Books by Mike Waller

* * * * *

The 'ECHO'S WAY Series

Solitude's End - Book 1 of Echo's Way

Dark World - Book 2 of Echo's Way

Enemy Ally – An Echo's Way Adventure

* * * * *

The FALCON Trilogy

Falcon's Call

Falcon's Ghost

Falcon's Bane

* * * * *

Other

Hawk: Hellfire

FALCON'S CALL

By

Mike Waller

COPYRIGHT

Published by Rampart Publishing
ISBN 9780645983005
Cover design by 100 Books
This book is written in United States English

Licence Notes

This is a work of fiction. All characters are fictional, and bare no relation to any person or persons living or dead.

For Rosanne

Clarke's Third Law

"Any sufficiently advanced technology is indistinguishable from magic."

Occam's Razor

"Given alternative explanations for an occurrence, the simpler one is the most preferred."

Chapter 01

NO LARGER THAN a baseball, it moved at a pace several times that of a high-velocity bullet. Spawned of a cataclysmic conflict between three larger asteroids, it streaked mindlessly through space, oblivious to either destination or destiny.

Far ahead, a swarm of small, sand-grain-sized meteoroids, the result of a freak impact between two of the adversaries, heralded its coming. An even more unlikely second collision, a glancing blow between the third contender and rubble from the first two, sent the rock in the swarm's wake, on the identical course despite odds in the trillions to one.

Contrary to popular belief, objects in the asteroid belt are not densely packed. They are in reality far apart and collisions are rare. The region of space through which this wanderer and its precursors now passed was almost empty.

But not quite!

* * *

A hot, tropical sun beat down on brilliant, white sand. Salt spray swirled along the waterline as a warm, murmuring breeze drifted in from the vastness of the South Pacific Ocean. The sounds of children's laughter drifted up from the water's edge, mixed with the raucous skirl of seagulls.

Joe Falcon half-opened his eyes. A young woman clad in a brief, suggestive, white bikini strolled across the beach towards him.

A glance in his direction.

A warm, friendly smile.

Helen, his beautiful wife of just a week, with her soft, gentle voice and the look of an angel.

A week? It seemed like a day.

He watched her approach. Life was satisfying, becoming better by the minute.

A split-second blink.

When his eyes opened again she was gone, the sand where she walked smooth and undisturbed. From somewhere nearby the rat-tat-tat, staccato rattle of an automatic weapon shattered the harmony, followed by the shrill, piercing whine of a siren.

Something smashed hard onto his head.

"What the f…?"

Joe's forehead struck the solid, unforgiving bulkhead of the captain's cabin. Weightless, he struggled to regain equilibrium, his eyes blind in the pitch dark, ears ringing to the noise of the ship's breach alarm. He reached out wildly in the darkness, one hand falling on the latch of the bathroom door.

Seconds earlier, he'd been reclining in the hot Australian sun, luxuriating in the soothing, caressing breeze of a time long gone but still cherished; a moment of bliss, a hard bang and a rude awakening.

The beach dimmed in memory as, with eyelids squeezed tight, Joe battled to silence the persistent gremlin breaking rocks behind his temples. Every few seconds a sharp, machinegun rattle echoed through the structure around him.

Something was not right.

The dim emergency lights flickered on and Joe's brain tumbled back to reality. The faint, ever-present vibration was absent, the accommodation wheel motionless. When rotation ceased Joe's body had continued, inertia launching him from his bunk. Deprived of the small but crucial centrifugal gravity he had drifted without waking across the tiny room and into the opposite wall.

With a gentle push against the bathroom door, he floated across to the crisis locker and his emergency suit, and then dragged the stiff fabric over his limbs as best possible in the zero-g.

Satisfied at last—he had not done this for a long time—he clipped the bubble helmet to his belt, planted his feet on the near wall and tapped the com-patch.

"Sarah? What in God's name…?"

"Meteor shower, Boss." The voice belonged not to his first officer but to Terry Caldwell, the second engineer. "We bin hit! Micro-m's"

"You're joking, right?"

"Wouldn't do that, Boss."

Joe whistled through his teeth. The source of gunfire in his dream now made sense; the irregular pings sounding through the toughened alloy structure of the ship were minute, sand-grain-sized meteoroids hitting the outside of the accommodation wheels.

Chances of being in the path of a meteoroid swarm were billions to one, a once in a lifetime event if at all. Unlikely, Joe thought, to happen again before he died.

"What's our status?"

"Not too bad, Boss. Sizes less than two millimeters, mostly. We got maybe three hundred hits overall but the old girl can handle it. Only a few bad ones: three on the reactor module, four on fusion-drive two, three more on the tanks, and six on the spine. No damage to the crew areas."

"The accommodation wheels aren't turning. What happened to the power?"

"We lost the feed from the reactor," Terry replied. "I got us on backup now."

"Good man. Engines?"

"Unit two's got a few hits. It can be repaired, I reckon, but we might need a dock."

"Anyone outside?"

"Yeah. The guys are out on the rock, 'round the back. They should be safe. External links are down, so Sarah's going out after them. She's in the lock now."

Joe grunted acknowledgment. The vessel was tethered to the surface of an irregularly shaped asteroid approximately three hundred meters across, the latest target in their never-ending treasure hunt through the Asteroid Belt. The 'guys', Carl Geddes and Peter Stanley, had been out taking core samples and soundings for analysis in the lab.

A rock like this was not generally worth the effort but Carl had requested more time to check it over, muttering something about it being part of a planetary body, probably Mars, which somehow ended up here in the Belt. Unlike the typical metallic or carbonaceous asteroids in the area, this one was igneous rock.

Chunks of Mars thrown off by meteor impact often turned up on Earth, but how such a massive piece found its way out here Joe could not imagine—hardly surprising since it was not his field. He was Navy or had been once.

"Are you alright, Sarah?"

"Yes, Captain," the voice of his first officer replied over the intercom. "Almost ready to go out now."

"Sounds like the shower's over."

"I wouldn't be going otherwise. Oh, hang on, I may not need to. The boys are coming around the rock now."

Joe smiled—his first officer was younger than every one of the 'boys' on the ship by several years. "Good. Be careful. Terry, I'm on my way up. Are all the crew in suits?"

"You bet, Boss."

Joe berated himself for leaving his com-patch off, stared at it for a moment, tapped it off again and then pulled himself through the doorway into the corridor.

Dim emergency lights illuminated the interior of accommodation wheel number one, throwing dark, surrealistic shadows on the curved walls. Near-silence haunted the motionless structure, the constant drone of the ventilation replaced by an almost indiscernible shush from the backup system.

Joe's nose wrinkled at the faint, 'canned' odor of the air. It felt cold. He shivered and then decided it was his imagination. The temperature was normal but the cool, bluish, secondary lights cast an unnatural pall that fooled the senses.

Opposite the door, a window looked toward the bridge and forward docking module. All was motionless beyond the polycarbonate pane, confirming the lack of wheel rotation. Joe launched himself at the exit ladder and floated up to the central spine, ignoring the rungs. Without gravity, they were superfluous.

An open hatch in the hub led up to the corridor within the spine of the ship. Joe glanced aft; a few meters away another rotating sleeve, also motionless, marked the ship's secondary wheel. The cargo-zone access hatch beyond was shut. Joe guessed Sarah had secured it on her way to the service bays.

Nothing else appeared compromised other than the lights, suggesting damage was limited to the electrics, tanks and engine. A lucky escape; the situation could have been far worse.

As Joe entered the bridge Terry turned, his battered, scar-covered face showing obvious concern. That face always intrigued Joe. At some point in the past, it had undergone considerable involuntary re-arrangement. Joe did not ask; it was not his business. That's how it was in the Belt.

"Any hull breaches?"

"The engine module, tanks and upper work bays," Terry replied. "The shower hit mostly aft of the wheels. Bit of luck, hey Boss?"

"Engineering?"

"We lost … oh, hang on … got a faint pressure drop in wheel two." Terry peered briefly at a read-out above his head. "A pinhole breach—easy fixed."

"Fine. Engineering?"

"Oh, right. One engine out. Reactor's okay. One of the bigger buggers tore straight through the casing on the primary power loom forward of the radiation shield. A broken piece of the case must've taken out the power cables. Mari and Sam are getting ready to go now."

Joe nodded. Marius Pine and Sam Bright, the ship's chief and electrical engineers, would sort the mess soon enough. Joe took a great deal of pride in *Butterball's* crew. They did their jobs expertly, neither needing nor expecting orders. Joe pulled himself into the command chair.

The mineral prospecting ship *Butterball* began life as a long-haul supply freighter built for the Earth to Mars cargo run before the Resources War. Little more than a long, spinal gantry connecting the bridge and docking module to the aft engineering units, she resembled a giant stick insect in space. The backbone contained an access corridor and formed the conduit through which ran high-voltage lines delivering electricity from the reactor to all other parts of the ship. Those cables now lay in shreds.

The view on the command screen currently looked aft towards the radiation shadow shield. Behind the bridge module, two counter-rotating habitat wheels contained the living and working quarters for the crew. With the loss of power, the vessel now functioned on batteries alone, and the rotation of both wheels had stopped.

Further aft, removable work and cargo flats sat around the spine. From there, the business of mineral surveying and prospecting took place. In the bottom, forward work bay Marius and Sam were getting ready to begin emergency repairs.

Long streamers of liquid spewed into space from two of the many tanks lining either side of the gantry between the upper and lower flats, diffusing into rainbow clouds of crystallized, frozen vapor. *Butterball's* lifeblood boiled away in a cloud of glittering diamonds.

"Xenon numbers three and seven," Terry confirmed. "There's still enough to get home once we carry out repairs, but only just. We still got one fusion engine, so we should be solid, Boss."

Joe's heart sank. The ship's main engine was a xenon-ion drive that provided low but constant thrust and used little fuel. This allowed her to accelerate at a slow, steady rate, ideal for her original intended purpose of freighting between Earth and Mars but useless for working the asteroids.

Above and below the primary engine were twin deuterium-tritium fusion boosters, fitted during the refit for faster maneuvering near targets in the Belt. One was now out of action, so *Butterball* would have to rely more on the ion drive, making close-quarters work more difficult.

Joe cringed as the proximity alarm let out a loud, chilling wail.

Something unseen slammed into the still functional number-one booster. At enormous velocity, the baseball-sized meteoroid punched through the unit, reducing it to a twisted mass of scrap metal as the impact wrenched it from its mountings. Alarms screeched as the ship automatically cut the wrecked unit off from the reactor.

Joe slumped back into his seat, took a deep breath and waited for his heart to stop pounding. If the rock had struck a meter or two lower, it would have hit the ion drive. A few meters further forward and it would have taken out the reactor and killed them all.

It was a frighteningly close call.

"Shit," he murmured. "Trip's over."

* * *

Allan 'Waldo' Pearce peered through the fogged windscreen as he maneuvered his brand-new Porsche into the darkened parking lot. Hoarfrost-covered gravel crunched beneath the tires as he turned into what he considered his personal parking space and killed the ignition.

Easing ample legs sideways, he struggled to extricate himself from the seat—the direct result of a large, overweight man in a sleek, underweight car. He peered up towards the ridge. In the darkness ahead, the massive, ghostly domes of the Franklin Telescope Complex loomed in the crisp night sky.

The facility perched far back on the western edge of the Mount Wellington plateau, over a thousand meters closer to the stars in the clear, southern skies of Tasmania. From here, the resident scientists enjoyed an unequaled view of the galaxy, but still with the nearby comforts of the cozy metropolis of Hobart. Little more than an hour away, the small capital city of Australia's island state sprawled along the lower, eastern slopes of the mountain and the beautiful Derwent River Estuary.

With the full bulk of the flat-topped mountain between, the city lights did not interfere with the telescopes, and the closeness of civilization compensated for the long hours of solitude with which Allan chose to fill his life.

"God, it's bloody freezing up here," he cursed. He hated the cold but accepted it for the sake of his work. Eager to escape the late autumn chill he reached in to retrieve his briefcase and bag, and then locked the door of the vehicle. For a man of his size the sports car was absurd, but he drove it regardless to remind everyone a man of his status could afford the better things in life. Without doubt one of the pre-eminent members of his profession, he found getting respect from his fellow workers the hardest part of the job.

He shivered, and crunched his way along the gravel walkway between the lot and the entrance to the observatory. With every labored step his breath streamed in curling whorls of frozen white drifting away into the night. A battered, old, leather jacket did little to warm him as he pulled it tight around his girth and pressed on.

Low, shielded footlights lit the way. The management permitted an absolute minimum of exterior lighting around this complex, to avoid interference with the array of giant optical telescopes. At the front entrance, Allan pushed his way through the swinging doors into the comparative warmth of the foyer.

"Evening, Allan," the security guard greeted, his eyes remaining glued to his newspaper and the steaming coffee in his hand. Allan ignored him, turning towards the reception center. The man annoyed him and persisted in addressing him by his first name. He shuffled across to the reception desk and the svelte, young woman with the misfortune to be tonight's shift manager.

He flashed his best, winning smile. "Good evening, Sophia. How are you tonight?"

"None the better for being here," she replied, casting a disapproving glare at the astronomer's yellow-toothed leer.

"You can always cheer things up a bit by agreeing to dine with me sometime."

She returned the sweetest smile she could muster. "In your dreams, Allan."

The University fawned over Pearce, one of the most prominent astrophysicists in his field, and considered itself privileged to have him at all. Sophia did not share that opinion. Only his unshakeable belief she would one day succumb to his charms allowed her to be so blunt without suffering the wrath of her superiors.

"Ah well, I live in hope." Wiping away a pretend tear, he lowered his head in feigned misery and shuffled in the direction of the control room.

On most nights, other scientists shared the complex, but tonight Allan worked solo. Of all the observatories he had worked in, he preferred this one. Possessing the latest in optical and computer systems, the lab had a small office in which he could work apart from the telescope's operational personnel.

He liked the solitude. Accepted, company through the long night hours could occasionally be pleasant, but he preferred working alone. Grateful for a chance to work undisturbed, he threw his bags to the floor and logged into the workstation.

With the system functioning properly, he waited as the telescope sought out the region containing his current object of interest. He had scanned the area several times in the past year but his latest, still unexplained discovery stemmed from a spontaneous decision to take a last look a few weeks ago.

An increasingly popular scientific endeavor in recent decades, hunting for asteroids, meteoroids and comets reflected an increasing awareness of the fact something enormous and soulless was inevitably destined to plow through humanity's peaceful and ignorant bliss in the near future.

First begun in the twentieth century, the field lost favor soon after, overshadowed by the more glamorous objective of finding exoplanets, particularly Earth-type ones. Forty years ago the search for near-space objects once again reached prominence due to a rock the size of a small bus slamming into the slums on the outskirts of the Indian city of Mumbai. Thousands died and a jaded branch of astronomy again became fashionable. Everyone suddenly realized there was an endless supply of cosmic bullets out there.

The trick lay not in finding anything new but rather, something changed. At regular intervals, scanners recorded a patch of sky and within minutes computers carried out a comparative analysis against previous records of the same area. Any variation triggered a report, flagging the anomaly for closer inspection. Any change in position indicated a body, a comet or asteroid, moving through near space.

The operations manager already had the schedule for the night, so while the hired help got the scope ready Allan shuffled over to the kitchen to brew a fresh batch of coffee.

In his mind, astronomy rode on caffeine. He intended to consume far more than considered healthy in the course of the night, sufficient to keep him tossing in his bed all the next day. With the first of many cups in hand, he returned to the desk and checked the screen.

"Ah, there you are my little beauty."

A dozen observatories were tracking this new target but Allan had found it first. In the last few years, using either Earth-based facilities or orbiting satellite telescopes, he had discovered numerous comets and other significant objects, a score placing him comfortably in the ranks of his field, he thought.

He always insisted his discoveries be in some way named after him; he never succeeded. It was against the current convention to have an astronomical body named after the discoverer.

The target tentatively designated *NE372BJ4* first appeared fifteen days ago, an uncatalogued object barrelling in from the far reaches of the Solar System. A bright blue flare on a single image first drew Allan's attention to this specific region of space. The phenomena did not re-occur, but the scan identified an unusual target moving near the coordinates of the original event.

Something about this one did not gel. Object *NE372BJ4* appeared slightly elongated by the vapor tail typical of all comets, but it was still well beyond the orbit of the planet Jupiter, much too far from the Sun for a tail to be developing. In addition, the light curve was wrong. Uniform and unvaryingly bright, it differed from other objects in deep space, which tended to fluctuate in brightness as they rotated or tumbled.

A week earlier, Allan had contacted a friend at the Outer System Exploration Laboratory. By sheer coincidence, *OSEL*'s latest mission was close to the target, so the university had lodged a formal request for the probe to take a photograph. The unmanned *Cox 24* spacecraft would pass *NE372BJ4* at a distance of less than five-hundred-thousand kilometers, a hop and a step in astronomical terms.

Intrigued by Allan's discovery, OSEL agreed to power up its systems as the two travelers shot past each other at breakneck speed. The encounter had come and gone hours earlier, and tonight Allan expected to see the results.

By the time the call came, he was well into his third game of computer chess and fourth packet of potato chips, the crumbled remains of which lay scattered everywhere around his chair. The monitor to his left flickered and Davis Clarke, a close friend and member of the *Cox 24* team, peered out from beneath long and untamed hair. Behind him a small group of fellow workers milled about, drinks in hand, as they smiled and waved in the direction of the camera.

"That you, Waldo?"

"Hey, Dave. What's with the crowd? You guys having a party or something?"

"Yeah, man. Got bad news for you. You don't get to name another comet after yourself. Hard cheese, old buddy."

"Shit!" Allan shoved his keyboard aside and turned to face Clarke, more than a little annoyed at his associate's lack of tact. "Why the hell not?"

"Check your data feed."

Allan turned his attention back to his workstation as a series of images began to scroll across the screen. As the first came up, he took his closest look yet at object *NE372BJ4.*

"You're going to be famous, buddy," Clarke said.

"I'm already…" For a few short moments, he stared at the fuzzy, elongated image. His jaw dropped. "Holy snappin' duck s…"

"You're a rock star, Allan." Clark's voice faded into the distance. "We're *all* going to be famous, man."

Chapter 02

IN THE FAR distance, the Gateway elevator rose from its sprawling base complex into a pitch-black sky. Cable Station, the principal entry point to the Martian cities, sprawled like a stain across the crater rim of Pavonis Mons, one of three colossal volcanic cones on the equatorial Tharsis Bulge of the planet.

Adam Palfrey leaned on the window ledge and gazed towards the gleaming shaft. His skin prickled as he took in the desolation. Double tapping the wall regulator, he dimmed the view into oblivion.

Cable might be the ideal location for his office but Adam hated the stark, oppressive landscape and the restrictions of living in a place so high the atmosphere beyond the domes was virtually nonexistent. Not that it was such anywhere on the planet that you could walk outside unprotected.

Sometimes in these warm, air-conditioned rooms, he imagined he was home in Hellas City, but his position as Minister for Space Operations gave him little choice in the matter. For the near future and despite personal preferences, this purgatory at the top edge of the world was home.

Adam ran fingers through his thinning, grey hair. "I must be getting old," he said. Almost two meters tall, he had been a native of Mars since the age of four. At sixty-one Earth years he still looked fit and healthy thanks to the low gravity, but had the typical pale skin of the Martian and a slight stoop developed over the years; Mars had been kind, a lifetime hunched over a desk had not. He turned to the portly individual sitting opposite. "So what are our options?"

"Option, singular," the other man responded. "One only."

Rob Billington, a short, jovial man, seemed to thrive in this mountaintop prison. He was Adam's personal assistant, long-time friend and the unfortunate soul appointed to spearhead the project responsible for the massive headache that plagued Adam.

Aware his colleague expected a response, Adam sat, scratched the emerging stubble on his chin, arched his eyebrows and peered expectantly across the opulent wood-paneled desk. Billington shuffled in his seat and with a nervous cough, opened the folder on his lap.

"We can't keep wraps on this thing," he said. "Those idiots at OSEL went public the second they confirmed the discovery and that astronomer Pearce is demanding they name the damn thing after him. By now every media feed on both planets will be downloading the images and writing its own set of facts to go with them. All we can do is ride the storm and concentrate on the task of getting a ship there. We have a suitable candidate, but only one. Not the most promising either."

Palfrey grunted acknowledgment. He tapped a paper on the desk, identified by its cover as an official memorandum from the Minister for Navy.

"The United Earth Space Force is organizing a fleet to rendezvous somewhere between Earth and Venus orbits, presumably to claim the target for themselves. I'm guessing they'll send Barrett."

Billington nodded. Commodore George Barrett had a reputation in the space forces. He was a man who got things done and never let anything get in his way.

"If they intercept first they'll lock us out," Adam continued. "It could re-ignite the war. What front-line ships do we have near the sector?" He did not consider himself an expert on navigation—he was a bureaucrat—but he understood the difficulties involved in making contact with anything moving through space at high velocity. To do so, you had to be in the right place at the right time.

"Nothing worth mentioning," Billington said, rubbing his eyes to keep himself awake. "Both planets are on the opposite side of the system at present, and the lions tend to stay close to the zebras." He grinned, waited for the laugh that did not come, coughed again, then continued. This was becoming a long day.

"There's a frigate at Copernicus in dock with a fused reactor. We also have a fleet patroller at Kepler, near enough and fast enough but with neither fuel nor cargo capacity to make a round trip of such magnitude. It'd be suicide for the crew. Our fleet's preparing to leave of course, but it'll arrive several days after the Earth contingent—too late."

"The *UESF* is sending a battle squadron. So what's our one option?"

"Yes, our other choice. We have a surveyor operating out of Kepler that can do the job, a converted C-5, ion-drive freighter with the necessary capacity for crew and cargo. It just got hit by a meteoroid shower and will be returning to base as soon as the crew can square it away. The basic configuration is suitable for retro-fitting, so an extra pair of boosters ought to be sufficient to push it up to speed."

Palfrey's brow wrinkled as he peered at his friend. "You're shitting me, right? An old, class-five hauler? What, sixty years old? We can't use a freighter; it has to be a naval vessel."

Billington glanced up from his folder. "I'm not so sure military vessels are appropriate, Adam. We need to rendezvous first in case there's any right of claim, but we can't risk a war over this. All we want is someone, anyone, to get there first. Once we land on the damn thing we have legal possession, which might make Barrett pause long enough for our ships to arrive. If not, the prospector and crew are expendable."

"You're telling me this old clunker is the only vessel available?"

"No, I'm saying it's the only one we have any control over. The ship operates for AMC."

"Will they play ball?" The Asteroid Mining Cooperative, largest Mars-based concern in the Belt, tended to be a law unto itself.

"Yes, but it's not a done deal. The damned ship's a private vessel owned by a man named Falcon. His contract lets AMC direct him to investigate targets outside his normal field of operation, so they can order him out and refusal would result in forfeiture of contract."

"Why would he refuse? This'll make him famous. A place in history and all that."

"Don't be so sure. The man's a hard-arse by reputation and he's not a fool. I don't think he cares much about fame. He may be a problem."

Palfrey stood, walked to a drinks cabinet and poured two measures of single malt, one of which he handed to his friend before returning to his chair. "Here's to headaches," he said, then took a long, slow sniff of his drink. The golden liquid burned as he drained the glass, scorching the back of his throat—exactly why he paid a fortune to lift the stuff from Earth.

"What do we know about him?"

Billington reached down, removed a thicker folder from his briefcase and placed it on the desk.

Adam pushed it aside. "Quick summary. Your words, and be brief."

Rob sighed again, retrieved the document and replaced it in his case.

"Joseph Barnes Falcon, fifty-eight, born in the West European Union on Earth, migrated to New Zealand with his parents when three years old. Entered the Pacific Federation Naval Officer's Academy in Australia at seventeen, graduated at twenty-one.

"He served on various oceanic ships including his first command, the patrol vessel *Huntington*. At the start of the Resources War, he transferred to the United Earth Space Fleet, age thirty-nine, and commanded fast attack destroyers followed by the heavy cruiser *Clinton*. An excellent commander—one of Earth's finest."

"So, how does one of our opponent's best come to be operating a survey ship out in the belt? What use is a Terran officer to us anyway?"

“He's one of us now. He moved here years ago, after his wife died. She left him an absolute fortune, old family money, and…”

“I doubt he decided to retire on his wife's millions to a life of ease and comfort prospecting in the asteroid belt. Why is he out there?”

Billington chuckled under his breath. Leaving his boss and friend on hooks was one of the small pleasures of this job.

“He didn't need her money. From the moment he entered service, he invested every spare cent in blue-chip investments on Mars. Almost lost everything in the Resources War, but in the end, the war demand made him a fortune. At the time of his retirement from the UESF his estimated worth, not including his wife's contribution, was seventy-five million. Mars talents, so do the math.”

“How does this affect our objective?”

“Stay with me. After the death of his wife, he resigned his commission, aged fifty-three, and emigrated to Mars. Had something to do with an attempt by his daughter—she's a lawyer in Hong Kong—to challenge the will in the high court. She wanted half but the will was quite clear. He wrapped her up in legal bullshit and transferred everything to the Hellas Bank. Falcon is now a citizen of Mars.”

“Fine, so our man’s wealthy, and Martian. Why the prospecting?” Adam wished again that Rob would reach the point so they could both go home and get some sleep.

“Yes, well, it appears he got bored. Spent a sizeable chunk of the family coin leasing and refitting a derelict long-haul freighter and somehow managed to secure a survey contract with AMC. I guess it's a kind of hobby to keep him amused. He's a natural, and he's done far better than average.

Owns the ship now. His crew is first rate and the Cooperative list him as its most productive prospector; *that's* our problem."

Thank God, Palfrey thought as he moved to refill their glasses. "Go on."

"Money's not a worry for him, and he doesn't care about fame. He's a loner who does things his way or not at all. The only hold we have over him is the clause in his contract requiring him to follow company directives to investigate particular targets.

"Failure to do so could mean cancellation of contract, but I doubt it would bother him; with his record one of the other companies would pick him up in a second. The situation suits AMC since he makes them a tidy fortune, so they let him do as he pleases." Billington sighed deeply. "He has nothing to lose by refusing this job. The journey is rather dangerous, wouldn't you agree?"

"Can we take the ship and put in our own men? The dispatcher crew could do it."

"Falcon owns the ship outright, and this isn't wartime. Short of an act of parliament, we can't touch it. He has to go voluntarily."

Palfrey spun in his seat and gazed at the blank, filter-glass windowpane for a full minute before commenting. He thought that perhaps he understood Falcon. The man sounded much like himself.

"He won't refuse," Adam said. "Someone like him—he'll go."

He stared at the glass for several minutes more, then turned and fixed his gaze on his friend.

"You sure there are no other options?"

* * *

Joe wedged himself deeper into the chair and digested the message on the computer screen.

2039 games played, 797 games won.

"I hate you," he muttered, clicking on '*new game*'. Mahjong was addictive, and Joe had lost count of the many hours poured into the god-forsaken thing. Not that he had anything better to do.

The ship remained anchored to the asteroid, the survey team outside checking a few last findings from the mineral sensors. Temporary repairs to the electrics and the engineering module were complete, and a patch now covered the only damage to the cabin areas, a microscopic pinhole in wheel two, captured by the foamed titanium lining the inside of the shell.

The damaged but now secure number-two fusion engine was barely functional, the remains of the first unit cut away and stowed above the cargo bays. The ion drive, helped along by the maneuvering jets, would suffice to carry them home and into dock. Thanks to the fuel loss, Joe had no option but to cut short the tour and return to Kepler as soon as the minerals team was finished with this rock. In the meantime, with little else to do, he played endless, boring games of Mahjong in his cabin.

It was boredom brought him to this circumstance to begin with. After Helen's death, his daughter the lawyer contested the will in a manner far too aggressive for his liking. She had pounced without warning, and with son Jake's help Joe had transferred the entire family fortune beyond her reach to Mars and moved there himself, hoping to teach her humility. The money would go to her regardless on his death, but in the meantime, she had a lesson to learn.

Jake had been a great help and a blessing during that time. A young man of acknowledged genius and undoubted talents, he needed neither his father's nor mother's wealth. He was a physicist and computer scientist, an entrepreneur well on his way to being a multi-millionaire in his own right. Universities fawned over him and governments sought his help. Joe was proud of the boy; he was much smarter than his old man.

Now, on a freighter in a less traveled part of the Solar System, Joe searched for a one-in-a-million El Dorado in the vast mineral smorgasbord of the Asteroid Belt, just to keep himself amused.

He grudgingly admitted he was running away from his past. Devastated by the loss of Helen, his path to inner peace had been a long and slow slog. The double blow of her death and his daughter's lawsuit threw him into a miasma of disenchantment with his life as it was.

Nowadays, the suffering of adults and children alike at the hands of uncaring politicians and the military was a constant subject of media reports, and tears came to his eyes with the acknowledgment he had once been part of that establishment. It was too much pain for one life.

He had seen two wars, first with the Pacific fleet and then with the UESF, lost the only woman he ever really loved and raised a callous soul for a daughter. The only thing of which he was proud was his son.

Enough!.

After moving planets, all Joe wanted was peace. The freighter had helped to relieve the boredom at first; a captain needed a ship—any ship. Life in the Belt came with problems but at least he answered to nobody and within reason did as he pleased. Now bored again, he prayed for a new distraction.

In this business, long, empty hours tended to be the norm rather than the exception. More often than not, the number of crew on a ship was as much a matter of social stability as operational need, and Joe maintained a larger-than-average crew to maintain that stability. A man alone would go mad out here.

With full automation of even the most basic craft, the crew always had plenty of spare time on their hands. The long hauls between Kepler and the target survey areas were the worst of all, and each crewmember dealt with them in his or her own way.

Some read, studied or viewed endless re-runs of old video shows. Carl Geddes and Pete Stanley ran a never-ending chess tournament in their laboratory; other crewmembers would sometimes sit in as game melded into everlasting game.

Terry Calwell, often addressed as 'Jailbird' because of his habit of wearing bright orange overalls similar to those of prison inmates, spent his time tinkering with any and every mechanical or electrical device he could find, and kept everything on the ship running smoothly. Joe suspected the young engineer had a hidden past—whilst friendly with everyone, he tended to keep to himself most of the time.

Huang Chan, the second officer, was a loner by nature. A tall, rangy man with black hair and piercing, almond-shaped eyes, he spent a lot of off-duty time in his cabin. Called Harry by everyone on board, he admitted to be writing a book and spent long hours alone at his console. Joe would have loved to read the book but refrained, since Chloe, the ship's computer mind, would have refused him access. He had a way around that, but the AI's privacy parameters were of his own making, so he respected them.

The ship's electrical engineer and cook, Sam Bright, spent his time in the galley providing everything the crew needed in way of food or drink—it amazed everyone what the man did with tinned, bulk rations—or occupied himself servicing and maintaining systems. Between him, Terry and Marius Pine the chief engineer, the old *Butterball* was in peak condition. Maintenance failures never occurred.

Joe spent most of his free time reading an infinite collection of classic literature, catching up on news from Earth or Mars, or playing this stupid computer game. Sometimes he mingled with the crew but never got in too deep.

It was good to be friendly with everyone, but also necessary to keep a minimal distance. The navy still leaked through the new and imperfect civilian shell, and required a certain degree of separation between captain and crew. Hopefully, the team understood and respected Joe's position.

The only exception to the rule was Sarah Cole, the first officer. Since coming on board she had become a close friend, their association filling a gap on both sides. She needed a father figure, and she was the daughter Joe wanted, rather than the one he considered lost. Long ago, it became clear the friendship would never affect Sarah's work, so she was allowed a little closer than the other crewmembers.

The girl first drew Joe's attention when introduced by a mutual acquaintance, her mentoring professor at the Mars Naval Academy. When she asked for a job he refused, considering her age, but later changed his mind after a discussion with the professor, realizing *Butterball* might be the best place for her, for a short while at least.

The way in which the services treated women was well known. In the male hegemony of the Navy, the opportunities she deserved would never come her way, despite her excellent academic record. Under pressure to follow her career-obsessed father into the space forces, she had rebelled.

Alienated from her family, Sarah's home was now the old freighter and although she would never agree, Joe intended to hand command of the ship to her on his retirement. If there was ever another war she would, as captain of her own vessel and with the best academy training, slot straight into a command position, circumventing the bias and prejudice she would otherwise encounter.

It was easy to like Sarah. The girl's physical attractiveness was a factor of course, but beyond privately acknowledging that, Joe never gave it much store, holding as he did a deep respect for the abilities of this intelligent, competent, young woman.

He had not let himself get close to any female since becoming a widower, but might have shown more interest in his first officer had he been thirty years younger. The age gap didn't appear to matter to her, but concerned him. Moreover, he was her captain and employer.

She made him sad at times, something he tended to dwell on more than he should. One was never too old to appreciate beauty in a young woman, but at his time of life he had nothing to offer or the right to try. The loss of youth never bit harder than when in Sarah's presence. Still, she was the daughter he always wanted, and so unlike the one he had.

A chime sounded from the wall behind him.

"Boss? You down there?"

For a moment or two Joe did not respond. After months in space the mind started to slow, drifting into a void where intelligent thought ceased and the specters of one's life emerged. He called it *'sitting in parliament'*. Almost a minute passed before he reached out with a pencil and tapped the com-patch.

"No Terry, I'm on vacation. What do you want?"

"Got an incoming for you, Boss."

"What's it say?"

"The tag says Security 107, Captain's eyes only."

Joe stared at the little white rectangles on his computer screen for a few seconds more and clicked off a tile or two while he mulled over Terry's words.

Captain to receive - no other personnel to be present.

"You still breathin', Boss?"

"So what else does it say?"

The engineer replied without hesitation. "Stand by to accept a follow-up package in fifteen minutes."

Joe sighed. "I'm on my way up."

The code was senseless, an old UESF directive and not a thing you sent the captain of a Martian mineral surveyor. Pushing himself away from the desk, he stood and headed towards the bridge.

* * *

"Coming in now," Terry said, nodding towards the communications console as Joe floated through the hatch. "You want I should leave?"

"No, stay where you are."

"The tag said…"

Joe pulled himself down into the command seat. "I'll decide who stays where on my ship."

It was strange that Terry knew the meaning of the transmission tag. The lad had never mentioned being in the navy and it was unwise to ask too many questions out here in the middle of nowhere. That code would be unknown to anyone but a service member, and not necessarily even then.

An image appeared on the monitor. The jovial, smiling face belonged to Marcus Bond, the coordinator with AMC and technically Joe's boss, a fact he tried never to acknowledge to Marc's face. The executive was a friend of several years standing and one of the few men in the company Joe trusted. After fiddling for a few seconds with something unseen to one side of the camera, Marc spoke.

"G'day Buddy. Hope you're there. Sorry about the urgency. I'm home on Mars at the moment and we have roughly a twenty-minute time delay each way, so this can't be a normal conversation, I'll say my peace and have dinner while you respond. You're alone of course. Sorry about the old navy security thing but we don't want your crew in on this yet and I figured you would understand the code where they wouldn't."

Joe smiled to himself and glanced up at Terry. Marc could not have been more wrong. Joe trusted his people, kept no secrets from them, and now was not the time to start: they were family.

"The company is activating clause 139 of your contract. Okay, we've never done it before, but we've found something rather unique and want you to go out and have a sticky. No doubt, you'll be as excited about this as I am. The full package is downloading to you as I speak, with photographs and data on an object located out beyond Jupiter.

"The target is heading in towards the Belt on a direct course for Sol. The trajectory is just below the ecliptic and closing. Considering its vector, we anticipate a swing around the Sun and back out into space, but we aren't sure. We need to get up close and yours is the only ship we have in the sector able to pull it off."

Joe opened the data package and brought up an image, then heard a faint gasp behind him. Terry sat bolt upright in the helm seat, arms wrapped around his shoulders as he stared, wide-eyed, past Joe towards the monitor. A childlike grin almost split his battered face.

"Jeez. Oh shit!"

"Calm down, Terry." Joe turned his attention back to the message.

"You know the conditions of the clause," Marc's image continued, "so I won't waste your time. Finish your repairs and get home as quickly as you can. Kepler's commander is up to speed and he's preparing to retrofit your ship for the trip. The full details are enclosed, so I'll leave you to read through and reply to me when you're ready. Oh, and Buddy, this is a first, mark my word. Over for now."

Joe diverted the package to his personal directory, deleted the record from primary memory and turned to face his Cheshire-cat second engineer. The man's smile stretched wider as he pretended to zipper his mouth.

"Settle down, Terry. Tell the guys outside to drop everything and load their gear back on the ship in thirty minutes. No arguments and no delays. I want us on the way home in sixty. All personnel in the common room in two hours. You already know, so you stay here to get us away. You got that?"

"Yes, Boss." Terry snapped to attention, almost flying from his seat.

"Good. Wipe the smile and keep your mouth shut. Nobody hears about this until I tell them. My orders, nothing else."

"Sure thing, Boss," The second engineer's grin remained undiminished as he turned back to the console.

* * *

In the privacy of his cabin, Joe worked through the information in the data package, studied each report and scrutinized every photograph. He had sent an acknowledgment back and now took careful note of the logistical summary of the voyage Marc wanted him to undertake, and mulled over the consequences for himself and his team. When finished, he called up a copy of his AMC contract and examined clause 139, then re-read the entire document for the umpteenth time.

Sounds of the gathering crew came from outside the cabin and around the drum. Several loud voices dominated; the geology team apparently did not appreciate the interruption without notice to their work.

Switching off the monitor, Joe stood and entered his private bathroom cubicle. He tried to sort through his uncertainties as he wiped his forehead with a wet cloth. He glanced up at the mirror, something he rarely did. An old, tired face stared back.

Surely, that was not him?

He studied the reflection. The man looking back was a stranger, still in good health but somehow jaded. The hair was greying and a once handsome face showed the vague softening of the years.

Those green eyes still held the faraway gleam that first attracted his wife all those years ago, and thanks to regular sessions in the ship's gymnasium and hours spent on vibration plates, his muscle tone was still acceptable.

Jowls? Yes, just the first trace.

Physically fit, and in reasonable shape for age, he was nonetheless unsure of taking on something of this magnitude. The lines and the jowls told the story. He was getting old.

The Company wanted him to undertake an epic journey and he doubted himself capable of pulling it off. Pounded down by a life he preferred to forget, he no longer had the confidence of his time in the forces. God knows why they would consider him suitable for this task, but presumably, it was a choice of last resort. There was no other vessel available.

They didn't need him. They needed the ship.

The *Butterball* would be fine; she was an old girl but in first-class condition. The crew was the best in the Belt, but was it fair to ask this of them? It was clear that for some reason AMC wanted to exclude them, but if Joe accepted the job that was not going to happen.

Many people believed space to be dangerous—and it was—but in many respects, it was safer than living in civilization. *Butterball* was like a secure womb, and Joe could not help but wonder if he had been here too long—whether he'd lost his edge.

Unsure if it wanted to accept the task, the doppelganger in the glass stared back for a long, drawn-out moment. No one could escape age, but perhaps it was time for a new adventure and a chance to relive the excitement of youth. Perhaps that was necessary. It might well be the last magnificent voyage to cap it all, or the final act.

How could he not go?

Chapter 03

THE COMMON ROOM, the largest space in the ship's primary accommodation wheel, occupied a quarter of the structure's diameter and was the only place with sufficient room for the entire crew to gather in relative comfort.

Voluntary mass gatherings were rare. One could never truthfully say that the 'Belters' were entirely normal, or even fully sane. Living in a small, confined, tin can for months on end was difficult at best, and in their off-duty hours, each crewmember tended to withdraw into his or her private world. Full assemblies were the exception and when they occurred, usually indicated something unusual was on the wind.

The room required a little psychological adjustment. With a wheel diameter of only seventeen meters, the floor curved dramatically. To stand at one end of the common room and talk to someone at the other meant looking and speaking several degrees above one's normal line of sight, the angle decreasing as the participants moved closer. At first, it was an unsettling sensation, becoming second nature after a time until the odd alignment ceased to be a consideration.

A secure table and seating filled the center of the room, with desks and lounge chairs along the sides. A massive video screen at one end served for anything from movies, computer displays and pleasant visual scenes, to communication with home.

Typical of any shipboard living space, data sheets, rosters, message boards and pictures concealed large parts of the walls; most of the images showed views of Earth or Mars salvaged and taped up by various crewmembers to remind them of better past lives.

Seven individuals, the remainder of the crew besides Terry, waited in expectation as Joe entered.

"Are we clear and away?" Joe asked. He already knew the answer—the ship was en route to Kepler Base as ordered, a journey of thirty-one days.

Sarah Cole sat at the front of the group. "Yes, Captain," she said. "All secure."

"Ok. Those down the back might like to bunch up so they can see the screen better."

"Why are we leaving in such a rush," Sarah asked. "What's going on?"

Joe took a seat at the head of the main table. "For anyone who isn't aware, our contract contains a clause allowing AMC to order an investigation of anything they deem worth the interest. It's never been activated, until now.

"Astronomers on Earth have located something moving in towards the Sun. The object is beyond the orbit of Jupiter at present and we've been directed to attempt a rendezvous somewhere between the Belt and Mars."

"What sort of object?" Carl Geddes interrupted. Carl, the ship's mineralogist, was a stick-thin man with prematurely greying hair and steel-grey eyes—everything about him was grey: his manner, his conversation, his general view on life. Of all the crew, he was the least sociable, keeping company only with Peter Stanley, his geologist workmate.

Joe often wondered why a man like Carl was in the Belt at all, but he was intelligent, reliable and very good at his job. He sat at the center of the room with his arms folded, a frown indicating he was not happy.

"Image one please, Chloe," Joe lifted his eyes towards the ceiling, as was his habit whenever he spoke to the ship's artificial intelligence.

"Yes, Captain," a soft, feminine voice spoke from the wall speakers. 'Chloe' was the name everyone used to address the AI system that controlled every aspect of the vessel's day-to-day functioning. To Joe, the term 'AI' meant 'almost intelligent'. She was good, but not genuinely cognisant; it was all just clever programming.

A fuzzy image appeared on the screen, resolving to a thin, tube-like object swollen at the mid-point and flattened to a shovelnose at one end. At the other was the hint of a bulge before the shape tapered into a spine. It resembled a shining, white minaret lying on its side.

For a long, drawn-out moment, the silence was deafening. Harry Chan, the second officer, broke the spell.

"Ah, April first, right?"

"Not even close," Joe said. "That is an object of intelligent origin. It's a hundred kilometers in length, give or take, and about ten in diameter at the widest part of the midsection, so not human—too big. Its current velocity is one hundred kilometers a second, or three hundred and sixty thousand per hour." He paused as gasps came from around the room.

"That's slow in astronomical terms, but we have few ships can come close other than naval vessels, and none anywhere near the size. I can say with confidence we're looking at the first confirmed visitor from beyond the Solar System."

An instant babble erupted throughout the room, everyone speaking at once. Joe held up his palm and motioned them to stop.

"Are you saying they want us to rendezvous with an alien ship?" Sarah asked, her eyes wide with wonder. "Us? The first humans to make contact with aliens?"

"Something like that. An alien artifact at least—there's no guarantee it carries life. You can all read the reports later, but the consensus is that long-distance interstellar travel is impossible for living life forms—too many associated problems. From the approach vector, astronomers think it's been out in space for a long time and is most likely either deserted, dead or a computer-controlled machine."

"Why would anyone send something that size to another star without a crew?" Maeve Pedder asked.

Maeve was the ship's trauma officer. A heavy, large-framed woman in her early fifties with short-cropped hair, her cheeks puffed with good humor. On first impression, she had struck Joe as being a hard, unyielding woman who would not give an inch to anyone, but that could not have been further from the truth. Underneath the steel shell was a soft and gentle soul, universally liked and trusted by all the crew. Many of the others confided in her and she had come to be considered the 'mother' of the ship.

"The Solar System was explored with unmanned machines," Joe replied. "We sent automated probes to the near stars—not quite so enormous, I grant you."

He surveyed the room. Silence reined, the expressions on the crew's faces ranging from disbelief through uncertainty to sheer consternation. Maeve's expression was, as usual, one of vague amusement, but others showed distinct unease.

"I've given it some thought," he continued, "and decided to abide by the terms of the contract. I would prefer a crew I know and trust, but I warn you this will be a lengthy and dangerous journey—a minimum of six months, probably more.

"To reach the necessary velocity for intercept, *Butterball* will be retrofitted with extra engines and fuel, and we'll empty the tanks to make rendezvous. After we leave the target we'll refuel from a navy tanker, loop around the Sun and head for home again. I don't have the exact details at the moment, but an idiot can work out a dozen different ways we might never get back." Joe paused so his full meaning would sink in.

"I'm giving each of you a choice whether you want to go or not. Anyone who wants out can step off at Kepler, no questions asked, and no judgments. We'll pick you up again if we return; can't be fairer than that. I'm putting the data on the open system. The company has told me not to do so, but I don't accept they have the authority to give such an order and I believe you deserve to see it before you make your decision. Kepler is four and a half weeks away, and I'd like answers from everyone before we arrive."

"Count me in," Sarah said without hesitation, her gaze locked on Joe. That was expected; the girl was devoted to him. Although she tried not to be too obvious about it, nobody on the ship was fooled and everyone knew she would stick by him on a fast trip to Hell if need be.

“Me also,” said Harry Chan, the second officer. Like Sarah, he would never abandon the *Butterball.* Since moving out to the Belt, he had devoted himself to working in space and the ship had become his sole purpose in life.

The others remained silent, their eyes fixed on either the captain or the images cycling on the screen.

“Fine. Some of you will want to discuss this with family, so communications will be available as needed. You can tell them you’re going on a mission and the rewards could be substantial, but nothing more until I say otherwise. I'm giving you access to this stuff, but it stays on the ship. A transmission lock will be on the file, so you can talk to your families but nothing you read goes over the com-link.

“Chloe will pre-record all communications and edit out unacceptable content. I appreciate this may make it difficult for your loved ones if they want answers, but until we know more, that's the way it is, I'm sorry. You can come and see me at any time. Any questions?”

Nobody raised a hand.

Joe nodded, rose and returned to his cabin, with Sarah close behind. Once inside he directed her to a seat and moved to shut the door. Before he could do so, Maeve popped her head through.

“I'm in,” she said. “Hey, I have nowhere else to go. *Butterball’s* my home.” With a wide grin, she disappeared again. Joe closed the door and sat down at his desk.

“Chloe?”

“Yes, Captain?”

“Move the last ASM package to public access, and restrict access to all files. All crew may view the information but nothing is to be copied, or transmitted outside this ship.

Any vocal reference to the data in communications is to be edited out, and reported to me."

"Yes, Captain."

Joe turned his attention to his second in command. Sarah was the most capable flight officer in the Belt, and at twenty-two years of age, the youngest person aboard. At one hundred and sixty centimeters in height, she was also the shortest, and with her heart-shaped face, enormous blue eyes and short, bobbed, dark hair appeared almost child-like at times. Every member of the crew respected her, knowing she would back them without question if need be, as would Joe. She could also, and if necessary would, nail any one of them to the wall if they stepped out of line.

"What's wrong with Carl and Peter?" he asked. "I get the impression they're not happy about being ordered off the asteroid. Did they find something?"

"No, it's a rock, maybe thrown out from Mars by a meteor impact, volcanic, mostly quartz. Carl says the mineral content isn't worth the effort. He's annoyed because he just finished setting up the core cutter when Terry told him to dismantle it again. Terry isn't very subtle."

"Fine, tell Carl to log the coordinates. Someone else can play with it if they want."

"Already done."

Joe studied the young woman opposite. "Thanks for your show of support. You know you don't have to go. Someone your age—your whole life is still in front of you."

For the fleetest of moments, uncertainty flashed across Sarah's face. "You don't want me to come?"

"I didn't say that."

"Then I'm still in. This is my home, my family." For a moment, she sat and gazed at the floor, her expression one Joe had seen many times before when she thought no one was looking. Vulnerable, a child with no way to turn in a crisis.

Joe realized he was the only one on board who ever saw this side of the girl. At least that was his impression; when in the presence of others she was always the total professional.

"Why us?" she asked. "We're just a bunch of prospectors. We don't know how to do this, do we?"

"I wondered that myself," Joe replied. "It would make sense to send an official Navy emissary, and I can't imagine why they would choose us instead. I can only assume there's no other ship in the region that can make an intercept."

Sarah nodded. She also knew the difficulties of such a rendezvous. "I never believed in extraterrestrials. Do you think it could really be alien?"

Joe pondered for a moment, staring at the cabin ceiling. "I see no reason why not. Scientists say our galaxy has at least two hundred and fifty billion stars. That adds up to; let me guess, oh, one hell of a lot of planets. Some of them are bound to have life."

"Yes, I suppose so. Kind of sobering, don't you think?"

"I think if a planet is capable of supporting life, it probably will. Given the basic ingredients are present, life might occur spontaneously as an inevitable part of a planet's evolution. Little green men could be everywhere out there."

Sarah folded her arms and stared at the wall, deep in contemplation. "Is a rendezvous even possible? I mean, no ship of this type has ever done that speed before. It's way above the supposed maximum for our drive systems. We can't go that fast."

"I'm not sure about that either. Definitely not as we are, but they intend to give us extra tanks and boosters. Some naval boats can do it. With constant acceleration for an extended period the old *Butterball* might make it."

"Yes, but will we?"

Joe thought of the long hours in an acceleration couch. In the wheels, gravity was only sixteen percent of Earth normal, and the crew were adapted to that. Weeks at full 'G' were not a pleasant prospect for anyone accustomed to limited gravity and gentle accelerations.

"Excellent question," he said.

* * *

After the Captain and Sarah left, the other crewmembers dispersed to their various private spaces. Carl Geddes and Peter Stanley returned to the laboratory, deep in whispered conversation. Others went to their cabins or duty on the bridge.

Only Sam Bright remained. For many minutes, he stared at the image on the wall screen, his face expressionless. Eventually, he rose and walked into the galley to begin preparing meals for the next twenty-four hours.

Chapter 04

KEPLER SPRAWLED LIKE the rubbish dump it was, one of five such complexes, each the domain of a separate mining concern. Between them, they and their vast fleets of prospectors, surveyors, tugs and transporters accessed but a fraction of one percent of the estimated resources of the Asteroid Belt.

"Locator for dock thirty-nine active, Captain," Chloe announced.

On the bridge of *Butterball*, Joe watched and waited as the ship's AI handled the approach.

"Dock thirty-nine signal acquired, Captain."

When Joe first re-commissioned the ship he gave the AI a smooth, sophisticated, male voice inspired by a classic science-fiction film about a computer gone mad. After a while, all agreed Chloe's voice was easier to live with. Joe was not the only one to have seen that movie.

"Take us in, Chloe."

"Proceeding. The tug is arriving now, Captain."

Joe nodded. Under normal circumstances the *Butterball* maneuvered without assistance, but with two inactive drives, her ability to move in close quarters was compromised. The risks of navigating the maze unassisted were unacceptable. Ahead, the small tug drifted into position and a flexible towing cable snaked back towards the ship's nose.

The base, headquarters of AMC, was a virtual colony, a loosely packed morass of thousands of different structures arranged over a spherical volume of space one hundred kilometers across.

The array consisted of three shells, or districts, around a central space station. The outermost, fifty kilometers from the center, contained the dumping yards where raw asteroid material waited to be processed and waste was compacted for firing out of the ecliptic. Scattered among the dumps were the general cargo docks, fuel depots and service bays, including the one where *Butterball* would undergo her re-fit.

With Sarah in the pilot's seat, Joe watched on as the ship and escort moved through the maze and lined up with one of the massive maintenance structures.

The bay, a tube-shaped scaffold laced with floodlights, crane gantries, servicing pods, workshops and offices, contained an office and shuttle-dock module at one end. With careful precision *Butterball* eased into the structure until its forward airlock linked to the module. Within seconds, service tubes and cables snaked towards the hull, connecting it to the dock's systems.

"Clear us in, Sarah." Joe handed command to his first officer and then reached for the ship's intercom. "We're now docked at maintenance," he announced. "Once cleared, crew are free to go *Core*-side according to the roster in the common room, when not involved in the re-fit. The rule about passing on information concerning our mission remains in force until I talk to the station commander. Sam, see me in my cabin in ten minutes please."

Sam Bright had yet to give Joe an answer. All the others had responded and all had chosen to stay with the ship. Only Carl Geddes and Peter Stanley, the minerals team, expressed doubts; their skills lay in the analysis of asteroid material and they doubted they would be of any value, but Joe had assured them otherwise.

Like everyone in the crew, each acted in several different positions. Peter filled in as cook behind Sam, and Carl did general maintenance on the ship's accommodations and elsewhere. Either of them could pilot *Butterball*, and both were capable at standing bridge watches.

Carl also had emergency medical skills and sometimes assisted Maeve in the infirmary or gymnasium. Responsible for all asteroid surveys, the two men had more extra-vehicular experience than anyone else on the ship.

According to rumor, their decisions to come on the voyage were the result of much heated and colorful discussion. In truth, Joe wanted them along through sheer stubbornness. His own reasons for accepting this voyage were personal and possibly had a lot to do with an awareness of growing old, but he intended to take any member of the crew who wanted to go. Regardless of the outcome, the mission would go down in history and he would not deny any of them the chance to take part if they so chose.

Under the terms of the contract the decision on who made this voyage was Joe's alone, and he was damn sure it would not include people he did not know and trust. He knew his crew as well as one could in the Belt.

Like himself, his people had no obvious qualifications for the task, but no person could claim to be an expert in dealing with aliens and he knew his crew's strengths and weaknesses. The last thing he wanted was a pack of officious scientists and simpering glory-seekers.

Sam Bright waited for him as he dropped down the ladder. Sam had been one of his earliest appointments to the crew and was technically a citizen of Earth. Of solid, southern Italian heritage, his stocky figure, brown eyes, dark-olive skin and curly black hair made him stand out amongst the crew, several of whom had the more delicate, tall, thin build and pale skin of the Martian native. Sam was a gentle soul, and a friend to everyone without exception or favor. Joe doubted the man would lose his disposition under even the worst provocation.

"Decided yet?" Joe directed his electrical engineer to a chair. Sam sat and gazed at the floor. After a moment, he looked up.

"Are you really thinking that thing is alien, my captain?"

"I don't think there can be any doubt about it. We don't have the technology to build a ship that size. That doesn't mean there'll be life on it; whoever built it may have been dead for thousands of years. Is that your problem, aliens?"

"No, my captain. I talk to *mia moglie*, my wife. She is extremely devout … Catholic. I know you tell us to say nothing, but the visitor is common knowledge back on Earth … is all over the news feeds. When I tell my wife I am going away, she figures out the rest."

Visitor, Joe thought. *As good a name as any for the aliens.* "Smart woman. She doesn't want you to go?"

"She is not believing there is any such thing as aliens. To her, it is the work of the demons. My wife, she is a little … traditional."

For a second, Joe was not sure how to respond. "I didn't think the major faiths believed in that sort of stuff anymore."

"My Ellie, she does. She is very 'old school'."

Joe had never met Ellie. The couple were long estranged but had never divorced, and had children to whom Sam was utterly devoted. He still supported his family, and Joe suspected that despite their separation the man still loved his wife.

"So, you're not coming?"

"Of course I come."

"But your wife…"

"…has no say in it. We see each other not so much anyway since I decide to come out here. She is happy with the money, but I am not letting her stop me from taking this opportunity. I am not letting you and the crew down either, and not wishing to be responsible for mutiny."

Joe flinched at the remark. "I'm sorry, mutiny?"

"If I am not going, you are eating Peter's cooking for six months. The crew are not standing for that, I am thinking."

* * *

A quick shower and a change of clothes saw Joe through the airlock to the maintenance-dock, and aboard a taxi waiting to take him to the *Core*. As the little shuttle moved away, he noted that preliminary retrofitting work on the *Butterball* was already underway.

Despite strict orders the ship not be touched until he gave the go-ahead, tugs were moving a number of massive tanks into the dock in preparation. Sarah was in command during his absence; Joe suspected anyone touching the *Butterball* before time would return home minus the family jewels.

Modified for attachment, the tanks would add fuel capacity to allow continuous acceleration on the voyage out, driving the ship to a velocity never achieved by any but the fastest military craft.

For normal operations, the ship carried four massive container bays above and below the central gantry, between the accommodation wheels and the shadow shield. The refit plan involved removing the rear bays and replacing them with extra tanks. Two additional thirty-meter tanks were to be fitted along the sides, outside the remaining bays.

In addition, four new engines awaited fitting, two fusion units to replace the damaged ones and two chemical reaction boosters to provide an immediate, rapid increase in speed. Combined, these would accelerate the vessel for weeks on end, allowing it to reach a velocity equal to that of the *Visitor*. By the time they reached the target, the fuel would be almost gone: Despite those huge tanks, *Butterball* would need a resupply before the long journey home.

The shuttle cruised through the middle 'shell' of the base, located forty kilometers out from the center. The district contained over four hundred structures, where robotic factories processed raw asteroid rubble and turned it into a thousand different products ready for shipment direct to the consumers of Earth and Mars.

The base had grown dramatically in past decades, thanks to increasing acceptance that the removal of heavy industry from planetary surfaces was to everyone's benefit. That single insight had been a big factor in the saving of humanity's home world, although the job was far from complete.

Inevitably, money played the winning card; value-adding at the source was far more profitable than shipping raw materials. Every voyage between the Belt and the planets was expensive, and the greater the cargo's worth the higher the return.

The innermost shell of the base contained multiple accommodation sub-stations and a variety of plants servicing the main structure further in.

The *Core* was the largest space habitat ever constructed. Two kilometers in diameter and five in length, the inner surface of its drum provided almost twenty square kilometers of living area.

Joe considered the structure to be the space equivalent of an old, frontier-mining town. Like those historical localities, it attracted every kind of business venture ranging from professional and retail, through leisure, entertainment and general support, all the way to the seedy underworld establishments nobody discussed but all knew about and many patronized. AMC's offices and those of any other business with reason to operate at Kepler were all located in the drum.

Constructed in situ, the habitat was a wonder of engineering and yet the most basic of space-habitat structures, a single huge barrel spinning roughly once every two minutes. The rotation provided close to normal Mars gravity, a figure chosen decades ago as the best compromise for an exotic mix of local employees, spacers who spent months in zero or almost zero gravity, and officials and buyers from both planets.

For Joe, it was not so good. Accustomed to the gravity of *Butterball's* wheels, he found living in the *Core* for extended periods tiring. Sometimes it was unavoidable.

The shuttle approached the space station from the rear, moving in past a long spine that stretched three kilometers aft to the station's nuclear reactor. Rows of heat radiators, communication antennae and other nondescript devices radiated from the spine like the bristles on a brush. At the front of the structure, the transporter approached a counter-rotating center section containing several docking bays, each a massive airlock.

Glass-fronted elevators ran down the inner, end wall of the station from the central axis to the perimeter floor. Weightless, Joe pulled himself into the first available car.

"Please be seated," a soft voice advised over the intercom. "Seat belts must be worn to avoid injury during descent. Gravity will increase from zero to Mars normal as you descend. The management of this facility accepts no responsibility for any injuries incurred by failure to follow these instructions, or for any health problems resulting from the sudden increase in gravity. The management does not…"

Joe smiled to himself. Bureaucracy never changed.

He had taken this short ride dozens of times, but with the elevator located at one end of an enormous two-kilometer diameter pipe, the mind-blowing view never ceased to fascinate him.

Far below, the floor curved up and over on either side, joining in an arc above Joe's head. Across every inch of this surface stretched square kilometers of structures, rail lines, walkways, parks and bodies of water—a city built on the inside of a drum.

At the extreme far end, on the edge of visibility, the floor curved up to the aft wall, simulating irregular hills and mountains used for recreational purposes. From high on the wall, water poured in shining ribbons—Joe could see the long, curved arcs where the outflow tumbled in a series of falls and pools as part of a massive recycling system. The water entered the rivers and lakes where it remained until pumped through the filtering systems back to the top again.

An artificial star, suspended at the center of the structure by three thin radial arms, illuminated the vast interior. High above the habitat's floor, it appeared to be a solitary, sun-like ball. In reality, it was a composite of thousands of smaller lights. For reasons of security it never darkened, but dimmed on a regular cycle to the circadian rhythms of the occupants.

Buildings of all sizes and configurations were scattered across the floor of the habitat, some a single story, others extending as many as ten floors in height. They differed from those planet-side only in their materials: plastic, carbon and metal, rather than stone, cement or timber.

At the end of the descent, the elevator doors slid open and Joe stepped out to the reception room, careful to maintain his balance in the higher gravity. He stood still for several minutes, allowing his body to adjust before moving on.

Chapter 05

THE JOURNEY TO the AMC administration building took only a few minutes in a small, golf-buggy shuttle. A petite, smiling secretary, flustered by Joe's presence, ushered him into the office of the station administrator.

Henson 'Henry' Braithwaite was a short, balding, middle-aged man, his ruddy cheeks and growing paunch marking him as the exception rather than the rule in an environment that did not normally include the excesses of life. To the inhabitants of the base he was the 'Count of Kepler'.

The stereotypical bureaucrat, which was in truth the definitive description of his job, Braithwaite ensured the *Core* functioned from a financial perspective. Responsible for the entire base, he employed a score of sub-managers to deal with absolutely everything, from the processing and shipping of products to the maintenance of peace and harmony amongst the thousands of personnel.

The only time he took a direct hand in things non-financial was if they were of particular interest to him or when ordered to do so by his superiors on Mars, both of which circumstances applied to the present situation.

"You lucky bastard," he greeted as Joe entered the room. "What I would give to be in your shoes."

"Nice to see you too, Henry." Joe sat in an armchair without waiting for an invitation. His feet hurt from the short trip to the office; it would take time for him to adjust to the *Core's* gravity.

They weren't alone. A young man in his late twenties or early thirties, wearing the uniform of a commander in the Mars Naval Space Command, leaned against a cabinet in the corner of the office.

"Allow me to introduce you," Henry offered, noticing the direction of Joe's glance. "This is Commander Alaine Parish of the MNSC, but of course, you know that from the uniform." Joe nodded at the young officer, who stepped over and took a seat beside him.

"Commander Parish is the captain of the patrol ship stationed here at the base. He'll be your second in command on this little jaunt." Joe raised an eyebrow but remained silent.

"Commander Parish's orders are to sit in as your first officer. His men will replace yours where appropriate—they are the best."

"Thanks," Joe said in his calmest voice, "but no."

"I'm sorry?" Braithwaite's brow furrowed as his face flushed a mild shade of pink. It had never entered his mind Joe would disagree with an official directive.

"I already have an excellent first officer and the best crew in the Belt. They'll be accompanying me on this trip, as usual."

Henry shook his head in bewilderment, but took the response in his stride and pressed on. "No, Joe, I don't think you understand. This is on direct orders from the Mars Planetary Security Council. It's not up for debate."

"I agree; it isn't. We aren't at war, so neither the Navy nor the Council holds any authority over me, my ship or my crew."

Henry slumped back into his chair, his eyes boring into Joe. Commander Parish said nothing, the smallest trace of a smile on his lips.

"You can't go out there with a bunch of miners and misfits," Henry snapped. "You need skilled and trained people on this mission. Experts!"

"Tell me in what way my crew is unskilled or untrained." Joe arched an eyebrow again. "They're the best, and I'd stack them against fresh-faced navy hacks any day. No offense, Commander."

"None taken," Parish replied, his smile unwavering. He would be, Joe knew, well aware that most personnel in the Belt were there for a reason, hiding from the law or their past lives, running from someone, something or everything. He would also know these men and women survived by their wits and their skill, and were without equal in that regard.

"You're asking me to do something never done before," said Joe. "I have to get my old girl to a speed greater than she, or any non-military ship, has ever achieved. What I *need* is a crew that knows her inside out, knows the feel of her and how to nurse her along if necessary. I want people I can trust and rely on."

Joe looked at the young officer. "Also, I will not take on a second in command who answers first to an authority beyond my own, or crewmembers who answer to him and not to me."

"Nevertheless…"

Joe sighed. "If you care to read my contract, Henry, you might notice I am employed by AMC and not by the Navy or the Government. They may have talked the company into cooperating, but they have no authority over me. You can direct me to take this trip, but my contract gives me complete autonomy over my ship and its operation—including whom I choose as crew—and over any other persons who come aboard her. She's owned by me alone, under private Mars charter, so she can't be commandeered except in times of war. If you're not happy with that, you can find someone else to go on your little excursion."

"That would mean forfeiture," Henry blustered.

"Not at all. I'm not refusing to go on the mission, so I'm not at fault. You will end up paying me out in full since any attempt to replace my crew against the terms of our contract represents a breach on your part. I'll have another job within a month. My crew stays."

Commander Parish leaned forward and motioned Henry to silence. "You're quite correct, Captain. Unlike Mister Braithwaite here I *have* read your contract and I'm aware of your rights." Henry blushed as the young officer placed a copy of Joe's contract on the desk. "My superiors, and Henry's, insisted he at least try. Let me put an alternate proposal to you."

Joe sat back and waited, noting the nervous twitch on his old friend Henry's brow. This was starting to be enjoyable.

"There'll be room on board for some … mission specialists, shall we say?" Parish said. "I'd like to join your crew as such. I'll be answerable to you alone and I do possess skills that will be of use."

"Such as?" Joe tried to give an impression of outcome independence; he could take or leave the offer without any lessening of his position.

"Whether we like it or not this is an official mission, so you'll be dealing with the authorities and navies of both worlds. Earth is sending a fleet to rendezvous and they won't like it if we claim the target before them. Mars will send ours to counteract, but I doubt it can get there first considering our current dispersal. I can make it easier by acting as a liaison.

"As a serving officer, I'm familiar with the current bureaucracy and I know the current leanings of the bear-cats you need to deal with. I can serve as an official representative of our navy—that might help keep the Earth fleet at bay until ours arrives. Also, my knowledge of ships may be useful to you."

"I doubt if you know anything my crew doesn't."

"Perhaps not about *your* ship, Captain—that's not what I mean. The patrol vessel here at the base is my first command. I'm not long out of the Academy, I admit, but my engineering major was in advanced drive systems. I'm familiar with chemical boosters, ion drives and fusion engines. Until now you've never had chemical units on your ship, so I can act as a backup to your men if need be. More importantly, I have knowledge that may be useful when we make contact with the *Visitor*."

"Such as?"

"The primary objective is to learn as much as we can about the alien vessel. Since it comes from another star, it must possess engines far more advanced than ours, something like a Bussard ramjet, a photon or anti-matter drive. I'm fully versed in the theory of those and if it's something else, I might be able to figure out enough about it to be of value to us. I'm the nearest thing to an expert on that ship you will find out here in the Belt."

Joe studied the officer for a moment. Tall and lean, he was clearly Mars born or at least raised, and like all members of the space force, in the best of physical condition. As a serving officer, he no doubt spent much of his life in the gymnasium attempting to counter the effects of long periods in zero gravity. His short, almost blonde hair was a whisker away from a crew cut.

True, he was young—Joe refined his estimate to late twenties—but he had the confidence and self-assurance of an older man. Ice-blue eyes held Joe's gaze with intensity, the mouth curled at one side in vague amusement. This man was convinced he belonged on the mission.

"If you set foot on my ship, you answer to me alone," Joe said. "You exercise no authority over my crew and you will be classified as a technology specialist."

"Agreed." Parish showed no hesitation.

Joe nodded acceptance and redirected his attention to the base manager, who was still steaming as he saw his control over the situation plunge towards zero.

"Alright," Henry agreed, shaking his head with annoyance." I'll confirm with the MPSC. How many passengers can you take?"

"Four, three after Commander Parish, in two cabins. I could take more if I double up the crew, which I'm not keen to do under the circumstances. *Butterball* is their home, and we're going to be out there for a long time."

"Can't you drop some of the less necessary members of your crew," Henry pleaded. "Perhaps the mineral payload specialists?"

Joe had already considered this. At the top of his mind was his determination not to give Henry a grip on any of his authority.

"No."

"But there are a lot of people who want to go. I have a stack of official requests."

"I'm sure you do, but I'll only take someone who can contribute. No sightseers and nobody who wants to go so they can get a few minutes of fame."

"That's a little unreasonable considering the qualifications of some of your crew. Some of these requests come from very important and knowledgeable people."

Joe shook his head, the comment further fuelling his desire not to let Henry get the upper hand. "When you asked me to do this I could not for the life of me work out what qualified me for the task. I know nothing about aliens, but then I realized that neither does anyone else. Nobody is qualified for this, so my crew and I are as good as anyone else. I suspect the only reason they picked me is that there is no other ship in the sector able to make an intercept in time. I have no doubt I am also considered expendable."

"Well, I…"

"Bottom line, Henry. You put me in this position and I will do it my way. Nobody goes unless I think they can contribute."

Again, Henry's eyes flared as he slumped back in his seat. Commander Parish placed his hand over his mouth to stifle a laugh, drawing a black stare from the administrator. Joe decided he liked the young officer. Rubbing Henry Braithwaite the wrong way was a national sport amongst the asteroid crews, and anyone who enjoyed doing that could not be all-bad.

"I would like to go myself," Henry said.

"What could you possibly add to the mission, Henry? You're a bookkeeper; admit it." Braithwaite's mouth twisted in annoyance.

"This is a mining and manufacturing station," Joe continued, "It has little in the way of scientists other than in mineralogy, chemistry, engineering and manufacturing-related areas. I have the first three covered and don't need the last. I doubt you'll find anybody I'd be prepared to take."

"One, actually," Henry said, resignation in his voice. "Please ignore the fact she is my niece. I think she still qualifies. Her field is exobiology, alien life and that sort of thing. If you do find anything out there, I suspect you will need her expertise."

"How can she be an expert in something we've never seen?"

"I think she deals more with the theory: what aliens might be like, how we might recognize them, how to communicate. The theory, not the practice. She came here to investigate another report of bacteria fossils out at sector nineteen. Looks like there's nothing in it as usual, but she's still here and keen to go. She's the best option we've got."

"Alright, tell her to contact me and we'll talk—no guarantees. I'm staying at the lakeside dorms for the next couple of days while I clean up loose ends. Commander, I want you and your gear on board twelve hours before we leave. Get the details on departure times from Henry when his team finishes getting us ready. Now, let's talk about remunerations for my crew."

Henry gave Joe the blackest stare yet.

After several hours of debate, Joe nodded farewell to both men and left the room. Once again, the secretary looked at him with a mixture of fear, admiration and pity. As he walked from the building, he let out an audible sigh. Attempts to take control away from him were predictable, but he did not intend to let that happen. The *Butterball* was *his* ship, and she would remain so. *You're just too bloody stubborn, Joe Falcon*, he thought, a thin smile on his lips.

* * *

Joe soaked in the sunshine and relaxed for the first time since returning to Kepler. His skin felt a touch sweaty from the warm breeze but the soft, gentle caress was pleasant. A faint smell of flowers drifted in the air. He cracked his eyelids a little.

This wasn't real, of course. In truth, the artificial sunlight produced no warmth, just light. Colossal electrical conditioners provided the heat while recycling, filtering and regulating the atmosphere of the *Core*. The flowers, fragrant and real, were in a garden a few meters across the piazza.

Joe had learned to fake it long ago. He sat with eyes closed, a golden glow filtering through his lids, surrounded by the warm, gentle draft from a ventilator not more than three meters away. It was not hard to imagine sitting under the real Sun on a fine, Earth day. That was something he missed.

His 'sunbaking' spot was a small bistro table beside one of the station's artificial lakes. It ran a poor second to reality but compared to life in the sunless, soulless cabin of a spaceship it was a pleasant deception.

With a deep breath, Joe sucked in air scented with the rare, earthy odors from the nearby gardens, and listened to the drone of people going about their business. When on board the ship he missed the sounds and smells of everyday life and the passing parade. Two days after the meeting with Henry Braithwaite, it was time to return to *Butterball.* Yesterday, two recruits, each of whom he interviewed at this table, joined the crew.

Patricia Grace, Henry's niece, was the first. Tall, thin and the exact opposite of her uncle, she was a native of the red planet. A typical Martian, her grey-green eyes, pale skin and intense look caught Joe's attention the minute she sat. Her blonde hair was short in the common style of the Belt, indicating she had been out here for some time.

Patricia was a pleasant, intelligent, young woman. At first, Joe had the impression she was unsure whether she was doing the right thing, but despite a tentative and nervous disposition, she impressed him with her reasons for wanting to go on the voyage.

It was unlikely there would be life on the alien vessel considering the time experts thought it had been in space, but Patricia insisted they should proceed on the possibility there was. If so, it represented the most momentous event in human history, not to be ignored.

If they met living creatures, she possessed a greater understanding of how to communicate with them, if it was even possible. Joe always assumed it would be, but Patricia pointed out they might have different senses, and communicate in ways humans could neither imagine nor understand. Even normal, human-style, vocal communications would be difficult without a long and involved learning process beforehand.

Recognition might also be a problem. People always assumed alien life would possess at least some characteristics in common with terrestrial life and therefore would be recognizable, if strange, but there were no guarantees.

"What if they evolved on different lines to us?" Patricia asked. "They could be so strange we might not recognize them at all. For instance, if you saw something like a lump of slime, would you acknowledge it as an intelligent being, or would you see it as something from a Petri dish and pass it by?"

"I would assume slime could not create a technology capable of producing a star-ship. Unless, of course, it had opposing thumbs."

"Yes, I know that's unlikely, but you see my point, don't you? Suppose the aliens replaced their organic bodies with artificial ones. Could you distinguish an alien from a machine?"

"Could you?"

She grinned. "Possibly, possibly not. I would work on behavior, not appearance. I think I have a better chance of finding and recognizing intelligent life on that ship than anyone else out here, and if it turns out to be slime mold with opposing thumbs, or a robot, then we'll all be surprised, won't we? If there's no surviving life and we find the remains of a crew or anything biological, I should be the one to examine and catalog it."

Pat Grace became *Butterball's* second mission specialist after Alaine Parish.

The third recruit was an elderly scientist, Walter Tyrell, until recently the manager of the Kepler Data Complex. A tall, solid, bear of a man, he was about to return to Mars following retirement at age sixty-six when word of the mission reached his ears. Walter's reason for coming was quite specific.

The vessel would be under computer control, he argued. Systems belonging to an alien race were unlikely to be recognizable or user-friendly to humans, but would likely operate on the same basic principles of physics. To access them, Joe would need someone with a deeper knowledge of the underlying principles of artificial intelligence than the crew of the *Butterball* possessed.

Walter believed even alien computers would function on basic parameters he might work out; Kepler had nobody more qualified for that kind of investigative task.

"I'm fit, healthy and available," he added, waving his AMC discharge over the table.

Agreeing in principle, Joe accepted Walter's application.

Only one of the four passenger positions remained vacant. Joe had spoken to twenty-seven other 'want-to-go' applicants, none of whom convinced him they had anything of value to add to the mission. On such a long voyage, every individual used resources. Nobody was going just for the ride other than crewmembers he stubbornly considered had an inherent right out of loyalty to him.

Sometimes he wondered why the authorities were allowing his intransigence on the subject of personnel. It did not overly surprise him; apart from the contract he was able to hold over the company's head, there was a sneaking suspicion it did not matter. This was about getting there before Earth—as long as a Mars ship rendezvoused first, he doubted anyone of importance cared who was aboard.

Three of the rejected applicants were astronomers. Two insisted they were essential to determine where the aliens came from and their destination, but Joe remained unconvinced. If Walter Tyrell accessed the ship's computers, he would stand a far better chance of discovering that. If not, scientists on Earth and Mars could do as well, and with better resources.

The third, most amusing application came in the form of a 'directive' from the astronomer who discovered the alien craft. He pointed out his 'god given' right to go and was currently en route to Kepler. Joe was to await his arrival, and he would require a private cabin and unlimited computer access.

Joe laughed when reading the message. The man might be a good astronomer but was ignorant of the mechanics of space flight. The *Visitor* would not wait for him, and neither would *Butterball.* Out of arrogance, he was wasting a great deal of money and months of his life for nothing.

There was also a metallurgist—"I can determine what it's made from"— a cafe worker who offered to cook just for the chance to go, and many others with reasons equally non-compelling and even unsavory.

Now he was tired and wanted to sit and relax for one final hour before returning to the ship.

A soft 'clunk' disturbed his piece.

Opening his eyes he saw a delicate, female hand push a fresh coffee across the table to replace his empty cup. Looking up he watched the hand's owner, holding a second beverage, withdraw the chair opposite and sit down.

"Can I help you?"

"Good morning, Captain." She appeared to be in her late forties or early fifties, of medium height and average build. Her long brown hair hung back in a ponytail, unlike that of most women in the asteroid belt. Warmth radiated from her smile, her laughing, hazel eyes sparkling with the wise intelligence of one who had seen life, fought, and both won and lost.

"Can I help you?" he asked again.

"No, but I can help you, besides the fresh coffee."

"How do you know what I drink?"

"Flat white, no sweetener, not too strong."

Joe paid a little more attention.

"There is one space left on your ship. I am the person you need to fill it."

"And you are…?"

"My name's Ruth Carvalio. I'm a writer."

Joe sighed and pushed his seat back. "I'm sorry, Miss … Miz Carvalio. I'm not taking any journalists on this trip."

The woman did not seem perturbed. "I said 'writer', not 'journalist'. I write history books. I've been in this god-forsaken place for the last three months researching a book on the development of asteroid mining."

"I don't need a writer of any kind. If you will excuse me, I have to get back to my ship." He began to rise.

The woman leaned forward. "Five minutes. It will be worth your while."

Impressed by the woman's forthright manner and the intensity of her gaze, Joe paused for a moment then sat down again. "Five," he agreed.

Ruth smiled, her confidence obvious. "Ok. You do need me, even if you don't yet know it," she said. "You need a media liaison. You and your crew are about to write one of history's most significant pages, whether you realize it or not. This will be the first contact with alien life, or at least proof of life if nobody's home. Historians and a million so-called experts on two planets will note and record every step you take—every action, every movement, and every word—then pick them apart for centuries to come. You'll be subject to the most intense scrutiny in history, and the media will write about anything they find. Every. Last. Detail."

"Yes, so?"

"So, you will be plagued with requests for interviews. If I've researched you correctly, you'll refuse most of them, so the leeches will use their initiative. If they don't have enough facts to please, they'll dig up every dirty little secret in the lives of everyone on your ship, and anything they consider of interest will be published. Things like your court case with your daughter."

"How do you know about that?"

"Public record. I do my homework and so will they. That leaves you with a simple choice."

"Which is?"

"You can leave it to them to decide how your story will be written, or you can control the outcome yourself."

"With your help, I suppose."

"Absolutely. With me on board, you can tell it the way you want it. With an official historian and media liaison, you can refuse personal interviews without upsetting people. All press releases go through me, approved by you. I can document every aspect of the voyage for the record and posterity, and interview each crewmember for their true story. Everybody has secrets and skeletons—this is your chance to make sure they are properly handled before the press get their hooks into them."

"And yours to become famous. What do you want out of this?"

Ruth eased back in her seat and smiled. "Oh, don't misunderstand me, Captain. I expect to be the most famous historian in history, with a multiple book deal and bank account to match."

For almost a full minute Joe sat in silence and looked at the woman opposite. Her five minutes were up, but he remained seated. He liked her; she had balls and was not afraid to push her case. Her logic was faultless; the media was something he had given thought to, and he knew she was right in every respect. It didn't hurt that he also liked her smile.

"Anything else?"

"I play a mean game of Chess." She grinned, flashing white teeth. "And I'm a wonderful person."

"You're pretty sure of yourself, aren't you?"

A smile. *That* smile, again.

"Give me a contact," he said. "I'll think about it." Ruth pushed a small white square towards him without comment and then sat back as Joe took the card.

The address was 'Hab. 31' in the inner sphere of structures around the *Core*. One of several smaller habitats built to the wheel pattern, '31' provided accommodation for the less affluent and lower-paid workers. Life there came at a much-reduced cost—in an environment attracting both the best and the worst humanity had to offer, money was often the deciding factor.

"It's cheap," Ruth explained, circumventing the obvious question. "Writers don't make much."

Joe nodded, slipping her card into a pocket as he stood. As he reached the exit he looked back. She remained seated, sipping her coffee and looking confidently at him.

Twelve hours later, ensconced in his cabin on the *Butterball*, he directed Chloe to send a message to Ruth Carvalio's contact address.

Ship leaves 0800 Kepler time, Day period 1427, day after tomorrow. Be on board at least 12 hours before departure with all gear—maximum weight allowance 400 kilograms, including you.

Chapter 06

UNDER SARAH COLE'S capable hands, preparations for departure were right on schedule. Packed into every available space on the ship were enough supplies for a voyage of many months, along with whatever equipment Sarah deemed it prudent to keep. Unwanted gear had been off-loaded to await their return but Joe doubted, given they survived at all, they would ever be back to retrieve it.

As directed, all extra personnel boarded at least twelve hours before departure. Alaine Parish and Wally Tyrell bunked together in the primary wheel. Pat Grace and Ruth Carvalio took a larger cabin in the secondary wheel where Maeve Pedder, the ship's medical officer, had sole use of a bathroom she was happy to share.

Equipped for an extended voyage, *Butterball* eased from the dock and retraced her inward path through the maze of facilities and dumps. Her departure from Kepler was eight hours ahead of the publically advised time, watched only by official craft and a few lucky observers who thanked their personal gods they had taken up station early to avoid the rush for the best positions.

Joe always planned to sneak away ahead of the inevitable swarm of mosquito-like personnel carriers he knew would turn up to view and document the departure. It amused him that they bothered—it was just another ship leaving dock, regardless of its intended destination.

He had no desire to delay over an accidental collision with any half-witted fool attempting the photo of a lifetime. Avoiding the problem and leaving Henry Braithwaite to face the tide of protests that would pour into the administration office hours later seemed the better option.

Soon after departure, all personnel gathered in the common room where Joe introduced the passengers and explained their specialties. Alaine Parish was the Navy and AMC liaison, and officially represented the government of Mars. Media liaison and official documenter of the voyage was Ruth Carvalio, Patricia Grace the exobiology and alien artifact expert, and Wally Tyrell the computer technology guru.

Several crewmembers including Sarah and Harry Chan the second officer, expressed concern over having a fully-fledged naval commander aboard in any capacity at all. To ease the tension the young officer assured them he was there as a private individual and that his uniform was in storage back at the *Core*. He wore a dark blue flight suit, devoid of insignia and typical of those worn by most civilian flight crew.

Hours later and with *Kepler* far behind, Sarah handed over to Harry Chan. Joe checked the ship's status one last time and then settled into his seat to read. Always an avid reader, especially of science fiction, he had personal library files of over a thousand books, including works from many great masters.

Under normal circumstances, none but naval and emergency vessels operated under constant, heavy acceleration. Any other ship gathered pace slowly until reaching operating speed. This journey was an exception; to reach a velocity of one hundred kilometers a second—the speed required to rendezvous with the *Visitor*—the voyage would begin with a long period of rapid acceleration compliments of the reaction boosters and fusion drives.

During this period, every crewmember would stay in his or her assigned acceleration chair. In space, severe injury from inertia was a distinct possibility if one lost balance and went flying across a cabin. A full 'G' was hard on those who rarely experienced anything above one-sixth Earth gravity. For the Mars born, it was particularly hard, their bodies having developed from birth in a forgiving, low-gravity environment.

The new chairs installed during the refit each had a communications screen and computer facilities, plus compartments for food and drink, making it possible to stay comfortable for extended periods. Every few hours, acceleration would drop for toilet breaks and other essentials. At best, *Butterball* was makeshift for the purpose; unlike high-speed military craft, her facilities did not extend to allowing all such activities to take place while still in the seats.

Four of the crew including Joe, his command team and Alaine Parish were on the bridge. The others were in the common room, but with full connectivity, each individual could follow the ship's progress and cross-communicate at any time.

Now that they were clear of Kepler and on their way, Joe settled in to relax for the first time in days.

* * *

Marcus Bond's jovial face grinned from the screen.

"Hello again, Buddy. By the time you listen to this, I should be well into my second course of lunch, so I'll get your response when I finish. It's a done deal now—I'm your liaison with AMC, and through them, with the Mars Government.

"The official word is Earth is sending a fleet out to meet the *Visitor* led by the heavy cruiser *Constellation.* You might remember her; she's 'Ball Buster' Barrett's boat. And yes, he's commanding the mission as expected. They'll rendezvous about halfway between Earth and Venus orbits, so you'll get there first. This is critical because if the target is derelict or abandoned we can claim it lawfully and there's nothing Earth can do about it."

Except take us to war, which they will, Joe thought. More than a century ago, laws had been drafted to set protocols for ownership over extraneous bodies in space. Intended to cover asteroids, meteoroids, comets, human ships and unspecified bodies, they excluded planets, moons and planetoids, all of which were common property.

The law said nothing at all about derelict alien vessels.

As a newly discovered object entering the Solar System, the target was claimable under existing legislation and the courts would argue over it for the next century, by which time any benefit obtained would belong to Mars. Joe also knew that in the vastness of space, laws were hard to enforce and did not always hold sway.

Wars started over much less.

The legal situation was far from clear and the possible outcomes were distasteful. This was potentially the first meeting between human and non-human intelligence; anything learned at whatever level should belong to all humanity and not to a specific political body. Joe would not allow the outcome to be another war. There were ways to deal with politicians.

"When you reach the target your priority is to determine if it's uninhabited or not." Marc continued. "If so, the committee wants an official statement from you claiming it in our name. You must do this before Barrett arrives so you can legally deny him the right to board the *Visitor*. I need confirmation with your reply, please."

Joe smiled at the intimation he could deny the Earth fleet anything at all, regardless of legality.

"You are required to consult with us on any major decisions regarding your actions or those of your crew, but you may take any action deemed necessary in an emergency. If you find intelligent beings, the board feels it may not be practical to negotiate through a powerless intermediary—that would be you. The *Visitors* might not understand if we sent an emissary with no authority, and the communication time-delay factor could become an issue.

"I've attached files outlining the official position on trade, military matters, colonization and anything else we could think of, and you will base your decisions on them. With that in mind, you're authorized to act as our representative in any possible dealings with the aliens, but please use your common sense. Obviously, you will only deal with preliminaries—you will not make any commitments we need to consult on, or which we may later regret."

Are you all completely crazy down there?

"That's about it, I think. I'll await your response and you will of course continue to report every twenty-four hours. Oh, by the way, your first-contact procedure is approved. Don't take chances, but don't waste time either. See you next time Buddy."

Joe stored the transmission and pushed back in his chair. He was not happy, but things were progressing much as expected. He did not intend to lose control of the situation, and a few loose ends still existed.

He wondered at times about the sanity of politicians. The chances of boarding an alien ship and immediately being able to negotiate anything were zero. According to Pat, they would be lucky if they could communicate with the *Visitors* at all, much less sit and discuss trade terms in English or Mandarin. The scientists had no doubt told them that, but it did not surprise Joe that being politicians, they would proceed on the present course regardless, just in case.

Nor was there much chance they would be able to influence the ship if it was just a machine. Scientists had already decided the blue flash that led to the discovery in the first place had been a maneuvering burn, proving the ship was under some sort of control. Unless Wally could access the ship's computers, it would continue on its mission regardless of anything he and his crew might do. In all likelihood, this mission would be one of observation only.

"Chloe, send a reply please," he said to the always-present AI. "Marc, I need you to understand I am and will remain the captain of this ship. I'll decide what happens regarding operational matters and the activities of my crew, and there'll be no negotiation. I sent my procedure for first contact to you for your information, not any committee's approval.

"You also need to remember I'm undertaking this voyage under contract between myself and AMC. I do not represent or answer to the Mars Government or any other official or political body. This job will be done according to my judgment, and not the bureaucracy's wishes.

"As soon as I'm satisfied the ship is deserted, you have my word I'll make a statement. Beyond that, I'll agree to consult with you on matters regarding alien interactions whenever possible. I will consider the guidelines, of course, but I want something from you in return.

"You say I have authority to act on my own cognizance in those negotiations as long as I give due consideration to the official policy. I want that in writing please, and before we make contact. Call it insurance. If you want me to represent Mars, I want a guarantee you will honor my decisions and nothing will come back on my crew or me. This is not negotiable, Marc—if I don't receive official confirmation in one hundred hours I will turn my ship around. Close and send, please Chloe."

Alaine Parish peered across from his seat, a nebulous, twisted smile on his lips. "You're a brave man, Joe Falcon."

* * *

Adam Palfrey scrutinized his new mission committee, ten men and women representing the Mars Government and Space Force, United Security and various commercial or educational institutions from across the planet. Present also was Carmichael Page, liaison to the Ambassador from the United Earth Council. In truth, Adam would have preferred not to have anyone from the UEC present, but it was a top-level political decree and not subject to debate or negotiation.

"Who the hell does he think he is?" Gordon Styles, the navy representative, snorted and slapped his open palm on the tabletop. "We sent him on this mission and he'll do as he's damn well told."

"How do you plan to enforce that?" Adam asked. "You of all people on this committee should understand a high-velocity rendezvous in deep space is not easy. This *Butterball* is the only available ship that can intercept before the alien crosses Mars orbit, and there's no other alternative. We're on the opposite side of the system and no suitable naval vessel is anywhere near close enough. Earth is also on this side at present, luckily for us."

Styles gave a grudging nod. Interplanetary relations were anything but cordial, and as a general policy, all capital ships on both sides remained as close as possible to home.

"At best, Falcon is a stop-gap to delay matters until our fleet arrives," Palfrey said. "After that, he ceases to be of value, but in the meantime, we have no way to make him follow our exact orders. The worst we can do if he ignores us is force AMC to cancel his contract. You all know what effect that would have on him."

"He'll be a pariah on Mars if he doesn't cooperate," Styles said.

"And a hero on Earth," Carmichael Page added. "If he drops out, the *Constellation* makes first contact. My governments are aware of your intention to grab the ship if you can, but I have their official word they will not do the same. Anything they find will be public domain."

"And of course they'll put that on public record, right, Carmichael?"

Page smiled. With his manicured appearance and expensive custom suits, he aroused a strong dislike within Adam. Still, he came with the job.

"So, what do we tell him?" another committee member asked. "We can't let him run wild and we can't give him authority to act on our behalf unrestrained."

"We have no choice." Adam stared down at the boardroom table. "If he doesn't get his way he might pull out. A bluff on his part will affect our chance of an intercept and as Carmichael said, *Constellation* would then arrive first." He raised an eyebrow at Page. "Naturally, once our fleet gets there we relieve Falcon, so the whole issue becomes moot."

Adam knew a great deal about the people around him. Some of them were loyal to Mars, others only to themselves. For him, avoiding conflict always came before gain. His priority was not to claim the target for Mars but to prevent a claim by the mother world, the unfortunate truth being either scenario could lead to renewed war. Although he did not voice the opinion, he agreed with the sentiment expressed by Falcon: anything gained from the alien spacecraft belonged to all humanity.

* * *

Three days later a communication reached the *Butterball* with the seal of the Mars Central Government on the front page. Joe scanned through until he found the paragraph he wanted.

Captain Joseph Falcon, master of the envoy vessel Butterball, *is hereby authorized to act as the official representative of the Government of Mars specifically and for humanity in general, in negotiations with inhabitants of the alien vessel* NE372BJ4, *referred to as the* Visitor, *until such time as those negotiations can be assumed by the mission authority convened for the purpose.*

He is authorized to take any steps necessary and to make any decisions considered appropriate in dealings with the inhabitants of said vessel, after having given due consideration to the official operational policy guidelines and any further requirements of the mission authority.

He will at all times...

Joe smiled to himself. Too old and wary to trust any committee or political double-talk, he knew that having no choice, they would agree. As expected, escape clauses littered the document. It did not precisely state they would honor or support his decisions, but at least allowed him some leeway to conduct the mission on his terms and would stand in court if necessary. It would be wise, he thought, to double-check that.

"Chloe. Send a copy of this to my son Jake, by secure transmission."

* * *

Joe glanced up as a fresh coffee appeared, urged on by the hand of Ruth Carvalio. Having sensed he was in need of a refill, she sat opposite and warmed her hands around her own cup.

The ship was mid-way through one of its brief respites from acceleration, and she had entered through the open door of his cabin while he was deep in concentration.

They had rarely been alone together since departure, and Ruth had become increasingly curious about the man she publically referred to as the 'enigmatic captain of this ship'.

She considered him deeper than generally suspected: interesting, but also a riddle. There was, for her, more to the man than the average, aging space jockey.

"You drink far too much of that muck," Joe commented.

"One of the perquisites for being a writer. You up for a chat?" she asked. Joe nodded absently. "If you don't mind my asking, why 'Butterball'?"

Joe smiled, his thoughts appearing to drift for a moment to something almost forgotten, lost in the past. "I named her after a dog I had as a child. A golden retriever. I loved that animal. It was either that or Peaches, after the cat."

Ruth returned the smile. She liked Joe Falcon. Despite his reputation as a stubborn hard-nose, he was human and reasonably sociable, unlike so many taciturn people she had met since moving into space.

"Fair enough. You lived on Earth when you were young." It was a statement, not a question.

"Yes, Born in France—shifted to Mars a few years ago."

Ruth took a long sip at her coffee. "You're something of a celebrity now."

Joe let out a sigh. "We haven't done anything yet. Won't even make rendezvous for another week."

He was a quiet, introspective man and plainly in no mood for a grilling. Ruth decided to move slowly. "So, tell me about Joe Falcon."

"Hmmm. Age fifty-eight, one-eighty-five centimeters tall, brown hair, green eyes, not married…"

"A widower," Ruth said.

"Yes, two kids. I've spent almost my whole life in the Navy, first on Earth and then in Space. I like music, chess, reading, Pinacoladas and walking in the rain."

"I'm sorry, I asked for that. I'm being nosey, aren't I?"

"Yes … no … I don't mind. I'm just being an ass."

"You have two children."

"Yes. I've already said that."

"Parts of the media have raised the lawsuit brought against you by your daughter, as expected. Before long they're going to request a statement."

"That's nobody's business. Are we chatting, or are you interviewing me?"

Ruth smiled at the remark. "Sorry, I didn't mean to intrude. But you did bring me along for a reason, after all."

"Yes, but not to grill me on my private life."

"Sorry again. I'm just trying to help. Court records are public, Joe, but they only record the technical details of the cases, not the human truths behind them. People love this stuff. Before you say anything, I agree it's none of their business, but if you don't give the media what they want they'll take the official records and embellish them to suit. According to my sources, at least one network has mentioned the case, and others will soon pick it up. Remember what I said about controlling this yourself?"

Joe sighed again. "Yes, fine. She didn't bring any case against me. She sued my wife's estate. Helen left her entire worth to me—Grace thought it should have gone to her and my son, Jake."

"But she didn't win."

"No. The will was very precise and ironclad. Helen did not want our daughter to inherit, and I chose to honor her wishes."

"Will you leave any of your estate to her?"

"Okay, enough," Joe said, starting to rise from his seat."You're out of line now, Ruth."

"Sorry, sorry. Please sit down. I promise I won't raise it again. I'm doing a lot of apologizing here."

After a moment's contemplation, Joe resumed his seat and returned to his coffee, his mouth set in resignation. "Ask if you must."

"No. If anybody digs, I'll deal with it based on what you've already told me, okay? And I promise I'll respect your privacy. Tell me about your son. I know you're proud of him."

"Jake? Yes, I am. He's a good man, smart, powerful … much wiser than me."

"I hear he's something of a powerhouse."

"In some circles, I suppose. He's made a few ground-breaking discoveries researching molecular systems."

"That's something of a holy grail these days, right? Very controversial."

"No idea. His work is way over my head; I know nothing about his level of physics and my knowledge of computers doesn't extend much beyond the words 'Chloe, can you…'"

"Yes, Captain?' the soft voice of the ship's computer enquired.

"Disregard please, Chloe." Joe turned his attention back to Ruth. "I know nothing about the field."

"Jake lives in…?"

"Brisbane, in Australia. Nice place."

"You like Brisbane?"

"Never been there, except the naval docks in the port."

Ruth grinned, leaned forward and propped her chin in her hands. "You know, it's an honor to be selected for this trip."

"I'm glad you feel that way."

"I mean you."

"I wasn't chosen for any honorable reason. *Butterball* was the only possible choice, and I suspect those in charge see us all as dispensable."

Ruth raised an eyebrow. "How do you respond to that?"

"No problem. Someone has to go. My ship can make the trip, and I was available at a moment's notice. Hardly an honor though."

"Why do you say that?"

"As I said, no one else can get there in time." Joe once again appeared lost in thought. "Better us than a warship, I guess."

"You think that's important?"

"I do. We have to work on the assumption the *Visitor* is inhabited. Any ship of war is identifiable as such, even by an alien, I would imagine. At first, I thought a Navy ship would be better, but not now. I don't think we, humanity, will be seen in a favorable light if our first ambassadors from the stars are greeted with a weapon of destruction, regardless of our intent."

"So you think the *Visitor* will be inhabited?"

"No. The odds are overwhelmingly against it."

"Alaine agrees with you. I don't really understand why."

"If you carry a crew, you also need the requirements of life—water, food, air, and heat. The trouble is, no matter how well you seal your environment, some loss—deterioration, leakage if you like—is inevitable. That limits the length of time the ship can carry living beings. Eventually, it'll become incapable of supporting life. You can recycle water, filter and renew air, and grow food, but there's always a limit. To maintain heat, you need a constant energy output—that's a massive problem."

"How so?"

"A crew needs a minimum temperature for the duration of the voyage. That's a big long-term power draw. That ship must have been out there for a long time, decades, even centuries. There's no heat signature, or at least nothing we can measure. It's stone cold."

"Carl was talking about cryogenic suspension."

"Oh, yeah," Joe said. "Alien popsicles—that one comes up a lot. I suppose it's possible, but unlikely; there are so many problems. Another option is deep hibernation and we can do that short term, but for decades or centuries it isn't viable, for us at least. Alien technology might be better, but we don't know yet."

"So you think it's dead?"

"Yep."

Ruth took a long draw from her coffee. "There is a rumor circulating on Earth that you agreed to make a claim for Mars."

"No. I said I'll make a statement, but that's all. I'll decide what line to take when the time arrives. You'll keep that to yourself."

"So you won't claim on behalf of Mars?"

"Let's say I'll think about that one."

"The media call you a hardnose, and many other less than complementary terms."

"I wouldn't say I am. I admit I'm stubborn at times, and I've been going out of my way to make sure I keep control here. I prefer to run my own race. I'm the captain of this ship and my loyalties are to my crew first, my passengers next and then humanity as a whole."

Ruth grinned mischievously. "So I come second?"

"Don't…"

"Do you think they would have sent you if you had told them that in the beginning?"

"Probably—I don't think they had a choice."

A soft warning bell chimed through the intercom. Joe stood and grabbed his empty cup to return it to the galley. "Time to get back to the chairs," he said. Ruth nodded and pushed her seat back.

"Joe, I know it sounds like I'm grilling you—and I guess it's true to a point—but I want to say I'm not working every time I ask a question. I … I'm interested. Really. Just so you know."

Joe stopped and turned until his eyes met hers. Deep inside he was aware the woman attracted him, and that had influenced his decision to bring her. "Next time, you can tell me about Ruth Carvalio."

Chapter 07

JOE FOCUSED ON the small object at the center of the video monitor. "Distance?"

Sarah swiped a finger on the surface of her screen. "Ten thousand kilometers plus."

Butterball tore through space with the *Visitor* astern to starboard and drawing closer. At the right moment Chloe would decelerate the freighter, match speed and assume a parallel trajectory thirty kilometers away from the much larger alien ship.

This was, in Joe's estimate, the most critical phase of the encounter with a high possibility of negative reaction. How the other vessel would respond to the human presence was unpredictable: an attack could come at any minute or the *Visitor* might change course to avoid them. He hoped allowing the alien to overtake would paint *Butterball* as benign; it was also the obvious way to close on their objective at such high speed.

The voyage was at day twenty-five, time mostly spent under constant acceleration. For an antiquated craft, the old freighter was performing admirably, having clawed her way to a velocity more than double her previous best. She was moving faster than any commercial vessel in the history of humanity.

The piggyback fuel tanks were all but empty, but the primary tanks held enough in reserve for an end-of-mission rendezvous with a tanker. Failing that, they would drift helplessly in space until rescued, somewhere inside the orbit of Mercury and far too close to the Sun.

During acceleration periods, Joe had sought to keep the confined crew occupied swatting up on anything of possible use for the voyage. Alaine Parish had lectured on his personal holy grail, to determine the nature of the *Visitor's* engines. He exasperated all with the theory of advanced drive systems, expressing the opinion the Bussard ramjet remained the most likely possibility: photon engines or anything involving antimatter presented technical problems he, at least, considered insurmountable. Now, moments away from contact, the point came up again.

"The ship would need a scoop thousands of kilometers across to collect enough mass for a ramjet," Marius Pine pointed out. "I can't see one at all on the distance photographs. The nose of the *Visitor* shows no traces of a scoop or any sign of the intake opening one would expect."

"It might be formed by some kind of force field, a magnetic cone or some such thing," Alaine said. "We'll find out when we're closer, with luck. The idea can't be ruled out; we're dealing with a technology well beyond our own. They may have anchored a scoop in some way we can't see, and dumped it as they entered the Solar System."

"I sincerely hope not," Pat's voice interjected over the intercom as she listened in from her acceleration seat in the common room.

"Because?"

"On its current trajectory, the *Visitor* can't leave at the same point it came in, right, Captain? If they dumped the scoop, it could only be because they have no further use for it. That would mean they intend to stay, wouldn't it?"

Nobody responded to the question.

"I mean, as far as first contacts go, this is a worst-case scenario for us."

"How do you figure?" Joe asked.

"There are only three possibilities for a first encounter. If we were more advanced, the first contact would be in their system, which is bad for them and good for us. We would know where they lived, and everything else about them, while they would know nothing of us. If we were equal in development, the meeting might be in deep space and it would be a standoff. But…"

"…they are ahead of us," Joe finished for her. "They are here and may know all about us. We are completely ignorant about them."

"Exactly my point," Patricia said.

After pondering the point for a few seconds, Joe turned his attention back to the closing colossus. "Planetary observers predict it'll traverse the Sun and head back out again. That would go against the scoop theory. Chloe, begin rendezvous maneuvers now."

Butterball dropped back as Joe kept his eyes glued to the data readout. He prayed the AI was paying attention.

She was.

"Force shield detected, Captain," she announced as numbers streamed across Joe's monitor. "It is a dome-shaped electromagnetic field preceding the *Visitor* by thirty thousand meters. The exact composition is beyond my programming."

"Meteor defense? Can we avoid it?"

"No, Captain. The shield will reach us in ten seconds."

"Shit. Hang on everyone," Joe said. "This might get rough. Reduce the rate of closure, Chloe."

He grabbed the arms of his command chair and closed his eyes.

Butterball was too close.

It would have been wiser to stay further out and move in from the side, and now the entire crew might pay for his poor judgment. Chloe's soft, never-varying voice counted down.

"Three… two… one…"

For a moment nobody spoke.

"We're still here," said Sarah, stating the obvious. "We're through. We passed straight through the field without feeling it."

Joe opened his eyes and observed the white faces of his companions. "Chloe, are you still functional?"

"Yes, Captain. My systems are unaffected. A void opened in the shield to allow our passage."

"You think it knows we're here?" Joe asked. "An intelligent meteor shield?"

Alaine glanced at him and shrugged. "They let us through. If that was a collision defense, it should've destroyed us. They deliberately let us through."

Slowly the freighter dropped back, maintaining a speed fractionally below the velocity of the *Visitor*. An hour later, with the alien vessel alongside, another burst from *Butterball's* engines matched trajectory, placing her thirty kilometers off the port bow of the new arrival.

* * *

Sometimes Joe felt small. Now he felt microscopic and insignificant.

For the first time, the crew gazed upon the object they had come so far to see. The sight left them speechless, the ship's sheer size lending a majesty no human endeavor could hope to match. The scale relative to *Butterball* was that of man to mosquito.

Long and pencil-thin, the principal structure was a cylinder. Forward, the nose extended into a stretched shovel shape, flatter underneath and level with the bottom of the hull, the top surface curving down to meet it. The nose spread away from the sides by around one kilometer on either side, reminiscent of a species of shark Joe had seen during his time as a young naval officer on Earth. A small, flat platform tucked in against the fuselage behind the aft edge of the shovelnose.

At the stern the structure bulged like a bulb of garlic, stretching into a long, thin spire tapering away to a needle-like point.

"It's kind of like a minaret tipped on its side," Alaine said.

"That's a good name for it," Sarah commented. "The *Minaret*."

"I agree," said Joe. "*Minaret* it is. Chloe, log that."

"The astronomer who discovered it won't like that," Alaine said, a smile on his face.

Joe shrugged; he did not care at all.

The most impressive feature was at the mid-section where the hull passed through a separate tubular structure about twenty kilometers long, several hundred meters thick and twice the diameter of the hull itself. In the gap between, struts connected the two structures. From nose to tail, the ship appeared to be over one hundred kilometers long.

"One hundred and six, point seven-four-three, to be precise," Sarah read from the figures provided by *Butterball's* sensors. "Diameter is five thousand and nineteen meters over most of its length, and nine thousand and forty one for the tube section. The spire at the back is fourteen thousand three hundred meters from the base of the bulb to the tip of the tail. Impressive."

"Do we have any idea what she's made of?" Joe asked.

"No. Our sensors can't penetrate. Not metallic at all—carbon maybe?"

Joe studied the imposing image on his screen and considered his next move. The *Minaret* was a blank canvas. Nowhere on the exterior was there any trace of hatches, windows or platforms other than behind the shovelnose, or of openings of any kind. Nor were there visible any external extensions such as antennae, fins or weapons. Beyond its obvious variations in shape, the hull was smooth and featureless.

Joe shook his head, overwhelmed by a sense of insignificance and helplessness. This machine had to be centuries ahead of anything within human capability. He wondered what they would find, assuming they were permitted to board at all.

"Any sufficiently advanced technology is indistinguishable from magic," he muttered to himself.

Sarah glanced across at him. "Sorry?"

"Clarke's third law. A famous writer from a few centuries back—wrote several fiction stories based on the almost identical scenario we're now facing. Chloe, drop us back to the tail, underneath to the other side and forward to take position opposite our current location. Maintain separation distance. I want a serious look at this thing before we go any further."

For the next two hours *Butterball* drifted the length of the *Minaret*, photographing and mapping every square meter of its surface. She came to rest aft of the nose, on the starboard side.

"Nothing," Alaine said. "There's another platform on this side. No openings, no other structures. Nothing else. Bugger all."

"We didn't look into the space between the hull and the tube very carefully," Harry Chan said. "Could be something in there."

"Maybe," said Joe. "Not a logical place for entry points though, with the struts in the way. Anyone want to guess about that tube?"

"It looks like it should revolve around the main hull," Alaine said, "but there's no sign of a rotating sleeve. Those struts merge seamlessly into the hull. Doesn't make a lot of sense—why would you build something like that if it couldn't rotate?"

"Could the whole ship spin?" Sarah asked.

"Then you wouldn't need struts. There would be no need for a separate drum at all. The flat nose looks like it's always intended to be oriented as it is now, and that contradicts the rotation idea."

Joe sighed. "I agree. Chloe, begin transmission. Radio, directional laser and light array. Prime numbers two to twenty-nine, please."

Butterball began sending her greeting, flashed from the outside of the cargo module, broadcast on multiple channels and by lasers set at low intensity in the hope they would not be interpreted as a threat.

Numbers were the key. Patricia, adamant a space-traveling intelligence must understand the language of mathematics, insisted on beginning with a prime number sequence. "You can't create an advanced technology without mathematics. The universe is built on math, so the rules must be constant—the same everywhere. They have to be, don't they?" Joe wasn't so sure; the aliens probably had a mathematical system, but it might be based on completely different principles to that of humankind.

Sarah grinned at Joe. "We could broadcast a message in English or Mandarin."

"Seriously?" Pat's voice responded over the intercom. "Do you think there is any chance at all an alien would understand one of our languages?"

"I live in hope," Sarah snickered, holding a suppressing hand over her mouth.

For an hour, the transmission continued without response. Joe's attention hung on the distance readouts. "Chloe, move us in to twenty-five kilometers. One thousand meters per minute."

On his command, *Butterball* drifted closer, settling into her new position five minutes later. Joe did not intend to pose a potential threat—he would not be the accidental cause of the first interstellar conflict in human history.

For another sixty hours, the freighter paced the *Minaret*, maintaining a constant distance and broadcasting its greeting without pause. Mathematical and scientific equations followed the prime numbers, then information on the Solar System and humanity. Last, as a final resort, greetings were broadcast in both primary human languages, Mandarin and English.

A giant screen on the outside of the cargo module sprang to life with drawings, pictures and biological data about humanity and life on Earth in general. In addition, a diagrammatic invitation was broadcast to enter into orbit around Venus.

Four days after arrival, and with no response from the target, tension amongst the crew began to show.

“Don't you think it’s a risk telling them so much about us when we know nothing about them,” Ruth Carvalio asked, following the procedure from her monitor in the common room.

“Not at all,” Pat Grace replied. “Assuming the ship is occupied, they are aware of our presence and where we live. They’re more advanced technologically and the last thing we want to do is appear unfriendly. Their social level is bound to be well ahead of ours, considering the organization it would take to build that thing. Better for us they don’t conclude our evolution is somewhere around dysfunctional-kindergarten-anarchy.”

“Point taken,” Ruth sighed.

On the bridge, Alaine clung to the back of Joe's chair, peering over his shoulder at the screen.

“There isn't a mark on the thing,” he said. “That worries me a bit.”

"Yes?"

"That ship's been out there for a long time, perhaps centuries depending on how fast it can go. Space is not empty. The collision shield must be highly effective but it's only at the bow. I would expect at least some scars on the hull; the lack of marks suggests there's more we haven't seen yet. I can't help wondering what's next."

"Let's find, out shall we? Chloe, take us in to twenty kilometers please."

Over the next few hours, *Butterball* crept closer, finally coming to rest ten kilometers from the *Minaret*, aft of the nose.

"Sarah, is *Drummer* ready?"

"Yes, sir. Carl's in the lock now."

In the cargo bay, Carl Geddes prepared to launch an autonomous vehicle used to investigate objects too small or too dangerous for the ship to approach. *Drummer* could land on an asteroid, secure itself with magnetic or mechanical grapples, and examine the surface with everything from seismic pulses to physical drilling. Joe did not intend to make a direct assault on the *Minaret's* hull but the little robot could still discover a great deal.

"Let her go," he commanded.

The robot lifted from the deck and sailed through the hatch, drifting at a fast walking pace towards the massive alien behemoth. At its leading edge, lights flashed the same greetings broadcast from *Butterball*. The flat upper surface carried modules containing samples of food, water and air, detailed biological data on human beings of both sexes, images of Earth, Mars and life on the two worlds, and information on the Solar System. Once again, the invitation to rendezvous in Venus orbit was repeated.

It took two hours to cover the ten kilometers separating the two ships, quite fast enough for Joe. Chloe continued to broadcast greetings and probe the alien vessel for data, none of which was forthcoming.

Drummer reached the *Minaret* and came to rest on the hull aft of the platform behind the nose. Magnetic grapples dropped, attempted to secure a purchase and failed.

"Sorry, no luck," Carl announced. "Hull is non-magnetic. I'll try suction … hang on … yes … holding, but only just. The surface is as smooth as glass." With a tenuous hold on the hull side, *Drummer* began sending gentle pulses into the shell.

"Bloody hell," Harry Chan cursed. "Nothing. Well, almost. Hollow; hardly a quantum leap. Most of the sound is being absorbed. It's telling us zip."

Joe nodded confirmation. "Ok, let's try something else. The flat ledge—I want to see it. Chloe, send *Drummer* forward."

The level area, small in comparison to the size of the larger vessel, was almost half a kilometer across. The tiny explorer began to drift along the inner edge following the near vertical wall where the shelf joined the hull proper. Without warning, its transmissions stopped.

"Whaaa? Where is it?" Carl asked. "*Drummer*'s gone!"

"No," Sarah said. "I'm still reading it. It's still there—we just can't see it."

Joe stared at the video feed, now focused on the only flat surface on the exterior of the alien ship. The platform was empty—*Drummer* had vanished. "We can fit on there, I think."

"I think so, yes," Sarah said. "Chloe confirms the top side of the ledge is free of obstruction and plenty big enough for us."

Joe eased back in his chair and thought over the possibilities. Before vanishing, the robot had found landing a difficult proposition. Magnetic grapples were useless and there were no protrusions of any kind. Only suction plates worked, winched in as tightly as possible.

Butterball could land the same way, but with its greater mass Joe did not feel comfortable about perching on the outside of the *Minaret's* hull. The ledge appeared more suitable but was also the place where the little robot vanished.

"Okay," he said. "This is no different from docking on an asteroid. Chloe, take us in please."

Under the infallible control of the computer, *Butterball* closed on its larger companion then turned and slid sideways, coming to rest a short distance from the hull wall. Spider-like articulating legs descended from the ship until clear of the lowest arc of the rotating accommodation drums, and from beneath the cargo module, suction plates dropped to the surface seeking whatever purchase they could find.

"Down and solid, sir," Sarah said. "More or less."

"I'd rather be sitting in space," Harry Chan commented. "The old girl was never designed to land on anything like this."

"We haven't been blasted to atoms yet," Alaine said. "Always an excellent sign."

After an hour of waiting and watching, Joe pushed up from his chair. “Alright, bridge crew take a break. Get some sleep if you can. Yes, I know, impossible. Try anyway.”

He launched himself in the direction of the spine corridor. “Harry, you take the first watch. Chloe, I want constant scanning and monitoring of the *Minaret.* If anything happens, you know the drill. The first exploration party goes out in ten hours—Alaine, Carl, and me. Let's try to find a way in.”

Chapter 08

A PAUSE FOR THE briefest of moments, a deep breath, and Joe stepped through the airlock and drifted down to the platform. Touching down on the smooth surface, he took his bearings.

"I'm down."

"Is that the best you can do?" Ruth's voice asked on his headset. "A simple 'I'm down' won't sound so hot in my reports."

"What would you like me to say? I come in peace for all mankind?"

Sarah's voice interrupted. "Not sure, but I think that one's been done."

"Fine, dealt with. Alaine, Carl, come down."

Minutes later the other two members of the first exploration party joined him and together they followed the flat aft wall of the bow shovelnose towards the side of the fuselage proper.

"No doors," Alaine said. "Not even cracks or seams that might be a sealed entrance."

Carl pointed to where *Drummer* had vanished. "What about that?"

A large patch of discoloration, about sixty meters high and extending at least three hundred along the inner edge of the platform was visible on the hull side. A pale, shimmering blue, it contrasted with the off-white of the ship.

Joe drifted across to the wall. "I don't remember seeing that before. Didn't show up on the video images." For a moment, he paused and looked around the platform. A memory from long ago flashed into his mind, from a time when he was a junior naval officer.

"You know what this reminds me of? Has either of you ever seen an aircraft carrier, the floating airstrips used by oceanic navies on Earth? They have massive hangers below the landing deck and the planes move up and down on little elevator platforms at the sides. If that darker patch is a doorway, this would be like the entrance to the hanger."

Carl stretched out a gloved hand and searched for cracks. "It isn't a door, just a color difference. No seams or joins…" He gasped as his fingers passed unimpeded into the shimmering surface, then snatched his hand back, the unaffected digits still attached to the end. "Shit."

Floating up beside him Joe reached out and repeated the process, watching his hand disappear. "This is an energy field of some kind."

He leaned in until his helmet touched the surface, and then eased forward another few centimeters. As the faceplate passed into the wall, a strange tingling sensation crept through the flesh of his face, spreading into his body as he continued inward.

Darkness.

Joe turned on his helmet lamp to light up the space beyond. Meters away, *Drummer* sat inactive on a broad floor. Programmed to traverse the hull at a set distance, it had changed direction when the solid surface gave way to the force field, and plunged through to the interior. Beyond the defined survey area, it then settled to the deck to await further orders.

Joe panned the lamp around. "You guys are not going to believe this," he said. "I think we found the front door already."

Seconds later, Alaine stood beside Joe as Carl examined his precious machine.

"Can you hear me, Sarah?" Joe asked.

"Loud and clear, Captain. We watched you go through. The audio is fine, and I'm trying to re-acquire visuals. Where are you now?"

"The patch on the hull side is an entrance covered by some sort of energy field. We're standing in a tunnel maybe three hundred meters wide. I can't see much: there's no light in here, and our lamps aren't that powerful."

"We can use *Drummer*'s floods," Carl said. "I'll switch it to manual control so we can float it further in."

"I'll work *Drummer* from here if you like," Sarah said. "I have a visual now."

"Seriously? Excellent." Joe turned towards the interior of the ship. "Let's take a gander inside."

Each member of the team wore a jet maneuvering harness, allowing him or her to travel the length of the entrance tunnel in seconds. From the inner end, they peered once again into darkness as if standing at the edge of a cliff on a black, moonless night. Beside them, *Drummer* waited obediently.

"I'm switching the floods on now," Sarah's voice announced. A blinding light illuminated the panorama below.

Joe's jaw dropped.

For a long, drawn-out moment nobody spoke.

Joe gazed out to where visibility vanished into black oblivion. Never before had he seen anything that came close in comparison to this. The light revealed a vast chamber stretching away several kilometers into darkness in all directions, the high ceiling barely visible.

Only part of the immense bay was visible. The floodlights, barely adequate to illuminate the deck several hundred meters below, covered just the area near the entry tunnel.

A checkerboard of squares and rectangles defined by black lines spread across the vast floor; the spaces varied in size, some as small as fifty meters square, others many times larger. Within many stood dull grey, cylindrical monoliths, each equipped with a thick horizontal arm at one side.

"Weird." Alaine peered down at the structures. "Kind of reminds me of something though."

"Are you getting this, Sarah?" Joe asked.

"Oh yes. I'm recording everything. I'll turn the floods up to maximum and pan so you can get a better view."

Joe guessed the space must extend the full width of the hull—they had seen a platform similar to the one where *Butterball* rested, projecting from the port side of the ship, so it was reasonable to assume a second entry point there.

Even the interior of the Kepler *Core*, with its gardens, buildings and pseudo-sunlight, lacked the cold majesty of this grandiose construct.

"A giant docking bay—it has to be," he said.

"Some docking bay," Sarah said on the intercom. "From *Drummer*'s scans, Chloe estimates at least twenty square kilometers in floor space—bigger than most airfields on Earth."

"And every spaceport on Mars. I want a closer look. We didn't see any hatches or openings in the tunnel walls on the way in, so if there is one, it will be somewhere down there."

"Yes, sir. Harry and Peter are suited up and waiting in the lock in case you run into trouble."

"Don't worry; we're only searching for an entrance this time. I don't intend to go any further inside this thing for now. Stay close, lads."

Joe stepped out over the precipice and floated towards the floor, with Alaine and Carl close behind. On reaching the bottom, he landed in one of the larger rectangular spaces below the entrance.

The nearest monolith, around seven meters in diameter and twice as high, stood nearby. Like the ones seen from above, this structure had a thick, horizontal, tubular arm extending out to one side and then forward, ending in a flattened, featureless, circular section facing the center of the delineated space.

"Skywalk!" Carl yelled.

"What?"

"It's like a skywalk. Earth airports had them a couple of centuries ago. You don't find them now except on smaller regional fields. Passengers would take a closed walkway from the terminal out to a boarding area and then through a skywalk to the aircraft. The end of the ramp would raise or lower to suit, and a skirt fitting against the side of the fuselage would seal the connection. This is the same basic configuration, but no opening at the end."

"Sounds reasonable," Alaine agreed. "So this is most likely a landing field, as we thought. Small ships come in through the tunnels, settle into a designated bay, and the crew leaves by a skywalk."

Joe surveyed the part of the field visible in the lights from *Drummer.* "That's as good a guess as any, I suppose. Not all of the bays have a skywalk. There are hundreds of them … thousands … so many."

"A ship this size can never land on a planet," Alaine said. "It would have shuttles, exploration craft, and service and maintenance vehicles."

"And military. This thing is too massive to maneuver in a battle. You would need a number of smaller ships for defense, like that old-fashioned carrier and its aircraft."

"Or for offense."

"Yep, that too," said Joe. "So where are they?"

Carl stared up at the overhead structure. "If it is a skywalk it might be our way in. I'll go up and take a look." Without waiting for Joe's response, he boosted up towards the end of the extension.

"It's a darker color, like the force field at the entrance," He pushed against the surface. "My hand won't go through. It's solid."

"Maybe it only works when connected to a ship," Joe said. "There must be another entrance; a bay this size would always be in vacuum, so there should be an airlock somewhere."

"No, nothing. No actual hatch and no opening mechanism on this side. No levers, wheels or panels of any sort. There's a faint grey line around the darker patch, circular, about two meters across. Nothing else."

"That tells us something about our aliens," Pat's voice interrupted on the intercom. "They're small enough to fit through a two-meter diameter door. They may be around our size if they walk upright."

"If they walk at all," Joe said. "Okay Carl, come down again. We'll keep looking. There must be a tradesman's entrance or whatever."

A block-like extension projected from the base of the column on the side opposite the skywalk. On the outer end, a second circular line surrounded another dark area, again two meters across. A smaller spot was visible on the wall beside it.

Alaine extended his hand to rest on the big patch. "This is solid as well. Maybe the little one activates it. A control panel or a pressure pad?"

Pat interjected again. "They must have hands, or something equivalent. Perhaps eyes of some sort; those darker patches indicate visual acuity."

"Let's find out if it works." Joe reached out to touch the smaller spot.

"Nope, still solid," Alaine's hand was pressed firmly against the larger patch."

"Dead," Joe said. "Stone cold. Not surprising considering how long it might have been out here. No power, probably."

"How come the force field at the entrance works?" Carl asked.

"God knows. Different system—different principle?"

Alaine pointed to one side. "There's something over there."

A cylindrical hollow, about twenty centimeters in diameter and ten in depth was set in the wall. A smooth bar stretched across the middle, merging seamlessly at either side. Alaine grabbed the crossbar in his gloved hand. "Doesn't look like it can turn." He gave it a hard twist. "Whoa, hang on."

The bar rotated easily, its ends gliding smoothly through the solid walls. In perfect concert with the rotation, a small dark spot appeared at the center of the large gray patch, expanding outward until it reached the circular line. What had once been a dull grey patch now shimmered with an oily blue-green-purple sheen reminiscent of the shell of an Abalone.

"I don't believe it," Alaine said. "This thing has no apparent mechanical parts. The bar merges into the cylinder, and the cylinder into the wall. No seams, joins, nothing. How can it move like that?"

"This hatch is weird," Joe commented. He extended a hand, passing his fingers through the shimmering patch with a tingling sensation similar to the one he had felt when entering the tunnel. "It just changed, as if the molecules of the material rearranged themselves to suit. It's open. There's some kind of force field but we can pass through. There's vacuum outside, so we might find atmosphere in there."

"We go in?" Carl asked, moving forward.

"Easy," Joe said. "Not yet. I won't risk anyone being trapped."

With a deep breath, he eased his head and one hand through the wall and shone the helmet light around the interior, feeling the same tingle as his flesh passed through the field.

The chamber within was the size of a standard freight elevator, but deeper. At the far end was another dark circle with an identical activation patch and manual bar. Turning his head, he spotted the same controls on the sidewall near the point he had penetrated.

"This has to be an airlock. Most likely, we won't be able to activate the inner door until this one is closed, for safety. We'll need to be prepared in case it won't open again from the inside. Alaine, close this hatch, please."

Joe pulled back and watched the wall change, leaving the original dark patch surrounded by its grey circle.

"If the force field keeps the vacuum out, why would they need an airlock," Alaine wondered. "Or an emergency safety on the doors?"

"Backup, maybe" Joe replied. "Any system can fail, given time. For now, we'll explore this bay further. Sarah, we're going to move over to the rear wall. *Drummer* will accompany us and light the way."

"Done," Sarah replied. Giant shadows shifted as the robot drifted down from the entrance to a position above and behind the explorers.

The maneuvering packs made short work of the two-kilometer sortie to the aftermost boundary of the hanger bay. After twenty minutes, Joe and his companions reached a vertical wall that stretched up into darkness.

In *Drummer*'s pool of light, dark patches were visible on the wall. A meter above the floor a row of hatches, each a dark grey circle around forty meters in diameter, stretched away to either side. Higher up was a second row of smaller hatches, then a third, smaller again, at the edge of visibility. All were closed. No opening mechanisms were visible.

"The only reason for so many accesses to an airfield," Joe said, "would be multiple levels of hangers. A hell of a lot of them."

For as long as their suits permitted, the three examined the wall, before turning back towards the entrance. If hangers occupied the space beyond, smaller auxiliary craft might be there, but with no apparent way through, it was a matter for future explorations.

"That's where I want to be," said Alaine. "On the other side of that wall."

* * *

Joe slumped into a chair in the common room, only half aware of the drone of voices as Alaine, Sarah, Pat, Ruth, and Wally Tyrell sorted through the shift's events.

"Captain Barrett of the *Constellation* sends 'greetings'," said Sarah. "He directed us to make no attempt to land on or enter the *Minaret.* If we do, it'll be considered an act of war against Earth."

Drawn into the conversation, Joe raised an eyebrow. "He has no authority to make that demand. How do you think we should respond?"

"I've already done so, Joe," said Alaine. "I thought you would approve since I'm supposed to be the official liaison. I advised we're an envoy of Mars, we carry a representative of the MNSF—that would be me—and are under no obligation to follow any directive from Earth or her delegates."

He grinned mischievously. "I pointed out they have no jurisdiction over the *Minaret* so our mission is in no sense an act of war, and that we've already landed and are exploring."

Joe rapped his fingers sharply on the arm of his chair as he sat upright. "And?"

"No response. They can't expect us to comply with their orders, and the threat is a bluff."

Joe dropped his gaze to the floor. "That's not quite how I would have responded. This is a commercial ship working within the laws of both Earth and Mars. As far as I'm concerned, we are a private vessel."

"Out here, private vessels have no rights or power over guns and soldiers," Alaine responded. "*Constellation* can make us disappear without trace and Mars can do nothing to back us up. They tried to bluff us, so we need to reciprocate. I had Chloe relay all communications to the Mars fleet just in case. If Barrett makes a move against us it will cause an interplanetary incident."

For a moment, Joe did not respond, mulling over Alaine's words. True, he was the official liaison, but he was exceeding his duty.

"Fine, but no more official statements without my approval. For now, we do not officially represent the government of Mars or anyone else. Am I clear?"

Alaine nodded, his grin gone, and changed the subject. "So, I want to see whatever's behind the aft wall. The landing bay is adequate for hundreds of smaller spacecraft but there isn't one in sight. It makes sense they'll be behind those doors."

"I think finding the control room is more urgent, gentlemen, and ladies," Wally said. He slapped the table with the flat of his hand. "Anything important will be there."

Alaine shook his head. "I don't agree. God knows how long we can stay here, so we need to find those ships. Imagine if we found one and learned to operate it. It would be the ultimate prize."

"And theft as well," Pat added, her voice calm in the growing storm between her two compatriots.

"Rubbish," said Alaine. "We tried for days to make contact with the crew of this ship. We landed at their entrance, walked—flew—over their airfield, and opened and closed a hatchway without a single response. They're long gone, or dead." He sat back and crossed his arms in defiance of Patricia.

"The problem, Alaine, is you're judging them on our terms. We can't assume the owners of this ship share anything at all in common with us; they might think in a completely different way. Our attempts to communicate may not have been recognized, or if they were, the aliens might not be interested. Their technology and social evolution may be so far ahead of ours that they regard us as insignificant. We could be the proverbial ants under their boots, and if we start stealing their picnic, they might decide to step on us. We should know a lot more before we do anything."

Pat sat back, mimicking Alaine with crossed arms and clenched jaw.

Joe eased back in his chair and sighed. "Enough, everyone," he said. "You're all forgetting one thing. This vessel is not dead. The force field at the hanger entrance still works. The hatch down at the skywalk also opens. I can't think of too many mechanical ways to rearrange molecules so in all likelihood the ship is still powered even if we can't find any heat sources. We can't make any assumptions about its capabilities."

"My point exactly," Pat said. "Everyone assumes it's dead after so long in space but that's not necessarily true. It might move much faster than we think, even a fair percentage of light speed. If so, it could get here from the nearest stars in decades, not centuries. It may have decelerated before it entered our system. Anything is possible."

"Doesn't mean there's a crew," Alaine muttered.

"That doesn't matter," Joe replied. "This thing could be automatic. If it *is* minus crew, there must be a controlling computer or the equivalent. I would prefer we didn't upset an artificial intelligence any more than an organic one. We may not be able to tell the difference."

"Ok, so what do we do now, Captain?" Sarah asked.

"We explore, we don't touch and we keep our wits about us. For the next team, I want some backup in case we can't get out of that hatch, so five of us will go this time. You, Alaine and I will enter the airlock. Harry, you will wait in the landing bay with Wally and if we don't re-appear within ten minutes, you'll try to open the hatch again from outside. *Drummer* will carry a rock cutter and you'll attempt to cut your way in and damn the Indians. If you can't rescue us you're in command."

For a moment, Joe considered the possible consequences of such an action.

"Either that," he said, "or we don't go in at all. We wait for the fleets instead."

Chapter 09

TWO HOURS LATER, five suited figures hovered above the hanger floor outside the docking hatch. With *Drummer* overhead to provide light, Joe gripped the manual bar and gave it a twist. As on the first occasion, the nearby patch within a circle changed, opening the way forward.

The interior was in darkness. Joe entered, followed by Sarah and Alaine. Once through, he floated up to the inner hatch controls and reached out a hand.

"Are we ready for this?" He turned the bar. Nothing happened.

"Dead?" Alaine asked.

Sarah turned back to the outer hatch in time to see it change from an oily shimmer to dull grey. "Hang on."

"Ok," said Joe. "Each hatch makes sure the other is closed before it opens. As expected."

"Yes, except it isn't happening."

Joe looked around. Both hatches appeared to be the same color, and the inner remained shut. "Harry, are you still with us?"

"Loud and clear, Captain. The walls don't interfere with communications at all."

Pat Grace interrupted from *Butterball.* "We can hear and see you as well."

A wave of relief washed over Joe as the inner hatch changed color. "Ok, time delay." He reversed the manual bar and as hoped, the inner door closed, followed a minute later by the opening of the outer.

"It looks like we can go in or out as we please," said Alaine. "That kind of scares me. What respectable alien lets someone just wander about like this?"

"Remember Pat's ants?" Sarah asked. "How much do you worry about ants wandering about your house?"

Joe was anxious to move on. "Focus, everyone. Harry, I want you and Wally to wait outside in case." He cycled the airlock several times until satisfied they would not be trapped. Only then did he step through the inner hatch.

A wide stairway wound around the inside of the cylindrical docking structure, the hatch opening on to a flat platform-like segment of the stairs.

"Our aliens have articulating legs," Pat said gleefully.

"And this part of the ship normally has some kind of gravity," Alaine said. "Otherwise steps wouldn't be necessary. There's no air in here and the temperature is close to absolute zero."

The wide, shallow steps curved down in one direction and up through a ceiling opening in the other. Through the center of the helix, a cylindrical tube of transparent, glass-like material extended through the ceiling and down into darkness. On the wall beside the hatch they had just entered through was yet another pressure patch and bar.

Joe floated up the stairway. In the room at the top, he shone his lamp around; the transparent tube filled the center of the space and on one side, an opening marked what he guessed must be the end of the 'skywalk' extension. At the front, a clear panel looked out over the landing field. The chamber was otherwise empty.

"I don't remember seeing that window from the outside," Sarah said as she floated across to examine the panel. "It's a transparent section of wall, not separate like a window at all."

"Smooth and featureless," Joe said. "Like everything else around here. Everything joins seamlessly as if it grew that way. Let's try going down."

Below the airlock entry, the stairway continued down for a considerable distance before ending in an empty, square bay with an arched opening leading into darkness.

The bottom end of the transparent tube stood at the center of the ground floor. Sarah shone her helmet lamp inside. "You know what this might be? An elevator—a way to lift cargo or crew."

"Or ants." Pat's voice added over the intercom.

"Touché."

Shut it, Pat, Joe thought. The cold chill spreading through his body was enough—he could do without the jokes. Deep inside, he suspected he and his crew were out of their depth.

Sarah tapped the transparent wall. "No door."

"The hatches in the airlock aren't separate either," Alaine said. "The walls just change so you can walk through. Maybe this is similar."

"So a door appears by what, molecular rearrangement?"

"Why not? That's as good an explanation as any."

Sarah stood back and studied the tube. "No controls either."

Turning away, the team floated across to the exit archway. Beyond, all was in darkness, the lamps illuminating only a small part of what appeared to be an immeasurable space.

From the doorway, a shallow ramp sloped down to where four parallel grey bands stretched away in either direction. Transparent, glowing arches, sometimes appearing solid and at others barely visible in the dim lamplight, sat arbour-like astride each band at regular intervals.

Taking a moment to orient himself Joe examined the road, assuming that was its nature. It crossed from port to starboard of the *Minaret's* hull. On the far side, a tall column stretched from floor to ceiling with a doorway and ramp facing out at its base. Joe assumed this was the entrance to the next docking bay; identical structures lined the route to the extent of the light.

Numerous box-like or cylindrical structures studded the spaces between the pillars, each smooth and featureless, blending seamlessly into the floor. From the tops of many, tubes extended up to the ceiling.

"They must be for servicing the ships," Joe said. "The ceiling is the base of the hanger bay, which makes this an access and service level."

"We aren't going to get far without some decent lighting down here," said Sarah. "What do we do now, Captain?"

"Well, I…" Standing in a pool of headlamp light, in a chamber possibly kilometers wide, the sense of solitude was overpowering despite the near presence of his companions. As the reality of the surroundings began to sink in, so too did the first doubts. He wondered how the other two were feeling. Never an anxious man by nature, he paused and took a moment to consider the next move.

In pressure suits, they could explore, but their efforts would be limited to the small area surrounding this immediate location and many important things would be missed or overlooked. In its current configuration the support unit of each suit could sustain life for fifteen hours, a little more for Sarah as her small frame made less demands on the suit's resources. In a vessel measuring one hundred kilometers in length, it placed an unacceptable limitation on the scope of their exploration.

"We follow the paths for as long as we can. Are you still with us on the ship?"

"Yes, Boss," came the response on the radio. It was Terry's voice. "Signal's still real good."

Joe frowned. A considerable amount of alien structure now separated them from *Butterball* and yet the audio from the communicators was unaffected, as were the images broadcast by their helmet cameras.

Floating above the floor, he drifted across to the roadway and then moved over the first of the two colored strips. Settling to the surface, he paused. "I guess we fly along the length." He turned to move and instantly felt himself speed up.

"Holy…" he cursed, using the backpack jets to push himself up from the path.

Sarah floated up beside him. "What happened?"

"I'm not sure. I moved, and something dragged me in the direction I was facing. When I lifted off it stopped."

"Wow," said Alaine, joining them. "What would you call this? Brilliant."

Minutes later the team glided along what they now accepted as a road, carried by an inexplicable force. The speed of movement varied, each individual able to move at a different pace according to desire, regardless of the fact they shared the same utility.

A second path, parallel to the first, worked in an identical manner, but in the opposite direction to allow two-way traffic. Motion across either band did not activate the system at all. Forward speeds of up to five kilometers an hour seemed safe but Joe intended to take no chances; the slightest hiccup and he intended to stop and return to *Butterball.*

For almost fifteen minutes, they passed through a metropolis of access pillars and service modules, varying from each other only in size. Some were colossal, others so small that if the internal cylinders were in fact elevators, they would not accommodate more than one passenger at a time.

Eventually, the road passed beneath what looked like a long, wide platform passing over the roadway. To one side a sloping ramp allowed access to the higher level. Joe and his companions floated up to the top.

Halfway along the platform and off to one side sat a spherical object about four meters across, its upper surface transparent and its interior featureless but for a flat, gray floor.

"What do you think?" Alaine said. "A transport system, maybe? I would lay bets on it."

Joe peered through the wall of the bubble. "It makes sense. Given that the old 'beam-me-up-Scottie' is impossible, a ship this size must have an efficient internal system. The roadways get you around local areas, and this may be some sort of shuttle going fore and aft. Don't ask me how though.

Somewhere, we'll find ways to move up and down between decks. You could go anywhere in pretty short order."

Sarah peered inside. "I wonder how it works. There are no rails or tracks. The bubble might float on magnets or something like that."

Alaine glanced at the readouts on the arm of his suit. "No magnetism here. Some new kind of field maybe, like the walkway."

"Hmmm," Joe said. "And no door, as usual."

"Maybe it's like the airlock hatches. You just walk through the wall."

Joe swept his eyes over the empty platform. No other significant features were apparent but the floating bubble was undoubtedly for transportation if one could work out how to operate it. With a complete absence of controls that would not be easy.

Feeling the cold shiver down his spine once again, Joe glanced at the timer on his forearm. Their suits still had plenty of capacity left but something about the current situation unnerved him.

"Alright. Back to the ship."

The return journey passed with little comment from anyone. Once at the entry arch, they ascended the internal steps to the inner door of the airlock. The airlock controls did not function immediately, with the same time delay as on the way in. All three explorers stood facing the hatch as they waited.

On the far side of the stairwell a multitude of specks smaller than grains of rice, emerged through the wall. Transparent, non-reflective and virtually invisible they passed unnoticed in the dim light.

The swarm settled on the back of Alaine's and Sarah's backpacks. As each landed, it slipped through one of the utility slots in the packs' outer casings. By the time the lock cycled to allow the three explorers through, the invaders were hidden, unseen and unsuspected.

Back inside *Butterball,* the party removed their suits and placed them in racks in the service bay, connecting them to the recharge station without once suspecting the presence of something that did not belong.

*   *   *

Once again, Joe took his seat in the common room and spread his hands in a candid gesture. "Any thoughts?"

Wally Tyrell spoke first. "I still insist the Bridge is the most important target, old boy. The computer interfaces will be there, so that's where I must go. If we can find out about these people anywhere, it's there."

"I second," said Sam Bright.

Alaine Parish predictably disagreed. So did Patricia

"So you would recommend?" Joe thought he knew the girl's answer already.

"Short of finding actual aliens," said Pat. "We have to locate the living quarters, assuming the *Minaret* has, or had, a crew. The people who built it are more important than the ship itself."

"Granted. Any other ideas?" Silence filled the room. "Ok, I want to see what's in the tube section around the middle of the ship. I can't help thinking it resembles a habitat drum, and if it is, that's where we'll find our aliens or the remains of them. We'll take duel approaches, I think."

"Two parties?" Sarah asked.

"Yes. Two groups of three will explore at any one time with the remaining crewmembers staying here. After every sortie we'll switch out one or two members, leaving at least one with experience in each team. To begin, we'll send one party forward to locate the ship's control deck. The second will search for ways into the hangers we think are behind those doors. After that, we continue aft to the drum, then on to the engine room if possible."

"This thing is a hundred kilometers long," Sarah said. "How do you propose we reach the engines, assuming they're at the rear end? Our suits won't keep us alive long enough for that."

Joe sighed. "Excellent point. We'll deal with that problem when we need to. The travelators still work, so I expect the platform-bubble-thingy does as well. We'll have to figure out how to use it. For now, we do what we can. *Drummer* can carry extra air for the longer trips if we can get it inside. Some of the other landing bays might have bigger airlocks."

* * *

After the meeting, everyone apart from the watch crew retired to sleep. In the cargo bay, hundreds of small, transparent micro-machines floated from their refuge in the vacuum-suit backpacks and crept through the ship, passing through open hatches, doors and passageways unhindered and unseen, following ventilation ducts and cable tiers into every part of the vessel.

Each device followed a pre-programmed agenda. Some drifted through *Butterball* recording and mapping the interior of every cabin and space. Others entered the service areas and worked their way into the computer console casings, where they attached themselves to various components and set about their tasks.

Within minutes, every byte of information stored in Chloe's memory banks had been accessed and transmitted, including the download links to every major data network on both Earth and Mars.

A handful of the tiny devices spread out to test the air and water, the food in the galley and any other substance of interest. Several penetrated the mechanical workings and sampled the fuel and all life support and utility services.

Others targeted the crew, homing in on each individual. On the bridge, Harry Chan and Sam Bright sat and chatted about their families on Mars and Earth, unaware as small intruders settled undetected on the backs of their necks, anesthetized their skin and took cell and blood samples.

In the wheels, off duty crewmembers received similar ministrations. Sound asleep on his bunk, Joe lay undisturbed as several intruders sampled his body tissues then exited through the ventilation grills and carried their precious cargo back to the maintenance bay to await departure.

A number of the alien mechanisms remained, taking up positions in dark, inconspicuous corners of each cabin and service space, and scattered throughout the electronic systems. Transparent, minuscule and undetectable, they began the task of recording sight and sound, transmitting it back to the *Minaret*. By change of shift nothing about the ship, its crew and the home worlds of humanity remained undiscovered.

Chapter 10

"SO, MARCUS," Joe began, staring at the camera above the monitor. "Here's the drum so far. We landed on the only flat surface we could find on the hull of the *Minaret*—the video I've attached shows that—and made our way into the ship. The sight is awe-inspiring. It's so immense you need to be here to appreciate it; a simple description won't do.

"Our way in was through what we think is the *Minaret's* main landing bay. Marc, the size of everything is off the scale. We usually build individual docking bays on our stations, but these guys just built a complete indoor airfield with tunnels leading out. I have no idea how this ship is constructed but I wonder what sort of material can work in such a massive structure.

"We found a transport system running under the airfield. We don't know what makes it work—how anything actually functions for that matter—but it's early yet, and I'm hoping we can use it to explore.

"There's something odd about all this. We still can't be sure if the *Minaret* is dead or alive. We've found no trace of a crew or any life forms, and we haven't made contact. The ship appears inactive and without power, but then we find an isolated system still working.

"The hanger force-field doors and the hatches, if you can call them that, still open. They operate by molecular rearrangement or something like it; the walls change to allow you to walk right through. The walkways also still function. None of us can guess how any of that works, but they must require power, so the ship is active. None of this means there is a crew; they could all be automatic systems.

"You'll know by now Barrett tried to scare us off. He sent an ultimatum that any landing or attempt to enter would be considered an act of war. Alaine Parish called his bluff; we had already landed and were inside by then. I would be a lot happier if you would give me some idea of the status of the Mars fleet that is supposed to be on its way here.

"Tomorrow we start to explore the *Minaret* in earnest. Our highest priority is to locate the bridge and the inner hangers where we think the ship's ancillary spacecraft, if there are any, must be stored. The hanger doors are on the video as well—there is no way to open them from the outside.

"Harry and Sam are busy trying to re-engineer *Drummer* as a mule for longer distance trips, so we can carry extra oxygen and so on. Our best hope is to work out how the transport system works, but I'm not holding my breath.

"Everything we've seen so far is way beyond us. We see what happens and we can sometimes work out the purpose, but the engineering behind it is a complete mystery. As an example, the self-propelling pathway is something you have to experience to believe. The technology is, well, magic.

"That's about it for now. I'll keep you informed as best I can. All I can say is, I still think the *Minaret* is sans crew. If there were living beings here, they would have made themselves known. Log and send please, Chloe."

Joe shut down the monitor and sat staring at the desktop. There was a lot he had not mentioned to Marcus, such as the fact the whole ship gave him the willies. Every crewmember who had been inside, including himself, reported the feeling they were being watched. He was convinced they were right but did not intend to say that to Marc.

With no sign of a crew, the ship was probably controlled by artificial intelligence. Joe wondered which he least would like to deal with, alien or machine. Organic beings at least offered the possibility of understanding, compromise, and mutual respect.

* * *

"Tell me you're not serious."

Carmichael Page stomped around the boardroom in his usual infuriating manner, clearly intended to intimidate the other members present. "It's bad enough that our first ambassador to an alien race is a rusty old relic called 'Butterball'. Now you're letting this man Falcon dictate terms to the naval fleets. Do you have any idea what they will do to him when they get there?"

"Sit down, Page," Adam Palfrey ordered.

"And for God's sake, shut up," Rob Billington added.

Page ignored them, staring out the window at the sprawl of Cable Station. "That ship is a private vessel, and according to my advice works for a private mining company and does not officially represent the government of Mars despite that silly little piece of paper you sent Falcon. Earth's fleet has orders to land and enter the ship immediately upon arrival, regardless of the message sent by this … Alaine Parish. Who the hell is he anyway?"

"He's an official representative of the government and of our navy as you well know, and as such, gives legal legitimacy to our claim," Adam responded. "Oddly enough, he was born on Earth and then moved to Mars, not unlike Falcon but as a small child. A fine, young officer."

Page turned towards the table, his eyes wide. "*Really*? His ordering Barrett about will create no end of problems."

"Will you *please* sit down," Adam barked. "If you would prefer, I can have you removed."

Page glared back at him and returned to the table. As he took his seat, Adam continued.

"We need to be constructive about this. And just for general information"—he waved his hand across the table to take in every board member present—"the *Butterball* is far from being a rusty heap, contrary to our earlier information. She's a perfectly functional converted freighter. We could have done much worse. At least we had a ship in the right position to make a rendezvous…"

"…before the *Constellation* could get there," Page finished the sentence.

"Okay, granted," Adam conceded. "You know as well as I do that Earth intended exactly the same thing."

Page waved a hand in resignation. There was no point in arguing that one—according to his brief, it was exactly what the Earth fleet had in mind.

"You do realize that some of Earth's governments are getting touchy about this," he remarked. "Several of them have expressed concern that a Mars-controlled mission has…"

"I'm not entirely sure we do control it," Adam said.

"…already landed on the *Minaret* and entered." Page continued with barely an acknowledgment. "They are demanding Mars issues statements that any and all knowledge acquired will be openly shared. The popular consensus among the common people is that the alien ship is a potential threat and that we should be sending warheads, not envoys."

"That is patently absurd," said Professor Alfred Brewer, representative of the Institute of Science, his soft, controlled voice in complete contrast to Page's. "The sheer level of technology needed to construct a vessel of such size dictates an extreme level of cooperation: there is no way the builders of that ship are aggressive."

"Wise words based entirely on known human traits," Adam said. "Nevertheless, most people on Earth are hoping our envoy comes to grief. Then their fleet just opens fire." He frowned across the table at his fellow board members. "Does anyone seriously think we could even scratch that thing? If it is inhabited, peaceful or otherwise, that approach will guarantee a war we would undoubtedly lose."

Page jerked his head up again. "Do you really think…?"

Julianne Devereaux pushed back her seat and stood, both hands firmly planted on the table. "Do *you* think we could get past this pissing contest and move on?"

Page nodded his head in grudging agreement. He had no wish to butt heads with the Martian Home Secretary.

Adam continued. "I suggest—and I hope you will all agree with me—that we officially ask for Barrett's fleet to stand off when it arrives. Ours will now get there a day later, so that will avoid any conflict between the commanders. Perhaps we could arrange a joint landing. The one thing we don't want is for this to escalate into a war between our worlds. The last one was bad enough."

"We have far more important matters to consider," Devereaux said, "such as the effect this is having on our respective populations. I fully appreciate the professor's line of logic, but the fact remains most people on both worlds are terrified this thing is an invasion craft. It's enormous. Imagine what kind of war fleet it could carry."

"The populations are the problem of our fellow politicians. Ours is to maintain peace out there and determine the intent of the alien ship."

"It will *not* be carrying a war fleet," the professor replied, maintaining a calm confidence. "In all likelihood it will not even enter our system."

"Pardon me?" the Secretary responded. "Has it not already done so?"

"No, Julianne. Our observations show that it is heading for a close transit of the Sun. We believe it is simply passing through and intends to use our Sun's gravity to change course, then leave as quickly as it came. At the speed it is traveling it is unlikely it will remain in our system, unless it decelerates first."

"Could it come here?"

"Oh yes, of course. It could use the Sun to slow down and then run a course around Venus and on to Earth or Mars, before settling into an orbit around one of them. There are several scenarios that…"

"Isn't all this just supposition?" Adam asked. "Falcon's already reported technology way beyond our understanding. Doesn't that apply to their drive systems as well? They may be able to decelerate rapidly, and they might be here in a matter of months."

"Yes, that's possible," the professor conceded. "But it is unlikely. I suspect the term 'they' is also an assumption that will not bear out. We cannot assume that the ship is occupied. Surely you've all read my paper on the subject of interstellar colonization?"

"Oh, of course," Page lied with a condescending smirk on his face. "Read it just yesterday."

The professor sat back in his seat and glared at his fellow representative.

"I haven't read it," Adam confessed, "but I bow to your expertise on the subject. Are there any other possibilities?"

"Yes, a few theories," the professor continued, "but that's all. Hibernation and deep freeze have been bandied about for centuries, but neither is practical in the long term. There is one other theory that might have possibilities, but it's even more unlikely considering the complexity. The idea is to record the mind of an intelligent being and then create a new body for it when needed. Never proved possible in practice. Hopefully, never will."

"You don't think that's a good idea?"

"Not for us, at least. That which we refer to as the individual, the person, is not the physical body you see. It's a collection of electrical impulses in a vast array of organic binary switches we refer to as the brain. Each of us is little more than a collection of accumulated knowledge, beliefs, opinions, mores, and so on. If we were able to record those impulses accurately, we could replace the matrix in which they were stored whenever we pleased. A person could become anything they desired—a new body, a change of sex, and even artificial bodies designed for particular environments. Imagine a spaceship with the mind of a human."

"And that's a bad idea?"

"It's a wonderful possibility," Brewer commented. "What is bad about it is that it opens the gates to immortality. Your old body wears out, just get a new one."

"And?"

"At our present level of development, it would be disastrous. Society would collapse without a major shift in social attitude. Birth control, for example: populations would grow beyond sustainable levels. We can't even get people to be responsible when it comes to maintaining a balance, two children for two adults, much less the other social impacts immortality would bring. Even if it was limited to the few…"

"Okay," Adam conceded again. "But for the aliens, the idea of recorded mentalities is possible?"

"Possible but unlikely. The amount of data we are talking about is immense, and that's just for a human being. Also, it would require a maintenance system under constant, powered operation for centuries. The possibility always exists, however."

"Fine. We already know the *Minaret* is still operational. Make up a proposal for consideration along those lines and Rob can send it to Falcon. Now, what about this Carvalio woman?"

Julianne Devereaux spoke. "Ruth Carvalio is a perfectly capable individual. Her books are first rate—I've read a couple."

"Yes, but does that qualify her to have a stranglehold on all and any news coming off that ship?" Adam asked.

"I prefer that, to be honest," the Home Secretary replied. "The alternative is to let the media handle it their way. I suggest we accept her as official historian since we have no choice anyway, and issue a statement that only official news from her—vetted by us, of course—is to be issued to the newscasts."

"Earth will love that," Page said.

"It's a Martian mission," Adam responded, slapping his palm down loudly on the table. He had known Page for several years and knew him to be a reasonable man who was now playing the devil's advocate, but it was starting to wear thin. "Your suggestion sounds reasonable, Julianne. All in favor? Okay, good. Now I want to talk about our beloved captain's son, Jake Falcon."

* * *

Jake stepped from the front portico of the office building to the small plaza fronting the street. It was early evening and the pavement steamed from the afternoon downpour. He loved the rain, and the scent of freshness it always brought to the city as it washed away the filth and debris of two million people living and working in the central business district.

At twenty-eight years of age, with pale green eyes and blonde hair, Jake was handsome by most standards and his appearance normally drew attention. At the moment his carefully cultivated, untidy hair and fashionably unkempt clothing gave him a singular anonymity, but he had to work at it. In a society where being on-trend was critical, the hair and general appearance were a common combination in the younger crowd and allowed him to blend in.

A good thing, he thought. With a reputation for being at the top of his game, he lived the way he wanted and worked wherever he wished, but when a face appeared in the media as often as his, public attention sometimes became undesirable.

Unlike the majority of people his age Jake did not like cities, but found them hard to avoid. Brisbane was better than most, especially with motor vehicles banned from the center forty years ago, but it was still too crowded. High-rise apartment living on a permanent basis appalled him. He preferred somewhere with space and trees—anything green.

Several years earlier, he found the perfect home on Mount Maleny, north of the city. The mountain was cooler and the house private, surrounded by six acres of what was once a macadamia-nut plantation. The property better suited Jake's peace of mind and always impressed him as the best place to raise children. Not that he had any; the right girl was yet to make an appearance.

Every city teemed with eligible young women, and in his immediate circle, Jake was an acknowledged catch. A suitable partner for any occasion never proved elusive, but he wanted more. The perfect woman would be his intellectual equal. There would be a connection—some chemistry.

"You're an Einstein, a Hawking, a Watanabe," a friend once remarked. "There is no such thing as a woman who's your equal."

Not true, he thought. *I'll find her, eventually.*

With the rain gone the office workers flooded to the maglev trains on their way to the outer suburbs. For a moment Jake considered joining them, but decided against it. He often made the journey home—only an hour each way on the Lev—but in recent days the ritual had become troublesome.

Within seconds of boarding, he would find other passengers staring at him. A week ago, one of the major news channels had splashed his face across every screen in the country, billing him as "the Einstein son of mankind's first ambassador to travelers from the stars." Several of the networks treated his father in a manner less than kind.

Someone would inevitably approach with "You're him, aren't you? The guy's son?" and then pester him for the remainder of the trip. Worse still, some wanted nothing more than to criticize his father, from the perception the man was betraying Earth in favor of Mars. The fact his dad grew up in Australia and served in the Pacific Naval Fleet carried little weight.

The evening had arrived and his current work project required him to be onsite early the next morning. With the return journey home taking two hours there was little time for anything but to eat and sleep, and he could do that here in the city. For now, he intended to stay near the lab during the week, traveling only in the off-peak periods or by private vehicle.

Perhaps a beard.

Two blocks away stood one of several 'pigeonhole' hotels in the business district. Common throughout the modern world, the concept originated in Japan centuries ago with 'capsule hotels' providing cheap overnight accommodation for travelers.

The majority of rooms were what the nickname suggested, a cubicle containing little more than a bed, a terminal, and room to sit. The smallest were stacked two deep on a floor, with steps to reach the upper row and with all amenities shared. The hotels also provided restaurants, overnight laundry services and a variety of social activities for their guests.

The cost did not concern Jake. This hotel, like most of its ilk, had a few more traditional, up-market rooms for its better-heeled clients, with more room, a double bed, and private bathroom facilities. Whenever he stayed overnight, one of these always served well enough despite his being able to afford the best in the city if desired.

In the lobby of the hotel by the check-in console, he spotted several other prospective residents. A young woman caught his eye as she stood to one side of the counter with her head down, rummaging through an oversize carry bag.

After a quick look of appreciation, he stepped forward and inserted a card into the payment slot, chose a room and retrieved a key. Turning, he discovered the girl standing behind him waiting her turn. She glanced up. Her face, an exotic blend so often found in people of mixed Asian and European heritage, immediately attracted him.

Instinctively he gave a broad smile, holding her eye for several seconds—much too long for politeness but perfect to express interest. She maintained contact for a moment, brushed her hair back with one hand, returned the smile and stepped past him to the console.

Ah well, he thought, heading towards the elevators. *Try not…*

Plain but comfortable, the room was more than adequate; these hotels maintained high standards from necessity. This one operated a restaurant on the ground floor, but there were better places to eat. Jake decided to go out for a meal and then settle in for a quiet evening.

On the media screen, he scanned his mail. One message was from his father, a request to have Jake's legal eagle pals examine a document. That can wait until tomorrow, he thought, flicking over to the entertainment menu.

Typical of these days, there was nothing worth watching—the networks showed little except reality garbage and repeats. With a sigh of resignation, Jake considered finding someone to accompany him for dinner. "Social, please."

The 'social link' was a site where anyone in search of company could register. The pigeonhole establishments were popular with travelers and new arrivals, people who knew no one in the city. The link provided a means for strangers to connect for whatever reason. Any legal activity was acceptable, from a casual dinner partner to a more intimate hook-up.

Jake flicked through the images of guests, looking for someone who might be an interesting companion. He had used the system before. Similar in operation to most network dating sites, it operated with the explicit understanding it was for the introduction only of residents. Following that, anything more was up to the participants and the hotel took no responsibility.

Jake wondered if the girl from the lobby would be listed, but did not expect so: many women avoided using these services. It came as a surprise when her image popped up on the screen.

The data line across the bottom introduced her as Akira Hirano, twenty-six years old, her selected preference, social company for the evening, unspecified, no strings attached.

Switching to the global census network, Jake typed in her name and location. The search results showed her to be a brand new arrival in Australia, transferred on a grant from the University of New Kyoto in Japan to the Technology University of Queensland, to work on promising new avenues in molecular mechanics.

You have to be kidding me, Jake thought. The girl worked in one of the most progressive and controversial fields in science, closely related to his. He read on.

Akira was twenty-seven—he knew that already—born of a European mother and Japanese father and graduated from Southern Hokkaido Tech. She was without doubt highly intelligent; they shared that much in common, at least.

Without hesitation, he logged in and sent her a request to accompany him for dinner, not in the hotel but at one of the better restaurants by the riverfront. He waited, aware that at this minute she would be checking him out on the net.

She would not have to search far; in his field, he was well-known worldwide. She might jump at the opportunity to have dinner with someone of his standing in a related area to her own. Then there was his father, the man who at this moment was exploring the first alien ship ever to visit the solar system.

Fame by association? Might prove useful, for a change.

Conversely, that might be too much and he expected her to turn him down flat. It was therefore all the more pleasant to find her face peering at him from the screen within seconds.

"Hello?"

"Hi. I'm Jake. Jake Falcon."

"Hello. I am Akira." She spoke in perfect English. "Are you *the* Jake Falcon?"

"Depends … yes, I guess I am. Would you like to join me for dinner? I thought perhaps Modigliani's. It's one of the oldest and best in Brisbane."

"I would love to. I was hoping you would be on here. I saw you downstairs, didn't I?" she asked, smiling.

"Yes. Sorry if I embarrassed you."

"No, you didn't. Can I meet you in the lobby in an hour? I look forward to talking with you."

"Wonderful. We share similar work interests, I think."

"Yes, but I hate talking about work. You can tell me about that spaceship if you like." Without a word further, she smiled and the image vanished.

Jake laughed to himself. All the effort put in over the years to make a name for himself and all she wanted to talk about was dear, old Dad.

Chapter 11

RUTH STUDIED THE individual seated opposite. "What I don't understand is what a beautiful young girl like you was doing poking around the asteroids with a bunch of older men. I mean you are, how old?"

"Twenty-two," Sarah replied, a frosty smile on her face.

It was nice, Ruth thought, to have other women on board besides Maeve, but this one was clearly wary of questions, perhaps from a natural distrust of strangers.

"The Captain hired me straight out of the academy," Sarah continued,

"You were training for Fleet."

"Yes, but I decided not to continue after I graduated."

"Why? The navy is supposed to be a first-class career. Why do all the work and then drop it?"

"My father's an officer in the Mars fleet; my joining was his idea, not mine. I went in to keep him away from my mother, but she died before my graduation and he could not make me do what he wanted anymore…" Sarah stopped suddenly, her brow wrinkling. "You're not going to report that." It was a command, not a request.

"No, I guess not. Don't worry. I promise your private life will remain so."

Sarah's mouth twisted with mistrust. "You insisted the Captain talk about his divorce."

How did you know that? "Yes, but that's all public record. The press would find out regardless. Your family is another matter. How did you meet Joe?"

When Ruth sat next to Sarah and asked if they could chat, she was only doing her job, and she expected the young woman knew that. Joe had asked everyone to be as cooperative as possible, but the first officer did not appear to like the situation. Ruth wondered if the fact she got on so well with Joe was the cause of the upset.

"He's a friend of Professor Ali, my mentor at the Academy. Just before I graduated, he came to visit while he was home looking for crew. I was in the office at the time, so the professor introduced us. I tracked him down later and asked for a job."

"And he gave you one knowing you were what, twenty or so at the time and fresh out of the Academy?"

"No, he turned me down—said I was too young. I kept coming back until he agreed to take me on, after talking to Professor Ali. One trip—a trial run. At the end of the tour, he offered me the permanent position of second; the guy who had the job dropped out."

"And now you're the first officer. Why would you want to be out here? A girl your age should be making a life for herself, having fun and meeting people, or having a family if she wanted."

"I *am* making a life for myself," Sarah spat. "And the guys on this ship *are* my family. They treat me like one of their own. I wanted to get away from Mars, and I like this job. Besides, I'm only twenty-two; I've got plenty of time to think about other things, and this is exciting."

"Do you like Joe?"

Sarah glared at Ruth. "Yes, of course. He's my captain."

"Do you like him as a person?"

For a moment Sarah did not answer, her face flushed cherry pink. "That's personal."

Minutes later, Ruth was alone. The young first mate had left abruptly with that last question.

A lot made sense now; Sarah had deep feelings for the captain. If she had problems with her domineering father, it would be natural for her to seek a substitute.

Ruth suspected the younger woman loved the captain, despite the decades between their ages. There was no accounting for human emotions, so in itself that did not concern Ruth. What did worry her was the effect the girl might have on Joe. He had to be aware of her interest, and any relationship between the two would be a potential tinderbox. Any older man or woman would feel flattered by attention from a younger person.

Sarah was young and resilient; having lost his wife not so long ago, Joe was the more vulnerable of the two and the most likely to get permanently hurt if the young woman pushed herself at him.

Ruth sighed. It was not proving easy. In the last decade, her career as a writer had gone reasonably well: three well-accepted histories on various subjects, and recognition gradually building, but the great breakthrough still eluded her.

This adventure was supposed to be her magnum opus, the work that would make her a household name for life. She wanted not just documentation of the voyage but a deeper insight into the lives and minds of the people on this ship. More often than not, she was finding the doorways to that goal closed.

They were an extraordinary group, tough, skilled and brave; more at home in the cold and deadly reaches of space than on the surface of a planet. Most of them had secrets, a desire to hide from something or someone, or to escape from a past life. Only Maeve, the medical officer, seemed to be here purely because she enjoyed being so.

Finding the deeper roots beneath the secrets without interfering or betraying faith was proving harder than expected. Ruth had never met such closed individuals before. Some answered her questions only when the interviews stayed at a superficial level, others not at all. Her great opus seemed further away than ever.

Standing, she made her way across to the galley for yet another refill of Sam's coffee.

* * *

Marius Pine settled to the deck. "So we turn this bar, and a door opens?" he asked, surveying the otherwise blank wall of the docking pillar.

"Yep." Alaine floated down beside him. "The spot changes color and you step through. Some form of molecular re-arrangement, or a force field which can be solid or not. I can't think of any other explanations."

Sarah placed a gloved hand on the smaller patch on the wall. "There's a pressure pad here we think opens it, but there's no power so it doesn't … whoa." Without warning, the hatch color changed to the same oily-shell pattern as before, indicating the way was clear. "Shit. That didn't happen before."

"It opened," said Alaine. "The power to the switch is on."

On the bridge of *Butterball*, Joe and Patricia watched the images from the incursion team. The manual system, Joe thought, must be for emergencies, but now the hatch was working as designed. It was a good sign, but troubling. It sent a chill up his spine.

Was the *Minaret* aware of their presence?

"There's air in here," Sarah announced minutes later as she stepped through to the stairwell platform. "And light. Scary."

"Not as much as this," Alaine said. The tube at the center of the helical stairs was no longer transparent, now the same shimmering color mix as the hatches. Directly opposite the inner hatchway was an opening in the tube, sufficient for a man to enter. Beside it, a small, shimmering, pillar-like console with two color spots on the flat upper surface, stood on the platform. Each spot contained a strange symbol.

On board *Butterball*, Patricia recalled the suggestion the tube might be an elevator as she pulled herself into the seat next to the captain. "Do you think the ship, or its hidden inhabitants, are watching us?"

"Something else," Alaine said. "There's gravity in here. How is that even possible?"

Joe leaned forward for a better view of the monitor. "No idea." The screen showed the explorers moving upright on the stairway, the image shuddering with each step. "The hull isn't rotating, so not centrifugal. How do you feel, guys?"

"Normal," said Sarah. "Like walking on Mars—about the same, in fact."

"No, wait," Alaine said. "Stop moving, everyone. Can you feel it?"

Sarah paused and concentrated, feeling a vague, base-level disturbance that extended through her whole body, unsettling but apparently harmless.

"Yes. A vibration, faint, like it's inside you, all over. You think it's caused by what's creating this gravity?"

"Whatever it is," Joe said, "if it feels all over, then your bodies are being affected by some kind of force acting like normal gravity. I can't imagine how they would do that." He sat back and pondered for a moment. "Well, at least it solves one problem. With light and air, we can explore more easily. We can go a lot further afield."

"Can't guarantee it'll stay this way," said Alaine. "If we get caught too far from home and the systems shut down again, we're dead."

"What's the temperature, Alaine?"

"I was hoping you would ask. Eighteen degrees Celsius. I'm not bullshitting."

A sudden shiver ran through Joe's bones. "Impossible. A few hours ago, the service level was at absolute zero and in vacuum. Chloe estimates the volume in there at around half a billion cubic meters. It can't be filled with air and the temperature raised in such a short time."

"We may never know how it works," Marius said. "The air is Earth normal. Doesn't that strike you as strange?"

"Bloody unbelievable would be closer to the mark. It makes no sense that all of a sudden we have gravity, atmosphere and lighting, all balanced to suit human beings. Where did that come from? What are the odds of an alien world having the same atmospheric mix as Earth?"

Hunched into the chair beside him, Patricia said nothing, her head shaking in denial, her expression dark. Joe suspected she saw it as more ominous than coincidental.

"This whole thing has been tailored for us," she said. "We've only been here a couple of days and this ship knows what we breathe, the right light wavelengths for our eyes, and what gravity is acceptable to us. I am not overflowing with confidence here."

"Why not?" Ruth Carvalio's voice came over the intercom from the common room, where several of the crew were listening in.

Joe ignored her. "Chloe, has anyone accessed your data banks, or compromised you in any way?"

"No, Captain. I have no record of unauthorized access."

"What do you want us to do now, Captain," Sarah asked from inside the alien craft.

"Proceed, but be careful and don't go further than the safe limit of your life support, just in case." Slumped in his seat with his eyes glued to the screens, Joe tried to find some logic to the new developments.

Sarah stepped on the travelator walkway. Turning towards the center of the *Minaret,* she took a step forward along the strip and felt herself accelerate. "This is so weird," she said, as an unseen force took hold of her body.

"I love this thing," Alaine said as he sped past. "Think what this technology would be worth in cities on Earth or Mars."

"Heaps. Every octogenarian could be the 'Flash'."

Minutes later, they walked up the ramp of the transport platform. The once-empty surface now contained a console at the exact center. Like the one at the entry, its surface shimmered with constantly changing color.

"This is live, I think," said Alaine, examining the top of the small pillar. "Two color spots. This can only be a transport system, so they'll be forward and aft, yes? For calling a shuttle, or whatever."

Sarah walked across to the bubble, still standing in the same position as on the last visit. Again, the once transparent surface was a multicolor swirl, now with an entry opening in the side facing the center of the platform. Peering through the doorway, Sarah saw yet another shimmering console on the circular floor inside. Without hesitation, she stepped in. "This one's live as well. The surface is divided into a square array of spots." She reached out to touch the console.

Alaine yelled. "Sarah, no! Stop right there. We can't assume it's safe yet."

"If they wanted to hurt us, don't you think they would have done something by now? They appear to be helping us."

"Maybe, maybe not, but you need to be cautious."

"I'm fine. There's nothing much in here, just these controls. This bubble may be the actual shuttle."

"Be careful," Joe said over the intercom. "Everyone else stay out for now. Talk to me, Sarah."

Sarah stepped back to the control pillar. "If this is part of a transport system it has sixty-four stations, Captain."

"How do you know?"

"The array is eight by eight. Each spot has a different symbol, starting with a single dot, then up to nine dots. The next is a bar, then a bar and one dot, all the way up to six bars and four dots. This is all very human, don't you think."

"Decimal system," Patricia yelped with glee. "These guys use a base ten mathematics, which means they may have five digits on each hand, like us."

"Two hands or ten tentacles," said Joe. "Or it could all be for our benefit. They've tailored the air and temperature for humans, so why not the transport system as well? Is there any indication of where you are now, Sarah?"

"The fourth spot is glowing so I'm guessing this is station four." Without thinking, she pressed a finger to the panel.

At the center of the platform, Marius and Alaine almost missed what occurred next. Faster than the eye could follow, the bubble vanished.

Alaine rushed across to the now empty place on the platform. "Sarah? Joe, we've lost her!"

"No, no, I'm still here," a breathless voice gasped over the suit radio system.

"What the hell happened?" Joe asked. "What did you do, Sarah?"

"I pressed another button. Sorry, Captain … I didn't think."

"Are you all right?"

"Yes, I'm fine. I'm … oh, hang on."

"Where are you?"

Sarah stared out of the bubble. Despite the multi-colored outer surface, the bubble was clear from the inside, the view unhindered. The transport was moving fast, the vast service bay already far behind. Seconds later, it came to rest in what resembled a terrestrial subway. Lights came on as it drew to a halt. The entire journey had taken only a minute.

"I'm out of the service area, somewhere in the nose of the *Minaret*, I think. Platform three. It's closed in like a subway station, a platform with ramps and stairs leading up and down to other levels, but no tracks."

"Come back now. Can you do that?" Joe was frustrated; he accepted someone would have made the trip eventually, but Sarah had done so earlier than he intended.

Seated beside him, Patricia saw the flush on his face. "If you're going to send teams out and they go any distance into the ship, they'll need to make decisions based on their judgment. Don't be cross with her."

"Sorry? Oh no, I'm not angry. I'm mad at myself for not anticipating this."

Sarah's voice interrupted. "Can you still hear me, Captain?"

"Yes, Sarah. What's happening?"

"Nothing. Nobody's home. This station is deserted."

Sarah stood motionless, too terrified to move. She stared at the platform outside, expecting a commuter crowd to appear at any moment. A deathly quiet hung over the chamber. Through the gloom, she could see the entrances to the ramps; the subdued lighting left the ends of the station cloaked in shadow, and tunnels exiting at either end were black as pitch. Despite the temperature reading on her suit sleeve, her whole body felt deathly cold.

A deeper chill rippled up her spine.

Not far away a vague, shimmering ovoid of glittering air appeared above the platform. The apparition had no distinct form, its shape fluctuating from second to second. Within it, a thousand minuscule stars glittered. It drifted closer, stopping nearer the bubble.

For a brief moment, Sarah thought she saw a face looking at her from the tenuous apparition.

A reflection?

Her face.

The specter vanished.

"Shit!"

"You all right?" Joe asked.

"Yes, fine. Someone walked on my granny's grave, I think." An overpowering sense of isolation washed over her like a wave, alone on an alien spacecraft of immense size, millions of kilometers from Mars. Not entirely convinced the phantom presence was a hallucination, her mind raced in anticipation of what might come down those ramps. Joe's voice broke her trance.

"Come back now, Sarah."

"I'm pushing button four. The bubble is moving forward. This must be a loop; I think I'm going to go to the end and back again."

"What I find amazing," Marius said, "is that she can even tell us that. The suit radios transmit only a thousand meters, but there must be several kilometers of ship between her and us. Has anyone else given thought to this?"

Alaine stood deep in concentration for several seconds. "Something is boosting or relaying our communications."

Without warning, a bubble appeared on the opposite side of the platform and a white faced first-officer tumbled out.

"Still alive," she gasped.

* * *

Several hours later Joe, Alaine and Sarah sat together in the captain's cabin. Nobody had been hurt during Sarah's unplanned excursion, but some things troubled them all.

Alaine glanced up from the digital pad in his lap. "I think what's bothering us all is that everything now works. All the experts swore the *Minaret* would be a derelict, and it's anything but."

"What concerns me is the air, light and temperature," Joe said.

"Yes, accepted, it's a worry."

"The ship's systems have come back to life as well. The symbols on the consoles are at least something we can understand. Do you realize how unlikely all that is?"

"It's responding to us," Sarah said. "Patricia thinks those things are being tailored specifically for us."

"Very likely yes, but how do the *Visitors* know exactly what we need?" Joe asked. "That's what scares me the most."

"I guess we accept that their technology, whoever they might be, is way beyond our own and move on," Alaine said. "I would love to know how the radio business works."

"Our units are inoperable over those distances," said Sarah. "Our hosts are helping us stay in touch."

"Why would they do that?"

"Why would they give us air and keep us warm?" Joe countered.

"A computer with a prime directive? Make sure the little fleshy things stay alive and well. We come along, and it can't distinguish between us and its creators."

Joe frowned at his companions. "I find that very, very hard to believe. Maybe they are making it easy for us to make sure we stay."

* * *

Seated on the *Butterball*'s bridge, Joe pieced together what they knew so far about the transit system. The stations apparently formed a continuous loop running throughout the alien vessel, the spheres moving from one station to the next. A passenger experienced no sense of acceleration or inertia and the vehicles revealed no visible means of propulsion or support as they flew at breakneck speed along a predefined course.

Bubbles departed a platform to starboard, traveled forward around the loop, then aft to arrive at the same platform on the port side. It worked like a duel-track railway, but faster by a quantum leap.

The console buttons might have been set up for the benefit of him and his crew, but the transport system was a fixed part of the ship. Despite the mysteries surrounding its function, it all seemed remarkably human, prompting Joe to wonder if whoever built it might have been organic creatures not so different from Homo sapiens.

Chloe calculated the system ran parallel with the central axis of the vessel, halfway between there and the outer shell. It was likely others were spaced through the hull cross-section to provide better coverage.

Joe turned as Alaine floated onto the *Butterball's* bridge, still dressed in work fatigues. The young officer had returned from another excursion into the *Minaret,* riding the bubble way as everyone now called it, to a point further aft in the ship.

A second team, led by Walter Tyrell, was in the bow following his holy grail—the ship's computers—searching for the control deck or whatever served the purpose.

Settling into a seat, Alaine grinned at Joe. "Told you we would find something if we went aft first."

Joe gazed at him, only vaguely aware of his words. The fact the *Visitors* were watching them, and worse, responding in ways beyond his understanding, preyed on his mind. He tried not to show it in front of his crew but the situation scared him more than he cared to admit.

"Yes?"

Alaine shuffled to a more comfortable position. "The first station aft of the rear wall of the airfield is like the one Sarah found the day before yesterday. Ramps lead to passages above and below, so we followed one of them. There are huge view-ports looking out into more bays, and you won't believe what they contain."

"Let me guess, ships?" To Joe, it was the obvious answer if the windows overlooked the spaces behind those doors.

"Ah yes, but wait for it. We saw hundreds, thousands of them in those hangers; everything from larger ones, possibly transports and work platforms, to what may be small personnel vehicles."

Joe nodded confirmation. "Not surprising. A ship this size could never land on a planet, or carry out any of the multitude of functions a colonization would require. The *Minaret* has a substantial fleet of support vehicles as we suspected. Did you get a close look at one?"

Alaine's face dropped. "Ah, no. We haven't been able to find a way in, but we will."

The captain said nothing, raising his eyebrows.

"The galleries let us see inside," Alaine continued, "but they pass right by and lead to other areas, vast mazes of rooms, all empty. The entrances to the hangers are somewhere else."

Chapter 12

THE FIRST PASSAGES accidentally discovered by the crew while exploring the maze of ramps, steps and 'elevator' tubes around station five, were high above the level of the hanger bay decks. Alaine's team took only a short time to access the lower levels.

At first, entry was blocked by the ubiquitous 'spot in a circle' hatchway. On the wall outside sat a keypad with sixteen small, circular, color patches numbered in the same manner seen on the transport system.

Marius Pine, the chief engineer, constructed a small, suction-pad device to sit over the panel. Under Chloe's control, pins began punching each possible key combination, from one, working up towards the highest combination of sixteen symbols.

Success came after only a few hours and eight digits. Once inside, Alaine called Joe to come aft and join them. "You really have to see this place from the floor," he explained over the intercom. "It makes the spaceports on Earth and Mars pale in comparison."

Joe finished composing the latest blast to Marcus Bond advising his only obligation to anyone was to investigate this ship—which he was doing to the best of his ability, so please stop making demands—and suited up.

Though the *Minaret's* atmosphere and temperature remained stable at Earth optimum, he still insisted everyone wear an exploration suit. In a worst-case scenario where the atmosphere or temperature vanished rapidly, the suits would keep an explorer alive long enough to organize a rescue effort.

The standing rule was that nobody moved about the *Minaret* alone, so he seconded Ruth to accompany him on her first sortie into the alien vessel.

Contrary to that rule, Alaine waited alone at station five and led Joe and Ruth up a ramp to the next highest deck, then through a maze of corridors. "We're on the airfield level here," he said, "and we can walk straight through to the hangers from here. This area"—he waved a hand around—"is for servicing, I think, with hangers on both sides. We can only access one so far."

"That should be enough," Joe said. "You don't have time to explore every hanger. Too much else to do."

"Agreed. I want to try for the engine rooms as soon as possible."

Alaine stopped inside the now open hatch leading into a long tunnel that stretched away into the distance. The walls and arched ceiling were transparent, allowing an unimpeded view into yet another enormous chamber.

Towards the front of the vessel, at what Joe presumed to be the other side of the airfield aft wall examined during the first sortie, a sheer, vertical surface stretched up to a ceiling far above. About ten meters up, Joe saw the inner sides of the massive first-level hatches.

"We haven't found any way to open one of those yet," Alaine commented.

The sheer number of spacecraft in the chamber boggled the mind; each sat in massive cradles, connected to umbilical lines leading into the floor. Those visible varied in size from no larger than a bus, to almost as large as the *Butterball.* Every craft gleamed, with polished surfaces shining as if fresh off the production line and never used. What struck Joe first was the nature of the ships.

"These aren't warships or passenger shuttles. They all appear to be work vehicles."

Alaine nodded. "Agreed. This is only one hanger though."

A hundred yards on, an opening appeared in the wall of the walkway tunnel allowing access to the hangar floor. Meters away, Terry Caldwell and Peter Stanley stood deep in conversation beneath a smaller ship, peering up and shaking their heads.

Alaine walked towards them. "No luck yet?"

Peter glanced up. "Sorry, no. There's no way into any of these things. The hulls are totally smooth."

Alaine examined the underside of the craft's hull. "Must be a way in. We need to find it. One of those molecular hatches, most likely."

"Yeah," Terry said. "With a remote control we don't got, hey."

Joe stepped away and looked around. As far as he could see, ships crowded the floor in all directions. Overhead, a series of apparently unsupported walkways stretched the length of the chamber and between them, also magically suspended, hung hundreds more craft. "How many do you think are here?

"A thousand or more," said Alaine.

"This is only one hanger. You say there's another on the other side of the service area, and judging by the three rows of hatches in the aft wall of the landing bay there are at least two smaller levels above us."

"Makes sense. Come and see this." Alaine led Joe until they stood beside another medium-sized craft.

Like a human assembly vehicle, the control cabin was forward and the engines aft. Between the two, a broad, thick platform supported an extending arm with an articulating claw.

Other devices of indeterminate purpose studded the platform, and stacks of sheet material similar in appearance to that from which the smaller craft were built sat at the forward end. As Joe had come to expect, every component of the craft's surface was seamless, with no cracks or joins.

"So what do you make of it?"

Joe ran his gaze over the odd-looking ship. "Designed for construction or maintenance purposes, I would guess."

"Yes, I agree, but it's intended for use in space, not atmospheric flight. So far, we've found several dozen like this or similar; if they are all like this it seems a lot for general maintenance. I think they may be left over from the building of the *Minaret*." He pointed to the materials stacked on the flat tray. "I want a piece of that."

"Why would they bring them? They would be useless once the construction was complete."

"Sure, unless they planned to disassemble the ship once they arrived at their destination. Or maybe the voyage is so long they expect lots of repairs."

Joe shook his head. Only one possibility came to mind. This was a colonization vessel; no other explanation for so many small craft made sense. The question was, did the ship intend to stop in the Solar System? Numerous support units meant a considerable number of colonists.

But where were they?

*   *   *

Two days later Joe and Sarah stepped from a transport bubble at station two to an enthusiastic greeting from Walter Tyrell. He had discovered his bridge deck and insisted they both come as soon as possible.

Again, Joe noted Wally was alone. Admittedly, he had been so only for a short while but Joe made a mental note to reiterate his orders regarding moving about the *Minaret* alone.

This platform differed from the others seen so far, having no ramps. Instead, passageways led away directly into the bowels of the ship. Wally led the way, chattering as he walked.

"You are not going to believe this place, kiddies," he said, turning into a foyer containing a helical stairway around an elevator tube, identical to the one at the docking bay. "Figured out how to operate these contraptions, you know."

He walked up to the now inevitable console and tapped it twice, then stepped into the seemingly bottomless shaft. He did not fall, standing suspended as if on an invisible glass floor. Unconvinced but trusting his own eyes, Joe stepped in after Wally, followed by Sarah. The trio began to rise.

"Scared the bejesus out of me the first time I actually found enough gumption to try it out," Wally mumbled.

Joe glanced down. He could feel a floor beneath his feet but appeared to be standing on thin air. Looking down to where the shaft vanished into the depths, he fought to stop his legs from shaking. "How far up have we come?"

"Almost two kilometers. Not bad for less than a minute. And no inertia."

Nobody had mentioned to Joe that he or she had worked out how to use the 'elevators' but it would make moving around the alien ship easier. Joe tried to ignore the incredible risk Wally had taken stepping into one of them in the first place.

"You think this is good?" Wally said. "What will really fry your noodle, old boy, is people can move both directions at the same time. If you are going up and someone else comes down, you're shunted to one side to avoid interference as you pass."

He stepped out at the new level and pointed along a side corridor. "We found another bubble way down there, about two kilometers. I conclude there are at least five, spaced through the hull section as we expected and running the full length of the ship. What I want to show you is through here."

Without further hesitation, he turned and passed through a large, circular doorway. Wally smiled and opened his arms wide. "Welcome to the bridge."

On the other side was a chamber unlike anything Joe had so far seen. He froze, unable to immediately accommodate what he was seeing, struggling to overcome the shock enveloping his mind.

The three stood on the mezzanine level of another enormous room. The floor, several hundred meters wide and at least fifty across, ended at a low barrier beyond which the chamber opened up to a void. The view beyond the barrier railing was overwhelming. The entire opposite wall was a window looking into the vastness of space, curved to optimize the view from the control deck. Ahead, a small star burned.

"This ship has no windows at the front," Joe said. "That's…"

"An electronic image of some kind, I gather. Makes our vid-screens a little mundane, don't you think."

Stunned by the immensity of the view, Joe had no answer. "That is *most* disconcerting," he said turning away."It's almost as if it's an open window to space.

Wally's face was alive with excitement. "Impressive, wouldn't you say Joseph? You get used to it soon enough."

"What are all those?" Sarah swept a hand across the floor of the mezzanine. Scattered everywhere were 'U' shaped consoles, within each, a long, narrow bench.

"My educated guess is those are control stations. There are dozens of them, and more down below." Wally poked a finger over the mezzanine railing at the main floor far below. "I expect the benches are seats."

"Pat's going to have a ball with this," Sarah said. "Benches for lying on rather than sitting. I can hear her now: our aliens are four-legged lizards and they lay down on those to work?"

"I heard that," Patricia's voice said over the intercom. "You forget I'm listening in. Captain, I need to be up there."

"You can come with the next team," Joe mumbled. "Have you found the computers yet, Walter?"

"No. The consoles are all featureless—completely smooth and no way inside. Whoever's in charge has given us the run of the ship but they're not letting us at the controls—yet."

His feeling of vertigo having faded to a manageable level, Joe moved over to the railing and surveyed the lower level. He felt more comfortable now; in his mind, the vast room was beginning to take on the aspect of an observation lounge of an old-fashioned ocean liner.

Below, more modules covered the floor, but unlike the ones on the upper level, these varied in shape. Arranged in small local groups divided by clearways, they were interspersed with what Joe decided were blocks of seating. "Reminds me of the waiting lounge in a spaceport."

Wally nodded as he stepped up. "It does indeed, apart from the fact everything here is smooth and featureless, as usual. It's almost like this ship and everything in it came from one gigantic mold."

"Any ideas?"

"This level is the bridge, I'm certain. I'm not sure about the rest of it."

Sarah stepped up, sniffing condescendingly. "Seriously? I think it's obvious."

Both men raised eyebrows.

"Look, Captain, we've decided this is a colonization vessel, so it should by rights have hundreds, maybe thousands of passengers. They're intelligent so they're also going to be curious. They'll want to see where they're going—view their new home when they arrive. What better place than here where the screens are? It may be as simple as it appears, a huge observation lounge. Occam's Razor."

Joe nodded slowly. The more he saw of this vessel, the more astounded he became, and the more questions piled up in his mind. "Why not? Occam's Razor. As likely an explanation as any."

"Think this is good?" Wally said. "You haven't seen anything yet, my little kiddies."

Taking Joe and Sarah by their arms, he guided them across the bridge to where another, smaller elevator tube extended up into the curved ceiling. Inside, they rose to a circular foyer from which a single corridor exited towards the front of the ship.

At the end of the passage, a door led to a chamber Joe found oddly familiar. The room was spherical, its walls a soft pearl grey but lit by a soft, muted glow. The actual size was difficult to ascertain but he guessed it to be about twenty meters in diameter.

From the entrance, a narrow walkway extended to a platform in the center. On it stood the inevitable console and two flat, bench-like seats identical to the ones in the control room.

"I've seen something like this before," Joe said. "A virtual reality sphere, right? Used to be popular for entertainment a couple of centuries back."

"Yes, it is. Probably the first thing I have seen on the ship that I can understand. However, this one is special. Walk out and sit down on those benches." Wally waved the way forward. "You're going to love this."

"What is this place," Sarah asked. "You could just tell us, you know."

"No, I could not. This, you have to experience for yourself."

Once seated, the elderly computer technician reached out and laid his hand on the top of the console. The upper surface immediately lit up. "Tighten your sphincters, children—this can be a bit of a shock. Almost wet myself when I did it the first time." He tapped the console several times.

The grey surface of the sphere vanished, leaving Joe, Sarah and Wally seated on a small platform surrounded by deep space. Again, the most prominent object was Sol, the other stars glittering with a clarity Joe had seen only from outside the *Butterball.*

He grabbed instinctively for the helmet on his belt then realized he was still able to breathe. Both hands grappled the seat hoping for some purchase. His head spun, unable to accept the idea he was in open space without a pressure suit, but still alive, warm and breathing.

Desperate to regain control he fought to calm himself, his heart beating hard, the blood pounding through his temples. With breath coming in fast, short gasps, he turned to his companions.

Sarah was fighting her own internal demons.

Wally sat gazing at the Sun, his face serene. "Beautiful, isn't it? I could sit here for hours."

Joe gasped. "What … what is this?"

"Don't worry old boy; you'll adjust in a moment. This sphere is a screen as you suspected, just like the one below but the image is so perfect the surface is undetectable. The walkway pulls back into the wall behind us. Don't ask me what holds this platform up—I have no idea. It's as if we were out in space, but we're still inside the ship somewhere above the control deck. We have nothing like this—nothing so clear."

Still frozen in place Joe sat and stared at the Sun, absorbing what no other human except Wally had experienced before, the vastness of the cosmos as if untarnished by a faceplate or video screen.

"Like being a bird," he murmured.

"How so?" Sarah asked, still battling to calm herself.

"Centuries ago man wanted to fly like the birds but he never got to do it. The best he could come up with was a variety of clunky machines or a virtual reality system. We went into space and had the same problem. No matter what we did, a ship or a suit was always between the infinite and us. Human VR systems have never been this good—never so perfect. This is as close to flying in space as we will ever get."

Wally smiled, never taking his eyes away from the distant star. "You might be right. You may very well be right."

"We're near Mars orbit now," Sarah said. "Pity we can't see it. It would be nice to see home again." Her words conveyed a sad, wistful loneliness.

Joe nodded in agreement. "Mars is around the other side, more or less."

"More, I think." A tear trailed from Sarah's eye. "A lot more."

Chapter 13

THE UNITED EARTH Cruiser *Constellation* bored through space like a shark through the ocean, surrounded by a small school of destroyers, fuel transports and support vessels. Both Earth and Mars were on the far side of the Sun from the target, and it had been a long voyage. Fifteen standard days remained until rendezvous with the alien ship everyone was now calling the *Minaret.*

Fleet Commodore George Barrett brooded in his cabin, picking over his orders yet again. He was not pleased at all.

After weeks of acceleration, *Constellation* and her companion vessels were traveling faster than ever before. The effect on officers and crew alike had been vicious but Barrett did not care. His men were navy; they thrived on hardship. The marines on the troop transport would live with it, since he had not given them a choice.

Acceleration was over and the fleet coasted to the rendezvous. The remaining days before the encounter would be busy indeed. To begin, that intractable survey ship captain, Falcon, had to be brought into check, as well as his jumped-up liaison, Parish.

How dare the little prick defy me, Barrett thought. He would not allow any pathetic junior officer to divert the mission. His orders were unambiguous: on arrival, an armed squad would land on the exterior platform and take control of the freighter, detaining its crewmembers 'for their own safety'. Once clear, *Constellation*'s shuttles would enter and occupy the *Minaret's* airfield bay.

Butterball's captain had so far made no claim of rights over the alien vessel, and if he did, Barrett would ignore it until ordered otherwise.

What concerned him most was the specialist team foisted upon him, fifty highly trained commandoes under Lieutenant Francis Manners. The man was an exemplary officer and his squad without equal, but Barrett sensed a potential problem. The mission was legally suspect at best and could lead to war. He wondered if Manners would carry the orders through without objection, or if the Lieutenant would exceed those orders. A loud rap sounded on the door.

“Enter.” He turned in his seat as the officer stepped into the cabin.

“Reporting as requested, Commodore,” Manners announced, snapping to attention.

“Sit down, Lieutenant. How is your team coming on?”

“Operational and ready to go, sir. Now acceleration is finished I'm drilling them in the hanger bay. Just need you to give the word.”

“You have another two weeks to iron out any wrinkles. I don't want mistakes.” Barrett leaned forward, beckoning Manners to do the same. “I want you to understand something.”

“Sir?”

"The orders, both yours and mine, direct that the freighter be boarded, its crew taken into custody and the whole shambles removed from the area. Some of the crew will most likely be inside the target so your men will go in after them. If you must act without the cooperation of Falcon or his people, you are to do so."

"Yes, sir. Those are my orders."

"Fine. I know you may not be happy about that. This mission amounts to an act of piracy depending on how you read the rules, and could precipitate another war between Earth and Mars if you screw up. But, we are under direct orders, so do your best and you have my word there will be no repercussions."

"Yes sir. We don't have a choice, do we?"

"The choice is a court marshal for each of us, so you *will* carry out your orders. In addition, I'm adding some of my own." Barrett casually tapped the screen between himself and Manners.

"Sir, I—"

"Shut up and listen. You will perform the task as directed but under no circumstances will you cause damage to the freighter, or harm any member of its crew. For their own safety, you will move them sufficiently to keep them out of harm's way while we occupy the *Minaret*, and then release them."

"They don't have enough fuel to reach home, Commodore."

"I'm aware of that. One of our tankers will deal with it."

Manners peered at his superior, his brow wrinkled. "You think Mars will react badly over this?"

"Of course, but as long as nobody gets hurt nothing will come of it. Falcon makes it quite clear to all that he is his own boss; that works in our favor."

"Sir?"

"Mars will object to our removal of the freighter and we will point out that Falcon, by self-admission, is working as a private individual. As such, he has no right to overrule an official diplomatic mission and is being removed for his own safety and that of his crew.

"He so far makes no claim on behalf of Mars, so our actions will not be an act of war against the Martian Government. They'll kick up a stink but they won't risk another conflict. Earth has agreed to share all knowledge of the *Minaret*, so we'll allay public concern by maintaining we're taking charge for all humanity."

"Yes, sir. What if Falcon makes a statement before we get there?"

"We'll worry about it if it happens. The Mars Fleet is behind us by twenty-six hours, so that's your window for this maneuver. You'll deal with Falcon's ship, occupy both landing platforms on the target and close off access to the airfield bay. Dismissed."

Alone again, Barrett removed a brandy bulb from his drinks cabinet and settled into his chair. Manners seemed a man with common sense, more perhaps than the authorities who gave orders on Earth.

The United Earth Council did not intend to share anything with Mars. The mother world was in desperate need of the red planet's resources, and the technology on the alien ship could be the key to regaining them. A fleet commodore in good standing, Barrett intended to carry out his orders meticulously, but he would not commit open piracy or be held responsible for murder.

He reached for his terminal and stopped the recording of the previous conversation. Manners had been warned—if he harmed any civilians, he would take the fall. Barrett closed his eyes, took another suck of the amber liquid and mulled over his plans.

He almost admired this Falcon character. The man had guts, or else was plain reckless; Barrett did not think the latter to be the case.

Unbeknown to Falcon, the Earth Fleet had a contact on board the *Butterball* and Barrett knew everything going on there. Falcon's communications had been intercepted and read, except a handful heavily encrypted with a code that Earth's best men could not crack. They could not even work out the ultimate recipient, although they had their suspicions.

What is Falcon up to, Barrett wondered.

* * *

"It's sad," said Sarah. "We're about to cross the orbit of Mars and we can't see the planet. So close, but so far away."

Wally glanced up from his note taking. "You sound homesick, my dear girl."

"A little, I guess. It's a long time since our last visit home."

"Yes, and it'll be a while longer, I expect. I planned to be there myself by now, but I couldn't resist volunteering for this little adventure. I'm beginning to wonder if it was a good idea."

"Still no luck with the computers?"

Wally eased back in his chair and sighed. "No, my dear, and I can't see that changing. This blessed ship is beyond anything we have, and I can't comprehend a thing. Those consoles on the bridge deck are featureless. I can't work out how to turn them on, much less figure out which are the computer and which the navigation systems. Can't even get inside them."

"Come on, Walter," Sam Bright interrupted from the galley. "You are knowing as well as I this voyage is a once-in-a-lifetime opportunity."

"Yes, but I would like to achieve what I set out to do. I thought I could contribute, but my efforts have been fruitless so far."

"Okay, suppose you are not working it out. You are still seeing things nobody is ever seeing, except us. This vessel is amazing, I am thinking."

"Yes Samuel, it certainly is that."

"It's mind-blowing," Sarah said. "The sheer grandeur is enough. Can you imagine what would be required to build a structure so enormous?"

Wally nodded his head in agreement. "Built in space of course, possibly by nano-machines judging from the lack of joins or seams. Nothing this size could ever land on or take off from a planet."

"I am still not understanding," said Sam. "Why build something so big and abandon it? If the crew is dead, there would be a sign of them—bodies, or something—but we are finding nothing. No trace. So where are they? Just like Marie Celeste, I am thinking."

"Like who?" Sarah asked.

"Many years ago back on Earth, a sailing boat she turns up adrift at sea with nobody on board. She is in perfect order, nothing amiss but everybody gone, as if they all jump overboard. It is one of the great mysteries of maritime history."

"You think this ship is abandoned?"

"I could not say. It is like the crew are never here at all. You would almost be thinking it was a robot, but then who is flying all those little ships we find?" Neither Walter nor Sarah responded to Sam's question, each lost in his or her thoughts.

Walter reflected on the amazing sights seen on the bridge deck and in the observation sphere. He wanted desperately to know how the alien craft worked, but perhaps it was akin to a Neanderthal wanting to understand the *Butterball*: he simply lacked the base knowledge for understanding.

At that moment, Joe Falcon slid down the ladder from the central corridor.

"Mars orbit," he announced. "We're crossing now. Calls for a drink, wouldn't you all say?"

* * *

"Do we have enough room to take her in?"

Harry Chan consulted the figures on his screen. "Yes Captain, with care. We should fit inside the entrance tunnel with room to spare. The old girl can go all the way to the docking floor if you want."

"No, I won't commit us too far; the tunnel will do for now. It'll make it easier for our away teams to function but still leave room for a quick exit if need be."

"Let's do it. On your command, Captain."

Joe tapped the intercom. "Attention all crew. I am about to move the *Butterball* into the starboard airfield entrance. We'll land in the tunnel and not enter the bay proper. Away teams, you'll find us there on your return."

Without waiting for a direct command, Harry turned to face the control console. "Chloe, prepare to relocate the ship. Be aware you may experience some unusual effects as we pass through the outer shield."

"Yes, Mister Chan." the smooth voice of the ship's computer replied. "Can you advise the nature of these effects?"

"I don't know, Chloe. It's unlikely since *Drummer* went through okay, but be ready in case."

"I will limit unnecessary activities and monitor all systems. If I sense any disturbance I will transfer control to manual and shut down all higher functions for a few minutes."

Butterball released the suction clamps from the exterior platform and moved tail-first towards the darker patch on the *Minaret's* hull. The ship would enter by the stern and settle in the tunnel, ready to leave again at a moment's notice. No resistance was registered as the engineering module penetrated the shield and the ship slid into the tight confines of the entry.

"Any problems, Chloe?"

"No, Captain. No negative effects detected."

"Fine. Bring us to rest as soon as the bow clears the shield."

"Very well, Captain. Aft motion stopped. Descending now." *Butterball* settled until the spider-like landing struts touched the flat floor. Suction pads dropped from beneath the ship, secured to the surface and winched tight.

"Too easy," Harry said.

"Yeah. It's a bit tight in here though," Joe moved to rise from his seat as Alaine Parish's voice came over the intercom.

"Captain. We've found something in the upper hanger levels. You need to see this."

"What is it?"

"More ships, but you'll want to come and look at them for yourself."

"Alaine…"

"Please, Joe."

* * *

Two teams were inside the *Minaret.* Alaine, Peter Stanley and Maeve Pedder were in the hanger bays, having found a way into the upper levels. Ruth Carvalio, with Walter and Sarah, was on her second trip into the alien vessel to experience the wonders of the bridge deck. Joe wondered how she would react to the observation sphere, assuming Walter gave her as much notice as he did everyone else.

With six crewmembers out already, Joe thought he might enter the *Minaret* alone. It was a breach of his own rules, he knew, but he thought that perhaps he was being a little too restrictive. No member of the exploration teams had experienced the slightest danger or threat. It was a risk worth taking—the *Minaret* was benign, so far. Finally, accepting he had to abide by the rules he set for the others, he called for Carl to accompany him.

The short descent from *Butterball's* new position to the airfield floor would take only a few minutes. Suited up, they left the ship and floated down to the docking pillar. Peter waited on the ramp at the inner airlock door, alone. Joe decided he would definitely review that rule and relax or reinforce it as necessary.

The three men took a bubble aft to station six and entered an elevator tube to ascend several levels, well above the airfield floor level. This part of the ship resembled others Joe and his crew had already seen, endless sterile corridors and empty bays stretching in all directions, with no trace of actual occupation.

"The hangers are on three levels," Peter said as they walked. "The big lower hanger you've already seen. The top level—we got in an hour ago—is full of machines about the size of a large drone. Not ships—we have no idea what they are. Kind of spindle-shaped with a flat disk and ball on one end. We're not going there—it's the middle level you need to see."

At the end of another long corridor, Joe stepped through a hatch. Alaine Parish was on the other side, intent on examining what looked like a small, streamlined spacecraft.

Joe walked up beside him. "Okay, so what is it I absolutely must see for myself?"

"Well, this." Alaine waved a hand across the machine he was studying.

Joe peered at the object. It was about ten meters long and a little less than two in diameter, tapered at the front with what appeared to be grills at the stern. The grey hull had small wings located at various positions on the shell, not unlike a small, futuristic fighter jet. There was no sign of a cockpit. The overall impression was of a fast and sinister dart.

"A missile, maybe?"

Alaine shook his head. "No, I don't think so. Not a piloted vehicle either; there's no canopy and no entrance hatch. Could be a robot drone. Come and see this." On the nose of the small craft, Alaine pointed out several small holes on the forward cowling. Joe lent in for a better view.

"So?"

"Doesn't it remind you of anything? No, of course it wouldn't—you're a civilian. Those have to be weapon ports—lasers perhaps, or something we don't know about."

"I haven't been out of the Service for that long. Your point is?"

"Small, streamlined, probably computer controlled and very maneuverable, with weapons. It's a fighter craft, Captain. I would lay odds on it."

"Well, the *Minaret* would need to be able to protect itself, wouldn't it?"

Alaine waved his hand in a wide arc. "There are thousands of these things in here."

Joe looked around and saw row upon row of the ships, all identical, stretching away into the distance. Above, two more layers of identical craft hung suspended, each extending to the edge of the light."

"Thousands," Joe murmured.

"I think it's a robotic attack fleet, Captain. Bet my life on it. This tub is a battleship."

* * *

Jake strolled along the sidewalk, Akira close by his side. In the last few days, they had become firm friends. Their relationship clicked immediately; both worked in the inner business district, so they lunched together and spent most nights in each other's company. For Jake, it felt right. He did not at all mind the way this amazing young woman grew on him.

Wandering around the city center in the early evening proved a pleasant distraction, stopping here or there for something to eat, watching the citizenry come and go, listening to the inevitable street entertainers and dodging the downpours of rain so common at this time of year.

Jake had not been to his home on the mountain for several weeks. In the past, he had often wondered about buying a unit in one of the inner-city high-rises, to save himself the trouble. Now he was not so sure.

The general vibe in the city was changing in subtle ways. People were less open and less inclined to talk or get involved. The nightlife crowds were declining as increasing numbers of people rushed home to their loved ones each evening. Despite the official government line declaring the *Minaret* benign, a groundswell of fear was on the rise.

Some of it was absurd. Both the Vatican and Mecca insisted *Butterball* leave the *Minaret*, stating it was insufferable to have a godless, faithless man represent humanity. Jake laughed at that. His father believed firmly in a God; it was the Church in which he had no faith.

Not quite so fatuous was the reaction of the world's governments.

In the Middle East, political one-upmanship was hard at work with a rising belief that the alien ship was a 'typical Western plot', designed to fool the people of the Arab World. Similar reactions were prevalent in various parts of Africa and Central America. Nobody believed them, acknowledging it as the game-play so beloved by the world's governments.

The attitude was predictable, as several centuries of political turmoil and resource misuse meant most of those nations had no technology capable of visually confirming the arrival themselves. Accordingly, they relied on Western scientists for news. The conviction that the West was trying to double-deal other, less advanced nations, however inaccurate, was centuries old.

India expressed serious concerns that the United Earth Council was behind what could only be a plan to gazump the rest of the world. The Council controlled Earth's space forces and nobody doubted they would keep, or attempt to keep, any technology discovered out there.

Representatives of the UEC denied this.

Nobody believed them.

The most thought-provoking of all was the change of attitude in the average person. Jake did not know about elsewhere—you could never believe a word of what you heard on the media channels—but in Australia, general discourse showed ordinary people had a mounting concern over what the future held.

Nobody knew whether the *Minaret* would use the Sun's gravity to enter the Solar System or leave again for places unknown. Logic dictated Earth or Mars would be the final destination if the alien stayed, but the assumption, Jake knew, stemmed from typical human arrogance. Nothing real was known about the ship's inhabitants or which planet they might consider attractive. For them, Venus could be a tropical paradise.

Concern was increasing daily and attitudes had begun to polarise. The previous night Jake had watched an interview with a survivalist guru who insisted everyone should stock up and batten down for the worst possible scenario. He could, Jake thought, have a point if paranoia continued to grow, but the danger would not be from the aliens.

Crime was on the rise, many of the lower elements taking the view that they could do as they liked and society would be in no position to punish them once the *Minaret* arrived. Murder, assault, rape and theft were all on the increase.

Jake had hoped the human race would put on its best face when first contact occurred. Reality was increasingly proving him wrong and the science-fiction writers of history right. Every nasty human failing of a million fiction stories was coming to pass. To those who noticed, the masses of humanity were so predictable.

Jake's mind wandered. Earlier he had created, at his father's request, a secure channel for them to communicate. Thanks to his unquestionable skills in the field, the link could not be blocked, broken or easily traced, using as it did any suitable carrier to piggyback the encrypted signals, and being able to switch carriers at will.

Only by stopping all data transfer between Earth and Mars could the messages be stopped, and that would never happen. Government officers had already visited Jake, claiming he was in contact with his father beyond the official communications channels. A few denials and a complete lack of evidence sent them away empty-handed. No laws were broken, but he knew they would be back.

In a world crippled by industrial, military and political espionage, encryption and data security was a major field and something at which he had excelled before turning his attention to molecular research. Communications with his father traveled across both planets via a variety of different pathways, hidden amid a vast network of servers set up onion-style, which only Jake could navigate.

The process used any server in operation and routed messages through thousands of private systems before sending them to their destination piggybacked on any one of a storm of commercial data transfers, including official government ones—the last place they would look.

To get them to the *Butterball*, he used the Council's communications. Encrypted with a unique system of Jake's own design, the content could not be read without a key, which changed with each message. Only he and his father's computer, Chloe, could decipher that key.

Data from the communications were stored piecemeal on myriad computers in the network, in a manner undetectable. Even the owners of the networks he used were unaware of their involvement. Nor would they ever know. Jake's systems served only as remote terminals, and he removed all traces of activity after every exchange.

Why his father should insist on such a secure link puzzled him. Joe never did anything lightly but Jake knew there was logic behind all of his father's actions.

“I'm thinking,” he said, turning to his companion, “that we should go to my place up on the mountain. Can you take time away from the university?”

“I just started there,” Akira said. “I don't think they would take very kindly to me taking a leave of absence so soon.”

Jake thought about it for a moment. “They've been trying to get me to work with them for years,” he said. “What if I sent them a request for your assistance as a co-researcher, the work to be done at my private lab in Maleny and the results to be jointly published?”

“You think they would agree to that?”

“They'll fall over their arses to help you pack,” Jake replied, grinning. “With the setup I have you can do all of your work from there anyway. I guarantee it.”

“Do you think it's important we leave the city?”

Jake did not reply, peering at his new friend. He sometimes found it hard to interpret those beautiful, huge, Asian eyes. He remained silent as they continued to walk.

One thing he knew very well: whatever the outcome regarding the *Minaret*, it would not be good for human society. Should the ship prove hostile, humanity could not compete with a species so advanced. Conversely, if it kept going, the next few months of uncertainty would still cause worldwide social disruption.

Stock markets were on a downturn as cautious investors succumbed to their paranoia and dumped shares, desperate to escape before the real collapse occurred. In so doing, they guaranteed that outcome.

There had been runs on the banks that would continue until they closed their doors. When it happened, the public would panic.

Religious fervor was boiling over in most of the major religions: the aliens were demons or angels, or the vengeance of God upon humanity. To others, they proved that God did not exist. It went on endlessly.

Another option: they were benevolent, or harmless, and would steer humanity towards a glorious future, as some desperate individuals hoped or believed. Jake thought that unlikely. So far, no trace of any living entity had appeared on the ship—it was a machine, deserted, most likely controlled by artificial intelligence and capable of anything. Having grown up as the son of a science-fiction fanatic, Jake could not imagine the savior of the human race being an alien computer. Empathy had to be a trait limited to organic beings who could know pain and suffering.

"In a few days, two fleets are going to intercept the *Minaret*, and I have serious concerns," he said to Akira. "Things are getting dangerous with everyone starting to panic or dig in. We need to get out of here as soon as we can."

Chapter 14

STATION EIGHT—NINE—TEN; Joe watched the light flash across the buttons on the console. He and Alaine, with Terry Calwell as the third member of the team, headed aft on the 'bubble way' searching for a route into what he suspected was a habitat zone, the enormous cylindrical structure sleeving the mid-section of the ship.

The preliminary survey of the *Minaret* on arrival had shown the tube to be twenty kilometers long and over nine in diameter. With a wall thickness of several hundred meters, there was enough room inside for several decks of accommodation.

Given the ability of the ship to rearrange parts of itself at the molecular level, a rotating drum to provide centrifugal gravity no longer seemed unreasonable despite the seamless connection of the spokes to the hull.

It seemed odd considering the artificial gravity in the fuselage; such a thing was technically impossible according to all the physics and gravitation theory Joe had ever read, but somehow the *Visitors* had managed to do it. He suspected long-term exposure might be a bad thing; several of the crew had already complained of general headaches and knowing them as well as she did, Maeve had commented on the possibility the strange force was the cause.

To Joe, the theory supported accommodation in the cylinder, where the artificial gravity would not operate. Centrifugal force, presuming the drum rotated, would do the job just as in the wheels on *Butterball.*

The trio had already checked every station leading up to the zone where Joe expected to find the entrance to the habitat. The area traversed was mainly hollow shell packed with spherical tanks of colossal size.

"What do you think is in them?" He directed his question to no one in particular.

"Hard to say," Alaine said. "Not fuel tanks—those are more likely to be aft, near the primary engines. Fuel for the smaller auxiliary craft, oxygen, water or some kind of material storage. Who knows?"

"Those are real big buggers," Terry said. "Must be over a kilometer across."

Joe gazed at the walls of the giant spheres. "Yes, even the smallest ones are bigger than most of our space stations."

The light from the 'bubble way' extended only a short distance, and small pinpoints of illumination moved through the darkness between structures.

"What do you think they are, Boss?"

Alaine answered the question. "Maintenance robots? They're beautiful, like fireflies."

Terry ignored him. Joe had become increasingly aware since they had left *Butterball* of some antagonism between the two men, something he would have to keep an eye on in future.

He pointed ahead. “There's another bulkhead coming up.” Every few kilometers the bubble passed through a wall that stretched away on all sides; after the second such structure, he concluded they were bulkheads supporting the hull. That aspect of the ship construction was at least understandable.

Seconds later, they stopped at another station despite Alaine's objections; he believed they should ride to the end and locate the engine rooms first. They were now in the region Chloe calculated as being closest to the structures that reminded Joe of wheel spokes.

A short corridor led to the inevitable cylinder elevator. Joe walked in and felt a solid, invisible surface beneath his feet. The exploration teams now routinely used the elevators, dubbed 'gravity tubes'.

“So, what do you think?” Joe asked as his companions stepped in beside him. “The spokes must rotate. If they are the way into the habitat, you would need a circular collar structure around the outer edge of the central hub, and it would be the only place you could get in.” He punched the lowest button.

The trip to the bottom took only seconds. The party stepped out of the tube and followed a corridor aft.

“I'll be…” Joe stopped in his tracks.

He stood on a broad balcony, the sight before his eyes once again mind-boggling. The ledge projected into yet another huge space and stretched away around the walls in both directions. The whole area was ablaze with bright light. The chamber, at least two hundred meters high and five hundred deep, extended away to either side, curving up until it disappeared behind the ceiling.

"A ring," Alaine said. "We must be at the outer shell. I expect this chamber extends all the way around like a donut; exactly what we wanted."

"Yeah," Terry said. "So how do we get in?" Alaine shook his head as he walked across to the edge of the balcony.

Spaced at regular intervals, small semicircular platforms extended out from the balcony edge, each with its own enclosing rails and open access on the side secured to the ledge. The team stepped onto one to get a better view.

Joe leaned over the end rail and looked down. "Does that floor appear to be moving to you?"

"Not sure, but that certainly is," Alaine replied, pointing away to one side. Far around the curve, a pillar a hundred meters in diameter and stretching from floor to ceiling glided majestically down the center of the curved hull space towards the team's vantage point.

"It's moving," Joe said. "It must be the top of a spoke. The drum outside is rotating."

"That's a concern," Alaine said, stating the obvious. "It was stationary when we arrived. Why start now? I think…"

Before he could continue, the section of floor on which they stood separated from the balcony and became a small, circular platform, floating out into the chamber and crabbing sideways to match the speed of the approaching column.

"Of course. The hull doesn't rotate and the spokes do. These platforms are how you get from one to the other; they match the rotation as they move out.

"Yes, it does seem logical," Joe agreed. "Pat? Are you with us?"

Seconds later the voice of Patricia Grace sounded through their headsets. "Of course, Captain. How far away are you?"

"Must be at least thirty kilometers now. Whatever is carrying our signal is still working. What do you think of this?"

"I'm concerned the drum is rotating all of a sudden, if that's what you mean."

"Yes. What's your perspective?"

"The only reason it would rotate is to create centrifugal gravity, and that means habitation. If it is a habitat, it's enormous. Twenty kilometers long and nine in diameter gives it more than five hundred square kilometers of space per deck, and there may be more than one of those. I find it hard to believe some computer started it up for the benefit of three lonely little explorers."

"I am inclined to agree with you."

"It's more likely," Patricia said, "the ship's computers did this as part of a pre-determined plan, don't you think? It could be coincidental you came along soon after it started."

"And that plan would be?"

"Maybe the crew are sleeping down there somewhere and are due to wake up now they've arrived at their destination."

"That's a worry," Alaine said. As he spoke, the platform closed on the moving pillar and entered through an opening in the side. Gently it settled to the floor at the center of a passage through the structure extended to a second entrance on the opposite side. On one wall, square color patches indicated doorways arrayed like elevators in a lift foyer. One of the doors opened, revealing a small, circular room beyond.

"Is that what I think it is?" Alaine asked.

"It must be," Joe said. "What else would there be in here?"

"What do we do now, Boss?"

"We came here to find a way to the drum, so we go down." Without another word, he stepped off the platform and approached the open elevator.

Terry hesitated. "So how many sleeping aliens fit in five hundred square kilometers?"

The elevator was like those on the Kepler habitat, a circular chamber with seating around the circumference. The seats looked so perfect for the human form Joe could not help wondering whether once again, this was for the benefit of him and his crew. It would not be the first time they had encountered things on this ship that could change shape at will.

As soon as the trio entered, the door closed. Unlike the molecular openings so far experienced on the *Minaret,* it simply vanished, replaced by a solid wall. A vertical line of color dots appeared on one side.

Alaine peered at the dots. "This thing could almost be on Mars. No numbers or symbols though."

Joe examined the row. "Three choices, three decks. Which do you suggest we should try first?"

"Bottom one, I think. We work our way back up?"

"Agreed." Joe stabbed at the bottom-most spot. Immediately the elevator began to descend. For the briefest of seconds, the team members' stomachs twisted. "The gravity has changed."

"You're right. It's been replaced by centrifugal gravity, getting stronger as we go down. Odd that a race so technologically advanced would revert to such an ancient principle."

"Sometimes the simple things are the best," Joe commented. "It's still very sophisticated if you consider the sheer scale and the use of molecular rearrangement technology where the spokes emerge from the hull."

"We don't know that. We can't see outside."

"No, but it's likely. The cylinder struts must move around through molecular re-ordering, same as the emergency opening bars on the hatches."

"So no weird gravity down here," Terry said. "Not once we are beyond the main hull."

"Right. I'm guessing the artificial type is unhealthy or disconcerting over long periods, so not used down here. We just transitioned from one to the other."

The elevator stopped and the door opened, the wall this time splitting to slide either side like an ordinary elevator door on Earth or Mars. The space beyond was in darkness, but the second Joe stepped through the doorway, lights flooded the immediate area. He stood in what looked like a service level not unlike the one below the airfield bay, stretching away to the edge of illumination.

Block-like and cylindrical structures, ranging in size from that of a shuttle car to a multi-story building, filled the chamber. Arranged row upon row in a grid pattern they were smooth and symmetrical, the corners rounded and the sides again flowing seamlessly into the floor. The air hummed with a faint noise sitting at the edge of consciousness. There was no sign of life and no movement.

"This is another service area," Joe said. "If the drum is a habitat then these machines—if that's what they are—will be for the support of the habitation."

"Which must be on the other two levels," Alaine said. "Do we want to explore?"

"No. Everything here looks sealed. If the whole place is like this, we won't learn anything in the time we have. We go up a level."

Minutes later, they entered into another, different scenario. Once again, lights came on the second they stepped from the elevator, revealing what appeared to be the foyer of a planet-side hotel.

They were on a raised mezzanine, at either side of which ramps and stairways dropped down to the main floor or rose to vanish through the ceiling.

The main room was at least fifty meters across with a high, vaulted ceiling. On one side, windows looked into complete blackness, as did a glass door positioned halfway along the window line. Low benches, perhaps intended as seats, sat in small clusters.

Scattered along the walls opposite the windows were doorways, wider than human doors but still recognizable. Between them, giant 'bas-relief' sculptures and murals filled the gaps, displaying what might be scenes from nature. Joe and Alaine crossed to the nearest.

"This is insane," said Joe. "Pat, are you still with us?"

"Yes, Captain. Still here. Always."

"You have to come down and see this with the next team. We've found murals—there appear to be stylized images in them, perhaps from the world this ship originated on."

"Seriously? Can you put a camera on them?"

Joe did as requested. For several minutes, silence reigned over the intercom, then: "From an alien world. Unbelievable. Our aliens have eyes similar to ours, and an appreciation for art. Do you notice anything odd about them, Captain?"

"Not really. They could easily be Earth."

"Exactly my point. It's just like Earth. Are there any living creatures in them?"

"I haven't seen any. Alaine, have you…" Joe turned to face his companion, but the officer was gone.

"Over here," came Alaine's voice from the glass doorway. "These are mechanical sliding doors. The molecular technology doesn't work down here as we suspected."

"Or they don't want it here," Joe replied. As the doors slid apart and floodlights lit the area outside, the two men stepped through into an almost unrecognizable scene.

A broad ramp sloped down to where a pathway wound across a vast space. To Joe, it resembled a park—all about were mounded areas of what appeared to be dark, chocolate-colored soil. Opposite the ramp, a second path led to a circular paved area, at the center of which stood what looked like a terrestrial fountain, a wide, raised dish with a strange, abstract creation sitting at the center. Around the edges of the plaza were more benches arranged in small groupings. Joe took a few paces and turned in a circle.

The floodlit area extended for perhaps a kilometer in every direction, pale, reddish light streaming down from somewhere high up in the chamber. The lobby from which the team had emerged was the ground floor of a columnar structure like an office tower extending to the ceiling high above. In the distance, visible at the limit of illumination, similar other edifices rose, some reaching the roof, others stopping below it.

Alaine stepped up beside Joe. "No doubt about it. This is a habitat. Residential buildings and so on, studded across parkland and recreational areas, in this part of the cylinder at least."

Joe bent down and examined the soil at the side of the path. A small purple shoot was pushing through, one of thousands visible in the near area.

"Are you getting this, Pat?"

"Yes, Captain. The reddish light is probably for the plants—maybe they come from a red star. That shoot is a living thing, the first extra-terrestrial life ever encountered by a human being. Congratulations." Joe heard a deep sadness in her voice, and realized he had unwittingly achieved a notoriety she would have liked for herself.

"Somehow, I kind of expected more from our first encounter. A little, wrinkly monkey with glowing fingertips, for example."

"This will do for now," Pat replied. "Who would imagine our first alien contact would be with a plant."

"It resembles something from Earth."

"Form follows function. Life forms filling a particular ecological niche can have a common shape. That plant may be alien, and it's probably different from Terran life at the micro level, but it could still appear similar. Then there's 'panspermia', the theory that life can cross through space on comets and the like, spreading a common biological base throughout the galaxy."

"It's just a shoot," Alaine interrupted. "Might be more interesting when it's grown a bit.

"It's much more than that," Pat said. "You have to bring one back for me."

"Not a chance," Joe said. "We are not disturbing anything here. Think about it—we're fast approaching the sun, the drum has started revolving and the habitat is starting to—things are growing, maybe to get this place ready for use. What does that tell you, Patricia?"

"This ship is not dead, just dormant and now waking up. Where are the inhabitants?"

Terry appeared in the glass doorway. "Boss, you might want to see this."

On a mural located at the far side of the foyer, the engineer pointed at an image. Joe aimed his camera for Patricia's benefit. It showed a creature standing on two legs, with a horizontal body. It had a short, tapered tail, small articulating limbs forward and a head not unlike that of an ancient Earth reptile, perched at the end of a long, curved neck.

"Dinosaurs?" Alaine said. "You're kidding me."

"No, not quite," said Joe. "The shape is similar, but it's not a dinosaur. Do you think that might be one of our *Visitors*, Pat?"

"Possibly—it's hard to tell. It has no clothes and it's not carrying tools or anything else. Nothing to indicate intelligence or technology, and it's standing in an open field. It could just as easily be an alien cow or chicken. The hands appear to be functional though, so who knows."

Terry leaned in until his nose almost touched the image. "Some people think the dinos was intelligent."

"Not enough to survive," Patricia's voice commented. "This is different somehow. Captain, I have to be down there."

"Next sortie, okay? We have to move on now."

Alaine studied the door. "It's different."

"Yes, it is," Joe agreed.

"Yep, sure is," Terry mimicked. "No entry."

The uppermost level of the habitat drum was a small, circular foyer, the walls smooth and featureless except for several closed doors. To one side of each was a color spot keypad similar to the one guarding access to the hangers. Sadly, Marius Pine's makeshift punch device was back in the *Butterball's* service bay, so for now this was the end of the exploration.

"We'll come back," Joe said. "For now we better get back to the *Butterball*."

"If this is a habitat area," Alaine said, "what's so important it needs to be sealed?"

"Maybe it's where the aliens are," Terry said. "I mean, they've got to be somewhere, don't they, Boss?"

Chapter 15

A BLADE OF GRASS, unspectacular, but enough to change everything; the *Minaret* was alive despite there being no trace of a crew. Back in his cabin, Joe gazed into his monitor and mulled over the new discovery. It would be so much simpler if there were no signs of life at all.

When *Butterball* first arrived, the alien ship was virtually inactive. Now it was alive, the temperature and atmospheric pressure were both acceptable to humans, and a gravity that defied all the laws of physics functioned at roughly Mars normal. Every part of the ship's transport systems, hatches and accesses worked, and the progressive behavior of the lighting system proved the ship was aware living beings were wandering its interior.

Strange globular objects displaying the same blue-green-purple, shimmering surface as the hatches had been observed floating through various parts of the ship; after considerable debate, the consensus was they were maintenance drones. They ignored the crew and went about their business unfazed.

The alien 'grass' discovery was a momentous event and a game changer. The vast spaces in the main level of the habitat were transforming into a landscape reminiscent of the domed cities of Joe's adopted world.

The only logical purpose of such an environment in a spacecraft was to enhance the comfort of an intelligent species that could appreciate its beauty and familiarity, so there had to be a crew and perhaps passengers, somewhere. Whether they were still alive was an unknown but the *Minaret* behaved as if that were so, and was preparing for them.

There were still too many variables for Joe's liking. To begin, the temperature and atmosphere both suited humans perfectly. It was improbable that a species evolving on another world around another star would need exactly the same requirements as man even given the concept of panspermia.

Of course, the vessel might, as suspected, be reacting to the presence of Joe and his team, with the original crew deceased. If the possibility of alien incursion—yes, Joe thought, to them we are the aliens—had not been included in the programming for the computers, they might simply accept any living beings and respond accordingly as Alaine had jokingly suggested earlier.

That theory did not seem likely either. No artificial intelligence so advanced could be so naive, surely. A gut feeling warned Joe the real owners of this remarkable ship were here somewhere. But where?

Patricia pushed constantly for samples from the habitat. Until some of the unknowns were answered Joe was determined no crewmember would take any action that might be seen as aggressive. Pulling up plants wholesale, or even nipping a few cuttings, could be such an act. For all he knew those shoots could be part of some larger organic structure, the exact nature of which was one of the many unknowns.

Then again, it could be just grass.

"Chloe?"

"Yes, Captain?"

"Record a message for me please, to be sent to Marcus Bond."

"Yes, Captain. You may begin."

Joe settled back in his chair to summarise everything discovered in the drum. Once the report was complete, he continued: "I've been asked to make a statement claiming this vessel as a derelict in the name of the government of Mars. I am no longer prepared to do so. It was my intention to claim it on behalf of all humankind, but now I don't think we have the right to do even that.

"The condition agreed to was I would make a statement once satisfied the ship is deserted or derelict. I am convinced more than ever that this is not the case. We have discovered the first-ever, extra-terrestrial life form, in the main level of the habitat. There is vegetation growing there and it cannot be terrestrial. I appreciate many people back home will say 'So what? It's just plants', but they need to consider this more closely.

"Why do we grow plants in spaceships? For food and to purify and regenerate air, and because we enjoy them for their beauty. Why else would aliens grow them if not for similar reasons? This ship is clearly under the control of a sophisticated artificial intelligence that would not require plants for either survival or aesthetic reasons. I do not believe they would be here for no good reason, so they must be for the benefit of a living, organic crew we have not yet seen.

"We may not have found them, but considering we are dealing with several thousand square kilometers of deck space, that doesn't preclude the fact of their existence. They are here somewhere, I'm sure of it. Therefore, it is my belief we have no right to make any claim at all.

"I am ordering my crew to explore, observe and record, but I will not allow anything to be removed or damaged at this time. We will stay with the *Minaret* as long as possible. If the aliens have not made themselves known by the time we are forced to leave, we will sample the plants in the habitat and try to take possession of one of the smaller ships discovered in the hangers.

"I would like to make it clear that if we do the latter—and it is unlikely, since we've so far been unable to work out how anything actually works here—we will be doing so for all humankind and not for the governments of either Earth or Mars.

"I am fully aware there is a fleet of warships from Earth nine days away, with another from Mars a day behind them. Although I've been assured the fleets are here in an ambassadorial capacity only, I have no doubt whatever that the second they make rendezvous the Earth fleet will try to occupy this vessel, and the Mars ships will do the same a day later. There is no way either force can stop the other from boarding without conflict. Consider that before you do something stupid. I do not have the power or the authority to prevent it, but I will say this.

"Neither party should board at all. Any attempt to do so could have consequences we may regret in the future. The *Minaret* is not derelict. I repeat, not derelict. It either has a crew yet to make an appearance or is controlled by a computer with a capacity beyond anything we can imagine. To assume the ship is ours for the taking is the ultimate folly.

"You gave me and my people the task of acting as ambassadors for the human race. We cannot do so with two war fleets fighting each other for control of something they have no right to claim. I respectively recommend both commanders back off and let us get on with our job.

"Chloe, send copies to the commanders of both fleets as well as Marcus, and to my son Jake through our secure link."

"Yes, Captain."

Joe sat back and gave a loud sigh.

* * *

With the faintest hint of a click, the largest door slid aside, opening the way to the yet unexplored top level of the habitat drum. The makeshift cracking device took two days to break the sequence of the security keypad, but finally, a signal came that the way was open. Beyond the door lay another passageway.

To Joe, the ship seemed little else but long, empty passages and barren halls. Apart from features with a distinct and obvious purpose such as the airfield bay, hangers, bubble way and bridge deck, every area not devoted to the actual functioning of the vessel—and even that was hard to assess—contained endless vacant spaces, ranging in size from small, human-scale rooms to vast, warehouse-sized bays.

It raised a puzzling question: why construct huge spaces and leave them empty? It was odd someone would build a mega-ship with so much unused passenger or crew space. That it was all for some future purpose seemed the only reasonable answer.

Adamant that when the upper habitat level was cracked he would be the first to enter, Joe now led Patricia Grace and Sam Bright into the corridor. As usual, light illuminated the section of the passage they were in, moving with them as they walked on. A short distance brought them to an opening leading into a room that was anything but empty.

Joe half-expected hibernation chambers for the alien crew, hence his inclusion of Patricia in the team, but the reality was far different.

At first, the floor appeared to be another service level. Arranged in rows stretching into the distance were small cube-shaped units about a meter square. On the top of each perched four cylinders, transparent and containing colored liquid. They glowed, casting an eerie blue-green light through the immense room. Something electric and unearthly permeated the place, a fact not lost on anyone.

"What in God's…" Patricia moved to the cube nearest the entrance. "Gel filled? And it glitters." She extended a gloved hand to touch one of the cylinders and then withdrew with a yelp. "It's protected," she whimpered, shaking her hand. "Some kind of electrical field."

Joe stepped up beside her and examined her glove. "Are you all right?"

"Yes. Whatever these things are, we're not permitted to mess around with them."

"Had to happen eventually, assuming this ship is aware of our presence. Even when we cracked the locks on the doors, we weren't stopped. We've been given unrestricted access to a point; this is that point."

"What do you think this place is?"

Joe passed on the question. "Sam?"

"I know not, my captain." Sam studied one of the flasks. "I think maybe we are finding the computer that runs the show. These flasks are memory cells of some sort, maybe. Have a look."

Joe leaned towards a flask, taking care not to come close enough to be zapped. Inside, faint flashes of light were visible, a fine tracery of energy shooting randomly through the liquid, each flicker lasting only a fraction of a second.

"There is electrical activity here," Sam said. "We have gel data cells at home, so it is a possible explanation for this. Walter should be here—he looks maybe in the wrong place."

Patricia gazed along the rows of modules. "This place is immense. You can see maybe a half-kilometer down that way"—she indicated the fore and aft orientation of the room—"before the light gives out. The floor curves up towards the ceiling on either side, following the curve of the drum, so it's wide as well."

"It could be one of many," Joe said. "Don't forget there must be several hundred square kilometers of space on this level, the same as the one below."

Patricia cast him a questioning glance. "So what do we do now?"

"We, um ... damned if I know. This place is vast, and these modules go all the way. If they all have protection, we aren't going to get far by exploring here. I suspect we would be better off using the bubble way to find other entrances. With such a massive floor space there are bound to be other ways in. Assuming every spoke has an elevator system, that makes—with five sets of spokes and three to a set—fifteen different places we can access the levels."

"So we go back up and come down in the next spoke around, yes?" Sam asked.

"Why the hell not." Joe turned back towards the foyer. With rooms stretching for kilometers in every direction and everything built on an immense scale, he felt increasingly lost. He understood little of what he had seen and now it was becoming overwhelming. Of the scientific or engineering principles behind everything, nothing was within his grasp, or that of any member of his crew.

He felt very small indeed.

* * *

Terry Caldwell shunted himself along the spinal corridor of the *Butterball* and launched himself through the entrance hatch to the number two habitat wheel. He floated down, grasping the ladder with hands and feet clamped on the outsides of the uprights. As the gravity increased, his free-fall became a slide.

The secondary wheel contained the medical bay as well as the gymnasium, minerals lab and several crew cabins. Desperate for relief from a crippling headache that developed during his last sortie into the *Minaret*, Terry sought Maeve Pedder. Doubtless, the cause was the strange pseudo-gravity everyone was talking about; whatever it was, it affected him more than anyone else.

This wheel was a duplicate of the first, but its observation windows faced the stern rather than looking forward. The habitats revolved around the central spine and from the viewpoint of someone standing inside, they appeared stationary while everything else rotated outside.

The view, mostly blocked by the cargo flat, tanks and radiation shadow shield, did little to help Terry's delicate head. Looking out, he watched as the entry tunnel spun around him. It was enough to make a body feel sick in minutes. He walked around to the infirmary entrance and peeked inside.

Maeve was not there; a gentle knock on her cabin door also proved fruitless. Assuming she was either in the number one wheel or out exploring, he decided to go to the common room and check the sortie roster.

As he reached the base of the ladder, he turned towards the minerals lab, his attention drawn by loud voices. The door was open and Peter Stanley, the ship's geologist, stood inside.

"We could have resigned and hired a ship of our own," Peter grumbled. "Why the hell we had to come on this god-forsaken mission I will never know."

"And where do you think we would get the money," another voice responded. "After this, we will have enough to lease a damned ship. Then we don't have to include anyone else."

"If we survive."

"If we do, we could be so famous we can get anything we need."

Whoever spoke had a mouth full of food; Terry was not sure who it was but he had a reasonable idea. He began the climb up the ladder; it was no concern of his.

Peter turned to see him leave, raising a hand to his unseen opponent to cease talking.

* * *

The final station aft on the bubble way sat transversely across the hull of the *Minaret* at the end of a loop, marking the point where the invisible one-way track turned and headed back towards the bow.

From the platform, a broad-way extended further aft. Along the center ran one of the ubiquitous walkways found throughout the ship. It ended at a lobby containing an elevator tube, with a single hatch in the far wall.

Alaine was certain it was an entrance to the Engine rooms, or perhaps an associated control or engineering area. He savored the moment; this was the reason he had come on this voyage. Finally, he was where he most desired to be.

It was locked, like the hangers and the upper drum level.

Beside the hatch was the inevitable keypad, this time with far more options, one hundred spots arranged in a ten by ten grid. No amount of guesswork would find the way past it. He had anticipated such a lock and had brought the punch device along, but it was too small.

With nowhere to go, the team returned to the *Butterball*, where Marius Pine and Sam Bright joined forces to construct a bigger and faster version of their passcode cracker. Two days later, the new device was in place, with a radio to transmit its activity back to Chloe. The AI would advise them immediately the correct combination was discovered.

*   *   *

"Grass, for God's sake," Carmichael Page moaned, slumping into a seat against the wall of the conference room.

"Ah, yes," Professor Brewer confirmed, "but alien grass."

"Oh, shut up, Alf. Grass is grass. Just because they found it growing in that thing does not mean it's occupied."

"On the contrary, young man. It is not just grass. The shoots are alien life forms, and at this stage, we can't tell what they will grow into. They are the first extra-terrestrial life ever discovered, and concrete proof that life may be common throughout the universe."

"So take a cutting. Make a salad for all I care, but let's get on with it."

"Oh no, we can't do that. Falcon is quite correct—if the ship is preparing itself for habitation then there are aliens on board, perhaps in cryogenic sleep somewhere the Captain has yet to find. If we take over with military force it may not go down too well."

"Well, we need to sort it now. The fleet from Earth is only three days away from rendezvous, and Mars is not far behind it."

"The sensible thing would be for both of them to wait until we know better where we stand."

"Damn it," Page cursed. "There's no real evidence of intelligent life on that ship. Falcon's just guessing. There's no way the authorities on Earth are going to tell Barrett to sit on his arse and do nothing."

Adam stood, as was his habit, where he could gaze through the window at the darkened sky of Mars while pretending to ignore the squabbling council. He turned and looked at Page, a quizzical expression on his face. "So you admit now he intends to board regardless?"

"Well, I… Oh damn it, you know as well as I that he will. The man follows orders religiously."

Adam nodded. "Yes, accepted. Perhaps it's time we stopped arguing about this and started to concentrate on how we can stop both fleets from dragging us into another war. With an alien ship in the equation, it's the last thing either planet wants."

For a moment, Page stared at the floor and then nodded in agreement. "Falcon says there is a fleet of attack vessels inside the *Minaret.* Barrett will go after those regardless and he won't let a piddling little freighter captain stop him."

"Tell Earth to order him away."

"They won't do it. Nobody on Earth trusts Mars. The Terrestrial governments don't trust each other, for God's sake. By the time they come to a consensus the fleet will have arrived."

Adam turned towards the Earth representative. He had learned to hate the man but never lost hope there might be some common ground. At first, it had been all stubborn resistance with Page maintaining Earth had only the best of intentions, but now cracks were starting to show in the comments he made when he was not paying attention. Adam watched and listened, realizing the man had reached the point where his intelligence and common sense were beginning to overrule his sense of self-interest and loyalty.

Earth did not intend to cooperate.

Their fleet would arrive first and they would push their advantage to take control of the alien vessel, desperate to obtain the technology it held.

The red world fleet was no different but it would not get there first. Mars already had legal occupancy through an official representative in Parish. If Barrett ignored that, there would be conflict, the last thing desired but the most likely scenario.

Mars did not come close to Earth in population, but its massive resources and industrial power made it Earth's equal in military might. The Resources War had dragged on for a decade; the next one would be worse and with far less return. Adam returned his attention to the committee.

"You're all missing the point. We can't yet tell if the ship will enter into the Solar System or slingshot around the sun and go on its way. In the latter case, the argument is moot. Falcon's observations are enough to see we can't comprehend the alien technology in any short term, and before we can they'll be gone despite anything we can do."

"The plants…" Page interrupted.

"…indicate the *Minaret* is inhabited and also that it intends to stay, in which case any action to take over the vessel, remove the warships or anything else might well be seen as aggression or an act of war. Sit down and shut up, Carmichael."

Gordon Styles, the Mars naval representative, cleared his throat. "You are correct, Adam. I suggest we advise our fleet to stand by upon arrival and make no attempt to board. Carmichael, you might make official representation for the Earth contingent to do the same, regardless of what you think they will do."

"Yes, of course," Page said. He slumped into his seat, a look of resignation on his face. "Naturally, they'll take a great deal of notice of me."

Chapter 16

JOE LAY ON his bunk and stared at the overhead. The complete failure to glean any useful knowledge from the *Minaret* was starting to tell on the crew. He could not help thinking the mission was beginning to turn pear-shaped.

"So how many ships have they sent?" he asked, directing his question to the younger man sitting quietly at the desk.

Alaine slouched in the chair and poured himself another measure of the Captain's best whisky. "Enough—it doesn't matter. The *Constellation* is a fully-fledged *Hector*-class battleship, more than capable of making our life a misery on her own. The other ships are two destroyers, a troop carrier containing civilian personnel, and several navy tankers. They're irrelevant, considering the capability of a *Hector*."

"She can't enter the landing bay. Way too big, so she'll have to sit outside and send shuttles across."

"Agreed."

"You think they'll stand off and wait for the Mars fleet to arrive?"

"Not a chance. Left to his own devices Barrett might make the sensible choice, but he can be a hard nose. I'm guessing his orders are to board despite our presence, so that's what he'll do. His away-team commander, Lieutenant Francis Manners, is an unknown factor to a point but he's also a career man. He'll carry out his duty without question."

"How do you know about him?"

"We have an agent on that ship." Alaine spoke as if it was an everyday detail.

Joe raised an eyebrow; the young officer never ceased to surprise him. "So how do we stop them?"

"Not sure. We don't have to. Just delay them until our guys get here."

For a few minutes, Joe mulled over those words. He had hoped his last message might ease the tension and his opinion that the ship was occupied might prompt caution, or at least a little common sense. That did not seem to be the case. He tapped the wall communicator.

"Sam, where are you?"

"Yes, my captain?" Sam Bright's voice replied. "I am in the galley. What can I do for you?"

"The rock cutters. Did we bring them with us?" Joe referred to the high-powered lasers used during prospecting to slice pieces from small asteroids before bringing them aboard. It had always been part of Sam's duties to maintain them.

"Yes. They are in the lower service module."

The rock cutters were small, portable devices, of no value at all against a capital ship like the *Constellation* but easily able to make a mess of a man at close range, or even disable a small shuttle.

"Okay, I want them set up and operational, one in each of the landing bay entrances. As soon as possible please."

"You do not start a war, my captain?"

Joe sighed. "I might be about to do exactly that."

It seemed logical to change tack and declare that on behalf of all humanity he would deny all access until the Mars fleet arrived. He would only allow both parties to come across together. Only civilian representatives would be permitted and any unauthorized attempts would be stopped with the cutters.

Joe knew he could not enforce such a stance nor hope to succeed, but the presence of the lasers in the entrances might cause Barrett to pause. The man could not know with any certainty that the lasers were too limited to stop a concerted attack. With luck, they would cause sufficient hesitation to allow the Martian fleet to arrive, and then the two commanders could play watchdog over each other.

"We have three days before they arrive?" Alaine asked.

"Yes. Why?"

Alaine pointed to the message flashing on the computer screen on the desk.

"It looks like our little doohickie has found the passcode for the engine rooms. If we're about to start a war, I'd like to get at least one look at that place first."

* * *

Joe punched in the code for the entrance to what they hoped was the engineering section.

Two days remained until the arrival of the Earth fleet. With nothing more to be done, the exploration was a perfect way to take his mind off more pressing problems. At his request, Chloe advised Mars authorities of the intention to bar access to the *Minaret.* Despite the difficulties of enforcing such a ban, the committee issued a formal statement declaring the alien vessel a common asset with all exploration to be conducted by civilian personnel only, as a joint action.

Any attempt by Commander Barrett to land a military force would be considered an act of war, a bluff roughly equal in strength to Barrett's. The fleet from Mars was larger and more heavily armed, and Joe hoped the threat of conflict would be enough to stay the man's hand.

He did not want to waste what had now become precious time, so exploration of the *Minaret* proceeded regardless, with three teams out at once. Initially, attention focused on the top floor of the drum, but after discovering everything protected by the pain-inducing electrical field, Joe placed the deck off-limits.

Wally Tyrell's team continued to explore the forward sections of the ship and the command decks, having so far discovered nothing else as mind-blowing as the 'space globe'. He had made no progress accessing the ship's computers or even identifying an interface console. The strange bench-like structures on the bridge-deck mezzanine kept their secrets well.

The second team explored the main habitat level under the watchful eyes of Patricia Grace. She at last confirmed Joe's stance that the plants should not be disturbed at this stage, and contented herself with photographic images and non-invasive tests of the rapidly growing vegetation.

The areas between the tower structures increasingly resembled parkland. Patricia searched without success for sample material to remove safely, but despite the unbelievable growth rate nothing of the alien life died, dropped or wilted, and as the flora grew her frustration increased in proportion.

Besides Alaine, Joe had wanted Sam, *Butterball's* electrical engineer, to be with the engine room team, but with him busy with the laser cutters, Ruth Carvalio joined them.

The three followed the walkway through yet another vast deck covered with row upon row of featureless, multi-sized cubes connected by a maze of pipes and conduits, a common scenario in their explorations.

"Looks a bit like the service area under the landing bay," Alaine said.

Joe grunted and continued towards another door in the distant wall. As he walked, a strange static built around him. His skin began to crawl and he suspected his hair was standing on end. His companions appeared normal but the expressions on their faces betrayed awareness of the strange sensations.

Ruth wondered aloud, "Is this safe, do you think?"

"Well," Joe replied, "it doesn't seem harmful, just uncomfortable. We'll be mindful and keep going, I think. We may not have time to come here again."

Minutes later he was glad he had not abandoned the mission too early. Beyond the far door, the path extended into the largest and most astonishing space yet encountered on the ship.

The chamber was kilometers across. The exploration team entered through the forward wall, along a broad walkway enclosed by a transparent tube stretching a hundred meters into the void.

From the walkway, the entire chamber was visible. The engine room, assuming that was its purpose, was filled with astonishing and baffling structures.

Everywhere, gargantuan, multicolored spheres hung suspended like celestial orbs in space, connected by tubular umbilicals ranging in size from perhaps two meters in diameter to as much as fifty. In the immense space, even these appeared insignificantly thin.

Throughout the chamber glittering objects, presumably maintenance drones, drifted aimlessly from sphere to sphere, and small, shining lights floated everywhere like stars in motion.

The walkway ended at a featureless railing. It was empty of control consoles or anything that might have served as such.

"It's an observation platform," Ruth murmured, tilting her head to look up. "There are several others—look." She raised her arm and pointed to where the underside of another walkway stretched into the void a kilometer above their heads. "This place is spooky."

Joe nodded, lost for words. The second he stepped on the ramp his skin began to prickle, an unpleasant, crawling itch that impelled him to turn around and leave again. Only the awe-inspiring view kept him from doing so. There was incalculable power in this place.

"So, engineering do you think, Alaine?"

"Well, it has to be, I suppose. This is the aft-most chamber, and something is definitely going on in here."

"Any ideas?"

"See those domes?"

Joe gazed across to where, several kilometers away, numerous hemispherical structures, each at least a half kilometer in diameter, extended from the opposite wall. Their smooth, shiny surfaces made them hard to distinguish in the electric half-light. From each, tubes ran to other structures or the forward wall.

"Some of those pipes are glowing," Alaine said, "The domes could be part of the actual engines, and the pipes may be supply lines for whatever they use for fuel."

"So what's your best guess?"

"Just theories: I still don't have enough data. We can't see them very well from here, but I can speculate. I've given up on the ramjet idea, so some kind of antimatter drive, photons maybe."

"I thought antimatter drives were impractical," said Ruth.

"They are, for us. We did a lot of research on them a couple of centuries ago, with hydrogen-anti-hydrogen systems. We never got it to work though, for several reasons."

"Do tell," Ruth asked.

"Anti-matter reacts with any normal matter, so containing it in storage is difficult. Anti-hydrogen can be contained by magnetic force fields, so given time, we might have been able to get around that one, but we never made enough of the stuff to make it practical. In addition, radiation is a massive problem. Given the difficulties, research focused more on things like Ion and Nuclear drives, and interest in antimatter faded away. We're still playing with it, but not seriously since governments won't back it anymore."

"What makes you think this is an antimatter drive?" Joe asked.

"A vague impression is all. Think about those domes. If they were reaction chambers, you would need two types of fuel feeds, one for matter, and another for antimatter. The antimatter delivery system would be shielded so the particles could pass through without touching the sides. They could be lined, for instance, with potent magnets, which would require a much larger diameter.

"There are dozens of pipes running into each dome, but they're mainly two different sizes. The small ones run back to these spherical modules in the chamber, but the biggies go straight through the front wall, maybe to larger tanks further forward. Little pipes for matter, bigger for anti-matter."

"That's pretty thin evidence."

"Oh yes. I'm guessing, of course. They could all be full of chicken soup for all I can tell."

Joe said, "Those big pipes are shimmering, so the idea they contain a force field is believable. There's definitely something going on in there."

"They glow as well," Ruth added. "I think that's why there is so much light in here. Maybe the field produces light as a by-product."

Looking up, Joe realized the diffuse light filling the chamber had no discernible source, but came from everywhere. As Ruth had observed, it was brightest around the massive pipes and the domes. Every few minutes, blinding bursts of energy discharged, arcing like lightning through the vast chamber.

"That explains the covers over the walkway," Alaine said. "The force flowing around out there must be phenomenal. You would expect power like that around an antimatter drive, I suppose."

"You still think that's what we are looking at," Joe asked.

"Why not? Of course, my knowledge of the concept is only theoretical. I really … don't … know."

"Not a bad guess though. Those huge tanks we figured were for fuel were two sizes as well. The ones for anti-matter would be massive because of the containment field mechanism."

"Exactly. I…"

At that moment, a broken, barely discernible voice sounded over their communicators.

"Captain, come in … lost control … engines starting up … control … Chloe … return … once."

A shudder ratcheted its way up Joe's spine. "Bloody Hell. Back to the ship, now." Without waiting for a response, he spun on his heels and bolted back along the ramp towards the bubble way station, with Alaine and Ruth close behind. As soon as they cleared the door to the engineering section, Joe called *Butterball*.

"Sarah, come in."

"Captain? You need to get back here straight away. Something has taken over the ship. The engines are starting up and we have no control. Chloe isn't aware anything is happening."

* * *

The dash back to the landing-field station took under thirty minutes, but for Joe it was the longest half-hour of his life. Helpless to do anything but wait, he stood at the front of the bubble and stared ahead as the surrounding wonders flashed by unnoticed.

His stomach threatened rebellion. The possibility the *Butterball* might leave without most of its crewmembers sickened him. Trapped on an alien vessel heading straight for the Sun, with no chance of rescue if their ship became lost to them— a worse scenario was unimaginable.

Being marooned in space had always been his greatest fear since leaving the oceanic navy, but he had always imagined it being in a space suit, drifting helplessly into oblivion. This was worse: stranded in a spacecraft, surrounded by wonders beyond reach, with no chance of escape.

The old freighter's engines were constantly at operational status, but he hoped some of the other crew closer to home would still be able to return in time. Every few minutes Sarah reported on the radio. So far, the ship had not moved, remaining in the entry tunnel, but repeated attempts to wrest back control had failed.

Chloe continued to express ignorance, and commands to shut down the engines went unanswered. As the bubble approached the service-deck station Sarah's voice came again.

"Captain," she announced. "We're moving."

"Talk to me, Sarah."

"We are lifting off and … shit … we're entering the *Minaret.*"

Joe doubted he had heard her words correctly. "Say again?"

"We're entering the bay. Whoever or whatever is controlling *Butterball* is taking us down to the airfield deck. Where are you?"

"We're almost back to station four. Stay online—we'll be there soon." A surge of hope rose in Joe's breast, his heart pounding so hard the veins thumped in his temples. His worst nightmare was devolving into a bad dream.

Platform four was deserted, and Joe wondered if the other teams were safe. Motioning for the others to follow, he ran from the platform and along the walkway to the docking pillar through which they had first entered.

About halfway there, Sarah reported in again. "We're down Captain, at a dock. Not the one you went in by, the bigger one next to it. I'll send Terry to guide you. And Joe, you're not going to believe what's happening."

"Surprise me." A tide of relief washed through Joe's overactive mind. At least the ship was not leaving, but it was still a concern that someone took control of her so easily.

As they approached the entrance to the specified dock entry Terry stood by the path as promised, dressed in his normal, orange coveralls without the environment suit Joe insisted everyone wear off-ship. He saw the look on his captain's face.

"Sorry Boss, didn't have time to suit up. We're down and safe. I came in via a skyway; it connected to the forward airlock as soon as we landed."

Ruth drew up beside Joe, gasping for air. "Thank God for that." Her face was wet with tears.

"Worried about being marooned?" Joe joked half-heartedly, battling to damp down the fire of his own fear concerning exactly that.

"No, but I'm never going to get a megabucks book deal if I'm stuck here, am I?" She replied, forcing a strained smile.

"Fair point," Joe said, struggling to recover his breath.

With Alaine bringing up the rear the group ascended the elevator tube to the top level and entered *Butterball.* The *Minaret's* artificial gravity cut off the minute they passed along the skywalk. A minute later, they were on the bridge.

Joe peered at the monitors. "What's going on?" The ship now perched on its spindly legs on the landing field, the accommodation wheels still revolving. Towards the stern, long, flexible tubes snaked up from the deck to various service fittings. "Chloe, what is our status?"

"We're docked on the landing field of the *Minaret,*" Chloe's calm voice replied. "Engines are off, and all systems are nominal. *Butterball* is being refueled and reprovisioned."

"What?"

"Our tanks are being refilled," Sarah explained.

"Chloe, please give me a rundown of the last hour of events."

"I am unable to do so, Captain. There is a gap in my data. I have no record of any changes in the period prior to docking."

Joe slumped in his seat and stared at the readouts. The ship was fully functional, and would soon be refueled. Either this was an automatic response by the *Minaret's* computer systems, or the yet unseen owners of this inconceivable craft were preparing to expel them.

Chapter 17

JAKE FALCON GAZED from his veranda across an expanse of lawn to the macadamia-nut trees, all that remained of the plantation that once covered this entire area. Beyond them stood an electrified fence, high, secure and the first of several lines of home defense on the property. The world was polarizing to a place where privacy was something ignored by the vast majority but fiercely defended by those who sought it.

He much preferred here to the city. Perched on the southern escarpment of Mount Maleny, it was a place to escape from the hustle and bustle of normal life and the mounting chaos. Clean and quiet, it provided peace despite the mass of humanity on the nearby coastline.

Five separate cities once occupied this region, Brisbane itself and the smaller cities of Redcliffe, Ipswich, Gold Coast and Sunshine Coast. Now merged into one, the mega-metropolis stretched over several hundred kilometers along a shoreline of islands and sandy beaches. Here at the northern end, it squeezed along narrow coastal lowlands between the sea and the mountain.

Somewhere inside the house, Akira bustled about, rising a little too late to watch the sunrise. Conveniently, she had a remote-access account with the university's computer networks, which Jake had been able to use to advantage. As predicted, the university jumped at the chance to place one of their own with him on the understanding they would share in certain aspects of his research. Battling against the unlimited funds of private organizations, universities waged a constant battle to gain kudos, and ignored no good opportunity. Jake swore that if the world ever survived the current turmoil he would honor the agreement in a way the university would benefit from the most.

Akira's presence made him more at ease considering the events occurring in the major metropolitan centers. The morning news spoke of riots last night. Beginning as peaceful protest that the authorities were not doing sufficient to protect them from the approaching threat, the masses boiled over when confronted by the police and the demonstration became a rebellion in minutes. This morning the violence persisted.

Jake shook his head; it eluded him as to what the demonstrators expected the government to do. Nobody on Earth or Mars had any ability whatsoever to interfere with the alien ship if it wished to enter into the Solar System, and besides, the biggest danger came not from there. The likelihood of a conflict between the two planetary fleets was greater.

Rising from the veranda seat, Jake wandered into his office and noticed words flashing on his computer screen. It was a message from Dad. Joe Falcon had decided there would be no cover-ups concerning the aliens, and most of what Jake received ended up on the World Net. So far, they had been lucky and virtually everything had become public knowledge. The information might have contributed to the current public unrest, but as long as it was the absolute truth, it was better than the public being kept in the dark, a scenario that might eventually lead to chaos.

Jake felt sure the authorities had him pegged as the source of the leaks, but to date, they had not been able to trace anything back to him thanks to his convoluted private systems.

Curious, he booted the decryption program and settled back to view the message. His father's face appeared on the screen.

"Jake, something's happened here and it worries me." Jake raised an eyebrow, and listened on. "I can only assume it was either a computer or an alien presence we have not yet seen, but something took over the *Butterball* for a brief period. The engines powered up and Chloe was cut out of the loop; she's unaware of having lost control. I was in the *Minaret's* engine room about eighty kilometers away at the time, and I can't tell you what a shock it gave me. The thought of being marooned on an alien ship is not something I care to experience again.

"The weird thing is, *Butterball* came into the landing bay and docked at one of the skywalk structures I told you about earlier. Once she was down, the *Minaret* began the process of refueling our tanks—xenon, hydrogen, water, oxygen, the lot. They even restocked our cargo bay with food we can actually eat, can you believe? I don't know how you feel, but to me, that's the strongest sign yet that this ship doesn't represent a threat to us.

"After I got back I sent my second mate, Harry Chan—you met him a year ago—to check the tunnel where we came in. It's closed. The force field at the outer end is now a solid wall. Harry is crossing at this minute to the starboard side, but I'm guessing the other entrance is blocked as well. We're trapped in here, but I don't think we're in any danger. I doubt the aliens would refuel us if that were the case.

"I think we may have been brought in for our protection. Our relay dish is still out on the platform and we're still able to maintain communications with Mars. The only explanation is our hosts are relaying our signals as they have been throughout the ship. It makes no sense to me, but at least we can still communicate.

"The *Visitors* are preparing for something. We don't know what—maybe the arrival of the fleets. The whole situation is moot now, because neither force can get in. We can't get out either.

"Something else. The rock cutter we set up on the starboard side is disabled. Harry reports the firing panel is fused to prevent activation. The cutter would appear to be working to Chloe, but would not actually fire a beam. I expect the other one will be the same when Harry gets there. It's very clever, as if it was done by an accidental power discharge, but it does strike me as a little simplistic for a super-advanced race of aliens.

"That's about it. I want you to check a few things for me. I would like you to make discrete inquiries about a few individuals. I need to know anything and everything you can find out: their birth, history, education, the lot. The names are Alaine Parish, Patricia Grace, Walter Tyrell and Ruth Carvalio. Yes, my passengers."

* * *

"We have a visual now, Commodore," the duty officer said, directing Barrett to the view on the main screen.

As a ship of war, the flagship lacked viewports, all images of the outside coming from shielded cameras on the exterior. They focused on the platform where the civilian vessel had landed, empty now apart from a small transmission disk secured at a point near the hull.

"Where the hell is the freighter?"

"Not there, sir…" The officer hesitated as he realized he was stating the obvious. "Falcon may have taken her inside to the landing bay."

"Isn't the entrance supposed to be there?" Barrett spoke more to himself than anyone on the bridge in particular.

"Yes, sir. Reports from our man on the freighter describe the entrance as a discolored patch."

"Damned if I can … oh yes, I see it. Barely visible." Flustered, he glanced up at the data screens above his head. The *Constellation* was closing on the starboard side of the *Minaret*, level with the entry platform. The remainder of the fleet held position five hundred kilometers further out, and would remain so until ordered to close in. That would not happen until the unpleasant business of the *Butterball* was done.

"All right. No time to mess about. Please advise Lieutenant Manners he may proceed as ordered."

* * *

The *Constellation*'s massive shuttle bay doors slid open and a single vessel, insignificant in comparison to the battlewagon that spawned it, shot into the void towards the alien vessel. The little craft closed rapidly with none of the caution Joe Falcon exercised on his own approach, and settled beside the supposed location of the entrance tunnel.

Forewarned by the experience of the *Butterball* the shuttle lowered suction clamps to secure itself to the smooth surface of the platform. Inside the claustrophobic cabin, Frank Manners waited as the rear ramp dropped and his troops, suited and armed, lined up to exit.

He detested this kind of action, going in without a clue as to what to expect. The moral aspect of what he was about to do did not matter—orders were orders. All he could do was complete the mission quickly and pray this would not be the opening gambit of another war between his beloved Earth and Mars. As the last of his team stepped onto the ramp, Manners followed behind.

As planned, the landing site was close to the wall. As each soldier disembarked, he or she drew up to the hull, weapon at the ready.

The entrance was featureless and uniform in color, a little darker than the remainder of the shell. Frank raised his hand and touched the surface. It was hard, impenetrable. He pressed against the smooth wall and let out a long, deep sigh.

Closed, he thought. "Commodore, it would appear the way in is shut. The door is sealed."

"Unacceptable," came the response. "You will search the entire platform for an entrance. If you do not find one, you will move to the port side and try again."

"Acknowledged." Frank waved his troops to spread out and search inch by inch. If a way in existed they would find it.

* * *

Commodore Barrett stared at the monitor. For the first time in weeks, he sensed a feeling of relief. In his mind, his career was based on sound judgment and what he considered right, even when others did not. Never before had he initiated an action against civilians nor disobeyed a direct order. His first instinct had been to contest the orders for this sortie, but it would have meant the end of his commission.

With the media of two worlds watching no matter how secret or clandestine the operation might be, any attack on civilians inevitably attracted condemnation. Despite military authorities defending their actions, the careers of several high-rankers had been decimated by public opinion in the last decade.

In this instance, Barrett was following strict orders, so there was no danger of official reprimand, but there was no doubt his reputation would be dragged into the deepest, darkest corner of hell if a civilian, even one of Mars, was injured in the process.

To make things worse, Joe Falcon was a retired officer in high standing of the Earth fleet, and since the beginning of this business, his entire career had been scrutinized by the press. To many, he was a hero.

Now the point was possibly immaterial. Without access to the *Minaret,* he could report to his superiors the task could not be completed, with no blame attributable to either himself or the away team. Sometimes you could be lucky.

Two hours after the first failure, a subsequent confirmation arrived that the starboard entrance was also sealed. It was still unknown if this was coincidence or deliberate, to deny entry to his men. The latest word from Command's contact on the *Butterball*, received only minutes ago, placed the old freighter on the landing field inside the colossus, so Falcon and his band of cohorts were trapped. Barrett had thought to re-classify the mission as a rescue to achieve the original objective without public backlash, but with access blocked, that idea also became a non-starter.

The screen flickered and an old, wizened face on a head devoid of hair appeared. Barrett felt his heart sink as he recognized the man. That face could shatter the soul of the most stalwart individual.

"Good morning George. And how are we on this fine day?"

Barrett flinched, ignoring the incongruity of the question in a place where day and night held no meaning. It was many years since he had spoken with Admiral Hsiang Li, the man who trained him and raised him through the ranks before changing allegiance and becoming the senior officer of the Mars Space Force. Barrett had, of course, been advised by his bridge team of the approach of the Mars fleet, but had not expected that particular legend to be in charge.

"I'm well, Admiral. You're early, I think."

* * *

Smaller than Barrett's battlewagon, but more modern and more heavily armed, the *MSF Olympus* was the flagship of the most legendary of Martian naval leaders. Hsiang's immigration to Mars just before the outbreak of the

Resources War was, many believed, the main reason for Mars's victory.

The Admiral had been touring when the call to send a contingent to the *Minaret* came. In typical fashion and under great secrecy, he had overridden the demands of the politicos and taken command of the mission himself. Also typically, he had arrived ahead of schedule.

Two hours from rendezvous he observed *Constellation*'s shuttle with interest, his own larger boarding force ready to go if necessary. He watched and listened as Frank Manners's team landed, searched, and failed to find a way into the alien vessel. With the squad back aboard the *Constellation*, he chose to announce his presence, assuming Barrett already knew of his imminent arrival.

"I am pleased to see you have not entered the *Minaret*," he said, feigning ignorance of the failed attempt.

Barrett was not fooled. "It would appear the way is barred, to both of us."

"Really?" Hsiang rubbed his chin and leaned forward into the camera. "My boy, you and I need a long, hard talk … in private. As soon as my fleet is in place, I am coming across, yes?"

"Why am I not surprised, Admiral?"

"Perhaps you've known me for too long. I am an old man and this will be my last mission; I will not allow either of us to be the cause of the next war."

"You used to be Earth yourself."

"Yes, and I still love the place. I had good reasons for emigrating, but it broke my heart to fight against my old friends and I will not see it happen again. That is unacceptable, do you not agree?"

For a moment, Barrett did not reply. He had his orders, but with access to the alien ship denied, it seemed proper to look at all options. Despite the fact many in the services considered him a hard-nose, he thought himself a reasonable man. Besides, the Mars contingent was larger and more powerful.

"Yes, I do, but you and I are both under orders."

"True. However, *I* command my ships and my captains will support me no matter what. I am confident the Martian committee set up to oversee this affair will agree with my actions. Our politicians are reacting with their usual lack of foresight and will continue to do so until they create a mess we will all regret. You and I are the commanders on the ground; it is up to us to find the middle path. I will see you soon, yes?"

Barrett breathed a sigh of relief. "Agreed. I'll meet you when you arrive." He had no wish for conflict with a man he both respected and feared above all others.

Hours later, the Mars contingent dropped back to a position on the port side of the alien ship, placing the giant craft between the two fleets. As the ships settled into place and the obligatory refueling began, a single shuttle left the *Olympus* and curved its way over the *Minaret*, coming to rest in the bay of the *Constellation*. Commander Barrett waited as his old superior floated along the companionway and came towards him.

"It is good to see you," Hsiang said. "It's been, what, fifteen years?"

"Yes. At least."

"Far too long. Shall we go to your day room? We can talk there, yes?"

Accompanied by a contingent of armed guards as required when an 'enemy' envoy was aboard, the two men made their way to the captain's cabin. Once inside, the pair sat for a full minute and looked at each other without speaking.

"Unlike you, I have lived on both worlds," Hsiang finally said, his words slow and considered. "I know beyond a doubt the politicians on both are … hmm, lacking. I came here on orders to do whatever necessary to remove you from the *Minaret* if you defied Falcon's request to stand off. That is something I do not relish, so I am relieved the way is barred to us. It gives us the perfect excuse to take a different approach."

"You know my men tried to enter?"

"Of course. I also know you were under direct orders, so I do not hold it against you, my friend."

Barrett nodded. "What do you suggest?"

"I recommend we do as Falcon asks. We both know the only reason the freighter was sent was so Mars would arrive before Earth; the leaders of my world are no better than yours. My orders are similar to yours, to occupy the *Minaret* and remove Falcon. I carry official scientific and diplomatic representatives on one of my ships to take his place."

Barrett cringed at his adversary's words. A statement of that nature to the commander of an opposition fleet was a quick path to a court marshal; Hsiang clearly had no fear of his superiors. "You believe the ship is occupied."

"Of course it is. If not by actual aliens, then by machine intelligence. Both possibilities are sufficient to give me the shudders."

"Agreed."

"If the ship passes through the system there will be no time to discover its technology. If it is under control—by machines or organic beings—and enters the system, any attempt to interfere with it would be disastrous. Either way, we are wasting our time if we try to carry out our respective orders.

"So we do as Falcon asks. He considers himself a representative of humanity, and not of either world. I suggest, under the circumstances, we support him in that for now. He and his team are trapped but in no immediate danger, so let us wait and see what happens, yes?"

"To do so would be a direct violation of our orders," said Barrett. "We could be court marshaled, both of us."

Hsiang leaned forward as he always did when intending to drive home a point. "George, you must realize this is a no-win situation. If we do as I suggest we risk being disciplined if it does not work out, but since the *Minaret* has locked us out, I think that unlikely. If we try to proceed with our orders, we could start a conflict needlessly. Which would you prefer?"

"I…"

"You have a reputation, George, as do I. Let us surprise them all and do what is right for once in our lives. Put that to your superiors—under the circumstances I think they will accept."

"I, umm … fine, agreed." Before Barrett could continue, the voice of the duty officer boomed from the wall communicator.

"Commodore, I think you and our guest might want to come up here. Something is happening outside."

Less than a minute later, both commanders floated onto the bridge.

"What's going on?" Barrett asked.

"The target appears to be maneuvering," the duty officer reported.

One hundred kilometers away the massive bulk of the alien vessel was moving, rotating end for end like a monstrous pinwheel. The sheer size of the star-ship gave the event an unparalleled sense of awe and grace.

The *Minaret's* colossal hull swung through the arc, eventually coming to rest with the tail pointing forward towards the Sun. Barrett felt insignificant; the ship dwarfed man's greatest achievements and his mind spun at the thought of the resources available to a race capable of creating such a wonder.

He ordered the *Constellation* out to a distance of three hundred kilometers, anticipating what he was certain was about to occur. Seconds behind, under the capable hands of Hsiang's second in command, the Mars fleet did the same. As the ships moved to their new positions a beam of solid, bright blue light sprang from the spire of the mammoth spaceship, an iridescent blaze stretching a thousand kilometers ahead of the *Minaret* before fading to nothing.

Barrett gasped, grabbing for the arms of his seat. "What the hell…"

"She's slowing down," Hsiang said. "Perhaps we should prepare for visitors after all."

Chapter 18

JOE SAT BACK in his command chair. "Commodore Barrett. What can I do for you?"

"Captain Falcon. May I call you Joe?"

"If you must. Can I be of assistance?"

"No, but perhaps we can help you. You no doubt recognize the gentleman behind me?"

"Yes, of course. It is good to see you again, Admiral Hsiang." The old man smiled and waved an acknowledgment.

"Joe," Barrett said. "Li and I are in difficult positions, courtesy of politicians who should know better. Luckily for us, your *Visitor* friends have now made the situation less volatile by shutting us out, and you in."

"So it would seem." Joe battled to appear at ease.

"Both of our governments sent us here with direct orders to take possession of the alien vessel. Each wants whatever advantages there may be in the way of technology, and I suspect the major motivation here is greed."

Joe nodded. It was as much as he had suspected. "You realize your respective superiors will be listening in on this?"

"No. We're speaking to you on a tight beam directed at the dish you left on the outer platform." Barrett leaned forward until his face filled the monitor. "I doubt if it will be any surprise that your team is, and always has been, little more than an interim measure. The Mars government needed to make a rendezvous before I could get here, and you were the best available. My orders are to ignore your precedence and remove you and your ship regardless.

"Admiral Hsiang's were to support your claim and prevent me from boarding. I don't need to tell you, as an old navy man, the consequences should either of us fail or refuse to carry out our directives."

Joe nodded again.

"However, the *Visitors* have taken it out of our hands. Neither the Admiral nor I feel obligated to pursue those orders further given the current circumstances."

"So what do you intend to do?"

"We've been having a little heart-to-heart chat and have agreed on a policy we expect will be honored by both our governments, mainly because they don't have a choice. I understand you possess a document granting you ambassadorial status on behalf of humanity?"

"I do."

"You know, of course, that paper is of little value."

"I have it on good authority it will stand up in any court on Earth or Mars."

"None of which have any power out here. If a conflict should break out between Li and me, your piece of paper would mean 'zip', especially given no authority on Earth had any part in its granting. Nevertheless, you and your man Parish are official ambassadors of Mars and any action on my part against you would be an act of war. We do not need another war and neither Li nor I want that to happen. We will honor the intent of the document."

"Which means?"

"For now we'll take no further action. We will report we are unable to enter the *Minaret* and cannot affect it in any way. Each fleet will maintain position and not interact at this time. We have agreed that although under the flags of our respective worlds, we must represent humanity in this circumstance. We are quite within our authorities to take this stance. The treaty conditions from the last war allow us to join forces in any situation where we believe the interests of both planets are threatened.

"We will support you in your role as ambassador for humanity; based on your statement you will equally represent both worlds and not Mars alone. We will declare this a military emergency because the alien ship appears to be decelerating. That validates our stance and limits the control of the politicians over us."

Joe breathed a sigh of relief as the tension that preceded the interview drained away. "What do you want me to do?"

Hsiang Li leaned forward and peered over Barrett's shoulder. "Continue your exploration, find the owners of that ship and try to stay alive."

* * *

Joe slid down the side supports of the ladder until his feet touched the floor of the main wheel. He glanced through to the common room, beyond the door to his cabin.

The larger space was generally the center of life on *Butterball* but now, because of the bizarre view from the ports, it was almost deserted.

Only Ruth Carvalio was present, standing in the galley making herself coffee, a beverage she seemed addicted to. Looking up, she spotted him in the walkway and raised an eyebrow, coffee container in hand.

"Yes, please. We can drink it in my cabin. The view is less upsetting in there."

Ruth nodded, and a few minutes later joined him flasks in hand. She handed over one of the drinks. "I heard a rumor our unseen hosts are staying."

"Not sure," Joe replied, "but it does look like they at least intend to visit."

"What's happening?"

"The ship is slowing down. We can't see it from here, but according to the fleets outside, the *Minaret* flipped arse over turkey and is using its main engines to decelerate, or maneuver … something like that. They sent us a video of the event" Joe tapped his keyboard.

Ruth leaned in and watched the image on the computer screen. "Looks like a gigantic flashlight."

"Yes. Alaine is ecstatic about it. He thinks it's pure light, and must be some sort of photon drive."

"Photons? What, light particles?"

"Yes. You can in theory drive a ship with light. It has mass like everything else. Chuck enough out the back and voila, Newton's third law."

Ruth stared at her lap for a moment, lost in her thoughts. "What about the warships? What are they doing?"

"We seem to be in luck there. The fleet commanders are old acquaintances—most senior officers in both space forces are—and they've come to an agreement not to push the issue. The way in is closed so they're standing by, waiting."

"And you trust them?"

"Barrett, no. Hsiang Li I would trust with my life. He'll keep Barrett off, I hope."

"They're friends? Isn't that kind of odd? I mean, they fought a war against each other."

"No, it's not strange at all. You need to understand the dynamics of that conflict."

"I remember it as a child, but it's not a part of history I've looked into." Ruth twisted her mouth in a patronizing manner.

"The war was over resources and independence. When Mars was first colonized, Earth treated it as a source for exploitation, period. The first Mars colonists built vast manufacturing and mining industries and all the control, product and profit went to Earth. The colonists on Mars remained poor and life was dangerous, so eventually they rebelled—hence the war.

"The first Mars fleet was not manned by naval officers. They were mostly ordinary civilians—people like you and me—but thanks to the industrial might of the planet they had better ships. It ended up a stalemate, but many of the people in the Earth Navy respected what the people of Mars had done and after the war, a lot of officers resigned and emigrated. Half of the senior personnel in the Mars fleet are ex-Earth."

"Including you?"

"No, I was always Earth. I moved to Mars after I retired; you know that."

Suddenly Joe realized something was wrong. Not paying much attention, Ruth sat staring at her knees, fingers clasped around her coffee. Joe could swear her hands were trembling.

"You okay?"

Ruth lifted her eyes to meet his. At that moment he saw fear, not the mature, confident woman he knew.

"Not really. I'm having trouble dealing with all this." She put the coffee canister on the desk and pushed it away. "And I've drunk far more of that than is healthy. I'm a bit hyper."

"Are you worried about being shut in here?"

Ruth nodded in the affirmative.

"Well," Joe continued, "I wouldn't be too concerned yet. The fact they brought us in probably means they wanted to protect us during the maneuver. I don't think they want to harm us."

"Harry tells me that could have been an automatic function. What if they don't open the gates again?"

"Well, there is that. We could be in for an interesting ride if such ends up being the case."

"Hence my jitters," Ruth said. A strained smile forced itself to her lips.

For the next half-hour, Ruth rambled about her concerns. Joe had assumed that being in the asteroid belt she was comfortable with space, but now realized her experience was limited to the civilian comforts of Kepler Base. Being trapped in a tin can, inside an alien colossus, was more than her mind could deal with on short notice. Finally, she stood and turned to leave.

"I should go. I need to be getting on with my reports. You?"

"I'm taking a break."

Ruth stopped by the door, her brow furrowed. She gave Joe a long, steady gaze. "Maybe I have a better idea." Turning from the exit, she walked across and sat down on Joe's bunk. "What do you think?"

Joe was not sure how to respond at first. Ruth's intentions were quite clear and he could not say the prospect was unattractive. She was a striking individual and had made it clear on several occasions that she found him equally likable. He had not been with a woman for years, since the loss of his wife, Helen. Life out here, even surrounded by the crew of the *Butterball*, could be lonely.

"I'm a little rusty," he said, sitting beside her.

She rested her palm on his cheek. "Makes two of us,"

* * *

Carmichael Page glared across the table, furious his dilemma should be considered funny, or trivial. Adam Palfrey could have sworn there was steam rising from the younger man.

"You think this is amusing?"

"Hilarious, actually," Adam said, "Of all the commanders in both navies, we send two who happen to be best buddies. And now they decide to cooperate with each other rather than obey our governments' directives."

"What do you mean by that?"

"Oh, come on, Carmichael. You've already admitted your superiors ordered Barrett to board the *Minaret* and remove Falcon by force."

For a brief moment, Page sat and glared at his opponent, then shrugged his shoulders and dropped his gaze. "Fair enough. But you need to drop this crap about Falcon as well. We all know why he's there. I mean, what were you thinking sending such a bunch of misfits? Not one of them is fit to represent humanity."

"I'm not so sure anymore. How do you draw that conclusion anyway? We've never met aliens before so who determines what qualifications are needed? Falcon was one of the best commanders you ever had in your Navy, and now you're calling him incompetent?"

"Yes, well…"

"And Parish is one of our finest young officers. Falcon's first officer topped her class at the Academy. Then there's the Carvalio woman. As far as I can tell, she's doing an excellent job keeping the media at bay. If it wasn't for her, we'd be plagued constantly."

"Fine, I accept that. Neither of our fleets can get in since the ship has gone into lockdown, so it looks like we accept Falcon as our man on the ground."

"Exactly. Listen, Carmichael, we need to work as a team on this now the *Minaret* is entering the system…"

"Sir, that may not be the case," a voice interrupted.

Palfrey looked up at the ensign who had entered the boardroom unannounced. "Can I help you, son?"

"I'm sorry sir," the young man said. "I didn't intend to intrude. I thought you might like the latest updates." He waved a sheath of sheet plastic prints in Adam's direction.

"What did you mean, 'may not be the case'?"

The ensign shuffled his feet nervously. "Well, Commodore Hsiang reports the *Minaret* is not slowing down after all. It appears the maneuver was to adjust course, and she's rotated back to her original orientation."

"And?"

"The new course takes her very close to the Sun. According to the guys downstairs, she can still either swing around the star, pick up speed and slingshot out the other side, or go even closer and use the corona for aero … solar breaking?"

"Ridiculous," Page said. "It would burn up."

"Maybe," Palfrey said, "or maybe not. Everything we've seen to date puts their technology so far ahead of ours we can't tell it from magic. Who knows what it's capable of doing? Commander Parish thinks the ship's fuel is antimatter. If they can handle that, the force fields they use may be just as inconceivable. Maybe one that can protect them inside a star is not such a stretch?"

Page scratched the back of his head. "They still may or may not be here to stay. Where do we go now?"

Palfrey turned and gazed out the window as the ensign withdrew from the room. For a few minutes, he said nothing, digesting the new information. His major concern was now Falcon's ship and crew. The governments of both worlds would throw Falcon to the fates if need be, but he, Adam Palfrey, would not.

The fleets would remain in position as long as possible to cover every eventuality, but so far, no avenue for rescue had been forthcoming. Thirty-five days had passed since the *Butterball* intercept and the alien vessel was well within the orbit of Venus. In another seven days it would reach the Sun, and in five, the fleets would have no choice but to leave. They were humanity's best, but could not go closer to the star. The commanders had decided they would abandon escort duty and reposition themselves to reacquire the *Minaret* later, if possible.

If the alien vessel used the Corona to brake and enter the system, the likely destination would be Earth. The *Minaret* could swing around Venus to achieve that goal, and at that time both human fleets needed to be working as a single unit just in case.

"I think," Palfrey said, "it's time to put this interplanetary rivalry aside. If nothing else, this event proves we are not alone, so we need to start behaving for the good of humanity as a united species, rather than pursuing our petty individual agendas. We should combine our resources and prepare for the possibility our guest is heading for Earth."

Page sighed and nodded in agreement. "Good luck with that," he said. "It won't be easy to get our respective governments to cooperate. They're politicians; far too many of them have nobody's best interests at heart except their own. They'll argue the point for months without coming to an agreement. I certainly won't get my lot to cooperate on this."

"I agree, but maybe this is the time. Are you much of a history buff, Carmichael?"

"No, not at all. Why?"

"You can learn interesting facts from the past. For example, when two cultures of vastly different technological levels meet, the less advanced one always suffers."

"Where did that come from?"

"History. It has happened on several occasions in Earth's past. The *Minaret* is well ahead of us technologically, so if they stop here, where does humanity stand?"

Page stared at the table for a moment, considering the point Palfrey had made. "I can try; no promises. Where do we begin?"

"The committee will issue a statement and then you and I start work on our respective superiors and colleagues. We need to get cooperation within the next two weeks."

"And if we don't?"

"We still have Falcon, Hsiang and Barrett out there."

Chapter 19

"WHAT IN GOD'S NAME?" George Barrett stared in disbelief at the screen, trying to register what he was seeing. The *Minaret* was gone as was the Mars fleet. Instead, another *Hector* class battle cruiser, identical to his own flagship, sat off the starboard bow. "Where the hell did that come from? Where is the alien ship?"

"That is the *Constellation*, Commander," the watch officer responded, peering at the readouts from the ship's sensors. "It's us." Barrett glared at him until he clarified his statement.

"The *Minaret* has put up some kind of enclosing force field, a huge, elongated bubble. What you're seeing is our reflection on the surface, like a mirror image. The alien is there, but invisible."

* * *

Joe floated forward to the bridge and dropped into his command chair. It was day forty since the first venture inside the enormous star-ship, and the situation had not improved.

The airfield bay doors remained closed following what Commander Hsiang described as a course-adjustment maneuver. The *Butterball* and her crew remained trapped with no chance of escape.

Three days earlier Rob Billington had relayed an official announcement that the fleets of Earth and Mars would act as a single, united force representing humanity in totality. Not surprising, Joe thought.

Now two days from the Sun, the combined fleet was departing. The ships of humanity were incapable of approaching closer and the commanders had decided to withdraw, hoping to pick up the vessel again when it completed its traverse of the star.

The intent of the alien craft was still unclear, and re-acquiring it was going to be potluck. If the ship used the transit to accelerate, it would be well into space and gone by the time the fleet could get anywhere near again, so Hsiang and Barrett had agreed to work on the basis it intended to stay.

The best minds available confirmed that if the *Minaret* underwent solar braking the likely destination was Earth, and the plan was to intercept somewhere on the flight path between the Sun and Venus, assuming a transit of that planet.

The announcement devastated the crew of the *Butterball*. Despite almost all being loners and happy to spend endless months in deep space, the thought of being stranded, never to see home again, cut several of them to the core and cast an even deeper pall of depression over the entire ship. Most remained in their cabins, writing or sending messages to their loved ones—those who had them—or simply trying to come to terms with the situation.

Arguments had broken out, usually between Carl Geddes and Peter Stanley. Several crewmembers reported heated voices in the minerals lab, then silence when the antagonists became aware of an additional presence.

Not everyone had withdrawn. In an attempt to raise spirits, Alaine had declared he was going to continue his explorations, since there was nothing better to do. He had decided to forgo another expedition to the engine room; it was too far away from home in case of developments and from what he had seen, it seemed unlikely he would be able to evaluate the drives further anyway.

Convinced the ship's engines worked on antimatter, there was no way he could prove it either way by standing on the observation platform and looking. Other than more platforms, no access to the workings was forthcoming. Joe was not convinced it would be wise to poke around there anyway.

Instead, Alaine re-focused his efforts on gaining entrance to one of the ancillary ships without cutting his way in. At this moment he, Sam and Terry were somewhere below the landing bay on their way to the hangers.

Hardest hit by the news of abandonment by the fleet was Ruth Carvalio. She and Joe had spent a lot of time together in the last twenty-four hours and he now realized she had never understood the inherent danger in this voyage. Her sudden need to be with him was as much born of fear and insecurity as anything else.

For her the mission had been an adventure and a chance to be a part of history; the likelihood of death never entered into her mind until now. Joe blamed himself. The decision for her to come had been his and but for him she would not be in danger now. Her impressive forthrightness in their initial meeting and the fact she attracted him influenced his choice. He wished, despite their having become so close, that he had acted more wisely.

Admiral Hsiang's image appeared on the monitor, the old man looking even older. Joe had not served under him but knew him well by reputation, had met him several times and respected him deeply. Leaving would devastate Hsiang, meaning as it did the abandonment of the crew that he was supposedly here to defend.

"Joe?"

"Yes, Admiral. I'm here. Visual please, Chloe."

"I'm sorry, Joe, but we can't wait. If we stay longer we may not be able to pull away in time." The old man's voice trembled as he spoke the words.

"I understand." Joe did not know what else to say.

"There is one thing you might find comforting. The *Minaret* is still enclosed in its bubble. We can't see through it but the aliens are letting our communications through—how they do that I don't know. I suspect the field is to protect the ship while it travels close to the sun."

"So you think it's going to brake and enter the system?"

"I don't know. I am sorry."

Joe studied Hsiang's face. The old man was almost in tears, determined not to leave until the last possible minute.

"I think you better pull out before you lose the chance," Joe said, seeking to alleviate the tension. "You've done all you can. I don't blame you or anyone else for this. I chose to accept this mission and I chose to enter the *Minaret.* The responsibility is mine alone."

Hsiang nodded. "Here's something to think about," he said. "The aliens have given you unhindered access to almost everything on board and made no attempt to harm you or your crew. When the maneuver took place they moved your ship to a safe place and now the ship has what we must assume is a protective field around it with you safe inside. If it does carry out solar braking, you should come through safely, and afterward, you may have a chance to get away. I can't believe they refueled you unless they intended to let you leave."

Joe nodded absently. All that had occurred to him, but it did not ease the pain of being trapped, or abandoned.

"Joe," Hsiang continued. "I'm pretty sure the *Minaret* is looking after you, yes?"

* * *

Alaine Parish stood at the end of a line of small, streamlined ships in the upper hangers. Convinced they were some kind of fighter craft, he now referred to the sleek vessels as 'bayonets' due to their long, narrow, dagger-like appearance.

Despite his best efforts, he had failed to find a way into any one of them. The hulls were seamless with no visible maintenance hatches or panels. Shaking his head, he turned back to his companions, Sam and Terry.

"We might as well go back to the lower levels," he said. "At least the ships down there look like they are supposed to have occupants. We'll concentrate on those." Alaine had already examined dozens of the ships there but he refused to give up until he found a way into one of them.

It was easier now with the atmosphere and gravity allowing them to dispense with their helmets. On Joe's orders, they still carried them slung from their belts, but the new freedom made it possible to stay longer in any given place.

"Why do we not spread out?" Sam Bright suggested.

"Fine. We can cover more that way, but we stay within sight of each other." Alaine's companions nodded and made their way to nearby ships, searching the hulls for any sign of potential access.

Four stops later Alaine paused as he stared up at what appeared to be some kind of service vehicle, his mind wandering as he studied the hull shell. At first, the brain did not register what his eyes were seeing; if not for a vague, subconscious tug, he might have overlooked it.

The ship was clearly some sort of construction unit. Above his head was a pattern of discoloration, the typical array of nine spots in a grid pattern that guarded the entryways to the hangers and the engine room.

"Over here." He continued to stare up until his companions reached him.

"Finally," Sam said. "We find one."

"All we need to do is get in. Where's our punch pad?"

"Back in the ship," Terry Caldwell replied. "I'll go get it."

Alaine looked at his eager companion. "No, you will not. We all go. You know the rule: nobody moves around this vessel alone—the Captain has already dressed everyone down over that. There are three of us, so if we split up one of us *will* be alone."

"It's only one station. We're docked now, so I can be there and back in half an hour. I'm not scared of boogie men even if you are, boyo."

"No, I forbid it," Alaine said, turning his attention back to the ship.

Terry stared at the back of Parish's head. It was hard to accept the man ordering him about, or forbidding him anything at all. He knew the Captain's rules as well as anyone, including the condition that Parish was not to exercise any control over the crew of the *Butterball.*

The others, except the Captain, sometimes treated him like a child and it never bothered him; they were family and he knew they liked him. Alaine Parish was a stranger, and the idea he would treat him the same way was irritating. This was a chance to contribute something; getting into one of the little ships was a key objective.

"You don't get to forbid me nothing; you're not my boss," Terry said, striding towards the exit to the hangers. "I'll be back in a jiffy," he said to Sam as he vanished into the walkways. Sam glanced at Alaine and shook his head.

"Joe, can you hear me?" Alaine muttered.

"Alaine, this is Carl. Joe is asleep, I think. I have the watch."

"Can you advise him Terry's left to return alone? I couldn't stop him. We're going after him, but he took off pretty quickly."

For a moment there was silence, and then Carl replied. "Will do. We'll look out for him."

* * *

Fifteen minutes later Terry approached the base of the skywalk pylon. Now on the last stretch from the bubble way station, he regretted leaving his companions.

Alone in the vast chamber beneath the landing bay, he felt the same sense of isolation Sarah reported after her brief, unexpected, solo excursion on the train. The emptiness of the ship was oppressive, almost haunting. Terry could swear someone, or something was watching him at every turn. Considering how much the *Minaret* appeared to know about everyone, he expected that was most likely true.

"Are you there Terry?" Joe's voice came over the radio.

"Yeah Boss, I'm here."

"What is it you don't understand about my order nobody is to move around inside the *Minaret* alone?"

"Wasn't thinking. I … Alaine and me don't get on too good, and he started ordering me around. Sorry, Boss."

"Where are you?"

"About two minutes from the ship. I'll be back soon, and I'm fine, by the way."

"Straight back, no stops. Come to the bridge when you get here."

"I promised I would get the 'punchy' and take it back. We found a way into a ship."

"The others are on their way back on my orders."

"Oh, okay. Sorry. Be right there."

As he turned towards the entrance to the elevator, he saw a flash away to the left. A large, bubble-shaped maintenance drone floated along the walkway a hundred yards away. That was common; on many occasions, drones of various types, the nearest thing to life outside the habitat drum, had been seen. In each case, they went about their business and ignored the crew.

Turning, he saw a figure standing beside one of the service modules.

"What the … what are you doing? You…" A pale blue beam lashed out, and Terry dropped to the floor, a neat hole burned through the chest of his suit.

* * *

'What the … what are you doing? You …' Joe heard the words on the loudspeaker, and the silence that followed.

"Sarah," he shouted into the intercom. "Meet me at the forward hatch now!" Without waiting for a response he launched himself from the command chair into the central corridor and down to the forward airlock beneath the bridge. As soon as he reached the hatch he cycled the lock and entered, with Sarah only meters behind.

"What's wrong?" the first officer asked.

"Terry took it upon himself to come back to the ship alone. I think something has happened to him."

As they emerged from the service-level docking station entry, they saw a large object floating at the base of the sloping access ramp beside the walkway.

The strange drone resembled a bubble, the same blue-green-purple shimmer the crew had come to expect of every active molecular surface on the *Minaret.* From the side of the bubble, tendril-like extensions reached out, ending in long, flexible pseudo-fingers.

Clutched in their grasp was the form of Terry Caldwell. A dark stain spread across his chest, the dripping blood forming a substantial, blackening pool on the deck. As Joe and Sarah rushed forward, Terry's body passed through the shimmering wall and vanished into the object, which then moved to the path and sped away.

"Wait," Joe shouted. The drone ignored him as always. From the bottom of the ramp he turned and looked at Sarah, her face contorted in shock as she realized they had lost a member of the crew. Joe's heart sank, a vague numbness spreading through his mind.

The alien machine was already out of sight, well on its way to its home base. Pursuit was impossible even if they had known where it was going. The machines appeared and disappeared at will, and moved too fast to track on foot. Joe's chest heaved from the rapid dash from the ship; he was getting too old for this.

"What's going on?" Carl Geddes ran down the ramp behind them. "I heard you on the intercom. Where's Terry?"

"Gone," said Joe. "The *Minaret* took him."

* * *

A faint knock sounded on Joe's door. It opened a few inches and Sarah's pale face peeped through.

"Alright to come in?" she asked.

"Yes, of course. Sit a while." As she entered and lowered herself into the spare chair, Joe finished a report to Rob Billington, advising of Terry's disappearance.

There was no evidence the Second Engineer was dead, but having seen the blood Joe felt it difficult to entertain any other possibility. He reported his lost crewmember as 'missing, status unknown' and dreaded the reaction it was going to cause at home and on Earth.

Despite being benign before, the *Minaret* now appeared anything but. Neither hostile nor friendly, it gave them air, heat and fuel but there had been no attempt at contact and the drones ignored them altogether.

The moribund atmosphere on *Butterball* was growing. The pall of gloom through the ship had deepened, most of the crew rarely emerging from their private cabins. The common room stayed empty except at meal times, when each individual ate in silence and then left.

Everyone took Terry's disappearance badly, especially Alaine, who berated himself for having let Terry go so easily. He held himself accountable despite Joe's assurance otherwise.

Sarah took it hardest of all. Earlier, as he passed by her door, Joe heard the sound of sobbing and the soft and now familiar voice of Ruth Carvalio attempting to soothe and calm the younger woman. Sarah and Terry had been like brother and sister on a ship filled with older people.

Near the end of his last wake period, Joe overheard something similar while approaching Maeve's door in the secondary wheel in search of something for a throbbing headache. He did not knock, hesitating when he heard the voices of Maeve and Ruth deep in conversation.

The women were pulling together and helping each other, while the men withdrew each to their own council. Every man and woman on board had withdrawn to some degree, disrupting the *Butterball* beyond anything Joe had seen before.

Terry Caldwell, found tinkering with engines in a backfield maintenance shop on Mars, was one of the first appointees Joe made when purchasing the ship. One of a handful of men who assisted him in the conversion of the old freighter, Terry's genius with anything mechanical, coupled with his good humor and child-like personality, won Joe immediately.

The whole crew had loved his unrefined manner and the way the smallest thing excited him. Despite a certain naiveté he was, in his way, one of the best of *Butterball's* family. His action in striking out alone was not typical.

Now, in the privacy of the captain's cabin, Sarah still seemed lost.

"Are you alright?"

Sarah looked up and nodded in the affirmative. Joe saw the redness of her eyes; she had been crying again, or rubbing her eyes. "Are you sure?"

"Yes … no. I'm scared."

"Yes?" He reached across the desk and placed his hand on hers.

"This ship killed Terry. We could all die here," she said.

Joe shook his head. "We don't know that. Terry might have got too close to one of those drones. We know they ignore our presence and keep on going regardless; maybe he got in the way and it hit him. He sounded like he was talking to somebody when…"

"That thing took him away."

"Doing its job, I suspect, to clean up damaged things. We may never know for sure."

Sarah shook her head and stared at the floor; Joe said nothing more. He understood she just needed company. She was not alone in that; for almost everyone on board, this voyage had begun as a dream, and now it was beginning to unravel, slowly turning into a nightmare.

Chapter 20

THE COMMON ROOM was deathly quiet, despite the presence of the entire crew. Joe had requested their attendance to make an announcement.

"I know the last few days have been tough on everyone," he said. "Forty-eight hours have passed since we lost Terry and there's nothing further we can do about his disappearance, at least for now. There's something else we need to consider." Several sets of eyes lifted from staring at the floor.

"Today is the day the *Minaret* begins its traverse of the Sun's corona. It won't be long before we find out whether it'll enter the system or slingshot away to places unknown." Looking around, he knew he had their attention.

"The combined fleet left us two days ago, so we're on our own. We can't communicate with them, even with the *Minaret's* help, because of the radio interference from the Sun. We're still surrounded by the force field…"

"Is that meaning we are safe?" Sam Bright asked from his usual position in the galley.

“I don't know—I hope so. I'm assuming whoever built this thing would not guide it so close to a star unless they knew their protection was adequate.”

“Why did you want us here, Captain,” Sarah asked.

“The last few days have been hard on us all, and most of you have been holed up in your cabins. Now we’re about to experience something that may spell the end of this mission, or not. We can't see what's going on outside, we’re completely isolated and I think all of us are a little afraid.” Several heads nodded in confirmation.

“Terrified.”

“Petrified, more like.”

“Right. I thought it wise if we spent the next few hours together for support and peace of mind. I'm not saying you have to be here—if you want to go back to your cabins you’re free to do so—but I think it might be better for everyone to be with friends now, despite the view outside. Anyone who wants to leave may do so.”

Nobody moved. The room remained frozen until Carl Geddes reached into a cabinet, retrieved a chess set and slapped it on a table between himself and Peter Stanley. “Set it up, Pete,” he mumbled.

The crew sat around in small groups, talking quietly. Several watched an old movie on the big screen while Sam busied himself in the galley making snacks and endless cups of coffee for whoever would take them.

Four hours passed before Wally Tyrell slapped a hand on his knee, jumping from his seat so forcefully he almost took a tumble in the low gravity.

"I'll be damned," he said. 'Why did I not think of that before?" Everybody stared at him, convinced he had gone crazy. Joe raised a questioning eyebrow.

"We're still alive, and we must be well into the Corona by now. We probably *can* see outside. Captain, with your permission I would like to go up to the bridge—the *Minaret's* bridge. We may be able to see what's going on from there if the place is operational."

Joe considered for a moment. It never occurred to him the *Minaret's* vision systems would function while traversing the Sun, but the possibility did exist.

"Assuming this ship is where we think it is, is that something we want to see?"

An ecstatic gleam appeared in the old man's eyes. "I most certainly do, old boy."

"What does everyone else think?" Heads nodded and mumbled words confirmed the suggestion. Joe suspected the impetus behind the general agreement was boredom, fear, or not knowing; any targeted activity was better than sitting around waiting for whatever the fates decreed.

"Alright, one team will see if it's worth the trouble and report to the rest of us. I'm not going to allow everyone to go on a whim."

Alaine stood. "I'll volunteer."

"My idea, sonny boy," Wally said, moving across to align himself with the young officer. Sarah stepped up beside them.

"No," said Joe. "Not you, Sarah. I want you and Harry here in case of an emergency. If the team reports in okay then we can all go. Non-essential personnel only to begin with."

"I guess that would be me then," Patricia Grace announced, stepping forward.

An hour later, the voice of Alaine Parish came over the intercom. "Captain, I think you all need to come and see this." He was breathless, and his words conveyed a sense of awe.

* * *

Joe entered the *Minaret's* bridge deck, unprepared for what confronted him. The screens were still active, giving the impression of an immense window to space.

Beyond the window, the surface of Sol rolled towards them. It was like the view from a plane skimming low over a vast landscape, but there the similarity ended. This panorama was a sea of boiling light.

Inside the door, Alaine stood with his back to Joe. Wally was at the balcony railing, looking down to the lower floor. Joe walked up to Alaine, not for a second taking his eyes from the scene ahead.

"Can't be real," he whispered.

"No, it's filtered in some way." Alaine's words were soft and breathless, spoken with trepidation. "And probably a computer interpretation. If it was a genuine image, I doubt we would be able to see anything at all from the glare. The temperature out there is … I don't know … a couple of million degrees Celsius? Enough to fry us neatly."

Most of the remaining members of the crew walked in behind Joe, some continuing to the railing, all with their eyes glued to the astonishing images.

Only Sam Bright and Maeve Pedder had stayed with the *Butterball*, content to forego the chance of a lifetime. Joe thought he understood why: the medical officer did not believe she could cope, while for Sam there was a deeper issue. He refused to elaborate, but Joe suspected it might have to do with his religion. Perhaps Sam felt he would meet God, and his god was something he feared more than the star.

For an eternity, everyone gazed in silence. With no sense of scale, it was impossible to tell how far within the corona the *Minaret* flew. Joe was sure if the Sun were an ocean, they would be leaving a trail of turbulence. Perhaps they were.

The image of the photosphere below was overwhelming, a hellish symphony in brilliant red, orange, yellow and black, presumably tinted by the heavy filtering of the system. The hazy surface of the star roiled in an endless, grainy field of fire, rivers and bands of dark and light flowing and twisting as they streamed towards and disappeared beneath the screen. Gleaming mountains heaved upwards through a fog of glowing orange, some extending into peaks before erupting and collapsing back to the madness below.

Brilliant, scintillating streams of what could only be radiation, as interpreted by the *Minaret's* computers, stretched upward through the haze, reminding Joe of the sunbeams one sometimes sees shining down through a break in the cloud cover, but with an intensity no human soul had seen before.

The glare was so powerful the darkness of space could not be seen, whilst below, the entire scene sparked with points of sudden, piercing light, exploding in brilliance and fading in seconds. Far ahead, a giant arch of star-stuff arced across the horizon, reaching high above the level at which the *Minaret* was flying.

Joe walked up to the balcony edge and stood beside Wally Tyrell. Wally glanced at him briefly. "A path where no man thought?" he asked.

"What?"

"It's from a book written hundreds of years ago. You think we're going to fly through that?" His face gleamed with pure joy as he looked at the arch.

"If the ship stays on this course we will, assuming that thing remains up for long enough. It must be a hell of a long way off. We shouldn't be able to see the surface, by rights. The glare from the Corona would wash everything out, I thought."

"I agree with Alaine—it has to be a computer interpretation," Wally said. "I wonder what it would look like from the observation sphere."

Joe tore his eyes away and looked at his companion. The expression on the old man's face was that of a child given free rein in the world's largest amusement park. He remembered Wally speaking of his grandchildren on Mars; he hoped the old fellow would survive this voyage so the children could hear stories about this moment. Perhaps no other humans would ever know this experience, at least nobody alive today.

"I don't think I could handle it," Joe said. "Terry would have loved this."

"Mind if I go?"

"No. Some of the others might go with you. Don't go alone." Wally turned and approached Carl and Sarah, who were standing a few feet further along the wall. At that moment, Alaine stepped up to Joe.

"That's not all I wanted you to see," he said. "Look down at the main floor."

Joe dragged his eyes away from the view and looked over the railing. At first, it appeared just as on his first visit, a wide area scattered with low consoles, counters and benches. It took a moment for his eyes to register that there was something new. Positioned randomly, some alone, others in small groups, were … something.

"What the…" Joe looked more closely. The new objects were tall, ovoid masses of translucent mist, ghost-like and infirm, sometimes fading and then becoming more solid. He felt a touch at the sleeve of his environment suit.

"You were so focused on the main event you missed them when you came in," Alaine said. "They're so faint some of the others still haven't noticed them." Tugging Joe's shoulder, he turned him to look back to the control consoles.

At every station, one of the ghostly ovoids hovered. From each presence, long, sinuous arms of vapor snaked out to merge with the now glittering surfaces of the consoles.

"Looks like the owners of this tub have come to watch the show as well," Alaine said. "I tried to touch one but I can't. You get a tingling feeling and your hand stops, like touching a statically charged glass wall. They don't respond to us in any way."

Only then did Joe realize, of all the crew from *Butterball* Patricia Grace alone was not watching the main screen. She stood by a console, her attention on one of the strange presences.

"Are these our aliens? Ethereal creatures made of vapor?" He felt a chill run up his spine as if he had seen a ghost.

* * *

On the level above the bridge, Wally, Sarah and Carl walked out to the platform at the center of the observation sphere. The minute they sat on the bench and took a firm grip, the walls vanished.

The view left them breathless as they flew free in space over the vast, dynamic surface of the star, towards the arc so high the Earth itself could have passed through many times over. It was like standing on the extreme bow of a ship with nothing of the vessel within the line of sight. One might almost be a bird flying across a sea of fire.

Wally knew it could not be real. He doubted organic eyes could observe the reality. Nevertheless… He had always prided himself on not falling for religious 'claptrap', but at that moment, he knew he had come face to face with the handiwork of God.

* * *

"I can't believe we saw that," Ruth said, taking a long draw from a carton of juice. Sitting across the desk, Alaine stared silently at the floor, while Joe lay on his bunk and gazed at the overhead. The three had hardly spoken since returning.

"What concerns me most is those … things," said Alaine. "Do you think they are the crew?

"Hard to say," Joe said. "When we got back Sarah admitted she had seen one before, when she went for her first joyride on the bubble way. She didn't say anything until now because she thought it was her imagination. It had her face."

"She's not alone," said Ruth. "Wally saw one on the bridge earlier. Apart from confiding in me, he kept quiet for the same reason. The delusions of an old man, he said."

For a moment more, nobody spoke. There were no explanations for the strange manifestations. They could as easily be another variety of machine or artificial construct as they could be aliens.

Joe doubted that. He could understand a drone presence at the controls, but wondered why artificial devices would turn out in numbers to observe the transit. If they were the aliens, they were just like humans, curious and able to appreciate the awesomeness of nature at its most powerful. Surely, that was a trait of intelligence.

"We have our communications back," he said. "I guess it means we've finished our traverse. Chloe tells me we're on a direct line to Venus, so our host has entered the system and will most likely head for Earth after a slingshot. It'll be a while before the fleets reach us again."

"If she can't see outside," Alaine wondered, "I would love to know how Chloe knows what's going on out there."

"Good point," Joe said. "Maybe our gracious host is telling her."

"I want to know about that shield," Alaine said. "We just skimmed through the corona of a star and we're still alive. Do you get that?" The others shook their heads in denial.

Alaine looked intently at the Captain, "The Corona is hotter than the surface of the Sun itself. We have to find out how the shield works. It makes everything else irrelevant."

"We haven't been able to figure out anything else we've seen," Joe pointed out. "What makes you think this will be any different?"

Letting out a deep, wistful sigh, Alaine stood and turned to the door. "I need some sleep."

"Me too," Ruth added, standing, "unless you would like me to stay."

Joe smiled. Their friendship was now common knowledge amongst the crew, and everyone appeared happy with the arrangement except Sarah. Her attitude to the older woman had cooled distinctly in the last few days, and it concerned Joe.

He knew the girl felt strongly for him, and was no longer certain it was a simple case of his being a father figure. At his age, it was not something to encourage, regardless of how much he liked her in return.

"I think we could all use rest," he replied. "We can catch up later."

* * *

Joe awoke. He was not sure how long he had slept; it had been a restless sleep—the type where he was never quite sure whether he had been sleeping or not. The cabin should have been in darkness, but there was a faint glow.

"Chloe, turn my screen off please."

"Your terminal is not on, Captain."

Joe rolled over to face outwards, and then sat up so quickly his head collided with the low bunk overhead. Cursing, he slung his legs over the side of the berth.

He was not alone. In the far corner beside the door to the bathroom, one of the unnatural, misty ovoids seen on the *Minaret's* bridge hovered above the floor. It was a little over a meter high and so ethereal it was barely visible.

The faint light was indeed coming from the computer screen, despite Chloe's assurance it was off. Three familiar words blazed against a black background.

Captain Joseph Falcon.

Joe scrambled to the desk, his eyes flicking back and forth between the screen and the strange presence in the corner. A familiar chill crawled down his spine and spread into his body.

"What the hell?" He reached for the keyboard, but before he could touch a key, the message vanished and new words appeared.

I am of the spacecraft you call the Minaret.

For a moment, Joe was speechless. Of all the answers to his question, it was the one he least expected.

"Chloe?"

"Yes, Captain?" came the computer's soft, even voice.

"The message on my monitor. Are you aware of it?"

"Yes, Captain. The message does not originate at any other terminal. Nor is it coming from outside the ship."

"That's impossible. Extrapolate."

"The message is originating on your terminal, Captain."

Joe looked up at the ephemeral ovoid.

"Thank you, Chloe. Please record."

For several minutes, Joe sat and looked at the intruder. His skin prickled, his hands tightly clasped to stop them from shaking. Something deep inside told him this was the moment he had been waiting for since first arriving, but the circumstances were somehow ridiculous, like something from an old movie. Finally, he summoned the courage to talk.

"What do you want?"

The time has come for us to meet in person.

Joe felt his heart slam in his chest. "When? Where?"

You will come to the place you call the grotto on the main habitat level. You may come when you are ready. You may bring two of your crew, as is your habit. You may carry weapons if it will make you feel more comfortable.

"Who…? Why have you taken so long to contact us?" There was no response to the question. The screen was empty, and when Joe lifted his eyes, the strange visitation was gone from the corner of the room.

* * *

"I think I should relieve you," Sarah said with a grin. "On grounds of insanity, maybe."

"Sure you weren't dreaming?" Harry asked. The entire crew had gathered in the common room to hear of their captain's encounter, but even he would have questioned its validity if Chloe had not recorded the event.

"At first I thought I was," he replied, "but it was real enough."

"And you're going?" Patricia asked.

"Of course. How can I not? The question is who I take with me, if anyone."

"Me, of course. This is my area. You have to take me."

For a moment, Joe hesitated. He had doubts about taking anyone into a situation he might not be able to control. This was without doubt the most potentially dangerous moment of the mission.

Almost immediately, he realized how ridiculous that was. Patricia, and everyone else, had already shown they were more than capable of holding their own, and it suddenly occurred to him that in reality, he had no control whatsoever anyway.

He and his crew had been at the mercy of the aliens from the moment they set foot on the *Minaret*. He doubted that, should bad come to worse, any of them could do a damn thing about it.

"Agreed," he said finally. "And you, Alaine?"

"Yes. Do you want me to carry arms?"

"No. Somehow, I doubt it would serve any purpose. Their suggestion we could do so if we wished means they have no fear of our weapons or us. Better to show good faith and go unarmed, I think." General nods of agreement came from around the room. "The rest of you can follow us by communicator."

"When," someone asked.

"I have a few messages to send first, and then we can go. Why wait?"

"Fine," Alaine agreed. "Let's get to it then."

* * *

"Hello Jake. I have an update for you. I appreciate the ongoing danger in using this link, but I want you to continue while you can. Eventually they'll find a way to prove it's you releasing information to the global net, but things are reaching a head here, and I think it's more important that everyone know what's going on, if you are agreeable. We've safely traversed the Sun. I can't describe the experience; I'll try when we next meet. In the meantime, we're all alive and safe." Joe paused for a second.

"Now, are you ready for this? A representative of the *Minaret* contacted me—yes, seriously—and a meeting has been set up. I'll be leaving in a few minutes. Chloe will record the entire encounter and as soon as a link with Earth is re-established, she'll send the data to you with this message. I want everyone to know; it's important the truth gets out.

"I don't think we're in any extra danger by going to meet our hosts, although I am concerned. They've looked after us since our arrival, but the loss of Terry gives me some worry. We can't be certain they killed him, but we don't have a body and I can't help but wonder. I admit to being terrified considering what we've seen of their technology. I'm not even sure if the invitation came from an organic being or a computer."

There was a gentle rap on Joe's door.

"I need to go now, Jake. Wish me luck. Chloe, file and send when possible."

Joe turned to the door. "Come in."

Patricia poked her head around the door and stepped into the cabin.

He looked up as she entered. "Ready to go?"

"As much as can be," she said. "There's something I want to tell you before we do." She sat down on the bunk. "I think I know where the aliens are. On this ship, I mean."

Joe raised an eyebrow and cast an enquiring look at her.

"I started thinking when we were on the bridge. These beings don't have solid bodies. They almost looked … electrical? Do you remember the memo we got from the mission committee about the concept of how a large crew might cross light-years of space without straining the ship's resources? They suggested only the mentalities might be carried, in a computer or something.

"If the crew gave up their organic bodies and took on a virtual existence, the strain on the ship would be minimal, since only the computer facility would require support. We dismissed the idea at the time."

"Yes, I remember."

"Well, the *Minaret's* level of technology made me give it more thought. We don't have the ability to record a mind, nor to put it back into a new body when we want to, but considering they can fly through the corona of a star without harm, I think they might. It seems a simple accomplishment in comparison."

"I'm not so sure. The mind is an incredibly complex thing. So where do you think they are?"

"It's obvious, isn't it? If we accept the premise, then they're in the flasks we saw in the upper level of the habitat drum."

"There were millions of those," Joe pointed out.

"Yes, but not all appeared to be in use. Some were filled with greenish gel, others were clear. What if they are individual storage cells? Each green flask contains the mentality of an alien, stored as electronic impulses in a matrix, maybe."

"Yes, possible, I suppose. Have you discussed this with Wally?"

"Yes. He agrees with me. A conscious entity is nothing more than a collection of electrical impulses; the body is just the hardware the consciousness inhabits. In theory, it *could* be stored in an artificial brain, even if we can't do anything that complex yet."

"Not yet," Joe said, thinking of Jake.

"But they may be able to. Those flasks must be part of a massive computer system, and the aliens live inside it."

Chapter 21

THE GROTTO WAS the first place visited on the accommodation level of the drum, several weeks ago. Joe, Patricia and Alaine stepped from the elevator and strode across the foyer to the glass doors leading to the 'outside'.

The exterior had changed dramatically in the interval. Where once bare ground flanked the pathways, with only small shoots poking their heads through, there were now fields of alien vegetation. The 'plants', darker and more violet in color than the green of the terrestrial equivalent, grew lush and dense in patches whilst elsewhere a low, grass-like carpet stretched away into the distance.

"Apart from the colors, this could be any park on Earth," Alaine said.

"Or the dome gardens at Hellas, on Mars," Joe added. "There's nobody here."

Nearby was the place where a circular path enclosed what all agreed was a fountain. Dense clumps of vegetation now surrounded the feature and water ran from the center structure, confirming that assumption. The *Visitors* had similar tastes to humans, and perhaps a similar culture at some past time.

"Well," he said. "They know we're here, so I guess…"

Among the stone benches at the far side of the grotto where seconds before there had been nothing, a young and very human woman stood dressed in a loose-fitting, white robe that flowed to the ground. Too distant for her features to be clear, she was pale-skinned, her hair dark and tied back in a ponytail.

Joe's jaw dropped. He turned to look at his companions and saw the same skepticism in their faces. That the aliens were human in appearance was beyond all credibility.

Greetings, Captain Joseph Falcon.

The words sounded as if the speaker was beside him. They were in Joe's mind, and not spoken at all.

Please approach. You and your companions need not fear me.

From closer, the features of the woman became clearer. She was perhaps in her twenties and there was something familiar about the face. She was beautiful, and her deep blue eyes fixed on Joe as he drew nearer.

Helen. He was looking at the face of his long-lost wife. *It can't be. This is not real.*

"You can't be human," Patricia said as she stopped ten feet from the young woman. "It's impossible."

You are correct, Patricia Grace. This body is a construct created to interact in a manner acceptable to you. It is what you would call an artificial person. Its appearance comes from the memories of your captain in the hope it will provide a sense of familiarity. Do you find this unacceptable, Captain Joe Falcon?

"I, um. No. Yes. I … What do we call you?"

My identifier is not pronounceable in your auditory language. You may call me Io.

"Io? From ancient myth?" Patricia asked. "You know our mythology?"

Yes.

"What have you done with my crewman?' Joe asked. "He was killed by something, and one of your drones took him away." He could not help himself. It was the wrong way to start what might well be the most important conversation in history, but the words came unbidden.

We will return your crewmember as soon as possible, the android replied. *The drone was simply carrying out its program. We did not cause his death but we will provide you with as much information as we have when we are able. Please sit.*

Joe and Patricia sat on one of the stone benches as the alien took a seat opposite. Alaine remained standing behind the bench.

"Who are you," Pat asked. "Where did you come from? Where are you? We've been looking for you since we arrived. How can you possibly speak our language? How..."

"Pat, please," Joe urged, aware the young woman beside him was becoming hyper-excited. Of all the 'experts' who had ever studied xenobiology, she was suddenly the most famous, the first to meet an intelligent extra-terrestrial, albeit a humanoid robot.

Your curiosity is acceptable. You already know our location on this vessel.

"The flasks on the next level above us," Pat said immediately.

Yes. Your speculations concerning the inhabitants of this ship are correct.

"How did you know we worked it out?" Joe asked.

You have been observed and studied since you first arrived. We know a great deal about you and your worlds.

"Where are you from?" Patricia repeated. "How did you learn English?"

Our home is another star in the near region of this galaxy. Your speech was difficult to learn; we made progress only after your arrival, by studying the interactions between yourselves. We have also accessed your ship's mind, and language databases on your home world.

"You're watching us? Inside our ship?"

Yes.

"And you can access computers on our worlds?"

Yes.

"How could you do…?"

"Why are you here?" Joe interrupted.

We come to warn you.

For a moment, Joe's mind felt numb—he had not expected that response. "Warn us? Warn about what?"

I will explain, but please be patient. It is necessary to tell you a little of our history, to make my explanation clear.

Joe nodded. A thousand questions waited to be asked of this beautiful thing, but somehow now was not the time. He decided to wait and listen.

Your many questions may be answered at a later time. For now, our purpose in coming here is of primary importance.

Joe nodded again.

Our home world was not unlike your Earth, but very close to our Sun and much warmer. Our star is what you call a red dwarf. It is smaller and cooler than your yellow Sun. It is also much, much older. We evolved much earlier than your race and were exploring our near space before you had developed primitive technology.

Our species has been in difficulty for many hundreds of your years. Long ago, a rogue dwarf planet entered our system and collided with our world. Due to its size, we were unable to stop or deflect it. Our planet was rendered uninhabitable, with much of the surface becoming molten once again.

We survived and were able to move many of our people to safety further out in the system. Our star has only one rocky world, our planet, and two gaseous worlds. Those have many moons, several of which provided us with sanctuary.

We realized we could not survive indefinitely in the outer system, so we made a decision to seek out new homes on which to recreate our civilization. We sent probes to all the stars in our local group and beyond in search of suitable planets. One of them came to your primary world several hundred of your years ago. It reported your existence, so we determined not to come here, having no desire to interfere with you.

"So why are you here?" Alaine interrupted, attracting a piercing glare from Joe.

While the probes were away, we began the construction of ten colony ships such as this one. Each would travel to a star identified as having an inhabitable planet, carrying a contingent of twenty million individuals living in a virtual existence. Our intention was to create new bodies upon arrival, modified for the new world.

In addition, each ship carried a genetic data bank of life rescued from our original world before the collision, and a complete record of our history, everything that defined our civilization for tens of thousands of your years. We accepted the difficulty of such a task but believed if even one vessel succeeded, it would ensure the survival of our race.

"You said you had no intention of coming here," Joe said.

Our ship was the last. Nine departed in safety, and this one was almost complete and ready to begin loading its precious cargo. Before we could do so, another vessel entered our system. It was a star-ship not unlike this one in concept, but totally light absorbing. We call it the Blackship. *It used our star to decelerate as we have done here, and went into orbit around our abandoned world. Discovering it lifeless, the ship redirected its course to the moon where most of our remaining population was gathered.*

We constructed the colony ships at the outer edge of our system in our star's equivalent of your Kyper Belt. Upon becoming aware of the Blackship, *we shut down operations and made ourselves as undetectable as possible. We waited and watched as the new arrival went into orbit around our major moon.*

At first, they professed friendship and claimed to be colonists in search of a new world, like ourselves. Soon after arrival, they left again, having realized we had nothing useful to offer in the way of resources.

Before leaving, they bombarded our moons, destroying almost all that remained of our people and our cities. We believe that knowing us to be in a similar situation to themselves they did not want competition. We expected them to destroy us as well, but either they did not realize we were there or did not care. They left on course for another star.

A sinking feeling seeped into Joe's gut. "What star?"

The Blackship *comes here. It will traverse your sun in fourteen of your Earth days.*

"That's why you came here? You came to warn us?"

We knew of your existence through our probe and realized your planetary system with its yet untapped wealth of resources would attract the Intruders. *We knew your technology was inadequate to defend against them.*

With our people gone, and our genetic banks and heritage destroyed, we no longer had what this ship required to create a new colony. We also realized the inhabitants of the Blackship *represented a future threat to our other colonies. We decided to come here instead of going to the star we had been designated.*

"To warn us?"

We gathered as many of our people as had survived, little more than ten thousand individuals occupied in the ship's construction or scattered across other moons in our system, and loaded our ship with as much raw material as we could muster. During the voyage here, our factories used those materials to construct weapons, something for which we previously had no need. When ready to depart, we selected a high-velocity trajectory to arrive at your world before the Blackship.

"You only just made it, by the sound of it," Joe commented, a little overwhelmed by what he was hearing. "You did all this to help us? For what return?"

We intend to destroy the Intruders. *We will also provide your worlds with what defense we can. If we are successful, we will refuel our ship, and leave in search of one of our other colonies.*

"I don't know what to say. Thank you doesn't seem adequate."

Do not misunderstand, Captain Joe Falcon. We will defend you as best we can, but we did not come here for that reason.

Joe did not respond, unsure of what to expect. The young woman leaned forward and fixed her eyes on his.

The intruders murdered millions of our people and destroyed the hopes of this ship. They represent a threat to our other colonies, if any have survived. We must prevent that. We come here for revenge.

* * *

Joe stared at the two small objects. They appeared to be standard data cubes, indistinguishable from any found on Earth or Mars, but given to him by Io.

One would be transmitted to human authorities to help them locate the new ship as it traversed the Sun. The other was his, a gift for transmission to his son.

They know my son is an Einstein. They know I have a secure line. They are aware of everything we do.

According to Io, the second cube contained scientific data in a form Jake would understand, a goodwill gift to humanity without its source being obvious. It was, the android explained, an act of good faith. She required something in return for their assistance. Joe now struggled over how to break the alien request to Marcus Bond.

"Your last transmission is acknowledged, Marc," he began. "The data I am sending you will allow our people to locate the new arrival. The *Visitors* call it the *Blackship* in our language, so for now, I'll do that also. We can't detect it the same way we found the *Minaret*, from its albedo. Its hull is black and light absorbent.

"We are still yet to see a real alien, and that may not even be possible. Io is a construct, an android, a machine created to communicate with us. Looks like my late wife Helen damn it, but I didn't want to say anything unless they took offense. I suspect these beings can create any kind of body they like for themselves and I'm pretty sure the mind inside Io is your actual alien. At least we know where they are, and how many of them are here. What troubles me most is that they are telepathic, and they can apparently read our minds.

"Do I trust them? I'm not sure. So far, there's no reason to do so, or not to. The only thing I can judge by is the way we've been treated since we arrived. They've looked after us beyond expectation and protected us when necessary. I suspect they have also been testing us, with things like the access codes.

"There *is* Terry to consider. Io assures me they didn't kill him. It's likely the machine that took him was a simple maintenance drone that considered him a unit no longer functioning and took him away. It 'cleaned up'—did its job.

"The *Visitors* say they will protect Earth—I presume Mars as well—and do their best to destroy the *Blackship*. The *Minaret* contains vast storage spaces and factories not yet seen by us, built to carry stores for a new colony and manufacture anything it needed. Robbed of the ability to create a colony they filled the bays with whatever raw materials they could salvage from the star-ship construction facility and programmed their computers to make weapons on the voyage here. I can confirm that, I think. I reported earlier that the hangers are packed with what can only be fighting craft. Alaine found another hanger filled with spindle-shaped machines we can't identify, and we've explored less than one or two percent of the vessel.

"Here's the crunch, Marc. It took time to rescue survivors and load the ship, so they left their star sometime after their attackers and with less than a full fuel load. To get here first required acceleration to a much higher speed than anticipated, and this meant using most of what fuel they had. If they win the battle they insist is coming they will leave, but to do so they need to refuel.

"They've requested permission to build a base on Titan. They want to construct a facility to manufacture massive amounts of anti-matter, and it could be as much as a hundred Earth years before they are ready to leave again. Based on our past efforts with antimatter I find that quite believable. They want exclusive access to Titan for that time, bearing in mind we can't easily get out there yet anyway.

"In return, as well as defending us as best they can, they'll share some of their technology with us. They've not yet specified exactly what, but something that will advance our technological understanding without swamping our social development.

"So that's the deal. We give them Titan for one century, and they defend us from possible extinction."

* * *

Carmichael Page's normally flushed face was now ghost white. "An alien race enters our system uninvited and demands one of our moons, and we are actually considering giving it to them?"

"First," Professor Alfred Brewer replied, "they are not demanding anything. They ask only in return for protection against this new threat…"

"…which we are yet to locate. We have no evidence this damned 'Blackship' thing even exists."

Adam Palfrey interrupted. "Wrong. I've received a report a second craft is currently in a braking traverse of the Sun."

Page slumped back into his seat, a deflated look on his face. "Fine. So, what do we know about it?"

"Well … it is, as Io said, completely non-reflective, hemispherical in shape, approximately sixty kilometers in diameter—that makes it bigger in volume than the *Minaret*—and isn't answering any of our signals."

"Neither did the *Minaret*."

"True, but nor did it sneak up on us. Io's lot would have known they were detectable and may have delayed contacting us until they could speak our language. So far, everything they have told us about the *Blackship* checks out."

"We still can't give them Titan. Their technology is a millennium beyond ours and allowing them to set up a permanent base would be dangerous. They may never leave. They could take control of the entire system—sit out there and strangle us."

"That is the whole point," said Professor Brewer. "Do you honestly think we can stop them from doing anything they want? Anything at all? Our most powerful weapons could not damage a shield that can defy the Sun's corona. I expect they're trying to be friendly by asking our permission when they can easily go ahead without it."

"We have no proof they are genuine," Julianne Devereaux, the Mars Homeland Secretary said. "Only their word. For all we know they are the enemy and the other lot are our friends."

"Somehow I doubt it," Adam said. "The *Visitors* didn't hide their arrival. The astronomers spotted them months ago, whereas the *Blackship* was on our doorstep before we found it, and only with the *Visitors'* help."

"I vote we give them approval," the Professor said. "We can't defend ourselves against either ship, so we accept the offer."

Page shook his head. "I say no."

Adam leaned forward and propped his chin on clasped hands, moving his gaze from one to the next of his fellow board members.

"The choice is not up to us," he said. "This panel doesn't have authority to make a ruling on something like this. We can't accept or refuse help, and we can't give away Titan as much as I think we should."

Adam directed his attention to Carmichael Page. "You'll convey all the available information to your governments along with my recommendation we agree to the request. I will do the same for my people here on Mars."

"Seriously?"

"Absolutely. Listen carefully, people. This is no longer a matter between planets. It's now man against alien so we work together on this, got it? Tell them a decision is required immediately—none of their usual farting around, and feel free to quote me on that. May the gods help us if they get it wrong."

Chapter 22

"YES? NO? MAYBE?" Alaine asked. "Who knows what those fools will decide? I would expect Mars to agree without reservation but the governments of Earth are arguing the point. Some nations agree in principle but others say no. How can they not see this?"

"Politics," Joe explained. "If the *Visitors* are telling us the truth then logic says we should accept the offer. If we refuse they will go ahead and take Titan regardless, because they have no other option."

"Mars has a single, unified government," Ruth Carvalio said, "and the population tends to be more progressive with a higher average IQ. A 'yes' decision is more likely, but not guaranteed. On Earth, we have numerous nations and despite the protestations of the United Earth Council, each believes its opinion to be the correct one. The people making the decisions are politicians, not scientists or academics. They aren't interested in the long-term good, just the next election. To give away a moon in our Solar System would make them look bad in the eyes of their constituents, or so they think."

"But only for one hundred…" Alaine said.

"The average voter won't see it like that. A century is the rest of their lives and most of their children's, so they'll see it as a permanent alien presence in our System. Besides, the general opinion back home is the *Visitors* are untrustworthy."

"Xenophobia," Alaine spat.

"But real all the same. The average person has no more reason to trust them than the *Intruders*. Nor do we."

"Agreed," Joe said, from his seat in the corner. Everyone was present in the common room, having listened in to the meeting with Io. All were aware of the stakes and that they were now the focus of attention on two worlds.

He had said little until now, content to listen to the opinions of his crew. There was no dissent—all agreed there was no choice but to accept the *Visitors'* terms.

"I suspect the United Earth Council will be swayed by public opinion, and they will end up saying no. The UEC has always been a toothless organization, since any one of the most powerful nations can veto anything they don't like. In four centuries they've never learned that lesson."

"So the little red planet goes it alone," Alaine suggested.

"Not possible," Joe replied. "Mars does not own Titan. By treaty, all non-occupied bodies in the Solar System are common property, so both planets have to agree. Besides, our population is only one hundred and forty million—that represents one percent of humanity. Do we leave the other ninety-nine to their fate?"

"No, I guess not," Alaine said. "If Earth was attacked and we didn't come to its defense, that alone could start another war, assuming we survived at all, and this time it would be based on hate, not commerce or politics."

Joe said nothing. An idea was forming, something to force the issue in what he considered the right direction. The consequences would be significant, and needed careful consideration.

The first order would be to ensure his legal footing and the future of the crew of *Butterball.* Most importantly, he had to clarify whether or not his hosts could be trusted. Were they telling the truth, in which case the *Blackship* was the enemy who threatened humanity, or were they lying? If so, they might be the greater menace. Joe wondered also about their motivations: were they in truth acting from altruism and offering the hand of peace, or was there a hidden agenda?

Later, alone in his cabin, he sent another message to Jake requesting he run certain questions about the legalities of this mission past the best legal minds he could find. Joe knew the kind of power his son wielded, and an opinion from him would be reassuring.

Next, he began a course of action he prayed would set his mind at ease. He knew the aliens monitored every movement and spoken word on *Butterball*, but he needed to know more about their telepathic abilities.

Are you there, Io? he thought. There was no response.

"Are you there, Io?" he asked aloud.

Yes, Captain Joe Falcon. The reply sounded in his mind. Io had responded to his spoken request, but not to the mental one.

"I have a favor to ask. You and your passengers live in a virtual world, correct?"

That is correct.

"Is it possible for me to visit there?"

Is it important for you to formulate a response to our request?

"Yes. I need to understand you better."

It is acceptable. How many of your number wish to accompany you?

"There will be three of us, I think."

* * *

To accompany him, Joe chose Patricia Grace and Ruth Carvalio. Pat had an almost unassailable right to go; a tour of the aliens' virtual world might provide valuable insight into their society and civilization.

Like any good writer, Ruth was a skilled observer with an acute perception of human nature, and Joe hoped her skills would translate to useful insights. He needed information, details the aliens would not give but which might be forthcoming from pure observation. He would have preferred to have Alaine and Wally along as well, but thought it might push the issue.

Some hours later, the three stepped through the glass doors to the 'grotto', the de-facto meeting place. As expected, someone was there waiting. The young woman who appeared to greet them did not look like the one who had met them before.

I am Io, the android stated. *My facial features have been altered so they do not cause you distress. We did not know my previous appearance was that of a loved one lost. This face is a composite of the females on your ship. I hope it will be more acceptable.*

Without waiting for a response, Io walked up to the ramp and directed them back to the elevator.

They understand love and loss, Joe thought.

Their destination was the topmost level of the habitat drum, the same on which the 'flasks' were located. Instead of entering the vast storage chambers, Io led them to a smaller exit and then to another door. The room inside was small and grey, empty bar three very human seats.

Pat approached one of the chairs. "Is this what you used to put your people into the computer?"

No. This chamber is custom-built for you. From here, you may journey into our virtual worlds without leaving your bodies.

Joe was concerned about placing himself in the hands of an unknown but accepted he had asked for this. "Is it dangerous?" *Do we trust her?*

The experience will have no detrimental effects, Io replied, her voice filling Joe's mind. *Please each take a seat.*

This was done for us? Joe thought. There was no response from Io.

"This was done for us? In a few hours?" he asked.

This vessel is fully automated. Our factories are designed for use by a new colony and can manufacture any item upon request. These devices were a simple matter.

"You said you manufactured weapons on the way here."

Yes. Colonization has many requirements which cannot always be anticipated. We built facilities capable of creating anything, given only molecular pattern and the raw materials. When the Intruders *attacked, we studied and analyzed their weapons and by the time we were ready to pursue, we had plans for our own versions.*

"How long did it take to get…?"

Please sit back. There will be more time for questions later.

Joe eased into his seat as a diffuse column of light descended. His vision began to blur and grow dark. After only seconds, sight returned.

* * *

Joe looked around. He and his companions stood at the center of what appeared to be a broad piazza surrounded by tall buildings, gardens and fountains. The scene resembled the primary habitat level below, with the addition of a colossal multi-paned dome overhead. Beyond the dome there was empty space; the distant orb of a dull, red star hung in a black sky. Io stood to one side, appearing as she had in her android form.

This is a re-creation of the colony on the moon attacked by the Blackship, *she explained. It was our last permanent home in our native system.*

Ruth stared up at the aged star, but Patricia ignored it. Her attention focused on the 'people' moving around the plaza. There was no single shape or type: several appeared human, some insect-like, and yet others some variation on a robotic body ranging from mobile trolleys to iridescent spheres floating above the concourse.

"Why are there so many different types of inhabitants?" she asked.

This is a virtual world. Here, individuals take any aspect they desire and change at will. You may even notice that your physical form has become fashionable since your arrival.

Pat was about to ask another question, but Joe interrupted. He understood her interest in the physiology of the *Visitors*, but he had deeper concerns. This reality was not what he wanted.

"Your star. What do you call it?

Our name for it, as close as can be replicated in your speech, is Dinastys. *You know it only as a number. It is no longer the home of our species, but if you wish I can provide coordinates.*

"Yes, please," Joe said without hesitation. Looking around, he realized this was only an illusion. The *Visitors* could show him anything they wished to support their story. "You said you had several virtual realities. Is there one representing your native world? We would like to visit that."

Of course.

Once again, Joe's vision clouded and went black. When his awareness returned, the sight he saw could not have been more different. The new reality was a planetary surface that on first observation resembled old Earth, except the gravity was closer to Mars and the colors were all wrong.

Joe and his companions stood on a stone-paved pathway looking across a series of broad, sloping terraces. Small, strange figures moved between long rows of what must have been crops. A wide river flowed through the fields, beyond which steep hills rose to mountains with more crops covering the lower slopes.

Ruth looked down at her feet. "Is this my real body?"

No. It is a re-creation—what you would call an avatar. Have no fear. Your organic body is safe in the room you just left.

Gigantic, pale red and surrounded by a yellow-orange halo, the same star shone down from a dark, almost black sky. Towards the horizon, a faint, green tinge pervaded, stars glittering even though it was midday. The sky was dark, the landscape bright and vibrant despite the reddish hue and the deep, sharp shadows.

"No atmosphere," Ruth said, forgetting it was a simulation. "How can we breathe?"

"No, the air is here," Joe assured her. "Their Sun is a red dwarf, and we must be very close to it considering how warm this place is. Our Sun emits white light, and the blue waves scatter in Earth's atmosphere, giving it a blue color. There's no blue coming from this star, so the atmosphere looks different—more transparent. The local vegetation reflects the red, giving everything a reddish tinge."

You are quite correct, Joseph Falcon. Would you care to follow?

"Is this your origin world?" Patricia asked.

Yes, as it was before the disaster destroyed it. It is our most favored reality. Please come.

Io led them down the path to a nearby cluster of buildings, a village surrounded by crop fields.

"How like your original world is this re-creation?" Joe asked.

It is closer to our distant past than the time of its destruction. We were much more industrialized then, and our technology freed us from the burden of growing crops manually. In this age, much of our society was agrarian. Most of our people prefer this reality because of the peace and tranquillity it offers. When they want something else, they move to another.

"So, you create your realities to reflect aspects you find desirable?"

Of course.

"This one?"

No. This reality is as historically accurate as we could make it. There are cities elsewhere. Do you wish to observe them?

"No," Pat interrupted. "I would like to see the village, the people."

Io dipped her head in silent acknowledgment and continued along the path.

The town consisted of small buildings, none more than two stories high. Closer, it became apparent the impression of a primitive, rural settlement was only surface dressing. The structures had the identical seamless construction seen on the *Visitors*' ship.

Some paths had moving walkways, and everywhere small but obvious signs betrayed a vastly advanced technology, or at least the simulation of one. Joe suspected these technologies were so old and so ingrained in the psyche of these people that they even recreated them here, in their dreams.

As the group entered the town a number of the inhabitants approached. Their bi-symmetrical bodies vaguely resembled Earth-type raptor dinosaurs but with short, stubby tails. Powerful legs provided biped motion, and two smaller limbs ended in articulated hands remarkably like those of humans. Each had five digits, with three central fingers and two thicker thumbs, one on either side. Familiarity ceased there.

Evolved for low gravity, the creatures were fine-limbed and delicate in appearance. Forward of the arms a thick neck curved up swan-like to a broad, flattened triangular head. Two crystalline eyes, a mouth like a toothed bird beak and two ears that were little more than holes completed what seemed like a hodge-podge of various animal parts thrown together.

The creatures ranged in size from about fifty centimeters in height to almost two meters, and to Patricia were at least familiar. They had a clear family resemblance to the one seen in the image in the habitat foyer and the legs, arms and an obviously articulated spine showed they differed from Terran life only in minor details. Form followed function, and Mother Nature's solutions on this world were similar to those on Earth.

Suddenly the truth dawned. "This is your native biological form, isn't it?"

You are correct, Patricia Grace. In this reality, we prefer to take our natural aspect. I understand if you find it disagreeable.

"No, not disagreeable. We once had life forms with very similar shapes on our home planet, and they're generally considered by us…"

"Pat!" Joe spoke to stop her. She had a tendency to speak her thoughts, and he did not want her stating humans might find the aliens disagreeable because they resembled giant, flesh-eating monsters.

Our native forms are indeed similar to the creatures you speak of, but please do not judge us by that coincidence. Our native bodies are a product of the environment in which we evolved, as are yours. At first, we found your physical form just as unusual, but our studies of your species have shown that mentally, our two races are similar. Like you, we are family-oriented, have a strong desire for achievement and advancement, prefer peace to war, and place great store in cooperation and interpersonal bonds—what you would call love.

"These little ones are children, then?" Joe asked, noting a number of smaller creatures scattered among the larger ones. "How do you do that, here?"

They are, Joseph Falcon. We increase our numbers here by creating new base combinations from the personalities of our existing inhabitants.

We then allow them to grow. It helps with their proper development to experience the normal periods of physical childhood here in this reality. They find you curious. I hope you do not find their attention unwelcome.

"No. Can they speak?"

Our native form does not have speech organs like yours. We can create sound in various ways, but long ago, we evolved the ability to communicate with thought alone. It was a key step in our evolution, allowing us to fully understand each other through telepathic communication, and grow out of the aggressiveness of our early history.

Joe focused on the statement. The aliens, according to Io, embraced peace and family. She claimed that unlike humans they had outgrown the aggressive nature that allowed them to survive the process of evolution. But she—it—had also admitted their reason for coming to the Solar System was to seek revenge.

Io had stated their numbers were roughly ten thousand, but if they had the ability to create new children in the virtual reality, there was no telling how many existed here, or if they were capable of taking physical form in new organic or artificial bodies.

He wondered how much of what he saw was the truth.

For several more hours, Io walked them through different realities of her virtual world. From country town to metropolitan center, Joe and his companions observed, listened and tried to make sense. More than a little overwhelmed by what he had witnessed, he opened his eyes again in the small, grey room.

As he lifted into a sitting position, he glanced at his arm monitor. Despite the lengthy tour, no more than half an hour had passed. Time, it seemed, was also relative in the virtual reality of the *Visitors.*

Patricia sat up. “Wow. That was something else.”

Ruth Carvalio slipped unsteadily from her seat and flexed her body. “Yep, it's me alright.” She looked over at the Captain. “This little excursion is going to make us all famous, you know.”

“Yes, but that's not why I wanted you along,” Joe reminded her.

“I appreciate that, but I'm still going to have one hell of a story to write if we get home. And Patricia just became the only xenobiologist with first-hand knowledge of an alien civilization. Top that.”

* * *

Joe looked at the face on his desk monitor. It was worn, with tired eyes red from strain. This individual was a stranger, but Joe knew who he was, a man under great pressure with the weight of two worlds on his shoulders.

The face spoke. “Hello, Captain Falcon. You and I have never met, which I find regrettable. I'm Adam Palfrey, Minister for Space. I am also, as you are aware, the chair of the committee set up to oversee this … adventure … of ours. That means the final decision on anything comes from me, at least as far as you are concerned. Earth is represented on the council as well, but you are Mars registered and you're there at our behest, so they have had no real say in what you do, up until now.”

Palfrey ignored the fact that Joe had now proclaimed himself as a representative for all of humanity, and not just Mars.

"The data given to us by Io is correct. The second ship is on an identical course to the *Minaret*, but several days behind, and heading for Earth. The hull is black—must be coated with some kind of light-absorbing material, and that's why we didn't spot it. There's been no attempt to communicate with us and it ignores our efforts to establish contact. However, we can't take that as indicative since we know nothing about it at this point.

"I've decided to speak to you personally because the decision regarding the *Visitors*' proposal has become, shall we say, a little thorny. Do we allow them to have Titan for a century in return for their assistance in defending Earth and Mars from the new arrival, which for the sake of clarity we're calling the *Blackship,* as have you? The answer is proving to be more elusive than anticipated."

Palfrey stopped for a moment, his attention focused on the desk below the bottom edge of Joe's screen. Every few seconds a sheet of paper flicked upwards. Palfrey had a document in front of him and the flustered look on his face showed he was fighting to get a handle on the moment, to find words that would not come.

"My fellow bureaucrats are now taking the view neither vessel poses an immediate threat to our planet. It appears doubtful either ship could make a direct orbit around Mars unless they have capabilities we haven't seen yet. Both ships appear to be heading for Earth so whether they are friendly or not, Earth will be the first to know and we will have some warning.

"Some of my myopic fellow politicians believe we should not respond without more information. Just so you know, I do not support them. A unanimous decision, as much as I expected one, is not yet forthcoming. I find myself … disappointed.

"Earth's position is also unclear. The United Earth Council is prepared to accept the proposal, but before granting approval for the Titan thing, the member states want guaranteed access to the alien technology. They fear that with you on the spot, Mars will monopolize anything the *Visitors* give us. I think you will agree that is somewhat naive. I don't think they understand what a threat these ships pose.

"Problem is, not all countries are part of the United Earth Council, and at least a dozen have announced they will not tolerate any incursion, human or alien, in or above their skies. They'll meet any such action with force. Most of those nations are nuclear-capable.

"The official policy seems to be…"

Palfrey stopped mid-sentence and stared off to one side for a few seconds. Joe noted fine beads of sweat on the man's brow and a faint tremble in the one hand visible on-screen. Palfrey took a deep breath, followed by a loud sigh. A movement of his arm indicated he had discarded the papers he was holding.

"Damn it, Joe. This is all bullshit. I'd hoped this business would bring us together, but far from it. Politicians on both worlds are playing politics, and ignoring the simple fact we're helpless in this matter. I wonder sometimes if we'll ever learn to stop bickering among ourselves."

Joe nodded to himself. Scientists had speculated for centuries that man's first contact with aliens would unify the human race, but nothing of the sort was happening.

"So far the only ones showing any sense are our respective space-force commanders, Hsiang and Barrett. Our fleets have united and will be back with you any day. They have jointly declared a state of emergency, removing them from the control of the governments. Whether the *Minaret* is friendly or not remains to be seen, but a combined fleet will have more chance to defend us than two smaller ones operating apart."

Palfrey leaned forward and peered from the screen. For a second Joe almost felt the man could see him, but knew better. The video was recorded over an hour ago.

"Bottom line, Captain. If Io told us the truth, then the *Blackship* is a threat and no price is too big for the protection of the human race. Given the choice I'd let them have bloody Titan; damn thing's no use to us at this stage. If they are lying to us, both ships could be in cahoots and the whole proposal could be to lull us into a sense of false security. In that case, we are in deep shit."

As if it made any difference either way, Joe thought. The shield that allowed the vessel to pass through the Sun's corona was sufficient to convince him the chance of humanity holding its own against this one ship, let alone two, was zero. No weapon possessed by man was a match for something that could defy a star.

"It comes down to this," Palfrey continued. "Can the *Visitors* be trusted on their word? There is only one man who can make that judgment. We are not going to get any useful decisions from the political hacks—not until it's too late anyway. I can't say any more but I'm hoping you follow my line of thought. I suggest you re-read the last official document you received from me. Thanks to our military commanders, both governments now accept your position as humanity's representative. Good luck, Joe." The screen went black.

What in hell was that all about? Joe wondered. Was Palfrey trying to tell him something without actually saying it? The only person who could decide if the *Visitors* were genuine *would* be someone on the spot—Joe understood well enough who that would be.

The only document received with Adam Palfrey's signature attached was the one granting Joe authority to act on behalf of humanity in any negotiations with the aliens, an instrument he knew was never intended to be honored.

Palfrey's message had been tempered by the knowledge others would see the transmission, and the wrong words might carry consequences.

Suddenly, Joe understood what Palfrey wanted of him.

Chapter 23

WHEN THE SHIPS of Earth and Mars returned they came as one. Joe expected the massed fleets of both worlds but only the original envoy vessels appeared, having sailed from their earlier point of departure direct to a new rendezvous as the *Minaret* departed the Sun. The *Minaret* was well on its way to a slingshot around Venus when the flagships arrived and took up station, once again on either side of the space ark.

"I thought there would be more," Joe commented when the face of Hsiang Li appeared on his monitor.

"Sorry about that," the old man replied, a twinkle escaping from his wizened eyes. "The main body is on its way; it'll be here in three days. Do you think they will make a difference, son?"

Joe smiled. Hsiang was not much older than he was.

"To the *Minaret*? No, not at all. I'm more concerned about the fleets themselves. Being in such close proximity is dangerous."

"I can ease your mind on that. They'll arrive together as a single body, for humanity."

"I'm still finding that hard to believe."

"Ah, I see you're as much a cynic as I," the old naval officer observed. "Humans thrive on crisis management; sometimes we even manage to get it right. With the mess getting worse, Commander Barrett and I decided someone should take the initiative. He's consulted with his superiors and they're in full agreement."

"And you speak for Mars?"

"I do."

"I gather things are bad on Earth."

"Yes, I'm afraid so. Most of the terrestrial governments agree we need to act in unity, and pull together. Perhaps two dozen nations are refusing to cooperate. Several are still threatening military action if anything happens in their skies, as you know."

"Can they do that? I mean, can they put the threat into practice?"

"Most certainly, but I suspect their efforts won't bother the *Minaret* too much. The wider concern is how our alien friends might react if someone lobs a nuclear weapon at them, considering they profess to come in peace, and offer protection."

"To *try* to protect us. There seems to be some doubt."

Hsiang nodded his head to indicate understanding. "Have you decided how you'll respond to their offer?"

"Me? I don't have the authority to handle this. It's up to the planetary governments." The recent conversation with Adam Palfrey flashed into Joe's mind; the minister had all but stated the final decision would be Joe's.

"Yes, well," responded Hsiang. "You and I both know what a useless…"

"What about Titan?"

"They will never agree on this Titan business. Joe, you will not get a decisive response from the politicians, so in the end, I think you know what needs to be done. I want you to know that I, and Fleet Admiral Breen, commander of the UESF, will support you all the way. I'll leave you now; keep you updated, of course."

"Thank you, Admiral." Joe flicked the monitor off. Leaning back, he let himself sink into the padding of his chair. The most familiar place on the ship, it was the best place to think, alone in his cabin.

Mars had chosen to withhold its decision for now—sheer stupidity he thought, and from remarks made earlier Palfrey agreed—so the decision now rested with Earth. The homeworld would greet the *Minaret* first, and then the *Blackship*.

Joe scratched his chin. Humans were a contrary lot; they would cut off their noses to spite their faces. Most troubling of all, some politicians on Earth wanted to impose conditions. It did not concern them that the aliens had no obligation to agree. Assuming at least one of the two vessels proved hostile, the aliens held all the cards.

There was also the future to consider. Joe's vast collection of books, all stored away in Chloe's data banks, included numerous tomes on history, some of which related examples of advanced civilizations colliding with primitive ones.

When Europeans colonized the Americas, the Indian peoples died in droves, many sub-groups became extinct and several Palaeolithic civilizations vanished with little trace.

The same happened when Europeans arrived in Australia. Despite the best intentions of the English to treat the natives with respect, open hostility began within days and thousands were slaughtered.

Most tragic of all was the Tasmanian genocide. In the early history of the Australian continent, the earliest Aborigines spread south over a land bridge, where they became cut off by rising sea levels on the Island of Tasmania. When the English settled there to create a dumping ground for the worst of Britain's criminals, the effect on the locals was devastating. The last full-blood vanished after less than a century. In Joe's mind, it was the darkest chapter of the human story.

A primary driving factor in all those historical instances was the insurmountable technological divide between the parties. The European penchant for weaponry far exceeded anything the local inhabitants of those lands possessed, with inevitable results.

Joe stared at his desk. Was this to be the fate of humanity? Two scenarios were possible. If the *Visitors* did not stop the *Blackship*, humankind faced possible destruction at the hands of the *Intruders*, or reduction to either a state of slavery or the largest feedlot in the galaxy. Who could tell without knowing more about the invaders?

If the *Visitors* succeeded there might be a chance, but if they stayed, the overwhelming likelihood was man would still suffer and be integrated, become a lesser class of citizen in their own stellar system or fade away altogether. To Joe, it loomed as a bigger threat than the *Blackship*.

The *Visitors* numbered only ten thousand, but just a handful of men decimated the Incas. Technology made the difference, and humanity had no power to sway the outcome. In truth, it was unsafe to allow either of the two alien craft to remain, unless…

A loud voice sounded over the intercom. "Captain, Sarah here. You better come up to the forward airlock straight away."

"What is it?"

"You won't believe me if I tell you."

"Sarah!"

"Terry's back, sir. He's alive and apparently unharmed."

For a man in his late fifties, Joe never thought he could move so quickly; it took less than a minute for him to reach the airlock. Inside, Terry Caldwell perched on a storage module, overwhelmed by the attention.

Sarah knelt beside him, talking softly as Maeve began a medical examination. Peter Stanley, Carl Geddes and Alaine Parish stood nearby, Alaine shaking his head vaguely, his entire attention on the Lazarus-like figure of the engineer. Joe settled to the floor beside them.

"Terry, are you alright?" he asked. The younger man, still dressed in the sortie suit he had been wearing when he disappeared, raised his head.

"Oh, hi Boss. Yeah, fine, I think."

Joe stepped forward and touched his hand to the younger man's head. Until this moment, he had not realized how much he considered the members of his crew as family. The grief over Terry's loss had been bad enough, but now, to see him alive and well—he appeared normal.

"I thought you died. I…"

"Umm. I think I did, Boss," Terry replied, fingering a scorched hole in the chest of his suit. 'Not sure."

"What happened to you?"

Terry stared at the floor and shook his head slowly. “Sorry, last thing I remember is walking up to the docking bay. I woke up in a hospital room with a beautiful nurse; thought I was back on Mars. She looked a bit like you, Sarah.”

“Lad, I need…”

“You leave him alone until I'm through,” Maeve interrupted. “I'm taking him to the infirmary for a complete examination. You can discuss pretty nurses when I'm finished.”

Too wise to argue with his trauma officer, Joe helped her guide the patient to the central corridor.

An hour later, she backed away from her charge, allowing access again.

Joe took a seat on the bench. “So, how are you, lad?”

“Bit shaky, Boss.” Terry sat with his hands clasped in his lap, his fingers fidgeting, his glance jumping from one point in the room to another. A sheen of sweat pearled on his forehead. The boy in Terry reappeared, a child afraid.

“You said you died?”

“Yeah, that's it. I just had the feeling … can't explain it. I was walking up the ramp to the elevator bay, and the next minute I wake up in the room with the pretty lady.”

“Tell us about her,” Sarah said.

“She said I been sick but I was alright now. She had your eyes.”

“Human?”

“What? Course she was. I know a woman when I see one.” A boyish grin broke on Terry's face. He knew nothing of the android Io, having vanished before her first appearance.

Joe breathed a sigh of relief—the old Terry was still there. "What did she tell you?"

"Nothin' much. She helps me dress, gives me a whole bunch of pills, and then brings me down to the skywalk. Carl found me when I stumbled into the ship. Looked like he seen a ghost."

"He probably thought he had," said Joe. "We thought you were dead. Can you remember what happened to you?"

"I … nope, no idea."

"Several of us were listening in on the open line. We heard something about someone being present when you died. Someone you recognized?"

Terry stared ahead for a few seconds, trying to recall. "Nope, sorry, don't remember."

Joe took a closer look at Terry's body. The engineer was dressed only in his shorts, and Joe expected to see some kind of injury to his torso. There was nothing except small, faint discolorations on his forehead and chest. Joe approached Maeve, busy entering her examination results at the computer terminal.

"Any injuries, at all?"

"I'm not sure, Captain," she said. "It's a tough one. His ribs are, well, I don't know. If he suffered some sort of injury, the repairs are better than anything I've seen before. I'm sure they were damaged but they appear so close to normal on the scans I can't be positive. There are skin discolorations on his head as well, at the front and on the back."

"You think the aliens fixed him?"

"The marks on his chest and ribs may be from a repair process. If they resulted from injury, it could only have been something piercing the chest cavity. The trauma must have been catastrophic. He would have been dead without a doubt. I can't see how he could be sitting here in that case."

Joe sat on the desk and rubbed his unshaven chin as he watched his young second engineer. "We don't know what these aliens can do," he concluded. "God knows what their medical skills are."

* * *

"Jake," Joe began. "I hope everything's good with you. Adam Palfrey tells me trouble is brewing down there—social breakdown and all that. Perhaps for now, you and Akira—how is she, by the way—should stay at Maleny. From what you tell me your compound is secure now. Are the 'feds' still posted outside your gates?

"I want to ask one thing. The information I sent you, the stuff given to me by Io. Did you examine it? I need your advice as to whether you think it's useful or if it might pose some threat to humanity. Forget about the monetary aspect—I'm only interested in the social impact if it's put to use. Please."

Jake pushed his chair back from the desk. The data from his father had been easy to interpret and without question was more than useful, but also potentially explosive and politically disruptive.

It seemed innocent enough, but there were hidden dangers. The sections on atomic and molecular manipulation would make possible advances beyond anything yet devised by man. A new Society beyond recognition would emerge.

Nanotechnology researchers had been playing with molecular manufacturing on and off for the last three centuries, but the work had never achieved expectations. The specter of 'grey goo', with all life reduced to zero at the hands of nano-machines, and the equally scary 'green goo' with the world's remaining ecosystems overwhelmed by an unstoppable merging of nanotechnology and natural biology, had served to cause political institutions to ban the research. Funding for such efforts dried up worldwide on both planets and with the war, vanished altogether. The field stagnated, and in many respects almost died.

The alien cube changed the game. Its contents allowed the construction of self-limiting, ecologically and biologically safe molecular assemblers that, functioning on a grand scale, would reduce the cost of any manufacture imaginable, from food to spaceships, to next to nil—the end of the age of industrialization, and Capitalism.

The provided information would also alter the course of computer design. Jake wondered if a technological singularity was possible, a point at which progress advanced exponentially, reaching heights that could overwhelm society or worse, make humans obsolete.

Would it lead to computers capable of autonomous intelligent thought? It was unlikely; there was a lot more to intelligence than processing speed and storage capacity. The gift made him question his doubts. A new era of technological advance might be either a blessing or a curse.

Worst of all, Jake did not possess the courage to ignore the data. Part of him said to destroy it and let humanity make the discoveries in good time. Another part insisted it was a gift not to be refused. With the right care and forethought, science could leap ahead without overwhelming society.

Leaning forward, he began a reply to his father, aware Akira had entered the room and was now peering over his shoulder. That was good; she would stop him if he made a mistake.

"Dad, wonderful to hear from you again. I envy you your joyride through the Corona. It must've been quite a buzz. Life is still tolerable here, and yes, my minders are still outside but they won't make any moves to come in. They know I'm communicating with you but haven't managed to pin me down yet. I think they've intercepted a few messages but without the key, it would take a thousand years to break the encryption, and they can't trace anything back to me.

"Akira is well. She's taken a leave of absence from the university now. With so much unrest the city's a dangerous place for an attractive young woman."

A small hand cuffed him gently behind the ear.

"The data you sent me is dynamite. It'll give us the capacity and processing speed needed to revolutionize the computer industry. That's a good thing, but not without problems.

"It also provides information on nanotechnology and atomic engineering which will transform human society. Try to imagine a world where you can make anything you want when you want it. The potential effect is both overpowering and devastating. Millions of occupations will vanish as technology replaces traditional employment. Scientific advances will explode, and society will have to cope with a future unlike anything we can imagine.

"With jobs vanishing, I suspect the age-old tradition of working for a wage will become obsolete. The nature of manufacturing will change. The old system of factories and distribution will vanish when anything can be created as it's needed. Molecular assembly depots on every block will replace them and anyone will be able to book time to produce anything at minimal cost.

"The information puts a lot of other things within our immediate reach. Unlimited energy and space travel. I can go on. I see numerous benefits coming from it, but just as much bad if we're careless. That's true of any technological advance, I think.

"Key point. We're going to figure this stuff out anyway within the next century, so I don't think the data will have any consequences that were not inevitable. Some of it we are already working out now. I can't find anything pathological, no ill intent or hidden agendas, just a gift of things we are bound to have soon anyway. We need to be careful, very careful, about how we use it, but one thing we do well is survive our mistakes."

Jake sat back for a moment and then leaned forward again. "There's something else you should consider, Dad. If we can believe the *Visitors*, there are possibly as many as nine other fully-fledged colonies of their species in this district of the Galaxy. They are all way ahead of us technologically. The *Blackship* proves they are not the only advanced species out there and that places us in a precarious position.

"We have to boost our technology quickly or we may find ourselves up against the proverbial wall before too much longer, if we aren't there already. We need the advances on your data cube, and anything else we can get from them. We also need to stop our political in-fighting and unite, but that's another barrier to overcome. Food for thought, Dad."

Chapter 24

THE ALIEN CUBE was, Joe thought, a mark of goodwill. Given wise use, it would benefit humankind and was not so far ahead of current technology its effects would not occur within the next century anyway.

By providing information with inbuilt safety protocols, the *Visitors* might well prevent humanity from making catastrophic mistakes by introducing new concepts before they were proven and tested, something humans seemed adept at doing in the never-ending quest for profit.

A gift, nothing more.

Joe trusted his son without reservation. Jake would not release this information publically and would find a way to use it without abuse.

Give the data openly to industry, and thousands of corporations would attempt to cash in before their traditional activities failed, causing a sudden and irreversible collapse of society. Give it to governments, and it would most likely be diverted to the military. The benefit must flow to all, but by a better, quieter, safer path. Jake would find a way.

Joe concurred with his son's last comment. The new technology was necessary, but not for the reasons the various governments thought.

"So, I need your opinions," he said.

Present were all crewmembers with experience of physical contact with the *Visitors*. On the bunk in Joe's cabin sat Sarah, Patricia and Ruth. Alaine Parish occupied the only other chair.

"I particularly want your insights, everyone, of their simulated societies, their native forms, their lifestyles and their children—anything at all. Tell me what you think about them at a societal level. Are they peaceful, or warlike and trying to hide it from us?"

Alaine clasped his hands behind his head. "That's a hard call. How do we know the simulations are realistic, and not created for our benefit?"

"We don't, granted, but we have to draw a line somewhere. I don't think they expected us to ask, so they may not have had time to build anything new. The room we used was simple enough but the virtual worlds must have taken some forethought. I'm guessing it would be hard to create new ones in a hurry without some mistakes or inconsistencies. That's why I took you ladies; your perception is far more acute than mine. My personal view is they don't seem all that different from us."

"I agree," Patricia said. "I think their intelligence level is probably about the same as ours but their technology is more advanced. They're a much older species, but that doesn't mean bigger or better brains."

"They claim to have a technology thousands of years older than ours," Alaine commented," but it doesn't seem all that far ahead of us. A few hundred years, I'm guessing."

"Can we trust them?"

"I'm not sure," Pat replied. "Maybe—I hope so. Physical appearance aside, their society is very human. Their communities are like ours, they solve problems in ways we can at least comprehend even if we don't understand the technology, and they have social standards as we do. They engage in agriculture and various industrial and leisure activities, value family groups and personal circles of acquaintance, socialize, compete and play, and so on. Our societies are comparable in many respects."

"They love their children, and each other," Ruth said. "I talked to some of the mothers. I know it was a simulation, but apart from curiosity about us their main concern was the welfare of their families."

"They gave us Terry back," Sarah said.

"Yes, that they did," Joe agreed. "Did anyone spot anything indicating a problem, a hidden agenda?" There was a general negative shaking of heads all around.

Patricia spoke again. "When we first met, Io said they came here for revenge. In the simulation, she said they'd grown past their aggressiveness. A contradiction?"

Joe nodded his head; he had also noticed that.

"Perhaps the lack of aggression only applies to their kind," Alaine said.

"Or maybe," Joe said, "they've conquered spontaneous or unnecessary aggression but still acknowledge the need for defense. The *Intruders* destroyed their civilization, so they choose to strike back. We've done nothing to them, so they offer us friendship. That puts them ahead of us, in that respect." There were nods of general agreement. "My son tells me the information they gave us is not detrimental. It could be of great benefit, depending on how we use it. He believes it's given in good faith."

Alaine leaned forward. "They can do whatever they please anyway, so I think we should trust them. If it's all lies, we're screwed regardless, and if they're being honest, our acceptance may be to our benefit. I vote we say yes." Joe did not comment, again turning his attention to the girls.

"I can't see they're much different to us, as I've said,' Patricia said. "The physical form doesn't matter. The mentality's what's important. I haven't seen anything to indicate they're outright lying. Their virtual societies don't give any concern and look genuine, and the data about the other ship, the *Blackship*, has proven correct so far. Apart from her contradictory statements about aggression Io does not appear to have deceived us"

"As if we could tell," said Alaine.

"So I vote we accept their offer. And then start praying."

Joe turned his attention to Sarah. She simply said "Yes."

Ruth looked more concerned. "Has it occurred to you the big losers out of this could be us, and you in particular, Joe? Palfrey is suggesting *you* make this decision knowing Io will accept, and responsibility can be dumped on you if it goes pear-shaped. We aren't in any better position to decide than he is; he may be making you into a potential scapegoat."

Joe nodded. He did not believe Palfrey was setting him up, but knew that whatever the outcome, millions of people would label him a pariah. If he refused, people would blame him if the worst-case scenario came to bear. Should the second ship prove hostile there would be accusations he threw away humanity's only chance for protection. Corporations would label him a public disgrace for throwing away their shot at perceived technological advances beyond their wildest dreams.

If he agreed to the alien request, a massive faction would ignore the benefit of any protection the *Visitors* might provide. He would be blamed for allowing a war of vendetta in the Solar System as well as giving away its second biggest moon; no one would accept it was only for one short century.

Many would not accept the reality that the alien request was only a token act, and that it did not matter if he or anyone else accepted or rejected it.

Others would hail him as the hero who saved humanity, but either way, life would be difficult, assuming he survived this voyage.

If the *Minaret* failed to stop the *Blackship,* none of that mattered.

"Yes. I am aware."

"And you're good with it?"

"No, but I'm not about to make this decision based on my personal welfare. This is too important. So do I say yes, no, or sit by and let the governments of both planets screw us sideways?"

"Or the corporations that control them," Ruth said. "I vote yes."

"Let's think about what comes after," Joe said. "Suppose they *are* genuine and succeed in defending us. Do we trust them to build their factory, manufacture fuel and leave, or will they remain here?"

"That's a tough one," said Alaine. "I can't believe anyone would be happy staying on Titan any longer than necessary. The place makes an icebox look tropical."

"Your point is?"

"You've seen their original world. If they decide to stay, they will want to move to Earth or Mars. Their visit then becomes an invasion in its own right."

"I think they would have trouble fitting in," Patricia said. "Humans can be unbelievably xenophobic."

Joe nodded in agreement. He had given a great deal of thought already to this aspect of the problem and thought he had the beginnings of a solution.

It was clear Io could hear every spoken word uttered in this cabin, but he now had a better idea of her telepathic ability. She could project her thoughts into his mind, and receive thoughts directed at her by another telepath, but it appeared the ability went no further—she could not read his mind because he did not have the telepathic ability and could not project. For a two-way telepathic conversation, both parties had to possess the skills.

He was sure she could not read him at all and just wanted him to believe she could. The only clear evidence to support greater ability was her original face, but there was a picture of Helen on his cabin wall that could have been recorded. When he tried to communicate with her by thought alone she failed to respond until he repeated the request in words. *Perhaps not at all, then.*

"Io tells us they can create any kind of body they like," he said. "All they need is the base DNA, which they already have from us. It would be so easy and very logical for them to assume real human bodies. They would blend in, be adapted for the environment as we are, be able to use all our existing structures and so on. Io said our form was becoming popular with them."

"Many of them already looked like us in the simulations," Pat said.

"They would be invisible and medically undetectable in our society," Alaine added. "They would have the same resistances to our microfauna, diseases and so on, that we have, and the ability to use our medicines if theirs did not cover them. They could integrate without any problems—without our knowing it."

"Yes, there's that." Joe agreed, holding up a hand to stop the young officer from elaborating. "We would accept them, simply because we wouldn't be able to identify them as different to us. Biologically they'd be human, but mentally remain … whatever they are."

For a moment, he watched the reactions of his crew and wondered if it would be wiser to let them into his full thoughts on the matter. *Perhaps not now.*

"So be it. We agree that there's no real choice about Titan regardless. I'll advise Io we accept their help and agree to the use of the moon for one century."

After the others left, Joe mulled over his crewmembers' words.

You got all that, I hope, he thought.

* * *

Joe never ceased to be amazed when he set foot on the alien bridge. The sheer grandeur of the place was overwhelming, quite apart from the view on the panoramic screen. He walked a few paces across the mezzanine and stopped for a moment to drink in the intoxicating atmosphere. Shimmering ovoids hovered at several of the control consoles as they had since the transit of the Sun.

A meeting with Io was easy to arrange. Joe spoke a request in the privacy of his cabin and the acknowledgment appeared in his mind. He had begun by thinking the request, with no response. It made him more comfortable, confirming the conclusions he had already drawn.

He assumed the aliens had complete access to Chloe's memory banks, but a thorough examination of the hardware and software had failed to provide any clue as to how. The only anomalies found were inexplicable gaps in storage indicating recent data deletion. That discovery still puzzled him.

Io stood waiting by the railing. She was dressed in a flowing, white, Grecian-style toga. The outfit shook Joe a little: the only historical Greek references in Chloe's storage were books in his private library. Had they read those or were they accessing information direct from Earth or Mars? Perhaps it was a coincidence.

Do you approve?

"I do," he said as he walked up to the android, wondering if the question was a human-like reaction or an attempt at manipulation. Io turned and gazed towards the screens. The view ahead swarmed with a thousand small, insect-like spacecraft.

Your combined fleet has joined us. When you return to your vessel, advise them not to position themselves in front of or behind this ship. Our maneuvering may cause them harm.

"I was planning to recommend they drop back to intercept the *Blackship*. It would seem to be the greater threat."

Yes. I understand your people still view us as a danger, but you need not fear us. We have been completely open in our negotiations and have not attempted to deceive you in any way.

"I am yet to be convinced of that." Joe felt that at this stage it would serve his purpose better to be completely honest. Although he now doubted she could mind-read, he had no doubt she could easily interpret his emotions and mannerisms, and that this was the primary source of her uncanny knowledge.

Your fleet may remain with us if its commanders wish. Tell them no weapon they possess is of the least concern to the enemy vessel. They cannot hurt it any more than they can us.

"How do you know?"

We observed the Blackship in action when it attacked us. The Intruders *use a fleet of smaller attack craft for hostilities; your ships will be effective against them, but cannot breach the shields of the mother ship. Any attempt to do so would be a waste of your resources.*

"How do you intend to fight them? You haven't told us anything about your capability."

For a moment, Io gazed at Joe as if trying to make a decision, then directed her eyes back to the screens.

When the Blackship *entered orbit around our moon the* Intruders *began by professing peace. They offered trade and assistance. When they realized we were in the course of abandoning our system and attacked, they used the smaller craft, each carrying weapons that can destroy a city in a single blow. It took them only minutes to destroy our dome cities.*

"I don't understand why they did that." Joe interrupted. "It's illogical. You were no threat to them. They could have left and gone their way."

It is probable they destroyed us because they do not like or want competition, and thought we might follow them to this star, the next destination on their search.

"They were right."

Yes, but we did not intend to come here until they attacked us. Our enemy does not care that you are here. Your system is rich in resources, with several habitable planets and many moons, but you are a hindrance to their objectives.

"What do you expect them to do?"

They are aware of our presence by now and may or may not guess where we came from. They could not detect us during interstellar flight, but the presence of such a large and advanced vessel—equal to their own—in this system will give them pause. We believe they will either leave again or attack without warning.

"Where will you be?"

We must protect our ship. It has defenses but no primary assault weapons, so we will move it behind your moon out of the direct line of sight. Our presence there may cause them to be cautious.

"And then?"

The coming conflict is not of your creation, and we do not wish you to suffer because of our agenda. If you accept our offer of help, we will place a network of shield devices around your planet. At the first sign of attack, an impenetrable barrier will activate, a variant of the one in operation around this ship during the transit of your star. The Intruder's *weapons will not be able to penetrate it. There will be fatal damage to your space elevator and many of your satellites and space stations will be vulnerable, but the planet will be safe. Our defensive ships, the small craft you call* bayonets, *will be nearby. When the* Blackship *launches its fleet, we will respond.*

"The shield will protect Earth completely?"

As long as it remains undamaged. The generating devices will sit beneath the activated force field and are vulnerable only from below. We are aware several of the political powers on your world threaten to target anything in their skies. If a device is destroyed, there will be a gap until a replacement is in place. This represents a danger.

"Hmm. I can tell them not to attack, but I can't guarantee anything."

There is another concern, one that is only transient.

"Yes?"

The force field is reflective. Nothing, including light, can pass through it from outside. From Earth, the sky will be black, with no sun, moon or stars. All communication with your geosynchronous satellites will cease. The people of Earth will be unaware of what is taking place above the shield and will experience fear. In addition, the defense will remain active until the threat ends. Temperatures will drop and crops will be damaged if the battle continues more than a few days. Some people on Earth may view it as an assault in itself.

"Alright, accepted. Tell me why you are doing this. Why do you want to save us?"

For a moment, Io did not answer.

We choose to do so as an act of good faith. We have seen many members of our race destroyed and we do not wish the same to happen to you. Life is common in this galaxy, but technological intelligence is rare, and we believe it should be protected at all costs. For us, all intelligent species are precious; the Intruders *do not share this philosophy.*

Jo considered the response. The *Visitors* claimed altruism—it was exactly what he expected, but he was not sure he believed it. If the *Intruders* were indeed the enemy they did not share that conviction, nor had humanity throughout its history. Perhaps the lack of it was the galactic norm.

Do you agree then, to our offer?

"Perhaps. I expect you know I am authorized to represent my worlds in any dealings with you.

Of course.

"Then I have some questions. Please tell me the absolute truth; I think I will know whether you lie to me or not. I want to know whether, assuming you succeed in destroying the *Blackship*, you will leave or whether you intend to stay in the Solar System."

For a moment Io did not respond, turning away to look towards the main screen. Joe wondered if she was accessing some 'higher command' for instructions. A full minute later she turned back to look at him again.

Very well, Captain Joe Falcon. I will be truthful with you. We have no choice but to remain here. If we leave, our chances of survival are minimal.

Joe looked up in surprise.

The history I gave you at our first meeting is true in all respects but one. We came to this world because it is the only one with habitable planets within our reach.

This ship is not capable of easily making another voyage, as wondrous as it may seem to you. I appreciate it is ahead of your current scientific level and that you fear the technology it may carry, but in truth, it is barely capable of functioning. When we were attacked it was only partially complete and whilst able to fly, is incapable of another extended journey. Coming here was a risk with only a small chance of success.

It cannot reach our intended target system, even despite our lack of what we need to create a new colony. Nor can it reach the target worlds of our other colony ships. We lack fuel and most other resources, and many of the essentials needed to complete the vessel. Your star was the only option open to us.

It was our hope that if we offered to protect your worlds from the Intruders, *you would allow us to remain beyond our stated period of one hundred years. We have no choice but to stay. We are still deliberating how we may do this without disturbing your civilizations.*

It was as Joe suspected, an incredibly human response, but there was no way he could tell that to the people of Earth or Mars without mass panic.

"Your technology is well ahead of ours. How could we stop you?"

Your masses outnumber us greatly. Eventually, a war between us could only end in your favor.

"And if we did not want you to stay here?

We are not yet sure. We will perhaps attempt to complete our ship and refuel as advised, then return to our home star or try to reach a colony world. Despite your concerns, we are an honorable race.

Joe studied the android, and then slowly took in the amazing room in which they stood once again.

No, he thought. *I need you to stay here.*

"Thank you for being honest with me, Io. On behalf of humanity, I accept your assistance. I ask you to protect the planet Earth as best possible, and Mars if necessary. In return, you may have exclusive use of the moon Titan for a hundred Earth years. There are some conditions, however."

Yes?

"I've agreed to the deal, but I'm not naive. You don't need my permission nor anyone else's to do all this. You asked in good faith, hoping that would result in our voluntary agreement to your staying here, and you answered my questions honestly, I believe. I accept that. If your ship is incapable of another voyage, I understand your reticence in being open to begin with. I had already figured that with no knowledge of the fate of your other arks, it would be difficult finding them if they move on from their original target planets. A struggling colony might not welcome extra mouths to feed anyway."

You are afraid for your people. You fear the presence of a more advanced technology that could overwhelm your civilization.

"Yes. Humans are inherently xenophobic. It's doubtful we could cope if you stayed without consideration and negotiation. There would be war."

Io turned and gazed at Joe with soft, searching eyes. *Perhaps that is true, but your species appears remarkably resilient. You have not yet learned how to look after your worlds, and the planet Earth is rapidly approaching the point where it can no longer support life. We have no choice but to ask to remain, and we can help you change that.*

"How?"

We know many things you are yet to discover. You are a wise man, Joseph Falcon, and have your people's interest much at heart.

For the next few minutes, Io outlined possible future courses of action for humanity and her people together. Some of the aliens wanted to stay—the android was no longer even attempting to deny that.

From her words, Joe realized Io's people were afraid of humans. Their fear was not for themselves, but of the potential for harm to their other colonies if man, in his current juvenile state, was to spread to the stars. Humans advanced quickly but had not yet learned the arts of cooperation and peaceful coexistence.

Joe had already decided he needed these strangers to stay. In his mind lay the germ of an idea that would guarantee the future of the human species as long as people remained unaware of the truth. With Io's admission, he believed his idea would work and humanity would not suffer. The greatest perceived threat came from this ship and not from the aliens themselves, but that was a detail easily dealt with.

"I may have a solution to your dilemma," he said. "You and I need to discuss the future in more detail. It would be best if the governments of Earth and Mars were not aware of any of this; they must believe you will leave. In the meantime, I will pass on all you have said about the shield. Hopefully, the dissenting nations will leave it alone."

Very well. We will proceed, and you and I will talk again on this matter.

Io stepped forward and held out her hand. In it was another data cube, which she placed in Joe's outstretched palm.

This device contains images extracted from this vessel's maintenance records. I believe it will be useful to you.

Joe looked down at the small object. Here, perhaps, was an answer to something that still troubled him deeply.

Chapter 25

"I HAD A FEELING it was wise to put faith in you, Joe," Adam Palfrey said. "The board is in a complete state of confusion. Most of the members agree your course of action is the only one possible, but some maintain you exceeded your authority. They're whining about the little detail that you gave the *Visitors* a verbal lease on Titan. I don't think they appreciate our lack of options.

"I appreciate your confusion as to why any government would not accept the *Visitor's* offer when it is obvious we have no real say in the matter, but the only explanation I can give is that we are dealing with individuals. Every voting member of each government fears that if he or she decides one way or the other, it will come back on them personally, so they end up choosing the safe course, to say no or withhold their decision. Democracy has its advantages but fails when each representative puts their own interest first.

"We've released all the information you were given by Io to the authorities on both planets. Several Earth governments have again stated they'll shoot down anything appearing in their skies, so we'll wait and pray. The UEC has told them they do so at their peril—very diplomatic. The good news is North America and the Rus and Chinese Federations have agreed not to mobilize.

"If what you say is correct, the shield devices will be in low orbit and so will cause problems. Agricultural industries are being urged to prepare for a possible food shortage if this business goes on for too long. Farmers have been told to harvest any crops they can, even if not fully developed. We're also evacuating the geosynchronous space stations to either Earth or the Luna naval base. The low-orbit ones should be okay, but we'll empty them as well, just to be sure. We'll make sure no one is on the elevator when the time comes, but we're not sure what else we can do about that.

"Regarding you, well, it's difficult. Many people are hailing you as a hero; others are branding you the traitor who gave away Titan. Yes, stupid I know, but the moon isn't the issue. The idea of an alien civilization sharing this system with us for the next hundred years, or maybe forever, scares the hell out of people."

If only you knew, Joe thought.

"I hate to say this but you may never be able to return to Earth. The vast majority love you but there are plenty of crazies out to shoot you on sight. A permanent armed guard is stationed outside your son's property now and steps are in train to protect your daughter and other relatives. We'll look into the families of your crew as well, just in case. I'm sorry, Joe. I never intended to set you up like this.

"The attitude on Mars is different; since Mars has no sole rights over Titan, we're remaining neutral. The *Blackship* is following the same course as the *Minaret* and will rendezvous with Earth first. The Pollies are hoping the *Visitors* will deal with them before they get a chance to move their attention to us. So you're still welcome here for now.

"I must tell you this may be our last conversation. The likelihood is I'll be removed from this position; something to do with things I said in one of my earlier messages, I suspect. A few people around here are after my head.

"That's all for now. I guess you know information you send us is being released to the public, and not by us. We're not sure how, but we have a massive leak somewhere down here. Out for now." With a grin, Adam waved goodbye and reached over to turn off the link.

Joe leaned back in his seat. "Off please, Chloe." It appeared Palfrey was going to back him up, but the reactions of the populace were as he expected. He gave a loud sigh, closed his eyes and tried to shut the thoughts out.

* * *

"Chloe, tell me about the gaps in your memory."

"I have located thirteen instances of data erasure, Captain. Information has been wiped, and the deletion identifier removed."

"Any idea when, or by whom?"

"No Captain. All time and terminal data relating to the deletions have been erased."

"What about my private backup?" During fit-out Joe had insisted a new backup storage be installed, unknown to the crew and accessible only by him.

"That record has also been deleted, Captain. The gaps match those in my primary memory and backup."

“All right. Place a record of your search in my private files.”

“Yes, Captain. I have detected one other instance of deletion, made before we returned to Kepler after the encounter with the meteor swarm.”

Joe sat up, his attention caught once again. “My backup?”

“It is intact, Captain. Shall I restore it to your directory?”

“Yes, thank you.”

Joe turned his attention back to the cube. Like the ones Io gave him before, it was an ordinary data device. Joe rolled the small block between his fingers, looking for some small thing betraying it as an alien artifact. About two centimeters on a side, it looked like any of the billions found in human society.

It fitted the socket on his desk reader easily. Despite pressure from Sarah, he had put off looking at it until now, more concerned with what he had taken upon himself to do, and also from fear of what he might find.

“Chloe, can you bring the contents up please?”

“Yes, Captain. The device contains a single video. Do you wish to review?”

“Yes, thank you.”

The image was a view of the level beneath the airfield bay, taken from a viewpoint high above the walkways. A small figure in a sortie outfit appeared in the distance, drawing nearer along the molecular walkway.

The suit showed a band of green around the waist, identifying the wearer as Terry Caldwell; his was the only green ID on *Butterball.* As the figure drew closer, Terry's face became clear, until he vanished below the bottom of the screen.

The next sequence was from floor level and looked towards the entrance to the skywalk elevator. Terry was approaching the ramp when he stopped and turned his back to the camera. Ten meters beyond him, another figure stepped from behind one of the many service modules.

A cold shiver ran down Joe's spine. The new arrival was human, also wearing a sortie suit. A bright orange identification band was visible. He braced himself and raised a bulky device to point at Terry. A shimmering beam lashed out, and the engineer fell to the floor.

The video ended.

Joe shivered, raising a hand to wipe the sweat from his brow.

Terry Caldwell was murdered by one of his own.

For almost half an hour Joe sat glued to his seat, unprepared to accept the truth. Only two of the ship's suits had orange ID bars. Both owners were similar in stature, but the unknown figure wore a helmet. It could be either individual or any other crew member in a borrowed suit. Joe could not believe the people in whom he placed so much trust included a killer.

"Chloe, erase all references to this from your memory banks. No trace must remain. Relay nothing of this to any of the ship's crew without my direct orders. Am I clear?"

"Yes, Captain."

Joe sighed and slipped the cube into a drawer, which he locked. Nobody could know about this yet. It would be pointless without more facts to back himself up. That meant more investigations.

*　*　*

"My captain, you need to come to drum two at once. We have trouble" Joe recognized the tone. Sam Bright's voice sounded strained, and more than urgent.

The metallic stench of blood assaulted Joe as he dropped to the floor of the secondary wheel. Around the corridor, Sam waved him towards the common bathroom.

Chaos filled the small chamber. Inside the doorway, a pool of dark, sticky liquid flowed from beneath the partition of the toilet compartment. The door leaned against a wall, knocked clean from its hinges.

"What the hell's going on in here?" Joe demanded, trying to squeeze his way into the room. A blood-smeared Carl peered around the cubicle entrance. "It's Pete."

From inside the cubicle, Maeve shoved Carl aside so she could see the captain. "It's Peter. He's cut his wrists. Dead, I think."

Joe leaned in for a better view. Stanley's body lay curled up in the tiny compartment, his head and one wrist propped on the rim of the toilet. Blood was everywhere, running in thick pools on the floor, splashed on the walls and hanging in congealed, icicle-like formations over the ablutions unit, inside and out.

Joe knew his medical officer was right; nobody could lose that much blood and live.

"Help me pull him out of here and into my infirmary," Maeve said. "Don't stand around. Arses and elbows … now."

Half an hour later, Joe sat motionless in a corner and waited while Maeve fussed over the body of their late companion. She had cut away Stanley's overalls, and cleaned as much of the blood as she could. Joe hated the odor; he had become too familiar with it during the Resources War but he never got used to it. Once smelt, the metallic tang was never forgotten, an assault to the nostrils that stayed with one forever. He watched Maeve trying hard to hold back tears as she went about her duties. She had liked Peter.

"Clean cuts," she murmured. "Both wrists, neat and quick. For sure, he was aware of what he was doing. I can't do anything more. Dead when Carl called me, I expect."

"Carl found him?"

"Yes. He went into the washroom and saw blood on the floor. He smashed the compartment door open."

At that moment, Sam entered the infirmary and held up a small, bloody object. "Scalpel," he said.

"Where did he find that?" Joe asked.

"Here," Maeve said. "I don't lock the doors—you know that. A few things have gone astray lately."

"Things … such as?"

"Small stuff. Headache capsules, sedatives, bandaids, the obvious things. And this scalpel, it would seem."

"What sort of sedatives?"

"A bottle of Aprylone. I noticed it missing this morning. It's not so strange on a ship full of insomniacs. Silly, he only had to ask."

"He?"

"Chloe says there's a high level of it in Peter's blood. He must have needed a massive dose to be able to go through with this."

Chloe's voice interrupted the somber mood in the room. "Captain, there is a message for you."

"Who from, Chloe?"

"The message is from Peter Stanley, Captain."

*   *   *

Joe slumped into his desk chair as Sarah took a seat on the bunk. He could not believe the message came from a dead man, but Chloe did not lie—did not understand the concept.

"When was it sent, Chloe? And where from?"

"The message was entered at the workstation in Peter Stanley's cabin three hours and twenty minutes ago, set with a delivery time of three hours." Joe leaned forward as text began to scroll.

Captain. By now, I am dead. At least I hope so, for everyone's sake. An explanation is in order, so here you go. I intend to kill myself because I am guilty of the worst of crimes. I can no longer live with that.

The Visitors gave you a data cube that I am guessing shows Terry's death; I was in the common room when you mentioned it to Sarah. By now, you will have figured I am the one who attempted … no, who did kill Terry. He knew something about me I thought buried long ago.

When I was younger and a lot stupider, I did a stint in the Mars Space Force. Terry was there as well—we served on the same ship.

I was rather keen on a young female crewmember. One day we had an argument and I hit her in a fit of temper. She fell back and struck her head on a bulkhead frame. The impact killed her. I panicked, put her body in an airlock and blew it out into space. I snuck back to my bunk and said nothing.

The girl was reported missing. Foul play was suspected but no trace of a body was found. The log said the airlock had been cycled but they were never able to pin it on me. I was very thorough in covering my tracks.

Terry should have been on duty in the airlock bay that day. He snuck away for a few minutes for some reason, and I took advantage of that. During the investigation, his absence surfaced. At first, they tried to blame the disappearance on him, but without any evidence, they settled for dismissing him from the service for dereliction of duty. As soon as we returned from the tour, he was dismissed. I always thought he suspected me since he had seen me with the girl before.

I figured the authorities would work it out in time, and they did. A month later the charges against Terry were expunged, and a warrant was issued for my arrest. I was on leave and word got to me through a friend before they could find me. I disappeared and set out to make a new life for myself. I changed my face and voice, got new identification on the black market, retrained as a geologist, and went out to the belt. I figured it to be the least likely place I would be found.

Despite his exoneration, I gather the Navy never re-instated Terry. They do not do things like that; it would be an admission of error. Imagine my surprise when I got all the way out to Kepler, signed on with you and discovered him in the crew. He did not recognize me with my new identity.

Something gave me away—I do not know what. When I realized he would report to you, I panicked and decided to kill him. I succeeded.

He died and my secret was safe. I did not bargain on the Visitors being able to bring him back to life. It did not occur to me the area under the landing bay would be under surveillance. Stupid, for an ex-navy man.

Now that he is back and you are aware of what I did, you would have no choice but to hand me over to the authorities when we go home. I cannot let that happen. I have lived with what I did for too long and it has haunted me every minute. So there it is. Death is easy, prison is not. Thanks for the job, Captain. Sorry, I let you down."

"You're kidding me, right," said Sarah. "He kills Terry because he thinks he can pin him as a murderer, and commits hari-kari when he realizes he's failed? Give me a break."

Joe turned and looked at Sarah. True, there was no place to run on *Butterball*, but the suicide note itself was troubling. Something did not gel. Why type it? Why not the video recorder? Why had Terry not said anything? Joe decided to call him in and let him read the message.

The young engineer shrugged his shoulders. "I'm sorry boss. Don't remember. The whole thing about being shot … it's gone."

"You were drummed out of the Space Force?"

"Yeah. I didn't do it though, Cap."

"Yes, I accept that. It was before I hired you. How long?"

"About a month. I had nowhere to go, so I got a job in a workshop. A good engineer can always find work. Then you found me."

"You didn't recognize Stanley when he joined the crew?"

"Pete? No."

"And later?"

"Sorry, Boss. It's a blank."

Joe sighed. "Alright, we'll leave it for now." Terry had been shot in the chest, and though the *Visitors* had somehow restored him to life, the severe trauma should not have resulted in memory loss. There were, however, marks on his head. Did the aliens delete the event from his knowledge for his own well-being?

Terry nodded as he stood and left the room, closing the door behind him. Joe turned his attention back to Sarah.

"Well, what do you think?"

"It's so … bizarre. That suicide note is … it sounds fictional. You think all this is legit?"

"I don't know. The surveillance footage does show someone shooting Terry, and the suit is one of the away team's, but anyone on this ship could have taken it."

"Almost. Wally or Maeve wouldn't fit in the team's suits. Too small."

"We can discount you and me. Also Alaine and Sam; they were in the *bayonet* hangers and we had radio contact with them the whole time."

"What about Carl?"

"Unlikely. He was right behind us when we ran down to Terry."

"So, we don't accept the suicide note as gospel?" Sarah asked.

"We don't, but the crew will want to know what happened, so we'll stick with it for now. I plan to do a little more digging."

After Sarah had left, Joe tapped the com-patch. "Maeve?"

"Yes, Captain?"

"Question. If a heavily sedated man slashed a wrist, would he then have enough strength or control in that wrist to do as neat a job on the other wrist?"

"Doubtful, Captain. I wouldn't think so, but you never know."

"Thank you, Maeve."

Joe re-read the note. "Chloe, send an encrypted message to my son."

"Yes, Captain."

"Jake, can you please use your expertise to dig up any information you can find on my geologist, Peter Stanley? His education, qualifications and so on, and anything about his early life. Also, the same for Harry Chan, Carl Geddes, Sam Bright and Marius Pine. I'm sorry, but can you please let me know as soon as possible? This is very important."

"Message sent, Captain."

"Thank you, Chloe." *Why do I keep thanking a machine?*

Chapter 26

THE *BLACKSHIP* BORE little resemblance to the *Minaret*. A massive hemisphere, the rounded dome faced forward with a tapered spine extending at least thirty kilometers from the flatter aft side. The matt-black surface absorbed light, giving the gargantuan vessel a sinister appearance as it glided through space.

Like the first ship, its hull was smooth and unbroken with no openings or ports, no antennae, no trace of weaponry or any kind of protrusion. Only the lighter scars of small meteor impacts blemished the shell, indicating it had been in transit for a long time.

Hsiang Li wondered aloud where the ship might have come from, considering it must have been out there for so long. The ensign assigned to him, who stood nearby and hung on his every word, shook her head dumbly.

The Commodore smiled to himself. That young woman was anything but dumb; the posting as his personal aid meant she topped her class. Nevertheless, he delighted in giving her a hard time; his reputation demanded it. The ensign took it in good faith. Doubtless, she could see right through him.

"I suspect the spine means she has a similar drive system to that of our supposed friends," he said. "Damn it, I need a coffee."

"Sir?"

"Coffee. Coff-eeee."

"Oh, yes sir. Right away, sir." The smile as she dashed in the direction of the bridge galley betrayed her enthusiasm as the aid of a man nothing short of a legend on two worlds.

Hsiang made a mental note to ease off on her. She had put up with him without complaint for several months now and without realizing, had earned from him more respect than most.

Let us hope, my dear, you survive this business … that we all do.

The combined fleets of humanity now operated as a single entity under the joint command of himself and Earth Space Force Admiral Albert Breen, and had rendezvoused with the *Blackship* hours earlier. Over one thousand ships now paced the dark goliath, keeping close but not interfering.

Hsiang's flagship opened communications immediately after taking position. The usual attempts at identification began the show, with the standard mathematical sequences, and greetings in various human languages.

"Any reply yet?"

The first officer turned in his seat. "You're not going to believe this sir, but they are responding in English. Shall I put it up?"

"Why not," Hsiang said, skepticism on his face. "Any visuals?"

"Yes, sir." The officer nodded absently as his fingers imitated a concert pianist on the communications console. Within seconds a face appeared on the main bridge screen, an upper-body view of a middle-aged man. The image spoke calmly.

"…come in peace. I repeat, we are an envoy to your world and come in peace."

Debatable, Hsiang thought. *If the* Visitors *are telling us the truth, you're no envoy at all, and you come for war. And there is no way you can be human.*

"Safe escort is requested to your third planet so we may begin a dialogue for information exchange and future trade. Please confirm your fleet will not attack. This is a peaceful vessel."

Lies?

"Send a reply," Hsiang said. "Confirm that our ships will not interact unless provoked. Advise we will escort them to a safe orbit around Venus. Negotiations will be conducted from there. Let's test them."

"Yes, sir." The officer rushed to transmit the response. For a moment, the attention of the alien on the screen appeared diverted, as if being addressed from one side. As the *Intruder* turned his head, the face flickered and then re-stabilized.

"Sir, would you like to bet that image is a fake? Looks computer generated to me."

"I agree. Our Envoy wants to hide his real appearance. Not a good sign, I think."

Suddenly the alien spoke again. "We are unable to comply with your request. This vessel is not as maneuverable as your small ships, and we are on a set course for your third world. We have no option but to enter orbit there."

"Is that true? Hsiang asked, leaning towards his chief navigation officer.

"Unlikely sir. Observations confirm the ship could probably enter Venus orbit if necessary. They must think we're stupid. The computer analysis also confirms the individual is a generated image. They don't want us to see what they look like."

"Very well. We can't stop them, so advise we'll escort them. Orders to all ships—encrypted—to go to red alert, all battle stations manned and active. This fellow is playing us for fools. I can feel it in my bones."

"And your bones are never wrong," the first officer said. "They haven't failed us yet."

* * *

"Chloe, where's Carl Geddes right now?"

"He is in the lower cargo module, Captain."

"What's he doing there?"

"I do not know, Captain. I cannot read minds; I am a computer. I can identify images on my sensors, but at the moment he is not where he can be observed."

Joe screwed up his eyes. Sometimes the damned AI behaved like a real person. He pushed his chair back and headed for the secondary accommodation drum. The second wheel almost matched the first in layout, excepting that the space devoted to the common room in the first, here served as a metallurgy laboratory.

"Chloe, tell me when Carl leaves the cargo flat."

"Yes, Captain."

Joe stopped at Peter Stanley's cabin door and entered. He wanted to go through Pete's gear, hoping to find answers to some of the questions that needed answering, and did not want the mineralogist annoying him whilst doing so.

Since the geologist's death, Geddes had hovered like a botfly whenever the subject of his ex-sidekick arose. He clung to Maeve during her investigations, insisted on helping seal the body inside a freezer chamber for storage and always seemed to be present when conversation turned to the suicide.

It was possibly protectiveness, or perhaps something else altogether. The two men were the closest of friends, constantly in each other's company. Perhaps Carl was lonely, having never become close to any other crew member.

Joe had received Jake's response to his recent request. The findings did not sit easily in his mind. Peter's history prior to enrolment at the University of Mars proved easy to track. Birth certificate? Employment history? Yes, of course. Like most citizens, he served in the Navy but completed his term with an honorable discharge.

Records could be faked as the suicide note indicated, but they contained events Joe did not expect in a forgery, such as childhood sporting achievements and a brief marriage never mentioned to anyone.

Peter had always been reticent in discussing his personal life. Joe noticed this when he first employed him but assumed information was withheld for reasons of privacy. The Belt, filled with men and women hiding from something or someone, worked that way. Pete's qualifications looked legitimate at the time and with nobody else available, Joe gave him a trial run for one excursion. His work proved exemplary, though he did not mix with anyone other than Carl.

The cubicle was typical of the crew spaces, about six square meters with upper and lower berths, one in use and one not, a desk, chair and computer station, and a screen on the wall. At the back corner, a basin and lockers completed the layout.

Joe slumped into the chair and looked around. The space of someone deceased had a strange feeling about it, like the husk of something once alive but now empty once life had departed. Quiet, lonely and somehow depressing, not in a physical way but in the sense the entity giving it purpose was absent. Joe wondered how you rebuild the story of a man from the things left behind. He turned to the desk.

"Chloe, give me Peter's personal directory please."

"I cannot divulge that, Captain."

"Shit." *Remind me to reprogram you.* The requirement was a security and privacy measure; he did not want crewmembers digging into each other's private data files. Joe also insisted on the installation of a 'back door' in case of emergencies. He reached out to the keyboard and punched in a twelve-digit code.

"Override accepted."

The desk monitor flickered and Pete's home screen appeared. There was not a lot to see: a library of book files—normal with most members of the crew—several directories filled with mineralogical data and analysis programs, and a private diary.

"Chloe, I want every file here transferred to a separate directory. Captain's access only. Clear this space once completed."

"Yes, Captain. Transfer initiated."

"And open the locker for me please."

Without hesitation, a gentle click indicated Chloe's compliance and the door to Peter Stanley's private cabinet swung open. Each crewmember had a secure space, but in every case the override code would bypass the electronic locks, accessing anywhere on the ship should the need arise. Despite the security measures, there were no secrets from Joe on this ship.

The contents were typical: clothes, personal items, private documents, a wad of genuine paper money, and several books—real ones, with hard covers and bindings. Joe never considered Peter a reader, but this was a part of the man to which he could relate.

He pushed the books aside in search of anything he had overlooked. Nothing. As he withdrew, his fingers felt something gritty. A small scattering of dust and grains lay in the back corner. With care not to spill it, he swept the discovery into one hand and held it out to the light. It glittered.

"I'll be a…" The look and color of the substance in his palm were beyond mistake.

* * *

The arrival of the *Minaret* at Earth was more subdued than anyone expected. The vast bulk of the combined fleet was absent, several days away keeping pace with the second alien ship. Only a handful of capital ships escorted the gleaming white goliath as it approached the planet.

In the minds of many, doubt existed as to who was a friend and who was not, but the general unspoken consensus was now that Io's people were allies and the *Blackship* an enemy.

Like a giant torch in the night sky, the ship inserted itself into orbit thirty-eight thousand kilometers above the planet's surface. It had flipped tail over nose again during the approach, heralding its arrival with multiple firings of its drive, the extraordinary bright-blue blaze streaming away along the tail spine. The flare of incandescence filled Earth's sky, visible even in daylight. From the night side, it was spectacular, drowning out the full moon and bringing light to the darkness.

To the common people, most of whom were ignorant of the details, the sight brought both awe and fear. Some heralded it as a second coming, a sign from God or the Devil. All through the orbital insertion, crowds lined the sidewalks and watched, church attendance rocketing to a level not seen since the Resources War.

For those who knew what was occurring—a small percentage thanks to the misinformation spread by the Global Net—the arrival marked the dawn of a new era. Regardless of the outcome, academics and scientists recognized the civilization of humankind would never be the same again.

If Io was to be believed, a war was coming, one in which the citizens of Earth would be mere bystanders or the ultimate prize. If they did not survive, the future of humanity might rest with Mars or be nonexistent. Survival itself would bring change beyond recognition, considering the presence of the *Minaret.*

* * *

"How many of you honestly think we could take any other course?" Palfrey asked, fixing each of the committee members in turn with his stare. "Come on, I'm open to suggestions."

Alf Brewer sighed and held both hands up in surrender. "Nobody is saying we could do otherwise, Adam. I think we all agree we cannot stop them. I for one support Captain Falcon's decision—it shows strength and decisiveness as well as a willingness to accept these aliens at face value. At least this way they are committed to telling us what their plans are before they act, assuming they honor the deal. You've all read Falcon's last report?" A general nod of confirmation came from around the room.

As the oldest member of the group and the one with the least personal agenda, Brewer had in the last few weeks come to represent the voice of reason. Most of the individuals at the table valued his opinion. The attention was quite flattering; people usually dismissed him as nothing more than an eccentric, old professor.

"Titan for one hundred years," Julianne Devereaux said. "I suppose I have no problem with that, considering we can't use the damn place. Any guesses on their intentions there, Alfred?"

"Well yes. The robot…"

"Android," Adam corrected.

"Android, yes. The android stated they intend to build a factory of some sort to manufacture fuel for their ship."

"And we accept that?"

“It doesn't matter a toss if we do or don't,” the Professor replied. “It does sound reasonable though. Imagine the amount that ship must require. It *could* take a century—we don't know.”

For a moment no one spoke. Everyone in the room knew the old man was right.

Adam was the first to speak. “We’re bystanders in this business, so let's try to get through it with as little damage as possible. What can we say about the shield?”

Carmichael Page lifted his chin from his chest and looked at Palfrey. In the last few days, he had become somewhat subdued, and much more conciliatory.

“According to the data Falcon gave us,” he said, “the force field will consist of thousands of generators in a grid pattern around the Earth. When they are activated—apparently not until the *Blackship* makes an aggressive move—the devices will link fields to enclose the planet in a sphere reflecting everything that hits it, be it a high energy beam, a bomb or missile, or even light.”

“That's going to be a problem for Earth,” Adam said. “If light is reflected, there will be no sunlight while the shield is on.”

“Earth's citizens have been warned,” Page said. “People are preparing…”

Professor Brewer laughed. “Is that what you call it? They're panicking over there. Supermarkets are running out of stock, many businesses have stockpiled and are capitalizing or not distributing until they can demand the highest prices. The situation is getting worse every minute.”

“What do you expect me to…?”

"I don't think social issues are our problem," Adam said. "Several nations are still threatening to use missiles against the shield. The UEC warned them if they do they may be placing the Earth in serious jeopardy."

"Nothing we can do about it," Page replied. "They are sovereign nations. They can screw themselves sideways if they wish, and we have little power to stop them doing the same to everyone else on the planet without starting a war."

"What I would like to know," said Devereaux, "is why nobody is acting to protect Mars?"

"You and your wise and learned colleagues in government did not respond to the *Visitors'* offer," The old professor said, glaring at the woman who had asked the question. "What did you expect?"

Palfrey slumped back in his chair and shook his head. As a minister, he advised against that course, but the majority of the members decided otherwise. He felt ashamed and disgusted with the body of which he had once been so proud to be a part.

"I've talked to Falcon about that," he said. "He suspects the *Blackship* is not yet interested in Mars considering Earth has more to offer. If the shield denies them access they might move on to us and the *Visitors* may come to our defense."

"What about Falcon?" Rob Billington had remained silent until now, but the Captain's future troubled him.

Adam stared into the distance for a moment before replying. "It's not going to be easy for him. He'll need to remain on Mars, I think. Less chance there of someone taking pot-shots at him."

As Adam spoke, a knock sounded at the door and a young officer entered, walking straight to Gordon Styles, the Martian Navy representative. He placed a document in front of his superior, turned and left without a word. Styles glanced at the paper then looked at his colleagues.

"You will all be interested to know the *Minaret* has entered a polar orbit around the Earth, as expected."

Adam stood and faced the table. At this time there was little more to be said. From here on, everything was up to the governments of Earth, and the *Visitors*.

"And so," he said, "the game begins."

Chapter 27

"CAPTAIN? Can you come up? You need to see this."

Joe could hear the excitement in Sarah's voice. Outside his cabin, he glanced through the nearest window and stopped dead in his tracks. The landing bay swarmed with objects, whirling in a celestial dance as the *Butterball's* drum rotated.

Sarah looked up as he arrived on the bridge. "Those are the machines we found in the upper hangers. You never did take a look at them."

Joe took his seat and looked at the monitor. The view was clearer here with the rotation effect of the wheel removed. Outside, lines of small objects floated in ranks across the bay.

"The upper row of hanger doors opened about ten minutes ago, and these things poured out," Sarah said. "Must be thousands of them."

Each was about fifteen meters in length, spindle-shaped with a long pointed tail. At what appeared to be the front end, a short neck above a flat, transverse disk ended with a small sphere. The machines had no visible means of propulsion but they moved with purpose.

"Where are they going?"

"They're leaving by the entry tunnels," Sarah said. "The exits appear to be open again."

"Do we know what they are?"

"I would guess they're to create the shield Io promised," Alaine replied as he floated onto the bridge. "This is going to be an upset."

Joe nodded in agreement. The devices resembled weapons, and if the *Visitors* positioned them above the Earth, their appearance was bound to cause panic.

They flowed in ranks to the nearest of the two exit tunnels and over the next few hours spread around the curvature of the planet to position themselves at an altitude of fifteen hundred kilometers in a spherical grid pattern. Once in place, they remained motionless. Via live images sent from the ships outside, Joe and the crew followed the process from the common room.

"Look where they've stopped," Marius Pine, the chief engineer remarked.

"Does it make a difference?" Ruth asked.

"It will when they turn them on. It's below geosynchronous orbit, so most communications on Earth will fail. I seem to recall Io said nothing could penetrate the shield, and most communications satellites are above it. No radio, television, web, navigation, nothing."

"Everyone will know what caused it," Alaine said. "There are enough landlines down there to spread the word, and the low orbit stations and satellites will still be functional. People will panic if the media take the wrong view.

"Io did warn us," Joe said.

Sarah smiled, then sat bolt upright and frowned, as a sudden thought registered in her mind. "The tunnel is open; we can get out." A general murmur of agreement came from throughout the room.

"That may not be the best move at the moment," Joe said. "Home is Mars, and we're in orbit above Earth. We aren't so popular down there at present, so we're better off where we are."

"Especially if there's going to be a war," Alaine added. "Look out there."

In the landing bay, the devices had come and gone, and lines of the small *bayonet* fighting ships now streamed towards the exits. Joe watched the procession for a moment, and then retreated to his cabin, waving Sarah and Alaine to follow.

* * *

"Io, are you here?"

Yes, Captain Joseph Falcon. Can I be of assistance? As had now become commonplace, the voice appeared to float on the air, its source impossible to locate.

"Can you fill us in on what's happening outside?"

We are proceeding as previously advised. The shield is deployed and we are now positioning our robotic fighters. They will take up station away from the planet, but close enough to respond at need.

"What happens then?"

As advised, we will move behind your moon following the disembarkation of the fighting units.

"And then?"

The Blackship *is only days away and is undoubtedly aware of our presence by now. They will suspect we represent a threat. We hope this will cause them to hesitate before attempting an assault on your planet, and focus on us instead.*

"Your shield will create panic and a massive degree of hardship on Earth. Can't it be set at a higher altitude so the Earth's communications remain unaffected?"

We regret the interference with Earth's satellites, but it is unavoidable. The shield generators have a limited range of operation, and we have set them as high as possible to protect your low-orbit stations. Increasing the sphere of protection further would require more units than we have. Some must be kept in reserve, so the current deployment is the best possible.

"Captain," Chloe's voice sounded over the intercom. "I have a signal from Earth. Are you free to take it?"

"One minute Chloe. Thank you, Io. Can you keep us informed please?"

Of course, Captain Joe Falcon.

Joe nodded. "On my screen, Chloe."

The face belonged to a man he knew well by reputation, the eminent Waleed Sarraf, head of the United Earth Council. One look at the man's face betrayed his state of mind: perspiration pearled on his skin, his eyes wide with agitation.

"Falcon? What the hell's going on?"

"Hello, Mister President. Are you not aware of the defense plan?"

"Damn it man, don't screw with me. There are thousands of spaceships up there, and they're all aimed at the surface. The people are in a flat panic, as are the governments."

"Understood, sir. Those are not ships. They're the generators to create a force field around the Earth for your protection. The pointy ends aren't weapons, and you're in no danger unless someone tries to damage them."

For a moment, Sarraf glared at him. "How do you expect me to convince the world of that? The things look dangerous. Several nations are threatening to knock them down…"

"…and your job is to persuade them otherwise. Those generators will be your first line of defense if the *Blackship* attacks."

Sarraf sighed and leaned back in his chair. "Yes, all right, fine. We've begun steps in that direction."

"Then why are we talking, sir?"

The President did not reply for a moment, and then shook his head. "I'm sorry, I needed to be certain."

"Accepted. I have to warn you the shield will cut most satellite communications and all sunlight. You should ground all aircraft and keep sea traffic in dock. No system using our geosynchronous satellites will work."

"The planes will be easy, ships not so much. My concern is the panic in the cities."

"Tell everyone to stay home and prepare for an indefinite period of darkness, cold temperatures and isolation."

"You're not the first to say that. Adam Palfrey said the same."

"Is he still in charge of the committee?"

"Yes. Sanity has prevailed there at least."

Good, Joe thought. "There's not much else I can tell you, Mister President."

"I understand, Captain Falcon. My apologies. I suppose I needed to vent my frustrations. I will be standing down if we get through this, I expect."

"Your call, sir."

"Have you seen the size of that ship? How do you destroy something so big?

Joe shook his head. "I have no idea. Smash it with an asteroid, maybe? The *Minaret* does not appear to have heavy weapons, so I don't know what they intend to do."

Sarraf blinked myopically. "One thing more, Captain. Do you trust these *Visitors*, this 'Io'?"

"I'm not sure, sir."

* * *

Bad idea, coming here now, Jake Falcon thought. The city seemed a stranger to him, the mood shifting after the shield generators appeared overhead.

Explanations of the exact purpose of the devices were widely broadcast, but not everyone was reacting favorably. Official reports pointed out they could not—would not—attack Earth. Public decrees commanded the populace to stay home until further notice, and prepare for a week or two of uncertainty.

Almost continuous public media broadcasts crowded the airwaves, making life difficult for all official transmissions.

Some networks held the view the machines did not, according to the *Visitors*, represent a threat to humanity but at this stage, nobody should accept that explanation at face value. So far, Jake thought, there was no reason not to, but the press chose to follow the negative view regardless.

In several nations, the governments had shut down the media to minimize panic, and the same would soon happen in Australia with the possible exception of government-controlled stations. They alone tried to stick to the facts.

Despite requests for calm and responsible behavior, trouble haunted the streets and moving around was becoming dangerous. A minority stood apart as always and chose to believe the conspiracy theorists and panic merchants who swarmed the Global Net. Many believed doomsday was a hop-and-skip away and decided they could do what they liked without fear of punishment by a society that would soon no longer exist.

Crime had increased at an exponential rate. House invasion and theft skyrocketed and, of more concern, so did crimes of assault; the criminal elements in the streets thought nothing of harming another to get what they wanted. Violence was on the rise and no sane person would leave his or her home alone.

So what does that say about me? Jake walked along the footpath, glad he had not allowed Akira to come with him. His beloved remained safe on the mountain, behind the electric fence.

When first erected, the security enclosure raised the ire of the local council, who demanded its removal. A compromise saw the power disconnected but the structure itself remaining. Jake quietly re-connected it when this business began, with no reaction except from the military authorities now guarding his gates.

Jake's appearance had changed; he now sported a beard and his hair was darker. He did not want to think about what would happen if anyone recognized him. Most of Earth's citizens either lauded his father as a savior or accepted he was caught by forces beyond his control, but again the vocal minority posed a tangible threat. The media had no recent photos of Jake so for now, anonymity allowed him to move about unrecognized.

The streets were empty of traffic. The *Blackship* would enter orbit tomorrow, and with the city streets all but deserted almost no vehicles and few people could be seen.

The vehicle Jake used to get here sat in a private garage at the top of Spring Hill, one of the inner suburbs of the city. The owners of the house were close friends and would be returning to Maleny with him later in the afternoon. It was a more than half-hour walk to Jake's office but a safer option than bringing the car into the center.

His decision to come in one last time was driven by the need to rescue his friends and, depending on the situation when he got there, to retrieve private data from the business where he was currently working. Those data cubes now rested in the satchel slung over his shoulder.

For the first time in his life, he carried an automatic pistol. Guns were an abomination and until a few weeks ago he had not owned one; now he never went anywhere without it, despite its possession having been illegal in Australia for centuries.

Only once so far had he needed to use it, when a trio of unfriendly-looking men blocked the footpath. His heart thumped as he pulled back the lapel of his coat enough to show the pistol in its holster.

The change of expression on his assaulters' faces was dramatic; they crossed to the far side of the road and walked away. Typical, Jake thought: brave when confronting a helpless person but lacking the guts to stand their ground against someone prepared to fight back.

On the way back towards Spring Hill, he noticed rubbish blowing around the streets as the evening sea breeze funneled along the skyscraper canyons. Street cleaners had not been here for days, the drivers following the advice of the authorities to batten down.

The majority of roller doors in the malls were locked. A few shops had opened to fill the demand from many thousands of individuals who remained in the business center. Those shops that still traded had an armed guard inside.

Jake lifted his eyes to the high-rises. Several of the near ones contained residential accommodation and as the sun drew down to the horizon and darkness encroached in the city canyons, lights were starting to appear.

He pulled his coat closer against the cool wind and increased his pace. This was Australia, one of the safest and most peaceful nations on the planet. In some parts of the Middle East, Africa, the Indian sub-continent and South America, society had collapsed even further.

Some countries had already instigated curfews or declared national emergencies, as protestors rampaged through the streets driven by fear and ignorance. At least here, some sense of order still prevailed. Some things like lights and water still functioned but the trains, buses and many other services did not.

Jake crossed the road and began to climb the hill toward his vehicle. By the time the second ship arrived, he planned to be safe inside his private enclave.

* * *

The face on the monitors was the same as when the *Blackship* first made contact, an image Commodore Hsiang Li now knew to be false.

The huge, upholstery-tack-shaped alien vessel entered orbit, taking up the identical position occupied by the *Minaret* prior to its moving behind the Moon.

The combined fleets of humanity waited nearby, ready to react at a second's notice. A state of emergency was in place, removing the governments from the equation and handing control to the commanders, Hsiang and Breen. Both agreed the planetary authorities would do more harm than good, based on past performance.

"I greet you once again on behalf of all aboard this vessel." The image said, this time in flawless Mandarin, the most common language on Earth. It did not surprise Hsiang that the *Intruders* also possessed an advanced understanding of several major human languages.

He had always assumed communication would be an insurmountable barrier between humans and aliens, but such was not the case. The assumption was based on humanity's current abilities in that arena, clearly less advanced than that of the aliens.

"You are welcome here," he replied.

"Your war fleet is now positioned in near space. Please state its intentions."

"It is part of the planetary defenses of this world. It is no threat to you if you come in peace."

"There is a second body of vessels located between this planet and its moon, and an interstellar craft behind that body. Please state their intentions."

"I do not speak for the starship. It is a visitor to this system like yourself and has come in peace. It withdrew on your approach to avoid conflict of interests. The second fleet you refer to belongs to that ship, and not us. I expect they have deployed as a precaution. You are an unknown factor to both them and us."

Li could not help but notice the face remained impassive and unchanged, reinforcing the fact it was a computer generation. For a moment, the image was silent, while the entity behind it no doubt discussed the situation with others of its kind.

"Your fleet is in attack formation."

"It will remain so until we are certain of your intention."

"You have no reason to fear us."

Li turned to Admiral Breen on the secondary screen and raised an eyebrow, seeking confirmation for the approach upon which they had agreed in advance. Without hesitation, his co-commander nodded an affirmative. Li turned back to the alien image.

"We requested a rendezvous around our second planet," the Admiral said. "You advised this was not possible but our experts believe that not to be the case based on observations of your vessel. You have not shown us your actual appearance—the image I am addressing is false. You have stated you are friends but have so far told us nothing about either yourselves or your true intentions."

"Our true appearance would be undesirable to you. We do not wish it to influence negotiations."

"Show it to me now, please. I will not be offended."

The alien hesitated before replying. "The presence of your war fleet and that of the starship behind your moon make it impossible for us to accept your intentions towards us are peaceful. We request your fleet stand down and the vessel behind your moon withdraw its fleet of smaller vessels and leave the vicinity of this planet. We cannot negotiate until this is done."

"I have no control over that starship. I have no doubt they are listening to this exchange and will act accordingly if they wish to do so. Please show us your true appearance." *This is not going well,* Hsiang thought.

Without warning, the monitor went dark.

"So end-eth the lesson," he said to his associate.

Breen nodded again. "It would appear the *Visitors'* advice has been confirmed. At least they've been open with us; this lot has so far been anything but."

No further communications were forthcoming.

* * *

Jake strolled amongst the macadamia-nut trees at the front of his property, looking beyond the fence. An army truck was nearby but the occupants were not in sight. These soldiers, unlike the police, were friendly and insisted they were there for his safety.

All for little old me?

Jake smiled and turned back towards the house. He strolled through the Macadamia trees and looked up, catching the Sun's warmth on his face. In a split second, darkness descended like a black shroud.

Shit, he thought. *The shield is active. The Invader is attacking. It's begun.*

* * *

Breen leaned forward into the camera. "Here we go. The bastards fired something at the planet, right above India. The force field came on and deflected whatever it was."

"I saw it," Hsiang replied. "A ball of… something… plasma? You realize we're now cut off from Earth, my friend?"

"So is the enemy, old buddy."

Chapter 28

ON THE GROUND, all was darkness. Without the Sun, Moon or stars, the planet drowned in blackness absolute. In time, streetlights flickered on to ease the enforced night, creating scattered mosaics of light through the cities and towns.

Akira entered the room, her forehead furrowed with concern.

"We'll cope fine," Jake reassured her. "Not all our grid power is solar; with luck, the fusion, wind and hydro can keep up. There are bound to be blackouts though. The emergency batteries in the basement can run this whole place for a fair while."

"The gauge in the kitchen says we're at maximum capacity," Akira said. "We'll be fine if the mains electricity goes; gas for cooking, and plenty of tank water. It will get cold though."

Jake glanced at the television and the now unbroken news broadcasts. The networks were still functioning, somehow. All the news was to do with Earth—nobody knew what was happening above the shield.

The day following Jake's return with his friends the police and military had declared a national curfew, but with insufficient men to enforce it beyond the city centers many people were unprepared, panicking when deprived of daylight.

A travel ban was in force with citizens ordered to remain in their homes. Again, many ignored the warnings. At many smaller airfields, a number of private planes crashed while trying to land in darkness without normal electronic navigation. With the satellite-based systems gone, only radar guidance and emergency lighting along the landing strips prevented the casualty list from climbing higher. Thankfully, the major airlines had toed the official line and grounded all planes as soon as the *Blackship* entered orbit.

Most problems involved private individuals who chose to carry on as if everything was normal. Solar generation accounted for over half of the grid supply so when power blackouts did occur those persons were the ones stranded away from home, lost somewhere or trapped in elevators. Jake shook his head; some people never thought ahead.

In the city, the lights hide the sky, but here on the mountain, the absence of streetlights near the house allowed a better view. Nothing. Only pitch black disturbed by a handful of burning specks, navigation lights marking the low orbit space stations and larger satellites.

Jake wondered what was happening up there. The darkness proved the planet was under attack, but no sign of a battle, or anything else, was visible.

* * *

Thousands of kilometers above the mirror-like shield, the *Blackship* rotated until the top of its massive, curved dome pointed towards the now invisible Earth.

From previously unseen primary armaments, radiant, fiery balls streamed down to impact the shield, spreading like liquid fire across the mirror-like surface to no effect.

Farther out towards the moon, the *Visitors' bayonets* moved forward as a single body, streaking towards the enemy. From several points around the rim of the *Blackship's* hull, long lines of small alien fighters streamed into space, rushing to position themselves between the mother ship and the approaching human and *Visitor* fleets.

Swarms of deadly-looking machines spread across the shield, looking for a way through or a weak point to attack the generators. Small groups opened attacks on the now deserted high-space facilities, focusing on the largest, the now deserted Perry Station.

Within seconds of the force field activation the asteroid anchor at the top of Earth's only space elevator, released from its leash as the cable severed, drifted away on a course to places unknown with the larger portion of the cable trailing behind.

The combined fleet paused several thousand kilometers out from Earth as Hsiang Li watched the battle unfold. He glanced around his bridge, where everyone was on high alert as on each of the multitude of ships under his command. He noticed his young aide shiver.

I'm sorry, my dear, he thought. *You didn't expect this on your first posting, I know.*

He and Breen had anticipated this scenario and decided on a course of action well in advance. Io had advised the fleet's armaments would be ineffective against the shield-protected *Blackship*, and the first attack confirmed she was correct. The alien's primary weapons were unexpected, having not been used during the attack on the *Visitors*' moon. It was reasonable to assume the *Intruders* had adequate defenses against any technology similar or inferior to their own.

The combined fleet also possessed plasma weapons, but nothing compared with those of its opponent. The smaller alien fighters could not carry generators the size of the ones presumably powering the mother ship's guns and defenses, so they were vulnerable. Admirals Hsiang and Breen fully intended to address that weakness.

The ships of humanity withdrew as a single body, backing away from the planet and drawing a sizeable number of *Blackship* fighters with them. *Bayonets* swarmed in towards the shield, each one selecting a fighter and hounding its every move.

* * *

Joe stood on the *Visitors*' bridge with Io and most of the members of the *Butterball's* crew.

"How many?"

There are one thousand and seven ships in your fleet. Our unmanned 'bayonets' as you call them, number three thousand six hundred. The enemy's fighters are five thousand, one hundred and twenty-three.

The Earth was hidden behind the reflective surface of the force field. Besides the swarms of smaller craft only a mottled, grey ball—a reflection of the moon in the shield—

and the *Blackship* were visible. Everywhere, space flickered with lights darting in all directions as cannons, lasers and plasma weapons sparked in a grand concerto of cosmic fireworks. Everything was deathly quiet.

Off to one side of the main screen, Joe saw the combined fleet spread, allowing each of the capital ships a clear line of fire at the oncoming enemy.

Humanity had yet to invent anything equal to the alien defenses, but its warships had meter-thick, diamond shells capable of taking an unbelievable beating before failure. Every one of the fleet's ships bristled with offensive devices; against the mother ship they were ineffective, but the smaller fighters were a very different matter.

Whenever an alien fighter came within range, plasma bombs poured from a thousand ports, and every time one of them touched a target it gripped, spreading like something alive until the hapless craft began to disintegrate under the intense heat.

Most of Hsiang's ships carried rail guns as part of their offensive capability. The Commodore gambled on the alien fighters being too small to carry hull plating heavy enough to resist the phenomenal force of those projectiles, and prayed their shields were optimized to repel only energy weapons.

Swarms of shells and small, spherical mines streamed out as the enemy closed. Armed to detonate on contact, the devices contained small tactical nuclear charges, any one of which could destroy something larger and more heavily armored than the small alien ships.

Missiles designed to burn through a half meter of hardened alloy slammed into the oncoming enemy craft, penetrating easily through the thinner hull plating. Due to the high speed and constant weaving of the targets, few projectiles met with success, but each that did reduced the attackers by one, and the tough ships of humanity plugged away relentlessly.

The fleet also suffered losses. Every few minutes a stupendous explosion spread like a radiant fireball as the attacker's weapons found a path to the fusion reactor or armory of yet another of man's best.

Far away beyond the shoulder of the planet, the Perry Station, the most magnificent of all structures in Earth orbit, exploded in an expanding ball of flame and glass, steel and plastic shards. Joe forced himself to watch, his hands trembling as his madly beating heart sent blood pounding through his ears.

He raised a hand and wiped a film of perspiration from his forehead, aware of his fellow crewmembers reacting in similar ways. Ruth Carvalio turned her back on the screen and held her hands over her eyes. She was in tears once again; she had never witnessed a space conflict before or been trained in what to expect, unlike most of the *Butterball's* crew.

Io stood beside Joe, her eyes fixed on the battle.

"It doesn't look like we are doing too well. What if you can't beat them?"

We will not be defeated, Captain Joseph Falcon. We are losing many fighting ships, as are you, but the enemy's losses are greater. Your fleet is putting up a much stronger defense than we did when our home was attacked.

"So what happens now? We bash it out until no one is left?"

You are not as helpless as we first assumed. With luck, the fleets will hold their own and drive the enemy back. They will survive unless the mother ship brings its armament to bear. That is our main concern.

"So how do we prevent that? Your fleet may be robots, but our ships carry thousands of lives."

This vessel is moving position to become visible. The Intruders *do not yet know we are lacking major defensive weapons and will move to oppose us. We will lure it away from your world.*

"To where?"

To your fourth planet, Mars.

Joe felt his heart sink.

* * *

On Earth, nothing of the space battle was visible. At Cape Town, in the Democratic Republic of South Africa, the artificial night shattered as a quartet of missiles lifted from their pads, streaking skyward toward the generators.

None of them found their mark, but an exact hit was unnecessary. Three of the warheads exploded against the underside of the shield, their hellish nuclear energies deflected without harm. The fourth detonated meters from a generator and knocked it from position, the force from the blast sufficient to damage the device and send it plunging to the planet surface, leaving a hexagonal opening in the defensive network.

One of several hundred backup generators stationed below the main array streaked to close the breach. The changeover took less than a minute, enough time for a single enemy fighter to plunge through and dive into the atmosphere before leveling out on a northeastern course.

In the Mozambique Channel, a naval fleet under the command of the United Earth Council responded. The Republic, like many other nations, had been warned any attack on the devices would be met with retaliation, which now came in the form of missiles streaking towards the base from which the launch took place.

On the fleet flagship, the lone alien fighter's movements were tracked and aircraft launched. Four planes streaked southwest at several times the speed of sound, heading to intercept the *intruder* before it reached the nearest major center, the mega-metropolis of Johannesburg.

Far away to the northeast, missiles lifted from the Manas Missile Base in Kyrgyzstan, and within minutes another opening appeared in the defenses. Two alien fighters snuck through, one turned south toward the Indian Sub-Continent, the other flying east towards Mongolian China. A solitary *bayonet* streaked through in the enemy's wake before the gap in the shield could be closed.

Lieutenant Frederick Holt peered through the canopy of his aircraft at the darkness outside. He hated the situation. Instrument navigation was the usual procedure in night conditions, but with all communications blocked by the shield, that was lost.

In the most advanced, satellite-guided fighter plane on Earth, only the compass and onboard radar still worked properly, with a little help from satellites and space stations still functional in low Earth orbit. Efficient as those were, it was as good as flying blind compared to the lost systems.

Holt's destination was Johannesburg, the most likely target of the first enemy fighter. Of four aircraft, his would be the first to arrive. Two more followed close behind, the fourth, flown by a less experienced pilot, further back. Holt prayed the South Africans were in the air and that in the confusion they would target the alien, and not him or his fellow pilots.

How do you fight something you can't see? Holt glanced at his radar. Johannesburg was only a few hundred miles ahead, and the *Intruder* fighter was there somewhere.

Without warning, the night lit with a hemispherical blaze of blinding light. For a frozen moment in time, a glowing dome hung like a half bubble on the horizon, marking the position where the great city stood.

Holt had seen nuclear detonations, but nothing like this. No ball of radiant energy appeared, and no column of dark smoke rose in the sky to spread like a mushroom. His aircraft did not register any force expanding outwards as the glow faded. After the fire died, the darkness returned, and there was nothing.

The console in front of Holt began to beep. The alien fighter was dead ahead, and only minutes away.

"Target has changed course—coming straight at you," a voice announced over the radio. "You got it, Lieutenant?"

"Roger. Firing now. Fox three."

From three aircraft, active radar-guided missiles streaked to intercept the closing craft. All exploded harmlessly in the night sky. The enemy easily deflected the missiles; it would not be simple to destroy. As Holt concentrated on lining up for a second attempt, something shot by on the port side.

"It's through," one of the other pilots announced. "It got past us."

Several kilometers behind, the young rookie pilot spotted a bright pinpoint of light streaking towards him through the darkness. Determined not to let it through, he threw his aircraft into a bank, crossing the path of the oncoming fighter. A split second later the two machines collided, exploding on impact.

"It's gone," the flight commander's voice announced. "We got him guys."

"You're joking, right? It can't be so simple."

"That was Jimmy. It didn't do anything to avoid him."

For a moment, Holt said nothing, then, "Jim. He did it deliberately."

"Yeah," another voice replied. "It's done. It's over now."

Holt sighed. "Not quite. Twenty million people lived in that city."

* * *

Jake Falcon remained glued to the video feed. So far, the power still worked, and he intended to keep watching as long as possible. On the coffee table a tablet streamed news from the still-functional Global Net.

It had taken only minutes for bright individuals to realize microwave signals bounced off the underside of the shield without being absorbed, and the world began using technologies considered obsolete for more than a century.

With this, and the help of the remaining low orbit systems, fiber-optic and undersea cable links, news propagated around the globe feeding the hungry beasts of the networks. The lead stories on most stations—those still operating—were the events in South America, South Africa and Pakistan.

Disaster struck Ecuador from an unexpected source. Nobody believed the elevator, set on the coast at the westernmost point of the nation, would be fatally damaged, but like a razor, the force field sliced through the thick, woven nano-tube cable at an altitude of one thousand, five hundred kilometers.

The lower section of the structure buckled. Driven by the rotation of the Earth it collapsed into the Pacific Ocean along a line due west towards the Galapagos Islands.

With an impact of billions of tonnes, the cut end of the massive cable slammed down across the archipelago. The shock wave shook the islands, shattering the slopes of Isabella's active Wolf Volcano with a blast like a nuclear bomb, destroying the island's natural environment beyond recognition.

The cable hit the surface of the ocean with sufficient force to displace billions of cubic meters of water. The resultant tidal wave took only minutes to demolish the small seaside communities of the islands and the western coast of South America.

The tsunami spread in an ever-expanding ring of destruction. Hours would pass before it reached Australia, by which time it would most likely have dissipated, but many other places on the vast ocean were in danger. To hundreds of small island nations and the coastal cities of many larger countries, it would bring devastation as it progressed. The greatest toll was yet to be paid.

A few ships were still at sea, feeling their way to safe harbor with whatever navigation systems they still had.

Procedures were in place to intercept and guide any nearing shore, and all hoped those caught further out would survive with luck. Jake uttered a silent prayer for any small boats still on the dark Pacific in the path of the silently approaching wall of water.

Of more concern was word starting to filter in from Africa. The news was sketchy; following the South African attack on the shield the metropolis of Johannesburg had vanished in a single blast before UEC aircraft brought down the alien fighter causing the destruction. The responsible base in the republic no longer existed, destroyed by retaliation from the UEC Indian Ocean Fleet.

In the Middle East, the military in Kyrgyzstan had, like the Venezuelans, ignored the warnings of the UEC and allowed two more of the *Blackship's* fighters inside.

Flying south over the Himalayas, the second enemy fighter pounced on the first major target in its path. In Pakistan, a blackened wasteland now covered the site of the ancient city of Lahore.

Observed by local sources, the alien fighter then turned towards Ludhiana, in India, but was intercepted and destroyed by a *bayonet* that followed through the gap in the shield. The *Visitors'* craft then turned back over the mountains to Tibet and the third, remaining enemy attacker.

The latest news placed the last *Intruder* over the Korean Peninsula, heading east. Nobody knew for sure, but word from an unknown source advised the Chinese had scrambled and dozens of aircraft were in pursuit. Jake prayed China's modern air force could stop the fighter before it caused any more damage.

"They're going to blame Dad for all this," he muttered.

The electricity cut out. The lights faded, only to spring back as the emergency batteries took over. The computer and the video feed remained off, indicating the blackout was widespread.

"It looks like the whole region is down," said Akira, sitting beside Jake. She reached out and squeezed his hand. "No more news for a while. I suppose we have to hope sanity prevails," she said.

Chapter 29

THE LARGEST VESSEL of the Mars fleet took center stage on the *Minaret's* screen. The most powerful of the combined human flotilla, it was the personal flagship of Fleet Admiral Hsiang Li.

Dozens of the small *Intruder* fighters weaved like flies around a corpse, firing at the larger vessel in a concerted wave of harassment. Every time an enemy blast hit the diamond-plated hull, the shell grew thinner but withstood the assault.

Joe watched intently, praying the Admiral would survive. The attackers were concentrating on a few small areas towards the stern of their target, attempting to take out the engines or reactor.

They were not having everything their own way. Hsiang fought with every resource at his disposal, his ship the source of a torrent of laser beams, plasma streams, missiles, projectiles and mines. Every few minutes something found a target, and another firefly winked in a brief flash of annihilation.

The screen blazed with a ball of radiant light. When the view cleared, the flagship was gone, in its place an expanding cloud of debris. Constant battering from the enemy had cut through the armor and found the ship's fusion reactor. The explosion destroyed the vessel along with any alien craft within twenty kilometers.

Joe slumped on one of the benches of the mezzanine bridge, his legs refusing to support his weight. Commodore Hsiang was a man he admired, revered by all in the space services of two worlds, and a prime mover in the formation of the massed fleet.

For a brief moment, an image flashed through Joe's mind, of the fresh-faced junior officer who always stood behind Hsiang when he was communicating from his bridge. She was one of many such young souls on board—all gone now.

Another massive battlewagon, that of Albert Breen, moved to take the post position. The future of humanity continued to play out, but somehow Joe could not watch. He shook his head and turned away; it no longer felt important.

Despite all his years in the services he realized he had changed. He felt responsible, and unrealistically blamed himself for the undoubted suffering out there, regardless of the possible alternate consequences.

There was open warfare in Earth's near space, the elevator was gone and its anchor station lost, the geosynchronous stations were a memory, and hundreds of humanity's ships were damaged or gone.

A voice in his mind told him not to blame himself; all of this would have happened the same way without his acceptance of the *Visitors'* offering. They would have proceeded with their plans regardless, possibly without the shield. That would have been worse.

Joe noticed his companions had all left the bridge, except only Alaine Parish who sat nearby, his attention glued to the battle. Io turned towards Joe.

You should not blame yourself for this.

Damn it, how do you know that? Joe wondered.

Many of your ships have been lost, but the Intruder's *losses are greater. Your flagship destroyed almost two hundred of the enemy before failing.*

"We're winning?"

In the battle against the fighters, yes, we will be victorious. The problem of the mother ship remains.

"How do we deal with it? You said you were going to try to lure it away to Mars. That planet is undefended."

Yes, but it is our hope it will not need to be. The population of your fourth planet is only a small fraction of the number of your species; it was essential to put all our defenses at the service of the greater number—your primary world.

"What about Mars?"

We will do our best to prevent the destruction of your civilization there. Nevertheless, it is necessary to draw the threat away from this world and our plan of operation makes it necessary to lure it to Mars. Please remain here long enough to set your mind at ease.

The screen divided to show several different views. The center section focused on the *Blackship* while to either side were other scenes. In one corner could be seen the Luna base, located on the surface of the moon facing the planet.

Joe was relieved as he noted the complex had suffered little damage. With the body of the *Minaret's bayonet* fleet positioned between it and the alien star-ship only a few fighters got through, dismissed by massive ground-based cannon and rail-gun batteries.

The moon base was a legacy from the Resources War when Mars carried the conflict back to Earth. *Thank God,* Joe thought. Man was not totally helpless and there would at least be a place of refuge for the remains of the combined fleet, if any, when this was all over.

On another section of the screen a dozen ships, shaped like *bayonets* but many times larger, formed a ring around the nose of the *Minaret* and then began a barrage of fire greater than anything yet seen bar the *Blackship's* main armaments. Streaming across hundreds of thousands of kilometers of space, the plasma eventually hit, splashing across the enemy's shield with minimal effect.

"Those are yours? They aren't doing much damage."

That is not our intention. The Intruders *will by now realize they cannot attack the Earth, and are losing the fleet battle. They will also now suspect we have no ship's armaments, due to our use of these smaller ships. We hope they will follow and attempt to destroy us with their primary weapons, intending to re-focus their efforts on your worlds later.*

"What if they shoot back?"

This ship may have no offensive weapons, but it is well-defended. The same force field you saw deployed during the star transit shields the hull. It is a more sophisticated version of the Earth shield, impenetrable but allowing us the ability to see out. The Blackship *cannot breach it.*

"What about those ships?" Joe pointed to the screen and the ring of *super-bayonets* at the *Minaret's* nose.

When the Blackship *follows us, they will move to the stern and fire on it as it pursues. Whilst we are under acceleration, our drive is not fully protected by the shield and is our most vulnerable point; they will protect us.*

"And when we get to Mars?"

We will destroy the enemy.

"How?" Joe felt he was missing something. To him, it looked like a potential stalemate with neither ship able to defeat the other.

We will use the method you yourself suggested. You must wait, and have patience, Joseph Falcon.

* * *

There was a deathly silence in the common room. Most of the crew were present, some watching the video on the end wall, others staring at their knees. Sarah glanced up as the Captain entered, with Alaine seconds behind him.

"We lost Hsiang," Joe said.

"Yes, we know." Sarah raised a finger towards the screen. The images were a repeat of those on the *Minaret's* bridge, less intimidating due to the smaller size. "We have our external feed back again. Thanks to Io, I guess."

The mood in the room was heavy, oppressive. Everyone remained silent, overwhelmed by the events outside. Only Sam Bright, standing from habit in the galley area, looked like he had something to say, until finally he shook his head and turned away. He had the look of a man bottling something inside.

Ruth Carvalio sat alone, her face a mask of frozen indifference. For her the devastation was absolute; Earth was her home more than any other member of the group besides Sam. There was no doubt the people down there were suffering and would continue to do so. Sarah, having put aside her animosity towards the older woman, sat with her attempting to provide support, but failing.

Three enemy fighters had broken through because of stupidity by rogue nations. Nobody on *Butterball* knew exactly what destruction they caused, or whether Earth's forces had succeeded in bringing them down.

With nothing relevant to say, Joe slumped into the nearest seat and joined his companions in their vigil.

* * *

The *Minaret* moved to a position between the battle and the Luna base. Three hundred and fifty thousand kilometers away, the enemy vessel began to move forward. As it drew closer, a hellish conflagration lashed out across the vast gulf and pounded at the *Minaret's* defenses, to no avail.

The second the attack faded, the *super-bayonets* fired again. Massive balls of dense plasma surged at the oncoming enemy, hidden within its own shield. The midnight black hemisphere deflected everything that came its way. With both ships untouchable, the conflict between them was a game of bluff, with neither able to gain the advantage.

It was clear the *Intruders* now believed the greater threat came not from Earth or the combined fleet of humanity, but from the starship confronting them. They may not have known their opponent's origin but directed their attention against it nonetheless, leaving their fighters to determine their own fate. Joe wondered if the ease with which they abandoned their own meant they had far more in reserve.

The *Minaret's* engines fired and it slid away towards the distant point of light marking Mars's current position in space, the *Blackship* in pursuit. From his command chair, Admiral Breen observed the goliath's departure on his monitors. For now, the *Visitors'* strategy was working. His ship numbers were down to a few more than four hundred, the devastating losses greater than any other space conflict in human history.

The enemy suffered more. It was apparent they had not expected the shield or the presence of the *Minaret*. The small alien fighters were not well designed for battle against large warships, even ones less advanced, their intended purpose possibly to strike and destroy ground targets on the worlds they attacked.

The *Intruders* had underestimated the abilities of humankind. Forced to deal with the bigger, more primitive but still deadly human ships, the attackers had suffered significant losses, and would continue to do so in the absence of the mother ship that had abandoned them.

Many of the fighters attacking the Earth shield had now retreated and turned their attention to the moon. It was a mistake; the Luna base was the most heavily defended site in the human domain. The massed rail guns and plasma cannons of the base created a hemispherical zone of destruction, assuring the annihilation of any craft attempting to penetrate.

Breen breathed a sigh of relief. With the *Blackship* gone, the fleet would win this battle, given time. Then he would turn the surviving ships towards Mars and advance at maximum speed. He prayed there would be something left to defend when he arrived.

* * *

"Ok, Sam. Spill it. What's on your mind?"

Sam Bright shuffled in his seat. He rarely entered Joe's cabin, but after the captain left the common room he followed, and stood at the open door building up the courage to come in.

"Uh, I am not quite sure how I am to say this. I … I am letting you down very bad."

"You mean the laser cutters in the entry tunnels?"

Sam's mouth dropped, his eyes wide with bewilderment. "How…?"

"It wasn't hard to work out. There are only a couple of people on this ship with the knowledge to be able to disable those lasers without it being obvious. Why did you do it?"

"I am so sorry, my captain. It is worse than that."

Joe sat back in his chair and waited for Sam to continue. The man took out a square of cloth and wiped perspiration from his brow to disguise the fact he was almost at the point of breakdown.

"While we are refitting at Kepler, I take a day to go into the *Core*. I work on the wiring of the new engines, and I need a break. I am in the concourse when two men ask to speak with me."

Joe heaved a deep sigh. "Let me guess. They were representatives of some group on Earth?"

"Yes. I am not sure, but I think they are with the military. They never clarify exactly."

"What did they want?"

"They ask … no, they *tell* me that as a citizen of Earth, it is my duty to support my home world, and I am to act as their agent. They order me to provide reports on what we are doing, and to sabotage the mission if possible."

"You agreed?"

"They give me no choice. They say if I do what they ask, then if I get back from this trip I am wealthy for all of my life and will never be wanting for anything again."

"And if you refused?"

"I will be vilified, and my family shamed. My Ellie will be thrown out of her church and our children, they will be barred from entering university, or anything else. They will be publically shamed—social outcasts. I cannot do that to them."

"So you've been reporting our activities? How could you do that without Chloe knowing about it?"

"I use your security access. I am sorry."

"My override? How can you know that?"

"I help re-program the computers for the retrofit. You are employing me as electrical engineer and cook, but I spend years coding when I am younger; I still can do this. I find the code for your override—it takes me not long to figure out what it is."

"So you…?"

"Every time I send a report, I am using the backdoor to erase the entry from Chloe's log and backup. Only from a query within thirty seconds could someone ever know. I also remove all traces of my sabotage of the cutters."

Suddenly the gaps in Chloe's data storage made sense. "Why did you do that?"

"I am ordered to do whatever I can to stop us from entering the *Minaret*."

Joe stared up at the ceiling for a moment. Sam had been one of his most loyal crewmembers from the day of his hiring, but Joe always knew that despite the man's rhetoric he was devoted foremost to his family.

Thanks to the inquiries Jake made on his behalf, Joe knew Sam's real motivation for spending his life in the asteroid belt was money. In an overpopulated world, life on Earth was difficult at best, and Sam's prospecting activity was all that supported his wife and children.

He expected the engineer had done the things to which he admitted for lack of choice, and from love. That, Joe could accept, but it was still a betrayal. He doubted some of the other crew would be as understanding.

"With the cutters disabled an armed force is having no trouble boarding and taking over from us," Sam said. "They promise no one is to be harmed, and we will be safely removed and refueled for the trip home. I do not know the *Visitors* shut down the entry tunnels."

"Okay, so you sabotaged the lasers, and you sent a few messages. Are you still doing it?"

"No. The fleets leave us; by the time they come back, they are together, so it does not matter anymore, I think. I stop."

For a moment, Joe watched the other man. Sam shifted in his chair and ran fingers through his hair, staring at the floor, clearly having trouble looking the Captain in the eyes.

"Anything else?"

"Yes, my captain."

Joe raised an open hand towards his crewmember, offering an invitation to continue.

"You must come with me," Sam said. "There is something I show you."

Several minutes later, the two men floated into the engineering module of *Butterball.* The Captain followed Sam through a wall hatch into the cable duct where the electrics ran between the reactor and the remainder of the ship.

"This is the primary loom to the control deck," Sam explained. Joe eased forward into the confined space. Around the indicated bundle of wires was a small plastic frame."

"It is an explosive charge. Enough to cut the supply clean, without any damage to the ship structure. The second it go off, Chloe is losing all control. Also, the engines are shutting down, leaving us to drift in space."

"You planned to use this?"

"They tell me to set it off the minute it is obvious we will be able to make rendezvous with the *Minaret.* When that time comes, I … cannot make myself do it."

"What about your family?"

"I report the device is a malfunction. I am thinking if I put the blame back on them I get away with it."

"Why didn't you do it?"

For a moment, Sam looked at the captain, tears welling from his eyes.

"The crew are my family too."

Joe decided to keep the matter to himself for now. "Alright. We'll keep this between ourselves. You better get back to your work." Sam nodded dumbly and turned back towards the spine corridor.

Joe knew Sam's wife and children would still be at risk. An hour later, he sent a message to Adam Palfrey asking that he arrange extra protection for them. He was confident the man would be able to do that, assuming Earth survived the current conflict.

Chapter 30

ALAINE WAVED HIS arms. "Can you believe it? Earth to Mars in five days."

Joe tapped away at the screen of his computer station. "Hardly surprises me, considering all the other mindboggling things we've seen."

Sixty-three hours after departure from the moon, more than half the distance to the red planet was behind them. The alien vessel was traveling at over three times the speed it had been at when the *Butterball* intercepted.

"It proves my theory," Alaine continued. "This ship is powered by anti-matter."

"Hasn't Io admitted that?"

"Yes, of course, but it's still nice to have it confirmed. To get to Mars in five days we must be averaging around three hundred and thirty kilometers per second. Our ion and fusion drives just can't do it, but in theory, antimatter engines could reach speeds a hundred times that. There can't be any other answer. That's why it'll take a century to create their fuel. Antimatter is hard to make, right? We can't work out how to build an antimatter engine without unacceptable radiation, but they must have. I need to look into this more." The younger man stood and made for the door, a wide grin on his face.

The Captain nodded as Alaine left the cabin. He was finally happy he had something to work on, and that was fine by Joe if it kept him busy.

There was one thing that could be said about the *Minaret*—it managed to withhold all its secrets. The crew of the *Butterball* had seen many wondrous things: the molecular doorways, the artificial gravity; the walkways, elevators and bubble trains. The list was endless, but not once had they found a clue as to how those things worked.

Alaine Parish was frustrated with the lack of discovery, and if this small revelation made him mope less, it was good. Joe turned his attention back to the computer.

The latest transmission from Admiral Breen advised the Earth shield was off. Between them, the combined fleets cleaned up the enemy fighters in under forty-eight hours, and the force field switched off. Joe wondered if it was controlled from here, across eighty million kilometers of space.

After the battle, the survivors of the fleet had landed at the Luna base, itself barely touched by the conflict. Less than a hundred ships survived, none of them unscathed. The losses were devastating; there would be no support for Mars from that quarter.

The *bayonets*, also few in number, descended to a nearby crater and a force dome appeared over them, cutting off all access. The *Visitors* did not want anyone investigating their ships, which no longer had the ability to reach their mother ship unassisted.

Word was, a single *bayonet* that reached the surface of Earth in pursuit of the alien fighters had landed on a point high in the Himalayan Mountains, and upon the shield dropping, had lifted off again and rejoined its fellows on the moon. The shield generators remained in position, high above a stricken world.

Upon leaving, the *Minaret* had accelerated constantly, its blue torch streaming in its wake larger and stronger than ever before. Not far behind, the *Blackship's* massive dome plowed on in pursuit, also under full power.

Courtesy of its alien hosts, *Butterball* had an outside video feed again. The super-*bayonets* once stationed around the nose were now at the stern, facing aft and pacing the mother ship in reverse. At irregular intervals, Joe saw them fire with no effect, but now better understood their intentions.

The object was not to harm the *Blackship*—they could not do that anyway—but to get it away from Earth. The enemy was behaving as predicted; the *Visitors* wanted it to follow, but Joe still had no idea what they intended to do then.

Io had been adamant the enemy would be destroyed at Mars.

We will use the method you yourself suggested. You must have patience, Joseph Falcon.

What that meant, Joe could not guess. He could not think of anything he had said, and Io remained unresponsive to further questioning. The red world was two days away and he reconciled himself to the wait, hoping whatever the *Visitors* planned would involve minimal harm to his adopted home.

The covered surface cities were vulnerable; a single shot at the domes could have dire consequences for every inhabitant, as had been proven long ago by the war with Earth. Already, citizens were being evacuated to the underground habitats as a precaution, and the ground batteries around each settlement were on red alert.

There was also the Solar Shield, the giant array of reflectors positioned between Mars and the Sun to concentrate the light reaching the planet while blocking the solar wind from stripping away the new fledgling atmosphere. Structures in space were replaceable if damaged and the ecosystem rebuildable over time, but the setback would be immeasurable.

Let's hope they can keep the enemy away from it, Joe thought.

Post-attack Earth was in chaos. The damage to crops and vegetation had been minimal but the effect on humanity overwhelming regardless. Unable to see the conflict above, many people suffered severe mental trauma, and societies everywhere were in varying states of collapse. Disruption to supply lines was seeing starvation and the closure of factories and services. Most communities were under enforced government curfew, even during the daylight hours.

Several nations were on a hair trigger. The response to the missile attacks on the shield had been immediate. The South African Republic was in crisis, having lost not only its major city but also its largest air force base and all the surrounding built up areas to missile retaliation.

Pakistan blamed the destruction of their city on Kyrgyzstan and launched a full retaliation, devastating wide expanses of the smaller central Asian country. It took only hours for tensions to escalate. Incensed by attacks on a proud nation for what they considered self-defense, many neighboring countries declared war on Pakistan.

Luckily, cooler heads prevailed almost immediately and the conflict de-escalated from nuclear to conventional, but by the time the shield deactivated, much of the world was engaged in open hostilities.

Fools never learn, Joe thought, and some never see the truth. He shook his head and returned to the matter at hand. He needed to press on with the mystery of Peter's death while he had the chance.

"Chloe?"

"Yes, Captain?"

"I need you to find two things for me. I want all the information you can find about the asteroid we were working on when the meteor storm in the belt hit the *Butterball.* Also, I want a detailed breakdown of where every crew member was, and what they were doing when Terry Caldwell was attacked on the service level, and when Peter Stanley committed suicide.

* * *

Mars.

Five Earth days after departure from Luna, the *Minaret* cruised past the Solar Shield and closed on the red planet. On approach, it reversed orientation and reduced its awe-inspiring speed to orbital velocity. Close behind, the *Blackship* continued to dog its every move at a cautious distance.

Joe once again stood on the bridge, watching events unfold on the giant screen. Around him were most of the other members of his crew, drawn from their funk by the immediate threat to their home planet.

Ruth, who had withdrawn deep into her inner world in the last few days, was present, firm in the conviction it was for her to document whatever was about to happen.

The ship was in an equatorial orbit eight thousand kilometers above the surface. Little more than an observer, Joe had no idea what was happening.

The red-brown ball turned far below, traces of a dust storm building in the area of the Isidis Planitia. Few signs of civilization were visible. Martian cities were mostly underground, deep in the rock of canyon walls or mesas, or else covered by domes or atmospheric tents. Joe prayed the latter were emptied in time.

A small cloud of shield generators identical to the ones protecting Earth exited from the landing bay as the *Minaret* dropped into orbit. Within seconds they spread unseen into the volume of space between the two star-ships.

The *super-bayonets* moved further aft. Still maintaining formation, they opened fire on the now slowing *Blackship* with blinding force. Their weapons had no effect, the star-hot discharge again splashing harmlessly on the enemy's shield.

The enemy vessel took position only a thousand kilometers behind and in an identical orbit. Joe's mind numbed as the forward section of the pursuing ship's dome opened, revealing the weaponry beneath. A single, massive blast lashed out.

What happened next, Joe was not certain. The *Blackship* vanished. It took the better part of a minute before he realized what had occurred. An opaque bubble over a hundred and fifty kilometers in diameter surrounded the attacking vessel and its shield. The surface was dotted with small bright specks, the generators that had left the *Minaret* only minutes earlier.

Joe understood at last. The *super-bayonets'* purpose had been to provide a brief few seconds of distraction while the generators whipped into position. Unlike those around the Earth, these focused inwards, creating an enclosing sphere. Io moved up to Joe, an ambiguous smile on her face.

"What did you do?"

They have no weapon capable of breaking that shield bubble.

"So it's enclosed. What good is that?"

The ship is not just enclosed. The sphere can resist any energy source and will deflect anything hitting from within. The blast will ricochet if the enemy fires its weapons. Their primary drive cannot be used effectively as the photon stream will bounce back. There may be some forward movement if the ship itself pushes against the bubble, but they cannot see where they are going or what lies ahead of them, only themselves reflected in all directions. They are blind.

"So they can't move."

Correct, but we can move them. Their instruments cannot see beyond the shield, so they will have no idea we are doing so.

"How can we affect something that size?"

Be patient, Joseph Falcon.

With the enemy now enclosed inside an impenetrable bubble of force and stationary in space almost eight thousand kilometers above the Martian surface, the *Minaret* began to maneuver, positioning itself above the enemy ship and then turning until its stern pointed down at the planet.

At the nose of the ship, the *super-bayonets* landed on the *Minaret's* hull, noses pointing aft to use their engines to stabilize the larger ship's position against the power of its main drive. A blue-white blaze lashed out as the *Minaret's* engines fired.

Joe and his crewmembers watched on in fascination. The drive functioning at well below maximum, the reduced blast reached the *Blackship* and played gently across the outside of the bubble.

At last, Joe understood. The photon output was tenuous, insufficient to damage the generators, but with force enough to push the bubble, gently nudging it toward the planet. For twenty minutes the process continued. Trapped inside, their instruments unable to see out, the *Intruders* were helpless.

In a few minutes the target will be six thousand of your kilometers above the surface, Io remarked. Does that mean anything to you, Joseph Falcon?

Joe was puzzled by the question. There was indeed something about the distance, deep in the back of his mind, but he could not place a finger on it.

On one side of the screen, he could see the Pavonis Mons Elevator, the massive, woven, diamond-micro-thread cable stretching into space from the top of the colossal equatorial volcano.

Many thousands of kilometers in length, the structure stretched far higher than the present position of the star-ships. Joe watched as it began to bend. Suddenly Io's question made sense.

"You have to be kidding me."

At a point six thousand kilometers above the surface of Mars, the cable of the elevator was fitted with computer-controlled jets, designed to cause it to flex a small amount to the north or south. The slight flexing created a rotating bow, scribing a circular arc in space over two hundred thousand meters in diameter.

Several times a day the cable and its precious cargo of passenger and freight cars reached the northern or southernmost points of the circle, clearing the path to allow the passage of one of Mars's minuscule moons.

Joe turned to his companions. Only Alaine, besides himself, had worked out what was happening, a broad grin on his face. The others remained focused on the main view, oblivious to events only kilometers to the side.

The cable reached full deflection as a colossal grey form flashed past. Seconds later, the shield around the *Blackship* dropped, revealing the massive, dome-shaped, enemy ship.

Phobos, with a mass of over ten and a half quadrillion tonnes, and twenty-two kilometers across, slammed into the stationary vessel at seven thousand seven hundred kilometers per hour.

The *Blackship's* shield flashed back on the second its prison vanished, but designed to deflect energy weapons, it was no match for the physical onslaught of such a massive solid projectile. The field collapsed in a blaze of sparking light as the ship received an irresistible blow on the long spine of the drive unit. The shell of the vessel buckled and shattered as the moon glanced away on a new course, taking it to places unknown.

Joe gasped, and realized he had been holding his breath. He heard cries from his companions, most of them taken by surprise as the grey, pockmarked moon flashed through their view.

The *Blackship* rotated slowly, moving in towards the planet. Its drive damaged beyond use, it no longer had the capacity to pull out of a descent into hell.

The Visitors had used the red world and its minuscule moon as their weapons. With wide eyes Joe turned to where Io was standing, returning his gaze.

Your own words, Joe Falcon. 'How do you destroy something so big? Smash it with an asteroid, maybe? Your moon is not quite that, but it was in a predictable orbit and served us well.

Shit, Joe thought. *All the advanced technology on this ship, and they hit it with a rock!*

Unable to halt the inevitable or escape the grip of the angry planet, the stricken vessel descended, gaining speed as gravity took hold. A thousand or more small escape craft ejected into space and began the descent.

Another problem for Mars, Joe thought.

The thin Martian atmosphere was still enough to set the vessel burning, creating a fireball of immense proportions. By the time the wreck hit the surface, well north of the equator in the Utopia Planitia, its velocity was sufficient to form a new crater, despite being only a hollow shell.

Still battling the numbness encroaching on his mind, Joe watched as the impact on his adopted home world sent billions of tonnes of dust and rock into the air to create a spreading storm destined to blanket the planet for a year.

Damn. They're going to blame me for that, as well.

* * *

How do you cope with life when people on two worlds want to kill you? Joe pulled out a seat at the computer bench in the lab, and eased down, tapping at the screen to bring up his files.

Three days had passed since the *Blackship's* impact on Mars, the worst effects of the event now evident. The area where the ship crashed had been uninhabited; scientists predicted one day the region would be a shallow sea, so avoided placing permanent settlements there.

Only a few thoroughfares crossed the region, with scattered temporary outposts involved in mining, surveying or terra-forming activities. The roads were little more than flat, graded pathways lined with flashing guidance lights.

The dust was rapidly covering the planet. The sun still shone through, as even the harshest of storms did not totally block the light due to the thin atmosphere. The effect was still significant, as would be the damage to the fledgling, terra-formed ecology.

In the underground cities and under the domes and tents, effects were negligible. Artificial lights powered by the fusion plants compensated, climate control maintained temperatures, and the ventilation filters cleaned the air. The citizens continued as before, complaining about a cataclysm that had little practical effect on them—for now.

The storm would last for many months at best. In time, the accumulated effects, such as dust covering the solar farms, would create hardship and increased work for the smaller settlements.

Most damage occurred outside the cities. From the days of first settlement, a great deal of progress had been achieved towards making the planet more habitable. The atmosphere, whilst still unbreathable, was denser and so retained more heat. Carbon dioxide was down, and oxygen, nitrogen and water vapor up. The process had just begun, but this event would set it back by decades.

The first attempts at vegetation with plants engineered to survive in the thin, cold atmosphere still struggled to hold. They would be lost, but could be replaced in time. It would not be the first failure and the technology was there.

The refugees from the wreck were another problem. The Mars military had deployed forces across the face of the planet to capture any survivors. The aliens had other ideas; no *Intruder* had been brought in alive, and many human lives had already been lost.

Unprepared for stranding on a planet virtually devoid of air and reaching sub-zero temperatures at night, many of the refugees did not last the first twenty-four hours. Most human teams found only masses of strange, alien corpses.

Joe's personal concern was attitude, on both planets. Most of the populations associated him with the *Visitors* and the *Intruder*, and could not differentiate. Many were unable to accept that neither he nor any other human soul had any say in what had happened. Both Jake and Adam Palfrey had warned him.

The overwhelming majority understood, and praised the efforts of himself and his crew, but a vocal minority on each world chose to see the opposite view.

The situation on Earth was the worst. The *Blackship* had destroyed two cities and the elevator, and the entire affair had caused major disruption and damage to agriculture, the general environment, and more importantly, to societies globally.

Subsequent wars made matters worse. According to the last message from Jake, several conflicts were still underway. Lives lost numbered in the many millions, and the effect on the planet in cultural and monetary terms was inestimable.

There were some who accused Joe, the nations of Earth stung by the destruction of their major centers, or angered, despite their own culpability, by the retaliations from the rest of the world searched for someone to blame.

On Mars, many censured him for the storm, the inconvenience and the damage to the fragile environment. Some accused him of being responsible for the deaths that had occurred during the cleanup. A small number berated him for robbing them of their only remaining moon.

Joe smiled; human intelligence, like everything else, followed a bell curve and it never ceased to amaze him those at the bottom end could be so ignorant, yet so vocal.

The *Blackship* was a complete loss, but there was still a great deal of activity concerning it. Despite the dust and radioactivity, the first teams were already investigating the remains, and to avoid another war an agreement had been reached to form a joint venture between the two worlds, with each sharing any advances gained.

Joe doubted they would find much. Samples of the wrecked ship's materials did not automatically guarantee an understanding of what they were or how they were made. The same went for the technology if any remained. Like the wonders on the *Minaret*, everything might be easy to see but impossible to understand.

What concerned him most was, if these ships were driven by anti-matter then the wreck could be a time bomb. The explosion on impact had been far greater than one would expect from a hollow-shell structure like a spacecraft, no matter how enormous. Joe hoped it was because the fuel had annihilated the instant its containment systems failed, but there was always a chance…

Again, there was a vocal minority. The crater was dangerous—a valid point, Joe thought—and could contain all kinds of toxins, volatile substances or even infectious organisms. Any technological discovery could be detrimental to both worlds, which barely coped with what they already had. On, and on, and on—

None of the bad attitudes came from governments, but rather from private individuals, small fringe groups and extremist religious cults.

It was enough.

Joe was a marked man.

Chapter 31

A KNOCK SOUNDED on the door to the lab, and then Carl Geddes stepped through.

"You wanted to speak to me, Captain?"

"Yes, if you have a moment."

Carl pulled out a seat and sat down, clasping his hands on the bench top. "So, what's on your mind?"

The captain stared at the screen for a few seconds, then at the mineralogist. "I was checking some of the old entries in our log. I was wondering why the log for LRG 3402 is missing."

"I'm sorry?"

"The rock we were surveying when the meteoroid swarm hit us. The record appears to be gone. Did you write it up when you came in?"

Carl stared back, a faint bead of perspiration appearing on his forehead. "I asked Pete to do it."

Joe sat back in his chair. "Hmm, looks like he forgot."

Carl nodded.

"What puzzles me is," Joe continued, "the initial entry I logged is also missing, like it's been deleted."

Carl remained silent.

"Any idea why Peter would do that?"

"He didn't tell me everything he was up to."

"Fair enough. The thing is I know he didn't do it."

Joe paused for a moment, eyes fixed on the man opposite. Carl's clenched fingers tensed.

"Did you know Chloe keeps an extra backup log of everything going in or out of the system, a record accessible only by me? I know you deleted those files from this very terminal after you came back on board from the survey. What did you find out there?"

"Nothing, nothing at all. A rock blown off Mars or Earth billions of years ago by a giant meteor impact. Okay, yes, I wiped it accidentally. I went in to update it and hit a wrong key. It was a worthless rock so I didn't think it would matter and didn't say anything."

"This have anything to do with that accident?"

Joe reached across and placed a tiny item on the bench in front of Carl. A grain of yellow rock a few millimeters across gleamed under the glare of the overhead lighting.

Carl picked up the object and turned it between thumb and forefinger. "Where did you get this?"

"It was inside Peter's private locker."

Carl sat back, gazed up at the ceiling for a long, drawn-out moment, then sighed. He dropped his gaze back to Joe, his brow furrowed and mouth twisted in frustration.

Joe continued. "You and Peter had no secrets from each other. I figure anything one of you knew about the other did as well, so don't tell me it must have been something Peter was keeping to himself. What did you guys find?"

Carl sighed again. "Okay, fair enough. I told you it was a piece of planetary rock, right? It was igneous—volcanic, not carbonaceous or metallic like most of the stuff in that sector, so we decided to check it more thoroughly for the hell of it, since the guys needed time to repair the ship. We did find something."

Joe raised his eyebrows in expectation.

"A network of seams of almost pure gold. A bloody big one, running right through the backside of the rock."

Joe nodded—it was much as he had expected. "You thought you would keep it secret. You planned to go back for it later, right? How much of it is there?"

"A lot—a heck of a lot. Multiple thick veins, one of them over ten centimeters across at one point—the biggest I've seen. Maybe a cubic meter, estimated."

Joe let out a long, low whistle. "That would be worth… "

"About one-point-four trillion at today's prices, Mars talents." Carl stared straight at Joe. "Enough for two…"

For a moment, Joe said nothing, ignoring Carl's last sentence. The find was stupendous. Gold was not rare in the belt; most asteroids had some of it in their makeup, but always in small grains spread through the matrix of the parent body and difficult to extract without factories like those at Kepler.

A deposit large enough to remove by hand was a different matter, and when such was found, it was in most cases in a mass that had once been part of a planetary body. But over a trillion talents worth?

No doubt, Carl and Peter had intended to resign after the tour and then return in a hired ship to make the great discovery as independents. That way, the rock would have been theirs, and not AMC's."

"So, that's why you murdered Peter?"

Carl froze, his face turning white as he fought to maintain composure. His jaw trembled faintly, his teeth clamped down on the lower lip, tiny drops of sweat beading on his brow.

"Pete killed himself. You know he did. He committed suicide after trying to kill Terry."

"I don't think so. Maybe it wasn't the gold. Perhaps you shot Terry because you thought he had figured out your identity, and murdered Peter to throw suspicion elsewhere. Am I right?"

Carl shook his head, his gaze flicking from place to place—anywhere but the eyes of his accuser. "You're daft, and wrong. You couldn't prove any of this even if it was true."

"Oh, I think I can."

Joe tapped the computer screen and an image appeared of the service deck beneath the landing bay. It was a view of the service-level entrance to the docking pillar, and showed Terry moving across from the walkway. He stopped and turned to face away from the camera. Several meters further away stood a second figure, dressed in full environment kit, and carrying a portable rock-cutter. The suit had a bright orange panel, the color of the mineralogy team, with a dark scuff mark across the left shoulder.

"One of your suits, I think."

"Yeah, it's Pete, obviously. Where did you get that video."

"Complements of our hosts. The *Minaret's* computers are not unlike Chloe—they record what happens everywhere on the ship. It took Io a while to track down this bit of footage. I don't think it's Peter."

"Of course it is. That scuff mark is his suit."

"Agreed, but I don't think he's in it. Chloe tells me otherwise."

"That stupid machine doesn't know what happened down there. She … it, can't see beyond the *Butterball*."

Joe nodded his head. "True, but she does keep pretty accurate records of where everyone is at any given time. Thanks to her I've been able to pin down the locations of every member of the crew at that time except two, Ruth Carvalio and you."

"You think that proves it was me? Anyone can take any suit at any time, even the bloody reporter woman."

"She's not a reporter and she doesn't know how to use a laser cutter. Doesn't have access to them. You killed Terry to shut him up, and then Peter to cover yourself."

Carl pushed back from the bench and crossed his arms, a condescending smile creeping onto his face.

"You have nothing here," he said. "You've accused me of two murders with no evidence other than a video of someone in a suit, and a survey record that I accidentally deleted?

"Do I look stupid? Fine. Why don't we start at the beginning?"

Carl waved a hand in annoyance.

"Let's begin with your service in the Navy. You and Terry served at the same time and on the same ship."

Carl opened his mouth to speak.

"Don't deny it," Joe interrupted, "I know it was under a different name, so stay with me. There was a female officer you both liked. You assaulted her, and when she threatened to report you, you killed her and threw her body out of the airlock. Terry got the blame, but they could never pin anything specific on him. It did ruin his career though. You, meanwhile, abandoned the forces and underwent a little facial modification at a hospital on Mars."

"That was Pete. He admitted it in his letter."

"I don't think he wrote that. I have some excellent contacts and I've been doing a fair amount of research into the background of everyone on this ship."

"And?"

"Peter's history is clean; it can be traced all the way to his childhood, and verified. He was in the Navy but not at the time of the murder. I even have a photo of him taken in the Navy, and the face is the same. Your history, however, only goes back a short way to a point just after the girl's murder occurred. Prior to that, nothing in your resume can be confirmed: there aren't any prior school records for you, your qualifications fail scrutiny and there are no government records. I'm confident it was you who murdered her and ruined Terry's career. I'm guessing you used the true story in the suicide letter hoping that, if we swallowed it, it would free you from that little problem forever. Am I right?"

"You can't prove any of that."

"Yes, you're right, I can't. Shall I continue?"

Again, Carl waved his hand vaguely, his expression blank.

"Fast forward a little. After changing your face and creating a new persona, you went out to the Belt, the one place where you could start a second life without fear of capture or of anyone checking your background too closely. I gave you a job, and you joined my ship. You must've got a hell of a shock when you found Terry on my crew, but when you realized he didn't recognize your new face or voice, you decided to stick it out until the tour ended. I'm guessing you stayed aboard for this trip because it would have made you enough money in gratuities to go after that gold later.

"Sometime after we arrived here you thought you'd been discovered, so it became necessary to cover yourself. Alaine radioed in reporting Terry was returning alone, and you received that transmission. After reporting to me, you grabbed a suit and left the ship through the engine module emergency hatch. Chloe doesn't have a camera in there but she did record the manual override when you left the ship and again when you returned. You should have known that, but I expect you were in something of a rush at the time.

"You crossed the landing bay and entered the service deck by another dock, made your way across and waited for Terry. You used the laser cutter to kill him, and returned to the *Butterball* the same way you left. You dumped the cutter and suit back in their storage units, ran through the skywalk and came out behind me in time to see Terry's body carried away by the maintenance drone."

"This is bizarre," Carl grumbled. He began to rise from his seat.

"Sit down," Joe barked. "I'm not finished yet." The mineralogist slumped back spontaneously, unsure of whether to stay or leave.

"So, to continue. Terry returned alive and well, and you panicked. His memory was gone, but there was always the chance it would come back, and that he had recognized you through the faceplate of your suit. You gambled it wouldn't, and decided to set up Peter and fake his suicide. Since you had the foresight to use his suit, it was easy. We wouldn't bother to look further if we thought we had the killer, right?"

"Maeve tells me Peter took a lot of sedatives. He always was the nervous type, and he had trouble sleeping. I think you drugged him with his own pills, and when he was too doped to resist, dragged him to the washroom and slashed his wrists. A brief wait, and you called for help. Of course, your having discovered him accounts for the blood stains on your clothes. I imagine it would be hard to cut someone like that without getting splashed yourself."

"Are you finished?"

"That's about it, I think."

"Fine. The whole thing is rubbish. Clever, but none of it can be proven. It's just your opinion—speculation. I'll be off this ship as soon as we get home" Again, he moved to leave.

"One more thing," Joe said. The ship's protocols called for each man or woman to use their own environment suit, serviced and maintained by themselves, and no other.

"I suspect your DNA is all over Peter's suit, and on the sedative bottle in Pete's locker. I expect we will also find fingerprints on both, and on the laser cutter most recently used. I'm guessing you would not have had time to clean it, so yours will be there and Peter's will not. That alone will be sufficient to have the authorities back home start an investigation." It was a lie and a guess, but Joe suspected he was right, and Carl could not know otherwise. "So, how close am I?"

Carl glared across the bench. He appeared to shrink. His skin turned pale, his eyes blank and emotionless, his facial expression betraying a growing uneasiness. He shifted his gaze to Joe and leaned back, acceptance replacing the frown on his face.

"Close enough," he said. "You got the bit about Terry wrong. He didn't work out who I was. He overheard Pete and me arguing about the gold, and later told us if we didn't cut him in he would spill everything. One point four trillion … too much to let that happen."

"So you killed them for greed; nothing more?"

Carl stared into the distance as he tossed over his options. There was no way off the ship, and when they landed on Mars, the authorities would be waiting to take him into custody pending an investigation.

Joe was correct—he had cleaned the sedative bottle, but not the suit or the cutter. It had not occurred to him at the time, and he had been unable to do so later. There was also the scalpel. He knew about Chloe's airlock records, but prayed they would not be checked if he could divert attention elsewhere. On a spaceship, there was nowhere to run—no escape.

There was every chance he would face charges for two murders, and a third if the Navy got involved. There was also the certainty AMC would have him convicted of attempting to defraud them of more than a trillion talents if the gold discovery leaked out in the investigation. Either way, incarceration for life was the inevitable outcome. The prisons of Mars and a life of hard labor were not pleasant prospects. He would not let that happen.

A look of resignation crept over Carl's face as he seemed to grow smaller. Without warning, he stood and stepped back, reached into the pocket of his coveralls and removed a small pistol he had carried since the day Terry returned. He aimed at Joe's chest and pulled the trigger without hesitation.

Joe gasped and jerked backwards as Carl raised the weapon to his own temple. Before he could fire again a solid object slammed into the side of his head with a resounding crack and he fell forward, crumpled over the bench, and slid to the floor.

Terry stood in the doorway with a length of metal duct piping in his hands. By agreement with Joe, he, Sarah and Alaine had heard the whole thing via the intercom from the nearby infirmary. His face was scarlet, his body shaking as he lowered the pipe to his side. Sarah pushed in behind him, spotted Joe motionless on the deck and rushed across to help.

Terry reached out with his foot and kicked Carl's ribs.

"I liked that girl, arsehole."

* * *

Sarah sat in the common room, in the position usually taken by Joe Falcon at the head of the table. Two weeks after the alien impact on the surface of Mars, *Butterball* sat on the landing platform outside the entry tunnel of the *Minaret.*

In one hour, a cutter was due from the orbital naval dock on the far side of the planet, to escort the old freighter to the base for debriefing. Alone on the bridge, Terry awaited their arrival while the remainder of the crew gathered in the common room.

Sarah studied the faces around her. Expressions ranged from serious concern to resigned acceptance. Her own eyes were red from lack of sleep. It had been a hectic couple of weeks.

"So that's our story," she said. "Carl killed Terry to keep his past a secret, and Peter to cover his tracks when he thought he might be discovered. Then he shot Joe. The authorities will be waiting to take him into custody when we arrive at Mars base, and in the meantime, we keep him locked in his cabin under sedation. Maeve and Chloe are attending to that."

"So, what happens now?" Marius Pine asked.

"We go home."

"Without the Captain? What about us? What about the *Butterball*?"

"Joe left a will in his records, and the ship is now mine. He always intended to leave it to me; I told him I didn't want it, but he didn't change the will so it stands. I have to be honest with you all; I don't intend to take her back to the Belt just yet."

A murmur of concern rumbled through the room. Many of the individuals present had gone to Kepler for good reason, at least in their own minds. Several days of discussion and a newfound air of honesty revealed only Carl was hiding from the law, and Sarah felt sure the others would overcome their particular ghosts in time.

"For now, everyone will have to return to Mars—there's no way around that. We all know opinion about this mission is not favorable but the negativity was focused on Joe. He was our public face. It should be quite safe for the rest of us, according to Adam Palfrey, but we'll be provided with security in case."

"I'm going to have one hell of a book to write, even if it can't be the whole truth," Ruth said from somewhere at the rear. In recent days, she had kept to herself but now appeared to have reconciled Joe's fate and re-joined the crew. "What I don't understand is why the *Visitors* could not help him. They brought Terry back."

"Terry was a lot younger and fitter than Joe. Joe's body just couldn't cope." *True enough,* Sarah thought.

"The authorities will want to know what happened to him."

"The space casket is ready in the storage bay. We'll launch it and tell them we gave him a funeral as per the expressed wishes in his will. What can they do?" A general murmur of consent and nodding of heads rippled through the room.

Sarah continued. "Each of us will be officially interviewed, and targeted by the media. As long as we stick to our story and take care of what we say, everything should be fine. Limit your comments about Joe to what we have agreed—anything else, you don't know about. With care you can all make enough out of public appearances, books and so on, to keep you in comfort for the rest of your lives, if you want." She looked at Ruth, her eyebrows raised.

"Yes, that's correct," Ruth said. "The networks will pay a fortune to any one of us for this, especially our resident Lazarus, Terry. Stick to the story and there won't be a problem. Get it wrong, and they'll start to dig."

"Good," said Sarah. "If anyone thinks they can't do that, they should refuse interviews and keep their head down, or the consequences for us all could be very awkward. Anyone who wants to go back to the belt can do so as soon as they are released by the Navy. Everyone else, you can be famous in whatever way you choose."

"What about Terry and the gold?" Harry Chan asked. "He might get in trouble over his part in all this."

"What part? He did nothing but push Carl to stop him from shooting himself. Carl hit his head on the bench. Terry saved his life."

Harry dropped his gaze to the floor. "Yes, of course. The gold?"

"What gold?"

Again Harry nodded, a grin on his face. "Without the original record we couldn't easily find it again anyway. It's a big place out there." Sarah smiled to herself; a record did exist in Chloe's secret backups, and Joe left the override code in the documents with his will.

"We don't mention it to anyone. The last thing they need out at Kepler is a million treasure hunters. So, we all have the facts right? About Joe, Terry, Peter and Carl?" Nods of consensus came in reply.

"Good. Let's go home."

* * *

A small lead-lined casket launched from the cargo module. It sped away in the general direction of the Asteroid belt, lifting above the ecliptic. It would be centuries before the unrelenting will of the Sun brought it back to the inner system again, and even then nothing of worth would be found.

Soon after, the small contingent of *Butterball*, its escort and two naval cutters moved around the shoulder of Mars. The giant alien spacecraft broke orbit and left the red planet on course for Luna to retrieve its remaining *bayonets*, and then on to the distant orange moon of Saturn. The shield generators vanished, presumably drawn back into the starship.

Sarah had spoken at considerable length with Io before their parting. Within seconds of Joe's death, the android appeared on *Butterball* and asked permission to take the body, a request Sarah and Harry had allowed in the hope the miracle of Terry might be repeated.

In the captain's cabin, a folder of emergency instructions was found, from which it was clear Joe would not have returned to either Mars or Earth. At best, he would have gone back to the Belt. Sarah knew she would have accompanied him.

The situation was different now. After discussions with Jake Falcon, an agreement was reached with Io, and Joe's body remained with the *Visitors*. Sarah would travel to Earth, to carry his personal possessions to his son for safekeeping.

Chapter 32

JAKE PULLED HIS CAR into the long driveway of his home and watched in the rear-view mirror as the security gate closed. He was glad to have been invited to the recovery meeting at City Hall, but happier it was over.

Common sense returned about two weeks after the dropping of the shield. The news of the devastation in Pakistan and South Africa touched the hearts and minds of the people, and public pressure to stop the petty arguments became overwhelming, forcing a fragile peace.

Everywhere, support efforts were underway to assist those countries suffering the most, and for now, the governments of the world seemed to have learned something from the event. Deep inside, Jake suspected it would not last.

The local authorities had requested his assistance in restoring systems and services to the region, and he had been happy to help. Australia had not suffered nearly as much as other countries, the greatest damage being from social collapse rather than technological failure or warfare.

In the lounge of his home, Jake threw his keys into the bowl on the sideboard and collapsed in his favorite chair. A beep drew his attention. He hauled himself back to his feet and walked across to the computer desk.

A massive download was in progress. Several petabytes of information were streaming in and had been doing so for a considerable time.

Jake called up a list of the first files to arrive. They were coming from the *Minaret*, streamed via a thousand different pathways on the secure system he had set up for his father. This was clearly for his eyes only, but would attract the attention of the military; there was work to be done covering tracks.

Nervous with anticipation he selected one of the files. The information appeared on first analysis to involve something biological, or genetic. It was outside his field of expertise, but he was able to glean sufficient to have a vague idea of what it concerned. He chose another file, then another and another, his jaw dropping lower with each he opened.

The data contained basic information on a range of 'holy grails' from medical, engineering, astrophysical and many other scientific fields. Even at a cursory glance, he spotted file titles on high-temperature superconductors, semiconductor nano-crystals, plasma physics and fusion that would revolutionize humanity's current understanding of those fields.

Half an hour later he had seen enough to realize the effects of this knowledge on human science would be profound. Dependent on how it was used and how it was released, it could guide humanity to a glorious future, or cause the collapse of society.

Akira strolled into the lounge and smiled. "Hi. How did your meeting go?"

"Hmm? Oh, yeah, good."

"What are you so absorbed in?"

Jake turned the monitor towards her. For a moment she peered at the screen, her eyes growing wider with each moment.

"Is that…?"

"Yes. Sarah told me something would be coming, but I didn't expect anything like this. There's enough data here to make us the wealthiest people in history, if we want."

Akira assumed a studied pose of deep thought and then shook her head.

"Nah, don't need that."

Jake smiled. "Me neither. Guess we'll have to become global benefactors instead."

* * *

The view beyond the glass was surreal, reminiscent in some ways of Earth. The giant, dark dunes, interspersed with rocky stretches, extended many kilometers towards a distant shore, a dark lake visible only as a black line on the horizon. Heavy, swirling clouds hung overhead, marking the approach of a storm.

An illusion—it was all an illusion.

The sand was not silicon, but hydrocarbon grains.

The outcrops were super-frozen ice, and the expanse of liquid in the distance not water but liquid methane.

The temperature? Cold—so very, very cold.

An orange haze filled the nitrogen-methane air, beyond which loomed something vast and overwhelmingly dominant. The planet Saturn, in all its ringed might, glowered through the building methane clouds of Titan. Bolts of lightning crackled through the atmosphere as the storm broke. Liquid methane raindrops pierced the haze as they pounded the ground.

Not real.

The window was another vision screen, and whilst the image was a genuine live view of the surface of Saturn's astonishing moon, Joe was not there. That in which he now sat was a warm, comfortable suite in the habitat drum of the *Visitors'* ship, where he had lived for the past year.

Dead?

Yes, I died.

There was a small gap in memory. That was it: he had ceased to exist for at least a short time.

There had been many discussions with both Sarah and Jake since then, and he knew what had happened in those missing moments, though he had no personal memories.

The bullet hit him in the heart, and death came almost instantly. As with Terry, the *Visitors* claimed him and began to weave their magic, perhaps not as efficiently as he was much older and less fit, already suffering from the deterioration of age. Hope for survival was a slim chance at best. The body failed before Io's miracles could save it.

Joe's mind survived, downloaded and stored in the ship's virtual systems along with those of his hosts. Now, at his request, he inhabited a temporary synthetic body made especially for him, awaiting an even greater resurrection. Another month or two was all he needed.

The mind was strong, perhaps stronger than before, no longer drowned in the mire of an aging brain. Other than his death he remembered everything, each small event from a life lived long. Soon there would be an end, but then a new beginning. *Need consciousness ever die?*

After the final defeat of the Invader, events moved with increasing rapidity on both planets. Once the initial knee-jerk reactions died, societies had drawn together to rebuild and differences had begun to fade. The two worlds were just a little closer if anything. The damage to ecologies, economies and societies could be and would be repaired, perhaps for the better. Law and order were yet to be restored in many places but work continued.

Far below on frigid Titan a vast complex was rising. It too was an illusion, a projection created for the benefit of anyone from Earth or Mars who decided to turn their attention to the frozen moon. Many would do so; humanity would never forget the presence of aliens in their system.

Due to an agreement made so long ago by Joe and Io, the real factory was no longer necessary. The *Minaret* was not going far. For one hundred years, it would remain near Titan and then depart as promised, but only to the Oort cloud where it would park away from sight or detection until the time was right for humanity to find it again.

By then, the *Visitors* would be gone in a sense, and the ship would become a gift, one possibly outdated by the time of its giving, Joe thought.

No matter how he viewed it, the only certain conclusion he could reach was that somewhere in the galaxy were other civilizations with technologies well in advance of Man's. Two advanced alien races had found their way into the Solar System, one of them friendly, the other not.

Others would not be far away, including the *Visitors'* sister colonies. How many of them would be threats? Humanity now knew beyond doubt it was not alone, and needed to get its collective arse into gear. It would take time but all journeys began somewhere.

The solution was to boost humankind's technology to a level where it could compete or defend itself. Despite being less advanced in other areas, humanity's defense capability had proven to be not too far behind the aliens; raising it a notch or two quickly was achievable.

The information Jake received was sufficient to allow a quantum leap in many areas, but care was necessary. Across both worlds, facilities were being set up by anonymous trusts, to conduct research into many different fields from medicine to space travel. Initial funding came from the surprise find by an independent, prospector benefactor, of a massive gold deposit in the asteroid belt.

The knowledge would come in dribbles, at reasonable intervals. The social impact would be dramatic, the damage minimal. Various teams would make supposedly serendipitous discoveries resulting in major scientific breakthroughs, to be shared publically despite the wishes of governments. The benefits would belong to all.

The benefactors? Well, that was hard to pin down. Each facility belonged to multiple trusts registered through a convoluted tangle of shelf companies leading back to a small number of individuals: Joe's son Jake and his brilliant new wife Akira, in partnership with Adam Palfrey, the now retired Waleed Sarraf, and a few dozen trusted individuals on both planets.

The *Visitors* had never intended to leave as they had first stated. Due to the circumstances of their departure, they had neither the personnel nor the equipment or supplies to create a viable new colony on another world. Their only choices, assuming that at least some of their other ships had survived, were to seek out one of those new outposts and join them, remain where they were, or return to their home star. The chances of success were minimal either way.

Joe now knew that the *Visitors* had come to Earth not out of altruism, but because with a half-finished and poorly provisioned ship, the Solar System was the only viable one they could reach, regardless of its being already occupied, and despite the *Intruders.*

The ship that at first seemed a wonder from the gods was, in reality, just a machine and an incomplete, barely space-worthy one despite its technology. The most likely scenario was that if it left, it would die somewhere in space.

Joe had suspected the *Visitors'* intention to stay from the first moment he met Io, and when confronted, her answers confirmed it.

With a crew of only ten thousand, they could not set up a competitive colony in the human-occupied Solar System either. Their plan was, in Joe's opinion, destined to fail, causing terrible conflict on Earth and Mars. He had given a great deal of consideration to what seemed an inevitable situation, and he and Io had come to an agreement. He had proposed a minor modification, one that appealed to the aliens and would change the outcome for man.

At the far end of the room another, smaller screen played news from the broadcasts of Earth and Mars. In the last year, there had been a remarkable outbreak of peaceful cooperation between the various nations. It did not surprise Joe at all.

The current broadcast was a political speech by the Premier of the Russ Republic. He stood at a dais before a massive crowd. A few feet behind was a woman who bore a vague resemblance to Sarah, or perhaps a younger Ruth. She was the Premier's powerful new wife, and it was known publically his sudden tendencies towards peace and reconciliation were the result of her influence.

Several other major world powers, including the North American Federation, China, Iran and some European nations also had new leaders or old ones with new, young partners.

According to Io, at least five percent of the ship's contingent was now living on one of the two planets, hidden in positions of power amongst the people. By the end of the century, the *Visitors* would be fully integrated into the societies of man, and no true human would be any the wiser.

Io stepped into the room and placed a drink on the table in front of Joe.

"There you are, Joe," she said.

He touched her arm in a gesture of thanks. The flesh felt warm, and real. At their first meeting, her body had been an android. She now inhabited the real thing, a living, breathing body cloned from the genetic materials of the *Butterball's* crew.

The aliens on Earth and Mars were also clones. The genetics varied enormously with no two alike, but each was, in a sense, a child of Joe's people.

Io had mentioned several times her people always intended to create new bodies suitable to the environment of their new home, and many found humans fascinating. Their plan had been to use synthetic bodies to place themselves within human society, until they controlled it to a point where they could live in safety.

The dangers as Joe saw it were the potential the *Visitors* would end up ruling, and the certainty of total disruption if they should be discovered. With artificial bodies, the chance of that happening was extremely high. The possibility also existed that despite their technology, they might not be the most qualified to rule.

Joe decided to convince them of a different path requiring one, simple change. Long ago he had worked out his hosts overheard every word spoken on the *Butterball*, and made a point of mentioning that if they chose to stay, the genuine human form would be an obvious choice.

In conversation with Io, he had confronted her and reinforced that, with a logical and minor modification to their plan. Instead of androids and certain discovery, it would be better to go straight to organic bodies. For Io's people, the advantage of being one hundred percent physically human and therefore undetectable was irresistible.

Why should they do such a thing? Joe had pointed out that, considering humanity's rapid technological advancement coupled with a slow rate of moral and ethical evolution, mankind would spread to the stars very quickly and potentially represent a threat to the *Visitors'* sister colonies. By blending into the human race, the *Visitors* could guide its development to a better and more peaceful future, eliminating that risk in favor of cooperation between the civilizations of the near galactic region.

For the *Visitors* it meant continued existence in human form, and a guarantee of the safety of their species elsewhere. It was an obvious solution, and after consideration Io adopted the idea, accepting Joe's explanation he wanted to help with a smooth and non-destructive integration that would not destroy his people.

Joe knew the aliens' moral and ethical development was well in advance of that of humanity. The concept of foregoing the uniqueness of ten thousand to protect the tens of millions in their other colonies did not seem a great sacrifice to them.

A curious species faced with a grim future, they found the chance to adopt a new civilization from within, and to protect their distant relatives elsewhere, irresistible. Of course, Io agreed, they would always remain who they were, despite their human bodies.

Only Sarah knew of this arrangement. She raised the question of alien domination of society, sighting an old movie she had once seen about aliens taking over people's bodies. Joe knew it would never be a problem. The alien ship had only a few thousand inhabitants, whilst humanity on both worlds numbered close to thirteen billion.

Joe often considered, while talking to Io, how human her thoughts and attitudes were. They could grow any physical form they wanted but their minds differed little from those of homo-sapiens. He also now realized his hosts were not the mental giants he at first imagined. They were, despite more advanced technology and social evolution, on a rough par with humanity in terms of actual intellectual capacity.

The *Visitor's* civilization was vastly older than man's, and its technology consequently more advanced, but it had taken them many thousands of years to cover the ground mankind had traversed in less than one millennia. Their mental capabilities were not on par with those of Homo sapiens.

It did not end there. The ship's contingent did not include the best and brightest minds of their species. The intended passenger contingent had included exactly that, but most had died in the attack by the *Intruders* on their refuge moon. Of the brilliant minds that had created the *Minaret* and its amazing technology, few were actually on board.

The present crew, excepting a core group of scientists and engineers who worked on the ship construction, consisted of workers and their families, bureaucrats who managed the yards, and an odd assortment of individuals who had been rescued from the attack on their dying system.

With bodies for all practical and medical purposes human, they could not be closer to the real thing, differing only in knowledge and social attitudes. Those could and would change with time.

The one thing about humans that Io's people did not understand would be their undoing. By adopting organic bodies, they would also inherit all the things that went with them, including human hormones. It was clear that Io had never fully grasped the emotional makeup of Joe or his companions, and *that* failure would be the *Visitors'* undoing. Love and sex were powerful weapons.

They would breed with their human bodies, and even if they sought their own kind to begin, would eventually mingle with the inhabitants of Earth or Mars, if not in this first generation then future ones. With many of them already partnered with prominent citizens as a prelude to intended social and political dominance, the process of assimilation had unwittingly begun already.

By overwhelming numbers, the human race was immune to domination by such a small alien force, and nothing short of the destruction of both worlds would change that. One thing that could be said of humanity—it was impossible to impose singular control over its teaming billions.

In time, the *Visitors* would vanish. In a dozen generations, they would be gone without a trace, bred into oblivion in the same way Homo Neanderthalensis and Homo Denisova had been in the far distant past. Like those ancestors, the alien minds would in time become part of that which was human.

They would be absorbed and assimilated. For a while, they would be among Earth's greatest leaders and would do amazing things, but in time they would melt in and the civilizations of humankind would remain forever so, for better or worse.

Joe suspected Io and her kind knew this, but the benefit of securing the future of their kind against a dominant, aggressive human race still made it worth their while. Homo sapiens would change a little, and become better as the species had many times in the quantum leaps of evolutionary history.

The people of Earth and Mars would gain in many, many ways: technology would expand, society would become more peaceful and cooperative, and life spans and IQ might even grow from the mix.

By the time the children of Sol spread out to meet their nearby alien neighbors, they would be ready to do so in peace, and on equal terms. Now that, Joe thought, would be worth seeing, and he intended to do just that.

Somewhere deep in the laboratories of the ship, a clone was being force-grown, made from his DNA with the damage of age repaired with donations from his ex-crewmembers. Already approaching adult size, it remained isolated from all stimuli to prevent it from developing a mind of its own, and in a month or so he would wake as his new self. The process could be repeated, making Joe the first natural human to be truly immortal, should he so desire.

It had been Sarah's idea, drummed up in conversation with Io while Joe's continued existence remained doubtful. He had always known the girl loved him for whatever reasons, and he felt dearly about her. On the day he woke again, they would be about the same physical age. Perhaps there was a future there after all.

After returning to Mars and placing *Butterball* into temporary mothballs, Sarah had stayed on the planet incognito and now worked with Jake and Akira. With the help of a privately hired and unknown ship, she had retrieved the gold asteroid, and now waited for the day Joe would return with a new body and identity.

What would he do? He would join his son as a partner, but not indefinitely. Jake believed the data given him would soon lead to interstellar travel, placing a galaxy of wonder and amazement within reach. One man, or a couple, could spend many lifetimes exploring the stars without even leaving the immediate neighborhood.

The potential boggled the imagination.

Now that is something to look forward to, Joe thought.

End

One Last Thing...

If you enjoyed this book, I'd be very grateful if you'd post a short review. Your support really does make a difference and I read all the reviews personally, so I can get your feedback and make my books even better.

If you'd like to leave a review then all you need to do is click the review link on this book's page on your favorite on-line bookseller or book club.

FALCON'S GHOST

(an excerpt)

JOE FALCON BRACED himself against the unsettling shiver that wormed its way up his spine. The sound of his own breathing echoed back from the confines of his space suit as he smelt the canned tang of the air from his life support system. It was not something he enjoyed. The last time he wore a spacesuit was decades in the past.

This moon had an eerie, surreal feel, and something about it set his nerves on a razor's edge. To his knowledge he was the first human to land on Titan since the original exploration ship almost a century ago.

Not that he had any right to be standing here; by doing so he broke a convention that had dominated humanity's exploration of the outer planets. No one was permitted here. As Joe was instrumental in the formulation of that decree, he of all people should not be breaking the rules, but for him this was personal.

He thanked Thoth and Hephaestus, the gods of technology, for his suit, and prayed it would not fail him. The surface temperature registered at ninety-six degrees Kelvin, or minus one hundred and eighty Centigrade, far too cold for a flesh-and-blood body to survive.

The insulated suit protected him from the hellish environment, but a chill still filled his soul. He glanced down, scuffed a booted foot in the grainy sand and contemplated the mark it left, proof of his presence in this forbidding place. With a shake of the head to force himself back to reality, he began the trek around the ship towards the cargo hatch. He had seen all this before, but long ago and from a distance.

Giant, black dunes marched skyward beyond the dark plain at the edge of which he stood, but those high ridges were not normal mineral sands. Composed of fine, hydrocarbon grains that drifted down from the frigid clouds, they extended many kilometers to where higher mountain ranges of rock-hard, super-chilled ice stretched into the ever-present haze of a frozen sky.

On Joe's other side, the calm waters of a broad, liquid-methane lake spread mirror-like, reflecting the orange murk that filled the nitrogen-methane air. Dominating all, a colossal, multi-colored orb forced its presence through the overcast, the glow sufficient to bathe the alien landscape with an eerie half-light. The giant gas world of Saturn, unchallenged queen of the Solar System, brooded over its hellish, elder child Titan, its glowering visage counterpointed by multiple lightning flashes that crackled uninterrupted across the moon's sky.

In the distance, the near wall of a vast structure stretched for many kilometers from the edge of the lake to the distant dunes and soared several hundred meters into the frigid air.

Six decades ago the colossal alien star-ship known to all as the *Minaret* arrived to warn the people of Earth and Mars they were under threat of attack from a second vessel, dubbed the *Blackship*, which entered the system soon after.

The first arrivals, named by Joe's crew the 'Visitors', offered protection for the worlds of humanity in return for the exclusive use of the moon Titan for one hundred years. Joe helped to finalize that agreement and the decree went out that no human ship was to land there for one century.

Joe had arrived a little early.

He worked his way around the ship, the New Worlds Institute research vessel *Marco Polo*, until he reached the cargo hatch. The short journey was disconcerting, the only sounds those of his breath, the pounding of his pulse in his ears and the multitude of small, whirring noises from the servos operating the limbs of the mini-tank that was his environment suit.

A breath of warm air flowed over his face but did little to ease the chill in his soul. No decent human should ever be in a place like this.

It all began with an innocent observation.

The *Minaret* was missing.

The exact purpose of the giant structure ahead remained unknown, but the accepted belief was it was a giant cyclotron used to manufacture antimatter, the supposed power source of the vessel. The Visitors never quite clarified the matter, and most knowledge was based on speculation rather than fact.

The Visitors stated they had used all their fuel to reach Earth ahead of the *Blackship,* and after the battle needed to make more before they continued their quest to find a new home elsewhere among the stars.

Or so the people of both worlds believed.

Joe knew otherwise. The giant structure ahead was an illusion, a ghost, but of all humans only he was aware of that.

Io, the ambassador of the aliens, once made a secret admission her ship lacked the capacity for another star voyage. They were here to stay. The Titan complex was intended as a blind to make humanity think the *Minaret* was being refueled. After one hundred years the ship would leave as promised, but go no further than the Oort cloud where it would wait hidden until a future time when it might be rediscovered by humans. By then they would have developed sufficiently to cope with the sophisticated engineering the star-ship offered.

The Visitors possessed the technology to create or clone any organic body they desired, and it had been Joe who advanced the idea they take on human form and merge with humans. Subject to the same emotions and hormones, the crew of the alien vessel would in time become integrated into the race and after a few generations of interbreeding would be indistinguishable, a part of the varied patina of humanity.

Joe long ago began to doubt the plan. For reasons both deep and personal he now mistrusted the aliens, and this landing was the result. He deliberately chose to defy the embargo. The time had come for everyone to know the truth about this place, but he needed to reveal it in such a way that his duplicity in the alien charade would not be discovered.

From the moment the war against the *Blackship* ended, rumors began to spread. Some maintained the Visitors wanted the Solar System for themselves, and took the chance to destroy not only their interstellar rivals but also human opposition. The fleets of both Earth and Mars were decimated in the conflict, and many considered humanity unprepared to defend itself in the future. Joe had worked hard to correct that deficiency in the last six decades.

Others suspected the Visitors walked amongst them in artificial bodies indistinguishable from natural ones. Joe knew that to be true without a doubt, as he had been party to the deception.

Despite the rumors, nothing had been heard from the *Minaret* since it went into orbit around Saturn. Only days before the *Marco Polo* arrived, the alien star-ship vanished.

"You alright, Joe?" a static voice crackled over the radio. "Your heart rate's up a heap and a half."

"Yeah, still standing." Joe took a deep breath and tried to calm himself. "Suit's working fine. This place gives me the willies, is all."

The embargo on Titan landings did not preclude exploration of Saturn's other moons, and Joe's original objective was to carry out research and survey exercises on several of them on behalf of the New Worlds Institute. After his having spent years as a surveyor in the past, this trip was an opportunity to return to that simpler life for at least a short time.

His ship was one of the first manned vessels ever to come this far, the voyage costing more than most organizations beyond the Institute would consider worthwhile. As they approached Saturn the first thing the crew sought was the star-ship, but a survey of the system failed to produce any trace. Joe decided the Visitors had not kept their side of the pact, throwing the whole question of the agreement between them and humanity into doubt. He needed to confirm their absence, and so the largest of the planet's moons became the *Marco Polo's* first destination.

The crew were determined to see inside the giant structure. If the Visitors *were* gone, anything remaining might be of value to humanity, but that was not the motivation for Joe. The aliens' original plan had diverged, and that troubled him.

From the rear of the vessel, an exploration buggy rolled from its storage bay and waited, tail ramp lowered. One steady step at a time Joe shuffled aboard and locked into the pilot frame, designed to hold the thermal suit in a standing position. A minute later he was on his way, the vehicle leaving deep tracks in the black sand as it rolled towards the nearby monolith.

"This place is bloody enormous," Joe mumbled as the buggy rumbled on, drawing close to the high, black structure before stopping a short distance from the near wall. He demounted and walked nearer, then leaned back as far as practical in the confines of the suit to peer upwards. "Must be a couple of hundred meters up there."

"Any sign of a way in? A door or something? Anything?" asked the voice again. Chan Berry, the man on the radio, was the captain of the *Marco Polo* and a close friend to Joe.

"Nope, not here. I'll run around the base a bit."

He remounted and drove along the perimeter ten meters out from the structure. The ship had flown over the building on the way down, and there was no trace of an entrance on the flat, featureless roof. Any way in would be at ground level.

The monolith was far too large to circumnavigate in the time available, so an hour later, having given up and turned around, Joe returned to his original position. He stopped beside the wall, dismounted and stepped closer.

He reached out a hand, but did not expect to encounter an actual surface. As anticipated, the carbon-fiber glove of the suit passed through without resistance. He jerked the hand back, the faint, tingling sensation one he was familiar with. Memories flooded back of his first landing on the starship when he flew through a force field into the airfield deck; it felt just like this.

"Something's not right here," he said, continuing the pretense. "This wall is—I don't know—not real. I can put my hand through it like the hatches on the *Minaret*, but it's not the same. It seems different."

"Sure you're not imagining it, old buddy?" the intercom replied.

"I'm not. Legit, my hand went straight into the damned thing. I'll try walking through. This might be the way inside."

"Are you serious? What if you go in and can't get out again?"

Joe paused for a moment to consider his response. "What else can I do?" He had taken similar risks before and emerged safely, and he could not stop the charade now.

"Drop it and come back. I think we should get off this moon and get on with the job we came here for. This place gives me the willies as well."

"Yeah right, but I'm not giving up so easily." Joe stepped forward again, re-inserted the gloved hand and leaned in until the faceplate of his helmet passed through. He felt no sensation beyond the tingling, and no resistance.

The wall had no thickness. Hundreds of meters above, the ceiling of the vast structure was transparent, the dim light from the exterior filtering through to provide minimal visibility. Inside, the black plain continued unbroken.

Joe took several paces forward and stopped. He was in, but it was like he had not gone anywhere at all. Beneath his feet lay nothing but sand, in every direction only blank walls. The structure appeared to be a vast, hollow space.

"Can you hear me, Chan?"

"Yep, you're still coming in clear. I can't see you. Where are you now?"

"I'm inside."

"Cool. What's in there?"

"Bugger all. Nothing." *Fine, now it's common knowledge.*

"What, they stripped it when they left? Damn!"

"No, I mean there literally *is* nothing here and it doesn't appear there ever was. This place doesn't even have a floor. Wait, I can see something in the distance. The light's not so good but I can just make it out. It's a little block-like thingy on a raised platform. Might be worth checking."

Joe turned and walked back through the wall to his buggy, boarded and drove into the enigmatic structure, heading for the object sitting on the sand several kilometers ahead.

"Not sure you should be doing that," Berry said. "Something stinks to high heaven about this."

"That'll be your jocks, Chan. You haven't showered for a week."

"No, I'm serious. This whole thing is weird. I mean, why would we be ordered away from this moon if it's deserted?"

"We thought there *was* something here, but I guess we were wrong. I'm still going to check this out though. Almost there."

Minutes later the buggy reached its destination, drawing to a halt beside a platform about five meters square and one high, smooth, featureless and by all appearances made from some kind of plastic material. Joe placed a glove on the black surface and felt the slightest of vibrations.

In the ultra-low gravity of Titan, he flexed the knees of his suit and launched himself up to the platform, landing with a soft clunk and the slightest of wobbles. He steadied himself and straightened up.

At the center of the block, a thin pylon constructed from the same material rose to a cube structure, the surface of which was broken by dozens of rectangular irregularities that reflected Joe's helmet lamp like glass. He stepped forward and examined the device, moving around until he had viewed it from all sides. Standing tall, he could see across the top.

"Nothing. No access hatches or anything. Can't see any way to get inside. Smooth as a baby's butt. Nothing else here either."

"So, a waste of time coming here, hey."

Joe laughed to himself. "Yeah, I guess. There's something about it though; I don't know what. A feeling I've seen something like this somewhere else." He had experienced the same déjà-vu sensation before. The Visitors had a penchant for building things not unlike their equivalent on Earth.

"Come back. You can stew over it later. The power in your suit is down to thirty-nine percent and if it fails I can't reach you in time. You'll freeze in a minute or less."

"True. Alright, I'm on my way." Joe knew he shouldn't have come alone, but this little subterfuge was something he needed to do by himself.

The buggy was almost back to the ship when realization flashed into Joe's mind.

"Got it," he said. "It's a projector like you see in planetariums. That explains a lot. This building's a phantom, a projection of some sort—a holographic image. That's why I can go straight through it. It isn't real."

"Don't make no sense. Those aliens have been out here for sixty years. Why would they stay so long and put nothing but a hologram here?"

"Who knows? What puzzles me most is I watched them build the damned thing from orbit, and now I wonder if it's a massive charade. A trick, an illusion for our benefit to make us think they were making fuel out here. They weren't doing anything. They were never here at all." Joe hoped he sounded genuine, and that Chan would not realize he was aware of the illusion all along.

"Where are they, do you think?"

Joe hesitated, unwilling to say anything that might give him away. "I'm sure I don't know, but until we can find out I think we need to keep this quiet."

"Sure, but where are they?"

If you would like to continue reading FALCON'S GHOST, *you can find it at all good online booksellers.*

ABOUT THE AUTHOR

Mike Waller is a writer of Science Fiction and Space Opera adventures, including the 'Echo's Way' stories, the 'Falcon' Trilogy and other stand-alone works. He currently lives in Queensland, Australia.

Mike's online home is:
https://www.mikewallerauthor.com

You can connect with him on Facebook at:
https://www.facebook.com/AuthorMikeWaller/

You should email him at
mike.waller@mikewallerauthor.com
Mike answers every email received.

Follow Mike Waller on BookBub at
https://www.bookbub.com/profile/mike-waller

www.ingramcontent.com/pod-product-compliance
Lightning Source LLC
Chambersburg PA
CBHW020307030826
48979CB00029B/2290/J

* 9 7 8 0 6 4 5 9 8 3 0 0 5 *